Praise for
Island Inferno

"*Island Inferno* is a boy-meets-girl story. But in Chuck Holton's world, boy meets girl in the middle of a jungle at 25 mph, hanging under a parachute—a *reserve* parachute—with an assault rifle strapped across his chest. You'd better plan on reading this in one sitting. And once you're done, you'd better give yourself time for your pulse to calm down."

TOM MORRISEY, author of *Deep Blue* and
Dark Fathom

"*Island Inferno* has the fast-paced action of a Clive Cussler novel with all the solid research and authenticity of Tom Clancy's books and a spiritual message that drove me to search deep within my own heart."

JEANETTE WINDLE, author of *CrossFire, The DMZ,* and
FireStorm

"The years he spent as an Airborne Ranger bring a gritty, heart-pounding authenticity to Chuck Holton's writing. He was in the middle of live combat, which is why there is an air of believability to the exploits of Task Force Valor. Strap yourself in and hold on for the adventure!"

DAVE MEURER, award-winning author of
Mistake It Like a Man

"*Island Inferno* beckons readers to a tropical island bathed in raw beauty and veiled in mystery. They are drawn into the valiant world of Special Forces and catapulted into a plot laden with espionage and danger. Holton's surprise ending redefines the ultimate romance."

> LYNNE THOMPSON, radio personality and
> contributing author to
> *Stories from a Soldier's Heart*

"Lather on the sunscreen and spray on the DEET. *Island Inferno* is an eco tour de force!"

> JOHN OLSON, Christy Award–winning author of
> *Fossil Hunter*

"Chuck Holton's remarkable storytelling ability and military expertise make *Island Inferno* a must-read. Suspense, intrigue, and God's guiding hand permeate every page. The Task Force Valor series rocks!"

> MARK MYNHEIR, author of *The Void*

ISLAND INFERNO

OTHER BOOKS BY CHUCK HOLTON

FICTION

TASK FORCE VALOR SERIES

Allah's Fire (co-written with Gayle Roper)

NONFICTION

A More Elite Soldier

Stories for a Soldier's Heart

Bulletproof

TASK FORCE
VALOR

ISLAND
A NOVEL
INFERNO

CHUCK HOLTON

MULTNOMAH
BOOKS

ISLAND INFERNO
PUBLISHED BY MULTNOMAH BOOKS
12265 Oracle Boulevard, Suite 200
Colorado Springs, Colorado 80921

Scripture quotations and paraphrases are taken from the Holy Bible, New International Version®. NIV®. Copyright © 1973, 1978, 1984 by International Bible Society. Used by permission of Zondervan Publishing House. All rights reserved.

The characters and events in this book are fictional, and any resemblance to actual persons or events is coincidental.

ISBN 978-1-59052-503-6

Published in the United States by WaterBrook Multnomah, an imprint of the Crown Publishing Group, a division of Random House Inc., New York.

MULTNOMAH and its mountain colophon are registered trademarks of Random House Inc.

Library of Congress Cataloging-in-Publication Data
Holton, Chuck
Island inferno : a novel / Chuck Holton.—1st ed.
    p. cm. — (Task Force Valor ; bk. 2)
    ISBN 1-59052-503-6
    1. Religious fiction. I. Title
    PS3608.04944344185 2007
    813'.6—dc22

                                    2007003586

Printed in the United States of America
2007—First Edition

10 9 8 7 6 5 4 3 2 1

For Connie

———

Special thanks for this work goes to Kevin Riggs, Brad Kinney, and Trevor Williams, who braved heat, thirst, bugs, and crocodiles on an expedition to the island of Coiba with me in March 2006. The island scenes in this book are closely derived from the adventures we had there. Thanks also to Lynne Thompson for helping to clarify the female thought process, and to Mike Hare for his considerable help to ensure that the technical aspects of the book were accurate. And to Multnomah fiction editor Julee Schwarzburg, for a limitless display of patience as I wrestled with the story line.

Glossary

ANAM: *Autoridad Nacional del Ambiente*; the national environmental authority

EOD: Explosive Ordnance Disposal

HALO: High-Altitude Low Opening freefall parachuting

HUNTIR: High-Altitude Unit Navigated Tactical Imaging Round

IED: Improvised Explosive Device

ITEB: Iso-Triethyl Borane, a fictitious odorless, colorless liquid that reacts explosively with air

KLICK: Military term for kilometer

MIKES: Military term for minutes

MRE: Meals Ready to Eat

NCO: Noncommissioned officer

NVGs: Night-vision goggles

PT: Physical Training

RFID: Radio Frequency Identification

RPG: Rocket-propelled grenade

Aggressive fighting for the right is
the noblest sport the world affords.

Theodore Roosevelt

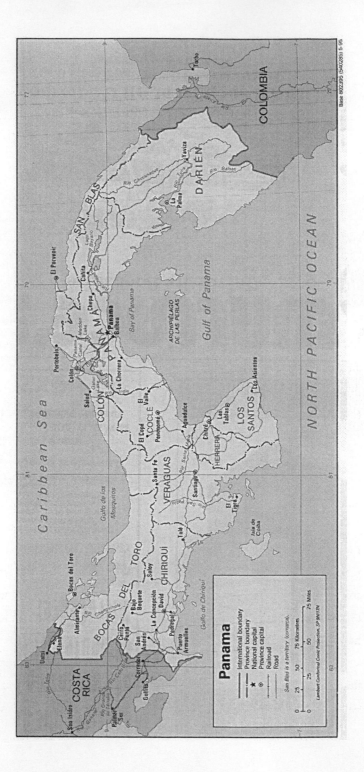

The Gulf of Panama. 2200 hours

MY LIFE IS WASTED.

The black-on-black sea stretched into nothingness before Naeem Bari, and he shivered. But it wasn't cold. In fact, even the breeze crossing the ship's bow did little to alleviate the suffocating heat of the tropical night as the vessel plied its way toward Panama. The humidity wrapped its fingers around Naeem like death itself. But still he shivered, because the bleakness of the sea before him mirrored his future.

If only there were one bright spot in my career, like the sliver of moon that now hides behind the clouds. Perhaps then I could hold out hope. But no. I have no future in this business. What am I to do?

There had been a time when Naeem was proud to be a mariner. He had been born into a poor Pakistani family, and as a teen, becoming a seaman had seemed an exciting alternative to sweating in his father's scrubby fields, staring at the desolate expanse of mountains that formed the walls of his prison. But he had simply substituted one bleak reality for another.

After spending twelve years at what amounted to little more than slave labor on a variety of aging merchant vessels, Naeem's youth had been consumed like the rusty hull of the *Invincible* upon which he stood. He often came to the ship's bow when he had trouble sleeping. It was the only place where he could think in peace.

The old vessel throbbed beneath his feet, as if the dark Pacific waters it had labored across for twelve days were the consistency of molasses. They had crossed the ocean three times in as many months. How many more times would the dilapidated ship be able to make the trip? Shepherding goats wasn't looking so bad after all.

He looked at his watch, pressing the tiny button to illuminate the dial. Nothing happened. *Cheap Chinese garbage.* He let out a disgusted sigh. Oh well. He could easily find another one in downtown Panama City, if they had enough time to go ashore while the ship's cargo was being off-loaded. He'd better try to salvage whatever sleep he could. He would be pulling watch on the bridge in a few hours.

As he turned away from the ship's bow, a shout sounded from somewhere high on the ship's superstructure. Naeem peered around the nearest container just in time to see the control room door slam open and the officer on duty come tumbling out and collapse on the landing.

Is Emilio drunk? Why…?

Before Naeem could wonder further, another man emerged from the control room and stopped under the doorway light.

Naeem felt as if his stomach and his bowels had suddenly switched places. The fact that the man was definitely not part of the ship's crew was almost as terrifying as the submachine gun he carried.

Pirates!

As Emilio struggled to his feet, Naeem started toward the stairway that led up to the bridge. More shouts echoed from the crew's sleeping quarters. Then a burst of gunfire erupted from the control room.

Naeem jerked his gaze upward only to see his friend's limp form topple down the stairwell.

He gasped. *Emilio!*

Angry voices approached, and Naeem instinctively stepped between two rows of containers, sure that his heart would leap from his rib cage. More gunshots sounded, followed by screams of agony.

They are murdering the entire crew!

His first instinct was to plunge overboard. But even though he was a decent swimmer, treading water for a few hours and then succumbing to exhaustion—or worse, sharks—might not be preferable to a bullet in the head.

More gunshots split the air. Naeem's breathing was as staccato as the gunshots. He pressed his fists into his eyes and tried to think.

He could hide, but the *Invincible* wasn't that big a ship, and the pirates were bound to find him eventually.

The orange lifeboat, located at the rear of the ship, was made to hold the entire crew, but the gunfire made it clear that most of the men were even now meeting their fate. Besides, the lifeboat required at least two men to launch.

Sweat flowed from every pore of Naeem's body, and his nightshirt stuck to him like cellophane. He promised Allah and himself that if he survived this night, he would never again step foot on a raft, much less a ship.

The raft! Two small inflatable life rafts in canisters were tucked beneath the forward stairs. Naeem peered around the corner of the container on the starboard side of the ship. He could just make out the dark shape of the fiberglass box that held the life rafts and several flotation vests, about twenty meters away.

He jerked his head back when two men emerged from the superstructure, but not before Naeem recognized the third man held between them.

Franjo Karovik, the ship's captain.

One pirate held the captain while the other, a huge, incredibly muscular black man, shouted a question. When Franjo didn't immediately answer, the pirate smashed his forearm into Franjo's face. Naeem heard the crunch of bone, then his friend crumpled to the deck.

A sob escaped before Naeem could stifle it. He clapped a hand over his mouth, turned, and ran between the containers to the port side of the ship. A peek aft showed no signs of movement. More shouts and gunfire drifted from the stern.

Time was running out.

When the pirates finished with the crew, they would most certainly search the ship, and he would be found. He must go now.

Hoping that anyone left in the control room would not see him, Naeem ducked around the side of the container stacks and sprinted for the stairwell. He quickly found the box that held the life rafts, and after fumbling with the latch for several seconds, he managed to yank open the lid.

Inside were a dozen life vests and the barrel-shaped pods that held the rafts. He heaved a pod out of the box and staggered over to the railing. The pod was heavy, at least forty-five kilos, but with the amount of adrenaline coursing through his veins, Naeem barely noticed. He hesitated.

Though the raft was self-inflating, it was meant to be deployed aboard ship, which in this case was impossible. For a moment he considered going back for a life vest, but when heavy footsteps sounded on the stairs above him, Naeem dropped the pod over the railing and followed quickly after, throwing caution and himself thirteen meters into the sea.

Naeem crossed his arms over his chest and hit the water feet-first. The impact ripped the air from his lungs. Panicking, he flailed toward the surface for what seemed like an eternity. He finally broke through, choking on salt water and bile.

Where is the pod? It isn't here! Terror redoubled inside his gut. When something broke the surface ten yards to his left, a new jolt of adrenaline shot through his already raw nervous system.

I am going to die.

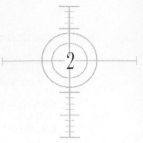

Los Angeles, California. 2207 hours

RIP RUBIO NEARLY DOVE headfirst into the drainage ditch at the sound of the explosion. But a split second later, he realized that the sound had come from a delivery truck running over a Coke can in the road.

Man, take it easy. This is L.A., not Lebanon.

He checked his Suunto t6 wrist computer as he rounded the corner onto Eighth Street, one mile into his run.

Seven forty? You've got to be kidding me!

He kicked it for the next block and a half, punishing himself for slacking off. He had never run this route slower than seven minutes, even when the cops weren't chasing him. Seven minutes forty was unacceptable.

You're getting old, Rubio. Old and slow.

He dodged an empty water bottle on the sidewalk, eyeing it warily. After his fiery introduction to the liquid explosive ITEB two weeks earlier in Sidon, Rip would never look at bottled water the same way again.

He frowned and ran even faster. Rip had purposely waited until late to start his run when the traffic had lessened and it wasn't so hot.

"Gonna do a little PT," he had told his mother as he headed for the door of the little apartment in Estrada Courts. In the shadow of downtown Los Angeles, it was the barrio where he had grown up.

His mother looked up from straightening the cushions on the dilapidated couch in the living room. Her face bore a tired, pained look. "I told your sister to be home before dark, but Gabi is worse at thirteen than you were at sixteen. If you see her, maybe you can send her home. She will listen to you, *mijo*."

Rip nodded. "You got it, *Mami*. Don't worry."

"*Cuídate*, Euripides. The gangs are worse than they've ever been."

He rolled his eyes. "Mom, I'm a Special Forces staff sergeant. I've survived four combat deployments to the Middle East. I think I can take care of myself in my own backyard. Besides, haven't you seen the commercials? I'm an Army of one!"

His mother made the sign of the cross and started muttering to herself in Spanish as he stepped through the rickety screen door onto the crumbling stoop to begin his run.

A rusty Oldsmobile passed by, belching exhaust. Rip coughed and realized he was practically sprinting. He made himself slow down a bit before his heart exploded. He would be heading back to Bragg tomorrow, his week's leave over. Some genius had scheduled his annual physical training test for Friday morning, the day after he returned, so it wouldn't do to wear himself out tonight.

He wasn't going to improve much in the next two days anyway. The run had really been more of an excuse to get out of the house. After a couple of days the place started to get depressing. He was worried about Gabi. Rip knew what the gangs were like, and so did she.

After his father had gone back to Jalisco to marry his mistress when Rip was seven, they had been forced to move from their modest home to the projects: Estrada Courts. His mother knew it was a bad neighborhood but had no choice. She had three cleaning jobs in the city, and while she worked, Rip learned his major life lessons on the streets of Boyle Heights—the kinds of things his father should have been there to teach him, and a few things no parent would want their kid to know.

His mom tried to make up for it by dragging him to the nearest Catholic mission every time the doors opened. The services at Nuestra Señora del Rosario de Talpa weren't all bad. It had always been a quiet place to think and had plenty of sweet-looking *chicas* to flirt with from the back row.

Things got better when his mother married the owner of the grocery store over on Olympic Boulevard. Within a year, Gabrielle was born, and two years after that their hopes of moving to a better home were dashed when their new father was shot in a robbery.

They never found out who was responsible. Some speculated it had been the Sentinel Boys; others blamed it on KAM. But when his mother rushed to the hospital to comfort her husband, his mistress was already there. They were divorced within a year.

Mom just never got a break…

Rip was jerked out of his reverie as two brightly painted imports blew past him on Eighth Street, swerving in and out of traffic, racing each other toward the freeway on-ramp.

Idiots. Bragging rights for the fastest car was a stupid thing to die for. Had he ever been that stupid? He was glad no one was around to answer that question.

He picked up the pace again and turned left onto Glenn Avenue. Any farther down Eighth and he'd be in Evergreen's turf.

He'd been ambushed by some of their gang when he was seventeen, and it had almost cost him his life. In a way, though, Rip was thankful for it. That incident had cemented his decision to join the Army.

A lot had changed in Boyle Heights in eight years. The government had pumped money into the neighborhood projects—new paint and landscaping were supposed to discourage the drug trade. Everything else seemed more run-down than he remembered it. And smaller.

Or maybe eight years in the military taught you that civilization didn't end on the other side of the interstate.

When he was a kid, this place had been his whole world. He still remembered riding his bike beneath the towering palm trees to Hostetter playground, a few blocks away from the projects. He and his *amigos* would climb around in the bamboo thicket that edged the soccer field. In their minds, it might as well have been a trek to the jungles of South America.

Later on, things became more complicated. All the neighborhoods in East L.A. had their respective gangs, and when he was fourteen, Rip was initiated into his: the Varrio Nuevo Estrada or VNE. Suddenly it seemed that enemies were everywhere.

Rip learned quickly how to take a punch—and to give one. He knew how to handle a nine-millimeter before he got his driver's license, and at fifteen he rode along on his first drive-by, just a mile west of where he was now jogging.

Rip pushed those memories from his mind, concentrating on his rhythm, pumping his legs and arms, breathing deliberately and deeply, feeling the sweat burning in his eyes. He couldn't outrun his past, but it might not hurt to try.

The tree-lined street was considerably darker and quieter than the one he'd just left. Apartment complexes lined both sides of the street. The smell of tortillas frying wafted from one side of the street, a dog barked on the other.

When the sidewalk ended, he ran down the middle of the deserted street, burning his lungs with exertion. Mile marker two was the corner just ahead. He checked the split on his watch again. *Seven-oh-two. Now we're talking.*

Rip had always been a strong runner, but he had definitely lost some of it on the recent string of deployments. *Spending too much time trying not to get blown up.* Well, that and playing Xbox with his teammates Sweeney and Buzz.

Three and a half minutes later, he came to the T intersection at Dacotah Street. The sight of his old elementary school just ahead brought back tons of memories: his first girlfriend, playing soccer at every recess.

He turned right, and the old soccer field came into view, now a baseball diamond surrounded by a high chain-link fence. A knot of kids gathered around two vehicles parked at the curb, Tejano music blaring from their souped-up sound systems.

That's the same two cars that were drag racing on Eighth Street.

Slowing a bit as he approached, he noticed something else familiar. The colors being worn by everyone.

VNE. The old gang.

Then he saw a girl with long black hair and a supershort miniskirt leaning against a boy, apparently the driver of the yellow import. He wore baggy trousers, a white tank top, and a black VNE bandanna tied around his head.

"Gabi!"

Rip's younger sister whirled to see who had called her name. She quickly dropped the cigarette she was holding. But that concerned him less than the object stuck in her boyfriend's waistband.

That's a Glock nine-millimeter pistol!

"Hey, Rip. *¿Qué pasó?*"

A girl in the group hissed appreciatively at his athletic, sweat-soaked frame. *"¡Ay, Papi!"*

Rip ignored her. "What's up?" Blood rose in his face, and his heart rate spiked again, but this time not from exertion. He walked to his little sister, grabbed her by the arm, and pulled her away from the boy.

"Go home, Gabi. *Now.*" He kept his eyes on the gun, which was suddenly in the right hand of the punk with the do-rag.

"Hey!" She jerked her arm away.

The older youth pushed off from the car and leveled the gun at Rip, staring him down. "Yo, *ese*. You got a problem with my chica?"

Rip didn't hesitate. His right hand snatched the pistol's grip while his left hand slapped the barrel to one side. With a flick of his wrist, the Glock was in his hands, now pointed back at the startled youth.

"Step back, *homie*." Rip glared down the barrel of the Glock. "You've got about two seconds to stand down or spend the rest of your life breathing through a tube. Your choice."

The kid couldn't be more than seventeen, with multiple facial piercings and a wispy bit of fuzz on his chin that he probably thought was a goatee. His hands shot up in surrender.

Five or six other Latinos crowded around, whistling in disbelief.

What had he gotten himself into? Rip had a feeling this was going to end badly. What could he do? Shoot the punk? That'd set a great example for his little sister.

"Whoa, whoa, hang on a minute, *vato*." Gabi put up a hand to stave off the confrontation. "Rip, this is my homie Chaco. Chaco, this is my *hermano*. Rip was VNE back in the day, before he went off to the Army."

The mood changed quickly, the tension melting like butter in a hot skillet. A few of the gang members grinned nervously. Feeling like an idiot, Rip thumbed the Glock's magazine release and dropped the seventeen-round clip into his left hand. Then he jerked the pistol's slide to the rear, ejecting the round in the chamber.

He handed the empty pistol back to Chaco. "Put it away, ese. It's not a toy."

The scruffy teen regained his tough facade. "You get that big mouth in the Army?" Chaco hissed.

"Nope." Rip turned away from the punk. "I picked it up on the block." He put a hand on Gabi's shoulder. "Come on. We need to talk."

Nobody followed as they walked away. They went several blocks before either of them spoke.

"Mom sent you out to find me?" Gabi asked quietly.

Rip stopped and looked at her. "No, she didn't; I was going for a run. But she said you were supposed to be home by dark. Look, are you *trying* to worry Mami to death?"

Gabi dropped her head and stared at her shoes. "No. She worries too much."

"Sure she does. Her thirteen-year-old daughter is out around midnight on a school night, running with the VNE, playing kissy-face with some punk who thinks you—and his Glock 19—are toys. What does she have to worry about?" Rip stooped and tossed the pistol's magazine into a storm drain.

They walked for another minute in silence.

"That was a really cool move, bro."

Fury welled up inside of him. He wanted to grab Gabi and shake some sense into her. "No, it wasn't, Gabi. It wasn't cool. It was stupid. And so is your hanging with the VNE."

She seemed genuinely surprised. "What are you talking about? It was good enough for you, wasn't it?"

Rip put his fists to his temples in frustration. "Being in a gang almost got me killed, girl! And I know how they treat their chicas." He flipped the hem of Gabi's miniskirt. "And what are you telling them by wearing this, huh?"

He shook his head. "Look, I know you want the boys to like you, but that's not the way to do it. You don't understand how a guy's mind works. You wear that, you're telling them you're in play, you know?"

Gabi looked hurt. "But Chaco loves me."

He snorted. "He might love parts of you, but not the way you think." *I can't believe I'm having this conversation with my little sister.*

He stopped on the sidewalk leading up to the front door of their apartment. "Gabi, the VNE is a dead-end street. Take it from me. Stay away from them!"

His sister's face was passive as she pushed past him up the steps. Before opening the door, she turned to him. "Sometimes a girl has to make her own mistakes."

The screen door slapped shut. Rip just stared after his sister for a moment, trying to decide if he should follow her inside.

He turned and started running again. Another mile might cool his emotions. But as he ran, a thought punched him in the gut.

Mistakes. Just like your father.

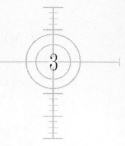

Panama City, Panama. 1103 hours

"YOU SHOULD NOT do this thing, *mija*."

Fernanda Lerida shifted her cell phone to the opposite ear and smiled at the concern in her mother's voice. "It will be fine, Mama. Really! This is the chance of a lifetime." She motioned for the taxi driver to stop.

"Traveling with three men? And in the jungle, no less. It is not becoming of a young lady from a family such as ours, dear one."

As if I'd never set foot in the jungle. Fernanda shook her head as the taxi rolled to a halt. Oh, how she had come to hate her mother's constant reminders of her social status.

"I won't be the only girl. Hedi is going too." She grinned at the tall blonde in the seat next to her.

"She is the student from Germany who arrived in Panama last month?"

"Right. She's with me now. Anyway, Carlos will look out for me, and Professor Quintero is…"

She knew the professor's status as one of the top entomologists on the planet wouldn't leave her mother nearly as impressed as Fernanda was. "He's a highly respected biologist and has years of experience in the jungle. We'll be fine."

"I do not care if Carlos is your cousin. He is an immature boy. What is that noise in the background?"

"We're headed to Avenida Central to pick up a few last-minute things."

Her mother's voice went from concerned to almost hysterical. "Avenida Central? What are you doing there? What could you possibly need in the Chorrillo District, the worst part of the city! The only people who—"

"Er…just a minute, Mama." She put the phone on the seat and asked the driver, "*¿Cuánto?*"

"*Dos cincuenta.*"

She quickly fished three bills from her purse and handed it to him as she opened the door.

"*Gracias, amigas,*" the man said appreciatively as the girls slid out.

"Don't forget your daypack, Hedi!" Fernanda reached in, retrieved the bag, handed it to her friend, then closed the door.

She turned back to her mother, who was still ranting. "Calm down, Mama. We're here because there's an Army Surplus store that sells camping supplies. Believe it or not, they don't have stores like that in Albrook Mall or the Multicentro Plaza downtown."

Her mother sighed. "Fernanda, this voyage…this island…it is a very, very bad place. You do not remember the Noriega years. You were too young. But during that time, we heard stories about the things that went on in the penitentiaries on Isla Coiba…unspeakable things. Many men who were sent there never returned."

Fernanda plugged her other ear as a brightly painted bus blasted its horn at the taxi, still sitting where they'd left it. Not that the car could have moved if it wanted to. Late morning traffic in Panama City was like a car wreck and a parade put together.

She and Hedi ducked into a shoe store where it was marginally quieter. "I'm sure it was terrible, but the prisons were closed down in 2004. Today the island is uninhabited, except for a small number of park rangers and environmental police. Oh, Mama! The island is almost completely covered with virgin triple-canopy forest. Do you know what that means?"

"The dead should be left in peace, dear."

Her mother wasn't listening. *As usual.* "That's just superstition talking. That island may very well hold the secrets to the cure for cancer or AIDS! If it hadn't been for the prisons there, the whole island would probably be inhabited by now. The prisoners actually saved the island from development."

"Perhaps, but you will miss the coffee harvest this year. We need you in the office to do the accounting, especially now that your father is gone. The coffee business this year…has not been doing so well."

Here it comes. When all else fails, pile on the guilt. It was point-less to argue. Fernanda stifled her anger. It wasn't fair to use Papa's death as a way to control her, but that was what her mother had always been good at—control.

"Papa would have encouraged me to go. I will only miss one week, and then I'll be there. I promise. This is a once-in-a-lifetime chance, Mama, and I am not going to miss it."

Fernanda hoped her voice sounded more resolute than she felt, but she needed to stand up for herself. Papa would have liked that too.

A short silence on the other end of the line stood between

them. Then her mother sighed. "Do what you must, mija. I will pray without ceasing. Please be careful."

"*Claro,* Mama. I will." She pushed the disconnect button, dropped the phone into her purse, then covered her face with her hands. Why did every conversation with her mother leave her exhausted?

"Everything all right?" Hedi patted her on the arm.

Fernanda dropped her hands and took a deep breath. "Yes. Sorry about that. My mother has a very strong personality. She knows what everyone should do and never hesitates to tell them."

Hedi smiled. "*Ja.* I have an aunt in Munich like that. She should have been running a company instead of a family."

Fernanda chuckled. "My mother does both."

Outside, the wonderful smell of vendors roasting meat mixed with the acrid odor of too many people, too close together. Street vendors crowded along the sidewalk on Avenida Central, mostly hawking variations of the same products: souvenir jewelry, cell phone accessories, and cheap hats.

Fernanda and Hedi walked south toward where the taxi driver said they would find the surplus store. Within half a block, Avenida Central became a pedestrian-only street, and throngs of shoppers replaced the noisy traffic. They passed two very short brown women dressed in brightly colored dresses and beaded leggings, with red scarves on their heads.

Hedi nodded toward the women. "Are those the kind of Indians your family hires to pick coffee?"

"No, these are Kuna Indians. They live on islands on the Caribbean side of Panama. My family lives in Boquete, in the mountains near Costa Rica. The Indians there call themselves Guaymi. They're very different from the Kuna."

"This is amazing. I never— Oh!" Hedi cried out as she spun around and went sprawling to the pavement.

Fernanda whirled to see two young men running away from them. "Hey!" Anger ignited within, and she started to give chase but quickly thought better of it. She turned back to Hedi, who was collecting the contents of her daypack from the sidewalk.

"What happened?"

Hedi was flustered. "I...I felt something tugging at my bag, and when I turned around, I guess I tripped." She pushed her blond hair behind one ear with a shaky hand. "I'm okay, though. *Ach*. It scared me."

Several onlookers encouraged them to call the police. Fernanda waved them off as she helped her friend to her feet. "Did they steal anything?"

"I don't think so."

They looked up to see two policemen in olive drab fatigues coming toward them. Fernanda had a short conversation with them in Spanish, and the men hurried off in the direction the two thieves had taken.

"What did they say?" Hedi asked as they started off again.

"That they've been having problems with pickpockets in this area recently. They said we should be more careful and offered to escort us to the surplus store. I told them that wouldn't be necessary."

Hedi snorted. "They probably wanted a date."

"Maybe." Fernanda giggled. "Your long blond hair and blue eyes really stand out around here."

"Are you kidding? I'd give anything to be thin and exotic look-ing like you are. And your green eyes are prettier than mine. Besides, I'm built like a rugby player."

"Well, Miss Rugby Player, the next time somebody tries to open your bag, tackle them!"

Hedi stuck her chin out. "I just might. Maybe I'll tackle us some cute policemen while I'm at it."

They laughed and locked arms as they continued down the busy street, passing a row of women selling lottery tickets. Hedi stopped to examine some of them. "Whose picture is on these tickets?"

Fernanda squinted at the tiny picture. "I think it's Jesus, or maybe one of the saints."

"On a lottery ticket? Why?"

Fernanda smirked. "I guess for good luck. It's part of the Catholic culture of Latin America."

"So you're Catholic?"

Fernanda smiled. "Well, no, actually my family is Protestant, thanks to some missionaries who came to Chiriquí years ago."

"Wow. In Germany, nobody goes to church. Well, almost nobody. The churches near where I live are somewhat like muse-ums—full of old, pretty things, but kind of cold and boring."

"Really? So you don't go to church?"

"Never. You?"

"Sure, when I can. School has been keeping me pretty busy lately, but there's a great church near the Albrook Mall I like a lot. "

Fernanda looked up at a huge red sign on the building across the street. "Here's our store, amiga. Do you still have the list Pro-fessor Quintero gave us?"

"I think so." Hedi fished in her bag and pulled out a folded note card. "Here it is."

Thirty minutes later, they exited the store with new backpacks, machetes, and various other items for the trip.

"Hey," Hedi said, "let's skip the taxi and ride a *Diablo Rojo* back to campus."

Fernanda groaned. "Nooo! I hate those horrible buses. They're so smelly and obnoxious."

"Come on. I've dated several guys like that, but it doesn't mean they weren't fun! Where's your sense of adventure?"

Fernanda looked into the bag she was carrying. "If this gear is any indication, we're going to be in for plenty of adventure on this trip."

4

Fort Bragg, North Carolina, 2100 hours

A HAND FIRMLY SQUEEZED Rip's shoulder, but he didn't turn around. His attention focused on the twin green circles defining his field of vision, all that was afforded by the AN/PVS 15 night-vision goggles mounted on his ballistic helmet.

Through them, he could easily make out the dirty, battered door three feet in front of him. A shiny new padlock hung from the hasp above the knob.

The squeeze said that the rest of the team behind him was ready. Rip crept forward to the door and carefully molded the puttylike C2 explosive charge onto the lock.

Then, as deliberately as he had approached the door, he retreated to his place at the head of the five-man stack, keeping his weapon trained on the lock and trailing a thin wire from the spool in his left hand. Sweat trickled down his back, and he tried to ignore the foul burnt smell in the dingy hallway.

Rip snapped a thumbs-up and his heart rate quickened as his headset crackled.

"Three, two, one…execute! Execute! Execute!"

Eyes shut tight behind his tactical goggles, Rip depressed the switch in his left hand, and the padlock evaporated with a loud pop, causing the door to slam open at the same time.

Before it could bounce back, Rip charged through the smoky opening with his silenced MP5 submachine gun leading the way. He cut left inside the door and scanned his sector, immediately locking on to a ski-masked form wielding an assault rifle emerging from behind a filthy couch in the corner.

A woman sat on the couch, bound and blindfolded. Rip instantly acquired his target using the infrared laser sight atop his own weapon and slapped the trigger twice in rapid succession. The nine-millimeter rounds exited the barrel with barely a *hiss*, and a microsecond later impacted with a double *thwack,* catching the terrorist somewhere in the chest.

Without waiting for the target to drop, he continued to scan his sector, hearing the same *hissthwack* as the rest of the assault team dealt swiftly with any threats they encountered. Then he heard a quick sequence of crisp reports from the rest of the team, signaling that their sections were clear.

An open doorway lay just beyond the couch in Rip's sector. A click of the thumb switch on his weapon created a short infrared burst from his under-barrel tac-light that showed cases of water bottles stacked up inside the small room beyond the door.

Bingo! We have a winner.

Rip gave his sector a quick secondary scan and then moved to one side of the open doorway. He made sure to keep his weapon focused on the area behind the couch that he couldn't see and called out, "Red zone, couch!"

A fleeting thought of Gabi, lying on a couch with that VNE punk flashed in his mind. He shook his head and put the thought away. *Not now.*

His team sergeant, John Cooper, was to Rip's right and had a better view of the back of the couch. "Red zone, clear," he replied, coolly.

Rip spun to face the doorway and had to wait less than two seconds before the rest of the team stacked up behind him, ready to clear the next room. They wouldn't use demolitions this time, even if there had been a door.

He checked his weapon, knowing it was loaded with special frangible rounds designed to break apart on contact without passing through the target. His gut tightened. One stray bullet was all it would take to blow them all to burning shreds. He imagined what might happen to his mother and Gabi if he were gone. Not like he'd been around to take care of them recently anyway.

As soon as he felt the pat on his shoulder, Rip took a deep breath and charged through the doorway. Before he made it three steps, a bolt of lightning seemed to strike him in the chest. The thunderous boom that followed slammed him to the floor, disoriented and ears ringing despite his advanced electronic hearing protection.

Something went wrong. Very wrong.

Flat on his back, staring at where the ceiling should have been, Rip saw only stars.

Then the lights came on.

Someone flipped his night-vision goggles out of the way, and then Coop's face came into slow focus above him. The dark-haired master sergeant's voice seemed tinny and far away. "You okay, Rubio?"

Rip shook his head and blinked several times. "Wow. What happened, bro?"

Coop smiled. "I think they got us, buddy."

The shriek of a referee's whistle cut through the night air. Someone outside shouted, "Weapons on safe!"

John shifted his own weapon to his left hand and offered Rip his right. "Better quit lying around. Here comes trouble."

Rip took the hand offered him and shakily got to his feet. Just then, a stocky man in black fatigues and a rumpled cloth patrol cap strode through the doorway, chewing a huge wad of tobacco.

The man surveyed the scene, then spit on the dirt floor. "Well, I'll be. Seems like Staff Sergeant Rubio here done got hisself blowed up and took the rest of y'all with him." He turned to face the rest of the men, who were still outside the small room. "Can anybody tell me what was his major malfunction?"

"Booby trap." Rubio coughed. "I forgot to check the doorway for a booby trap."

"Weeell," the rotund man's bushy mustache arched in a smug grin, "looks like my little present might have knocked some sense into ya. Only problem is, next time, this won't be no training run in the tire house, and that boom you hear won't be a little love tap like mine was. No sir, that'll be the sound of your soul leaving your body. You get what I'm saying?"

Nausea churned in Rip's gut. He managed a nod and a weak, "Yeah."

"Good. You musta got discombobulated after checking the red zone behind that couch and plumb went silly as a rooster wearin' socks!"

Rip's face was getting hotter, and his temper was approaching the "red zone."

Coop must've noticed. "Okay, point taken. Shall we do it again?"

The instructor looked at his watch. "Well, seein' as how I'm aworkin' here as a civilian now, and *CSI* is gonna be on in thirty minutes, I say we knock off for the night. Y'all go meet with Major Williams for an after-action review. He's waiting for you in the control room."

The other team members grunted assent and headed out the door of the tire house. Rip dropped the magazine out of his weapon and popped the snap on his chinstrap, then removed his helmet and headed for the door.

The instructor spit again and threw a beefy arm around Rip's shoulders. "Listen, don't let what happened tonight bug ya, Staff Sergeant. I've been workin' EOD for twenty-two years. I was a sergeant major over at phase three of EOD school at Redstone Arsenal before I retired. That's why they brought me back to work with you guys. It's my job to make sure y'all have what you need to survive out there."

Rip swallowed some water from his CamelBak—and some frustration with it. "No problem, sir."

Face it, Rubio. You got distracted. And distracted will get you killed.

The grizzled old noncommissioned officer smiled as they walked toward the control tower. "Hey, don't you go callin' me sir, now. Makes me feel all funny. Call me Jed."

"Okay, Jed."

"Now listen, it'll behoove you to remember something."

"What's that, Jed?" *I'll never understand what bee hooves have to do with anything.*

"The easy way in is always mined."

Rip nodded. "Roger that."

———

University of Panama Campus, Panama City, 0945 hours

"Ach! You've got to be kidding me!" Hedi staggered around the parking lot under the large backpack that had just been lifted onto her back.

Her classmates Carlos and Zack shot concerned looks at one another while Fernanda stood with one hand on the trunk of her car and the other stifling a laugh.

Zack stepped in front of Hedi and studied her contorted face. "Should I…do you want me to help you take it off?"

Carlos spoke up before she could reply. "Wait up, brah. I'm thinkin' she's gonna have to get used to it sooner or later." He leaned on Fernanda's Nissan and raised his eyebrows. "She hasn't even filled up her water bottles yet."

Hedi put a hand on Zack's shoulder to steady herself, blowing a loose blond strand of hair out of her face, and looked Carlos in the eye. "No. I am fine. The weight, it just surprised me a little."

She shrugged her pack higher and tried to stand erect, then squeaked as she nearly fell over backward and took Zack with her. Fernanda gasped.

Carlos just shook his head. "I'm telling you, man. We're gonna end up carrying these girls' stuff."

Fernanda shot him an icy look and then turned back to Zack and Hedi. "Maybe we should just stack our bags next to the car until Professor Quintero gets here."

Hedi dropped her bag with a thud. "Good idea."

Other than Fernanda's light blue Sentra, Zack's was the only other car in the parking lot. It was the first Saturday morning of spring break at Florida State's Panama City campus, and most people had already left.

"Dude, what kind of car is that, anyway?" Carlos raised his sunglasses to gawk at Zack's beat-up vehicle, which looked like some fifth-grader's attempt to build a go-cart out of pieces left on the field after a crash-up derby.

Zack shrugged sheepishly, stooping to hide the key under his front tire. "Dunno. I bought it from a taxi driver who was retiring."

"You bought a Panamanian taxi?" Carlos's eyes bulged. "Are you loco?"

A boyish grin lit up Zack's face. "My girlfriend thinks so. But, hey, it was the best I could find for three hundred bucks. I'm only staying here for a year anyway, then I'm headed back to Florida. Besides, it has a kickin' stereo system."

Fernanda wanted to mention that Carlos had no vehicle at all. Instead she said, "It's probably not a good idea to leave your key there. Somebody's liable to steal your car."

Everyone was silent for a second before they all burst out laughing.

Even though Fernanda hadn't known Zack very long, he seemed to be genuine and generous, if perhaps a bit naive. The best word she could think of to describe Carlos was *maleducado*, or poorly raised, which belied the fact that his father, Fernanda's uncle, sent Carlos to the best private school in Panama City.

She turned to Zack. "So are you a biology major like Carlos and Hedi?"

"Nope. I'm shooting for a degree in cultural anthropology at FSU in Tallahassee. I transferred here for a year because I wanted to learn Spanish. Well, that, and I'm fascinated with Latin America. There's so much cool history, especially here in Panama." Zack shoved his hands into the pockets of his cutoff cargo pants. "I figured this would be a fun place to spend a year studying. Besides, everything's wicked cheap."

Carlos gave Zack's jalopy a sideways look. "You get what you pay for, brah."

"But why is a nonbiology student signing up to spend a week in the jungle looking for unclassified species of lepidoptera?" Fernanda asked.

"Oh, that. Well, I've wanted to visit Coiba ever since I first read about it in a book about the buccaneers and pirates who conquered this area in the 1500s. It said that the pirates thought Coiba was cursed and held things like flying serpents and trees that would spit acid on you."

Hedi's mouth dropped open. "You're kidding, right?"

Zack shook his head. "No way. Coiba has an incredible history. It was a penal colony for something like a century. Panama would send its worst criminals there, and they'd basically just roam the island, killing each other off and surviving on whatever they could catch or grow."

Hedi looked at Fernanda. "What have we gotten into?"

Fernanda winked. "Don't worry, girl. They closed the colony a few years ago and moved all of the prisoners off the island. It's a national park now. Besides, Professor Quintero has been there several times. He says it's one of the last places in Central America that hasn't been explored. It probably has hundreds of new species of animals and insects."

"I saw that on the literature he sent out. Do you really think we'll find something nobody else has?"

Fernanda smiled at her friend. "It's very possible. The professor's already credited with discovering twelve new species of butterflies and moths."

"Really? So he's, like, famous?"

Laughing, Fernanda said to Hedi, "Well, sort of. I've read all of his papers, and he's brilliant. His most recent discovery is a bright red butterfly he named *Nymphalis quinterus.* I got to work with him on part of that project. As far as anyone can tell, it exists only in a microecosystem the professor discovered in a section of jungle on what used to be Fort Sherman, over on the Caribbean side of the country. He's one of the world's foremost lepidopterists."

Fernanda realized she was gushing and caught herself. "I'm sure he wouldn't take us anywhere unsafe."

"Anyway," Zack said, "I saw the ad for this trip in the school paper and figured this would be a great way to learn more about the island. And if I have to spend a week chasing bugs around the forest with you guys, I can handle that."

Everyone laughed. Then a shiny maroon SUV whipped into the parking lot and sped toward the group.

"All right!" Carlos said. *"Aquí viene el professor."*

Fernanda felt a flutter in her stomach. *That's the professor, all right.*

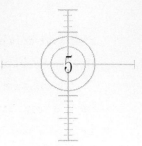

5

The Pacific Ocean. 1000 hours

SO THIS IS what it feels like to die.

Naeem grimaced in pain and struggled to get even one eye open. As soon as he did, the blazing sun made him shut it again. It didn't matter. There was nothing to see.

He lay in the inflatable raft, the saltwater sores on his back and legs seething like he was lying in a pool of acid. At least the hunger pains had disappeared.

When the ship had been attacked, he jumped overboard with the life raft still in its container. Fortunately, the barrel-shaped pod floated, and he clung to it until it had gotten light.

Naeem had been very proud of himself when he managed to deploy the raft and climb inside. But now he was fairly certain it would have been better to stay aboard the *Invincible* and die at the hands of the pirates with the rest of the crew.

He ran a swollen tongue over his cracked, shriveled lips. How should he die now? Staying in the bottom of the raft to be broiled alive by the tropical sun would take the least amount of energy, but that would undoubtedly take longer than if he rolled into the sea and joined his comrades at the bottom.

But dreams of their bodies being consumed by greedy fish haunted him every time he'd been able to escape the waking nightmare of being lost at sea. He could not bear the thought of them eating him too.

How long had it been? Three days, perhaps. At first he had held out hope for rescue, but when the plane came, it hadn't seen him, a tiny yellow speck in a vast expanse of blue. That was when he knew he would die in this raft. Alone. Forgotten.

Why had they taken the *Invincible?* Was it simply random chance? Why kill the crew for a load of lumber? Piracy was almost unheard of in these waters. Unless…

Perhaps they had come for the package.

The thought struck him like a bag full of mud. What if the owner of the package, upon hearing that his client failed to take delivery, chose to murder the crew rather than pay for the return shipping?

Naeem never liked it when the captain took on "special deliveries." Though he rarely knew what these shipments contained, that they were illegal went without saying. Perhaps Captain Karovik thought these shipments were an easy way to pad his pockets. But in doing so, he put the entire crew and the ship at risk.

This most recent shipment had given Naeem a particularly uneasy feeling. He eyed the metal boxes every time he inventoried the refrigerated provisions container.

When the client never appeared to claim his shipment in Sidon, Naeem wrote in his diary that transporting it was a bad idea. Still, he could not bring himself to hate the captain for what he had done. It was simply how things worked in this business.

He no longer wept for the family he would never see again. Besides, he had no tears left to shed. Being without water while surrounded by it was the worst torture imaginable. Allah once sent a short rainstorm, but even the water that collected in the bottom of the raft was so brackish it only made him thirstier.

He wondered about eternity. Had he lived a life that would please Allah? Deep inside, he feared the answer to that question.

Oh, he'd avoided gross sin—he never drank or smoked. He never visited prostitutes in the ports where the ship called. He sent as much money home to his family as he could spare. But it wasn't enough. The irregular work schedule on the ships where he'd served rarely left time for prayer. And he'd never completed the haj, the pilgrimage to Mecca.

As Naeem looked back, he realized he hadn't really been a Muslim at all. He had simply been born into a Muslim family and had done what he was told, without question. He had been so preoccupied with his suffering on earth that he hadn't really given what came afterward much thought.

Was it all a lie? Allah, Paradise, Mohammed? Now that it came down to it, what did it matter if death really was the end? What if he could slip into an unknowing, unfeeling sleep and just cease to be? Would that be so bad?

If Allah did exist, he had forgotten about Naeem Bari. What good did it do to pray to an unseen, uncaring entity?

If Allah would not hear him, perhaps some other God would. Part of him realized that even thinking such a thing would be considered the height of blasphemy in Pakistan. But he was not in his country. He was lost on the high seas and ready to take any help he could get.

A feeble prayer formed in his mind. *If there is a God who cares, please hear me. Please help.*

Nothing happened. No angel appeared. Not even a cloud filled the sky. Naeem sighed. *What did I expect?*

When the blackness finally came, he welcomed it.

Chorrillo District, Panama City, 1005 hours

The cockroach almost made it across the desk before meeting its fate at the end of a rolled-up magazine. Oswardo kept the periodical tightly bound with rubber bands for just that purpose.

He unceremoniously swept the smashed bug's remains into the trash can, careful not to disturb the electronic components arranged on his desk, remnants of his latest round of tinkering. He resumed reading today's copy of *La Prensa*.

The newspaper had gotten much better in recent years, and though he spent much of his time endeavoring to stay off its pages, he enjoyed reading about the other poor souls who were not so fortunate.

Another drug shipment had washed ashore on the San Blas islands, doubtless dumped at sea by Colombian smugglers after being spotted by Panama's border police.

He smiled and turned the page. *Good. Keep their attention in the north.*

Skimming to the bottom of page two, he read a blurb that made him jump like he'd been slapped in the face. Adjusting his glasses, he reread the short clip that had caught his attention.

A merchant ship due to enter the canal at Miraflores locks
failed to arrive last Wednesday at its scheduled time. The

ship was reportedly the *M/V Invincible,* a twenty-seven-year-old break-bulk carrier flagged in Liberia. According to canal records, the ship has visited Panamanian ports six times in the last three years to take on cargoes of sugar, coffee, and bananas, the last time on 6 March of this year. An official for the Panama Canal Authority told *La Prensa* that when the ship failed to arrive as planned and would not respond to radio calls, a search plane was sent to look for it along her charted course but found nothing. Officials are not speculating publicly on the ship's fate, but the possibility of foul play has not been ruled out. A formal search-and-rescue operation is being mounted.

Oswardo yanked a drawer out of his desk and dumped its contents—more electronic switches and activators—on the floor. Then, with the tip of a letter opener, he carefully pried up a false bottom in the drawer. Retrieving a spiral-bound notebook, he pulled from between its pages a bill of lading bearing a date three months prior. The form was filled in with barely discernable script.

Origin: Panama. Destination: Sidon. Pieces: 3. Weight: 40 kilos.

The space for shipper address and phone number bore only the name *Oswardo* and a phone number to a prepaid cellular phone now lying amid the heap on the floor. Under consignee address—the name Franjo Karovik and the words *M/V Invincible.*

A quiet curse escaped his lips. Karovik had phoned him several weeks prior to report that his contact in Sidon had not appeared to take delivery of the shipment.

Oswardo had stifled the urge to skip the phone like a rock across the mildew-ridden rooftop of the crumbling apartment building where he maintained a flat. He kept it for tinkering with his gadgets and for business that needed discretion. "Very well," he had said. "When do you return to Panama?"

"Not for t…onths," was the captain's static-laced reply.

"Did you say months?"

"Yes. We have …ps in Indone…a and Korea."

Oswardo sighed. "All right. Listen. Return the package to me. I will settle up with you once I have again taken possession of it. Call me when you arrive, and we will meet at our usual place."

Oswardo slapped the notebook shut and dropped it on the desk with a thud. Losses had to be expected in a business such as his. Perhaps his client in Sidon had been arrested. Maybe he was dead. At least half of the payment had already cleared his bank. He would pay for the return shipping and then resell the product elsewhere. It would be easy to find another interested party.

But now this? He picked up the newspaper and checked the name mentioned a third time, hoping he had been mistaken. But no, there it was. *M/V Invincible* vanished without a trace.

Any way he looked at it, this would be costly. As if he needed another burden, with a wife and teenaged daughter who despised him and were permanent fixtures at the Multicentro, a mistress here in Chorrillo who spent more money than she was worth, and a shiftless son who was presumably still in college. Oswardo could ill afford more setbacks. Life was expensive, but he hoped to soon be rid of most of his problems.

He picked up the throwaway phone and turned it on. Only three credits left. He would need to purchase some more.

He had many contacts. If someone had stolen his shipment, he would find them.

And they would pay.

Outside Panama City. 1015 hours

WHAT'S WRONG WITH ME?

The village of Chame sped past outside the passenger window as Fernanda tried to shoo the butterflies from her stomach. Something had her unsettled, but she hadn't yet figured out what it was.

Thirty minutes earlier, the expedition team had left the parking lot, after piling all of their gear into the professor's Rexton SUV.

Fernanda took the passenger seat, and Hedi started out between Zack and Carlos in the backseat. But it soon became apparent that she was going to take photographs of every square meter of Panama's sprawling countryside, so Zack offered to switch places with her. Carlos plugged in the earbuds for his iPod and was head-bobbing to the beat of Panamanian hip-hop.

"Let me apologize again for the late start," Professor Quintero said as he drove. "Although this is my fifth expedition to Isla Coiba, the permit process has become more difficult on every trip. ANAM has a new director, and I believe he'd rather not have anyone traveling to Coiba for any reason."

"What's ANAM?" Hedi snapped a photo of the back of the professor's head.

"It's the *Autoridad Nacional del Ambiente.* The National Environmental Authority. Ever since Coiba was designated as a World

Heritage site a few years ago, they've been in control of its administration. Now they're making it really difficult to visit any part of
the island other than the ranger station on the north end."

"Why?" Zack asked.

"I'm not sure." The professor stroked his close-cropped goatee.
"It's a huge island, larger than several Caribbean countries. The
problem is, plenty of corporations would like to get their hands on
the island's resources. And even if that doesn't happen, the tourists
are coming in droves now, and they could easily upset the balance
of the island's ecosystem."

Fernanda had heard this story before in some of Professor
Quintero's classes. The intense look in his eyes whenever he spoke
about the island revealed his passion.

She found it quite attractive. Most of the guys her age were too
busy pretending to be cool to show a passion for anything. The professor, on the other hand, was passionate in everything he did, and
it made him seem younger than his forty-eight years.

The only thing that bothered her was that he seemed to enjoy
bashing any religion. For this reason, she'd never really felt the need
to flaunt her faith in front of him.

"Professor?" Fernanda had been quiet until now.

"Please call me Alex." He spoke to the group but locked eyes
with her. "We're all going to spend the next seven days together, so
let's dispense with formalities, shall we?"

Fernanda nodded. "Okay, um, Alex."

"Just a moment, please."

Fernanda studied him as he changed lanes to pass a lumbering
semi truck loaded down with fresh-cut sugar cane. She was especially drawn to his hands. They weren't the pallid, effete hands of

your typical academic, but tanned and strong. She'd heard he was an avid runner and scuba diver. *And a staunch evolutionist.* But hey, she could respect his good qualities. He was self-confident, among other things. She liked that.

"Oh no!" Hedi shouted.

Fernanda looked up to see the semi truck drifting into their lane. She grabbed the door handle and stomped the imaginary brake.

"Idiot!" Alex hissed. But instead of braking, he floored the gas pedal. As the Rexton shot forward, rage exploded on his face, and he cursed the driver of the semi, one hand pounding on the horn.

Hedi squeaked again, and Fernanda braced for impact. The SUV surged past the truck, missing its front bumper by a few feet, then jerked back into the right lane.

For a moment nobody spoke. Fernanda glanced around. Carlos was asleep, still plugged into his iPod. Hedi peeked one eye open, then let out a huge sigh. Zack appeared somewhat annoyed but said nothing.

Alex looked at Fernanda, once again cool and confident. "Sorry about that. They let any moron who can reach the pedals drive those things."

She'd forgotten her original question, so she said, "How much farther to Santa Catalina?"

He turned up the air-conditioning a notch. "It's about three hours. Was anyone missing anything from the list I gave you?"

Hedi shook her head. Zack reached over and punched Carlos, who sat up looking bewildered. He jerked out the earbuds. "What's up, brah?"

"Alex wants to know if you have everything he told us to get," Zack said.

"Who's Alex?"

"The professor."

"Oh. Uh, I think so…except I couldn't find the brand of hammock on the list."

Alex frowned. "Hmm…so you didn't bring a hammock, Carlos?"

"No, I did. I borrowed one from my roommate, Trevor. He bought it from some Indian dude."

The professor pursed his lips, looking irritated. "Let me look at it when we get to Santiago. If it won't work, we'll see if we can find one for you there."

"That's cool." Carlos resumed jamming.

"What's Santa Catalina like?" Hedi asked.

Alex glanced at her in the rearview mirror. "Beautiful. It's a small fishing village, and until recently it took a four-wheel drive to get there. But they've paved the road, and the town is growing like mad. It used to be that the only foreigners you saw there were surfers. It has some of the best waves in Central America. But now, the tour buses show up on the weekends, full of fat American tourists."

Hedi looked puzzled. "I thought you were American."

"I'm an expat. But that only makes it more appalling when I run into Billy Bob from Arkansas here on vacation. Or worse, some blasted missions team scurrying around destroying the way of life for every indigenous group they come across."

"So where are we staying?"

"Oh, you'll love it, Fernanda. It's called the Oasis. It's a handful of cabanas owned by an Italian guy. You can step out the door of your room right onto the beach."

Hedi clapped her hands. "Oh, it sounds so romantic!"

The professor briefly locked eyes with Fernanda again. "You're right, Hedi. I suppose it is."

Fernanda blushed. The butterflies were back.

———

Fayetteville, North Carolina, 1800 hours

Rip was still frantically tossing dirty clothes and other assorted detritus from his recent trip into the spare bedroom of his apartment when the doorbell rang.

"Be right there!" He heaved a duffel bag down the hallway. Maybe it hadn't been such a good idea to cook supper for his new girlfriend, but since he never knew how long it would be before the team was sent on another deployment, it was important to make the most of every night he was in town. Besides, he'd been gone so much lately that Chelsea would kill him if they didn't do something tonight.

He quickly checked his close-cropped black hair in the bathroom mirror. It was still a little wet, but that was okay. On the way to the door, he picked up a remote control and pointed it at his iPod, sitting in its dock in the corner of the room. Flamenco music played softly.

He dropped the remote onto the brown leather couch, which faced the forty-two-inch plasma television on the wall, then turned the handle and jerked the door open with a flourish. "*Buenas noches*, amiga."

Chelsea emitted a little squeak and hugged him tightly. "Oh, Rip. I've missed you!"

"I've missed you too, *querida*." He stepped back and took in her long blond hair, normally up in a tight ponytail, but tonight it flowed over her shoulders. "Wow, you wore a dress."

She feigned offense. "Just because you've almost never seen me in anything but running shorts doesn't mean I can't dress up."

He smiled. "I *like* you in running shorts, but you look fabulous in anything." And he meant it. The form-fitting black dress showed off her incredibly fit athletic figure and dropped off one tanned shoulder.

Rip shook his head. "*Caramba*, you should have been a model instead of a fitness instructor."

"Oh, stop." She playfully slapped his arm. "So what's for supper?"

He bowed slightly and held a hand out to the coffee table sitting in front of the couch. "Your table awaits, *señorita*. I will have your meal shortly."

Chelsea's perkiness was just what he needed tonight. Time to forget about the problems back in L.A. and just enjoy not being in some foreign country for once.

Yeah, pretend to have a normal life. That's it.

He turned and headed for the small kitchen. "Are you planning to run the Cinco de Mayo 10K in Fayetteville this year?"

She bounced slightly as she spoke. "Actually, no. I'm going back to California to see my folks, and I'm running the redwoods marathon while I'm there."

Rip's eyebrows shot up. "A marathon? Hey, good for you, chica."

"So are you running the Cinco?"

He shook his head. "No idea. Don't know where I'll be then."

"It must be really strange, never being able to plan ahead like that."

"Sometimes, but you get used to it." He lied.

"What smells so good?"

He retrieved two plates of food he'd been keeping warm in the oven and walked over to sit beside her on the couch. "*Chilaquiles mariscos.*"

A cute little furrow appeared in her brow. "Chila...what?"

He laughed. "Chilaquiles. Say it slow. ChEE-La-kEE-Layce."

She looked at the plate and shrugged. "Looks like nachos."

He put the plate down in front of her. "Kind of, only better."

"Ooh, shrimp! I love those."

"Great! Plus it's good carbs." He winked at her. "Hang on, I'll get the drinks." He returned to the kitchen and came back a moment later with two glasses of wine.

"So what's the occasion?"

"No occasion, just wanted tonight to be special."

She gave him a flirtatious look. "Oh, really?"

"Wait! I have something for you." He jumped up and hurried down the hall to his room. A moment later, he returned with a small box.

"What is it?" Chelsea asked, wide eyed.

"Something I've had for a while." He sat down and handed her the box.

She opened it and gasped, lifting out a crystal pendant on a thin golden chain. "It's beautiful, Rip!"

He grinned. "Not just beautiful but rare. I had it custom made."

"What do you mean?"

He reached out and took it, turning it over in his hands. "That crystal came from one of Saddam Hussein's palaces."

Her jaw dropped. "This pendant belonged to the king of Iran?"

"Um…it's from Iraq. Anyway, the crystal was a part of a big chandelier in the palace. We got mortared there one night, and some of the crystals fell down. I picked it up and brought it back, then had a jeweler here in town make it into a pendant."

Chelsea looked like she was going to cry. "You did all that for me?" She threw her arms around him.

He hugged her back, figuring it'd be better not to tell her that he'd had several of them made and had been thinking of selling them on eBay.

Dinner was apparently over. Chelsea planted a kiss on him that would have given Fabio heart failure. She fell back on the couch, pulling Rip with her.

But for some reason, Rip wasn't into it. *I should be enjoying this!*

He mentally shook himself. *Come on, Rubio. Focus! Wasn't this the plan for tonight?*

But that was just it. What was he doing? He'd only been out with Chelsea twice, and one little gift had turned her into this—a cross between Anna Kournikova and a yellow lab puppy. All of this was too calculated, too easy.

Too much like Chaco.

Rip broke away from her embrace and sat up. "Hold up, chica. This isn't cool."

The cute confused eyebrows were back. "What?"

Then the doorbell rang.

He jumped up. "Hold that thought, Chelsea." He jerked open the door to see a tall, slender Puerto Rican woman.

His blood froze. "Nicole! Hey…I…uh… What are you doing here?"

The Latina pursed her lips as she took in the food, the music—and the blonde on the couch. "I just thought I'd drop by and see if you were doing anything tonight. I guess you are." She nodded at Chelsea. "Who's she?"

Rip looked from Chelsea to Nicole and back again. He could almost see the sparks sizzle. "Her? Uh…she's…this is my friend Chelsea."

Chelsea now stood, straightening her dress indignantly. "Your *friend,* huh? Is that what I am to you? Just your friend? I guess you give all your friends a necklace from Osama Bin Laden's castle?" She twirled the pendant with one hand.

"It was Saddam Hussein's palace," Rip muttered, feeling his face go hot.

"What?" Nicole screeched. "You gave her one too?"

Rip looked back at her. *Oh no, she's doing that head-shake thing.*

"You mean I'm not the only one?" Chelsea asked, incredulous.

"Join the club, sister." Nicole was staring at her long red nails.

"Ooohh! You…" Apparently Chelsea couldn't come up with a suitable word for him. She dropped the pendant on the table and stormed out the door.

"*Puerco,*" Nicole spat out, then turned and followed Chelsea down the stairs.

Obviously, Nicole had no problem finding the word.

Rip only wished he could disagree.

7

Isla Coiba, Panama. 0550 hours

IT IS TIME. Finalmente.

With one very black hand, Chombon absently ran a thumb over the jagged scar bisecting his left eyebrow and smiled. The low outline of the island was barely visible in the rising daylight. It looked lush and inviting, but he knew better; it was a dark, wretched place. A place not meant for humans. The scar over his eye was a reminder of its horrors. Untold numbers of souls had expired on that island, and he did not intend to join them.

From the stern of the *Invincible* he watched the last launch pull away from the ship and arc toward the place where the wide river met the sea. The tide was rising, covering up the long crescent expanse of beach that stretched off to the north for more than a mile.

Sixteen days of backbreaking labor had been required to clear the encroaching jungle away from the long-abandoned compound on the remote windward side of the island. But the location was perfect, tucked away from the shore, safeguarding his secrets. That was all that mattered.

He had never visited this side of the island when he was a prisoner here, back when the guards had first given him the name

Chombon and meant it as an insult. But he had embraced the epithet, determined to make it a name of respect, even fear, among the prisoners. And by virtue of his impressive size and strength he had succeeded.

Behind him, an old man stepped onto the aft deck from the stairway that led to the hold. Cesar Plinio was probably the only one of the sixteen men on this operation who Chombon trusted farther than he could spit. Cesar was a friend of his uncle and had fished the teeming waters around Coiba for twenty years.

With him were two of his men. "That is the last container, *Jefe.* Of the cargo, there is only the lumber remaining."

"Good. What about the provisions? I want the men to be rewarded tonight with a special meal, but only take ashore what we can eat tonight. Tomorrow we must begin repainting the ship. Then we must file the paperwork to reflag her under a new name."

Cesar nodded to his two lieutenants. "Take care of the food."

Then Chombon shouted at their backs. "And do not pilfer the best of it for yourselves, or I will be sure you have no tongues left to taste it with!"

He thought to say so only because he had already removed a bottle from one of four cases of bottled water that had been in the refrigerated container and had stashed it in his hut. After all, rank had its privileges. He was tired of drinking the brackish water from the river.

Cesar joined him at the railing and squinted into the late afternoon sun. "Have you decided what we will call her?"

Chombon had been watching the tide overwhelm the lazy flow of the river, causing a small but noticeable tidal bore that

momentarily changed the direction of the current. The phenome-
non amazed him. With enough power, even the forces of nature
can be reversed. It was a perfect picture of his life.

He turned to face Cesar with a satisfied smile. "We will call it
Asesino del Sino." The Fate Killer. For that's what it was. The few
containers of Chinese products that the ship carried would sell for
several hundred thousand dollars, and its main cargo of lumber
would net several million, enough for him to live comfortably for
the rest of his life.

He would no longer be bound by his past. He had overcome
his own destiny and created a new one, reversing the flow of his life.
He had been born a nobody—and should have remained so—but
he had been willing to do what others would not, and that great
risk had succeeded.

Or nearly so. Another two weeks and his life's new course
would be set.

Cesar nodded thoughtfully. "It is a good name. A Maltese flag
and new paint will make her all but untraceable."

Chombon saw the first *lancha* was returning with a load of
blue paint. "We must hurry. It will—"

The force of the explosion slammed the two men to the deck
and almost blew them overboard. A cannon of flame shot skyward
from the doorway of the galley below, singeing off any exposed hair
and sucking the oxygen from their lungs. The ship shuddered,
coughing flame and smoke from nearly every opening amidships.

Chombon struggled to stand, frantically scanning both sea and
sky for their attackers. Nothing. No warship. No fighter plane.
Confused, he staggered to the galley stairs.

Excruciating screams tore themselves out of the smoke and

assaulted his ears as flames lapped greedily at the walls and stairs.

There! A fire extinguisher!

He vaulted to the wall of the superstructure and tore the red canister from its mounts. He would not give up his dream so easily.

With a deep breath, he started down into the flames, extinguishing a path for himself as he went. At the bottom landing, smoke seared his eyes, but within seconds he had put out enough of the fire in the immediate vicinity to get another breath of air.

Just then one of his crew charged toward him screaming in agony and engulfed in flames. Chombon closed his eyes, raised the nozzle, and let fly, emptying its contents in the direction of the writhing figure until the horrible shrieking stopped.

When the white powder and smoke cleared enough for him to open his eyes again, the man lay still at his feet. Chombon crouched and turned him over, fighting a wave of revulsion when the man's charred skin sloughed off in his hand.

It was one of the men Cesar had sent to see to the food. His hair was gone, as was most of his skin. The man's breathing was rapid and shallow, and his bloodshot eyes darted back and forth, as if afraid the dragon that had incinerated him would return.

Chombon leaned over the dying man, trying to get him to focus. "Hey! What happened?"

The man's lips were moving, but no sound emerged. His eyes were wandering again, and he was rapidly going into shock.

Chombon grabbed his shoulders and shook him. "*¿Qué pasa?* Tell me what happened!"

Barely audible sound escaped the man's lips. Chombon leaned close, trying to discern his words.

"I told him…not…not to drink the water."

Fort Bragg, North Carolina, 0800 hours

You're a bonehead, Rubio!

Rip slammed the door on his wall locker but stayed sitting on the bench in front of it, alone with his thoughts.

His teammates Bobby Sweeney and Buzz Hogan had already finished their workouts and left to get some breakfast.

Sergeant First Class Frank Baldwin entered and began fiddling with the lock on the wall locker across from Rip. "'When sorrows come, they come not single spies, but in battalions,' eh, Rubio?"

"What are you talking about, Baldwin?"

"It's Shakespeare. Never mind."

Rip just grunted.

Frank opened his locker. "From one gadget head to another, here's something that might cheer you up." He reached into a green nylon kit bag, produced a cylindrical metal object, and held it out for Rip to see.

"A rifle grenade. Just what I always wanted."

A sly grin appeared on Frank's face. "Ah, your sarcasm reveals your ignorance. This is no ordinary forty-millimeter rifle grenade. Look more closely."

Rip took the round and turned it over in his hands. Frank was right. This was no standard high-explosive grenade. "What is it? Some kind of parachute flare?"

Frank's grin grew into a full smile. "You got the parachute part right. It's called the HUNTIR. That stands for High-Altitude Unit Navigated Tactical Imaging Round."

Rip shook his head. "What? You're missing some letters in that acronym."

Frank waved a hand. "Yeah, who cares. This baby gets shot out of a handheld grenade launcher, travels up to one thousand feet in the air, and then transmits up to five minutes of high-quality video back to us as it falls back to earth under a small parachute."

"Whoa! Really?"

"Yep. I haven't tried it out yet, but it ought to come in real handy for doing a quick aerial scan of a location before approaching a site—checking for snipers and such or seeing what's on the other side of a ridge, etcetera. I'm testing one on the range tomorrow."

"Wow. That's cool, bro."

Frank took the round back. "I'll let you know when I go if you want to come along."

John Cooper stuck his head in the door of the team room. "Hey, Rubio! You coming?"

"Yeah, Coop. Be right out."

"Okay, I'll wait for you in the truck. But get a move on before I eat the steering wheel!"

With a sigh, Rip picked up his black leather jacket and headed outside. It was just past Easter, and though the worst of the winter weather had passed, the mornings were still chilly. At the moment a light drizzle was moving in. He shrugged into his coat and stepped out the door of the shop. Coop's silver Tacoma was idling in the parking lot.

When he opened the passenger door, John was talking on his cell phone. It didn't take Rip long to figure out who was on the other end. Liz Fairchild.

"No, really! I loved your grandmother. Yes, I can see where you get it. Uh-huh. No, Philadelphia is fine. Well, listen, hon, Rip and I are going to get waffles. Call you later? Love you too."

Coop hung up the phone and put the truck in reverse. "Liz is already planning our next visit."

Rip was lost in thought. "Mmmm…sounds serious."

Coop smiled. "Could be. We had a great time last week. Went white-water rafting in the Youghiogheny and drove down to Seneca Rocks for some fantastic climbing."

"And you met her grandmother?"

"Yep. Stayed with her. She insisted."

"Sounds like fun."

Coop gave him a sideways look. "I detect a note of sarcasm."

Rip shrugged.

"What's the matter, Rubio?"

"Nothing. I'm fine."

"Well, anyway. I still can't believe Phoenix cut us loose for a whole week. I'd almost forgotten what it was like to eat a home-cooked meal and sleep past zero seven hundred."

Rip stared out the window. *I almost wish I had stayed here at Bragg.*

Ten minutes later, they were sliding into a booth at the Waffle House. The middle-aged waitress took their drink order, then left them to attend to her other customers.

Coop leaned forward in the booth and skewered Rip with a stare. "All right, buddy. Tell me what's going on."

Rip just looked at him. "What do you mean, bro?"

"I mean, you haven't been yourself since we got back. What's up?"

"It's nothing. Really."

Coop frowned. "Okay, sorry. I thought that we were like, you know, buddies who trust each other with our lives on a regular basis. Don't let me intrude or anything."

Rip felt the blood rising in his face. The red patent leather seat groaned as he sat back and crossed his arms. "I have a lot on my mind, okay?"

Coop raised his eyebrows. "Like what?"

Rip hesitated, chewing his lower lip, then nodded. "All right, you asked for it. For one thing, it's my sister, Gabi. She's only thirteen, and when I was home, I found out she's dating this gangbanger from the VNE. I caught her one night hangin' all over this punk who was messin' with a Glock 19."

The waitress appeared with two large glasses of milk. Coop smiled at her, ordered their waffles, then looked back at Rip. "Yow."

"Yeah. And it got worse. I show up and this bonehead punk draws down on me. Dude had one in the chamber too."

"Lemme guess, you found that out after you took the gun and fed it to him?"

"Something like that." Now that he was talking it out, he felt like the emotional dam he'd built was about to burst. Oh well. If it helped unjumble the thoughts ricocheting around his brain, then so be it.

He leaned forward, hands on the table. "I'm worried about my little sister, bro. I know how the gang treats their women. It feels like I get kicked in the gut every time I even think about that slimebag putting his hands on her."

Coop nodded. "So what are you going to do?"

"I don't know. Mom needs to get out of there. She's going crazy just trying to keep food on the table. I told her she should find somewhere else to live, even said I'd help with the cost of moving."

John took a sip of milk and set the glass back on the table. "Where is she going to go?"

Rip shook his head. "That's just it, man; she won't. She's been in that dump of an apartment for twenty years. No way she's going to leave."

"Hmmm…" Coop pursed his lips. "And Gabi?"

"That's what really gets me. She was only five when I left. In a way, that's still how I see her. But now she's runnin' with the VNE, and there's nothing I can do about it. I want to fix the problem, but I don't know how."

But there's more to it than that, isn't there? The emotions swirling inside him threatened to boil over, and Rip clenched his jaw to keep it from trembling. The waitress appeared with their order.

Coop was looking at his hands on the white Formica table and chuckling softly, which made Rip want to smack him.

"Dude, what about this is funny?"

One corner of Coop's mouth turned up slightly. "Nothing. I was just thinking that I know what Liz would suggest."

Rip spread his arms wide. "I'm all ears, man."

"She'd say we should pray about it."

Rip blinked. It was the last thing he'd expected Coop to say. Not that it didn't make sense, now that he mentioned it. Rip had prayed lots of times, usually when he needed a little extra luck. On his first combat deployment to Iraq, he'd even made a habit of crossing himself before every mission, praying at meals, and wearing a pendant inscribed with a picture of Saint Philip, the patron saint of the Special Forces.

Rip blinked again. "You mean like right here, right now?"

Coop glanced around. "Sure. Why not? I'm man enough to bow my head in public." He looked Rip in the eye. "Are you?"

Well, when you put it that way… "I'm gonna slap you, Coop."

John's smile had "gotcha" written all over it. "I take it that's a yes? Okay. I'll pray." He bowed his head. Rip did too but kept one wary eye on his friend. This wasn't like him.

"Lord, uh…thank You for this day. Please be with Rip's little sister and protect her from…uh…the bad things she's been getting into. Help Rip know what to do in this situation. Keep us safe too. Amen."

"Okay, ese, who are you, and what have you done with my team sergeant?"

Coop just threw back his head and laughed.

Rip was getting sorta weirded out. "Yeah, laugh it up. But like you said: We rely on each other to come back alive. So don't let this new girlfriend turn you into some kind of religious sissy, you know?"

Coop stopped laughing. "What, praying over my food makes me a sissy now? I've seen you do it!"

"Only if it affects how you do your job."

"And why would it?"

Rip shrugged.

Coop dug into his waffles. "I think it makes me better at what I do."

"Yeah?"

"Sure. I mean, it really is easier when I can trust that God is looking after the unknowns. Then I don't feel like I have to control everything. I can just focus on doing my job."

"And if you're wrong?"

Coop chewed for a minute. "Well, if there isn't a God but believing there is makes me a better soldier, then it's a net plus whether I'm right or wrong."

Rip nodded but said nothing. It was hard to argue with that line of reasoning.

Coop brought his napkin up and wiped his stubbly chin with it. "So anyway, what's your girl situation?"

Man, he's leaving no stone unturned today. Rip shook his head. "*Nada.* I'm swearing off them for Lent."

Coop's eyebrows shot up. "What? You're kidding."

Rip's reply was muffled by a mouthful of waffle. "Naw, just tired of their games, you know?"

"What brought this on? Things go badly with that girl, Naomi?"

"Naomi? Dude, that was three girlfriends ago."

Coop shook his head. "Wow. You change girlfriends like I change socks."

Rip put his fork on his plate. "Exactly."

The simple fact of the matter was that Rip had been a ladies' man since puberty, maybe before. Drugs and alcohol never appealed to him, two things for which he was thankful since it kept him from being disqualified for military service.

But girls were another matter. The real problem was the word *no.* He hated to disappoint a young lady. Even when it would have been best to do so, Rip couldn't bring himself to say that word. Combined with the natural testosterone of youth and the need to prove his manhood to his homies in the VNE, that weakness had resulted in a long string of bad choices and broken hearts.

Coop downed the rest of his milk, then gave a satisfied sigh.

"So why is it bothering you now? Most guys would kill to have that problem."

Rip felt like an idiot for even talking about it. "That's just it. Everyone thinks I'm a stud, but if you ask me, I'm a total failure. I mean, look at the major—he's happily married to the same woman for years. And you—I know you and Liz haven't been going out that long, but it's obvious you two belong together. I've never had anything like that.

"I was having dinner at my apartment the other night with this good-looking *mamacita* I met at the 10K I ran month before last. We were having a great time until my old girlfriend Nicole decided to pay a visit."

Coop grimaced. "Ooohh. That can't be good. Didn't she get the memo that her turn on the merry-go-round had ended?"

"Apparently not. But I'd rather play football with an IED than go through that again."

Coop gave a low whistle. "I can imagine. Nothing in the EOD manual for defusing angry girlfriends."

Rip sopped up the last of the syrup on his plate. "Don't I know it."

While the resulting scene had been all-out ugly, it had made one thing crystal clear in Rip's mind: He didn't really care for either girl. Both had simply been convenient ways to get his needs met, and he couldn't escape the feeling that he was little more than that for them either. There had to be girls out there who were deeper, but he wasn't sure he'd ever had a relationship based on anything other than basic hormones.

He was no better than Chaco, and images of his little sister with that greaseball made him physically ill. Talk about a mood killer.

Coop signaled the waitress for the check. "So what, you're not going to date for forty days?"

"Nope. Maybe longer. I think it's time to find a good girl. It might sound funny, but I think it would be awesome to have a girlfriend who I'd never laid hands on."

The burly team sergeant looked like he'd just heard the major announce he was giving up coffee. "I honestly never thought I'd hear you say such a thing."

Rip's laugh was curt and humorless. "Neither did I, bro. Neither did I."

8

Santa Catalina, Panama. 1700 hours

"FERNANDA! COME QUICK!"

The sound of Hedi's frantic shout caused Fernanda to nearly fall out of her hammock. She struggled to her feet, dropping her journal in the sand, and rushed through the open door into the cabana.

Hedi was standing on the bed, backed into a corner. A trembling hand pointed through the open door into the sparse bathroom. "Ww-what is it?"

Fernanda gave Hedi a concerned look, sweeping her wild black hair from her face with one hand. She adjusted her bikini top and tentatively peeked around the corner into the bathroom, half expecting to see a giant boa constrictor or saltwater crocodile. Instead, something small and very blue scuttled across the floor and hid behind the commode.

Hedi screamed. Fernanda started, more from her friend than from whatever critter was inhabiting the lavatory. "Just calm down, girl." Fernanda bent down to peer behind the toilet. Then she broke out laughing.

At that moment, Zack burst into the room, barefoot and panting. "What's wrong?"

Fernanda was still chuckling. "There's a land crab in our bath-room."

"A land crab. Cool!" Zack went into the bathroom for a closer look. Hedi collapsed on the bed with a groan and buried her face in the pillow.

Zack's excited voice echoed out of the bathroom. "Oh, man! This guy's feisty. He's showing me his karate moves. I wonder if—ow! Aaaahhh!"

Fernanda jumped out of the way as Zack streaked out of the cabana with the blue-and-orange crustacean attached to his right index finger.

"Problem solved." Shaking her head, Fernanda returned out-side to retrieve her journal.

Settling carefully back into the colorful woven cotton ham-mock, she retrieved her pen from the ground and shook the sand from the small, leather-bound diary. Opening to the current page, Fernanda laughed again as she reread the sentence she'd written just before Hedi's outburst.

I can't imagine a more peaceful place on earth.

Still smiling, she lay back and took in the beauty beyond her bright-red toenails. Two double rows of palm trees shaded her ham-mock, and five cabanas painted in sunny colors sat just a hundred or so meters from the water.

The primitive resort was situated on a long beach the color of campfire smoke, about two miles southeast of the fishing village of Santa Catalina. The professor had dropped them off at their cabanas and then gone back into town to find the fisherman he had hired to take them to Coiba tomorrow morning.

Just offshore, the large waves rolling toward shore reminded Fernanda of why she'd seen so many surfer dudes strutting shirtless around the town when they arrived.

Carlos had borrowed a bodyboard from the owner of the tiny resort as soon as they'd finished unloading their gear. An hour later, he was still out in the water, hotdogging it with a small group of Canadian surfers on spring break.

She brushed off the page and started writing again.

I can't believe I've lived in Panama all my life and have never seen this place. I spoke with David, the owner of the Oasis. (He's Italian and VERY cute, probably just a few years older than I am.) He says that the property values have gone crazy in the last year, which probably means he's a rich man. But he doesn't seem to have much need for money. I suspect he sees the Oasis as a good way to get paid to live here and surf.

The local fishermen had just returned with their daily catch when we arrived this afternoon. We stopped for a moment in "town" (one road that ends in the Pacific Ocean), and I watched the local kids playing futbol in the street. They were dirty, unkempt, and obviously poor, but they, like their parents, didn't seem to have a care in the world. Maybe having so little, there isn't much to worry over. Sometimes I wonder if it wouldn't be better to have such a simple life. In a way, I envy them.

Now that the road into town is paved, I'm worried that

the big corporations will come in. And if they get their way,
they'll soon destroy this incredible view with a string of high-rise
hotels. The professor—Alex—talks about the evils of corporate
greed often in his lectures. Papa would have undoubtedly
opposed him, having spent years working to build Casa Lerida
into a successful company. But Alex has made me look at my
upbringing in a whole new light. Our family's success in the
coffee business ensured that we always had more than enough,
but what right did we have to live in such luxury on the backs
of the poor Guaymi who still work our farms today? I guess I've
always known that poverty like this existed, but I never thought
about it like I have since meeting Alex. He's a very wise man.

"Hey, Fernanda." She looked up to see Zack heading her way.
"Hey."

Zack stopped short of where she was lounging and turned
slightly to gaze out across the beach when she sat up. She got the
distinct impression he was trying *not* to look at her. *That's strange.*
She only noticed because that was the opposite reaction she got
from most men.

"I, uh…I just saw the professor pull in. Didn't he say something about going out for pizza?"

She closed her journal and stood up. "I think so. Why don't
you go fetch Carlos, and I'll change clothes and see if I can wake up
Hedi."

Zack ran a hand through his blond non-hairdo. "Sounds like a
plan."

Ten minutes later, Alex, Fernanda, a very sunburned Carlos,
and Zack piled into the SUV for the short trip to the local pizza

joint.

"Where's Hedi?" Carlos asked, his black hair still wet from the surf.

"She's not feeling well." Fernanda shrugged. "I think the long ride down made her a little queasy. She gave me her camera, though, and made me promise to take lots of pictures."

"I hope she's better by tomorrow morning," Zack said. "She's going to have a hard enough time carrying that pack without being sick to boot."

"We'll convene after supper and distribute our food and other common gear," Alex said, as he powered the Rexton up the steep dirt road that led into town. "Regrettably, I was forced to make some last minute changes to our boat plans. The captain I normally use went to Santiago to get a part for his boat and won't be back until tomorrow afternoon."

Fernanda frowned. "Didn't he know we were coming?"

"Well, yes. But these things happen in an area without proper communication resources. It's easily remedied, though. Any of the fishermen in town will gladly take us. A trip to Coiba is much more profitable than fishing all day."

A moment later, Alex turned left onto a dirt path and slowed as they passed a gaggle of scruffy surfer dudes.

"Hey!" Carlos called out the window. "What up, brah!"

Alex looked puzzled. "Who are those boys?"

Fernanda smiled and winked at him. "Carlos's Canadian surfing buddies."

The SUV rolled to a stop in front of a small orange house with several thatch-topped umbrellas shading tables arranged about the front yard. A sign with the name Pizza Jamming hung above a walkway that led from the gate up to the side of the house. Lively Reggaeton music emanated from inside.

"This is a restaurant?" Carlos looked doubtful.

"What kind of a name is Pizza Jamming?" Zack asked as they got out of the SUV.

Alex shrugged as he rounded the front of the SUV to Fernanda's side. "They've got a brick oven pizza that's to die for."

"Rock on!" Carlos pushed through the gate, and the rest of the group followed him toward the entrance.

Fernanda caught the professor's attention and hung back as Carlos and Zack went inside. "Alex. I'm worried about Hedi. What will we do if she's sick tomorrow?"

His confident smile made her feel gooey inside. "We'll worry about that in the morning." He touched her elbow lightly with one hand as he motioned toward the entrance with the other. "You look beautiful tonight, Fernanda. Let's enjoy an evening together, shall we?"

The way he said it made the evening sound like a date. But something deep inside her didn't mind.

The place was packed, though few of the mostly younger crowd looked like locals. The two women who ran the restaurant— one waiting tables and the other behind the bar—weren't local either. Everyone sported the sort of half-dressed look that seemed to be the norm around here. Fernanda got the feeling that if you lived here, you'd rarely have need for much more than a two-piece.

The restaurant was open to the yard on three sides, with a brightly painted bar made of concrete strewn with decorative driftwood and seashells. Hammocks hung around the edges of the several picnic tables inside. Party lights strung in the eaves gave the place a festive atmosphere, and shirts and shoes were definitely not required. Even the waitress wore only shorts and a bikini top.

Once they found an empty table and were seated, Fernanda excused herself and went to wash up. When she returned, the waitress had apparently already taken their drink order, because everyone had a bottle of beer, except for Zack, who sipped a Pepsi.

"Ah, Fernanda," Alex said, half standing as she approached. "I took the liberty of ordering you an Atlas. We've got some ceviche on the way as well."

"Thank you, but I'd prefer water," she said as politely as possible.

The professor looked somewhat embarrassed. "Oh, of course. Forgive me." He turned and beckoned to the waitress. *"Agua, por favor."*

Carlos reached over and helped himself to her beer. "What, you don't drink either?"

She gave him a pasted-on smile. "I drink water."

"Why, is it a religious thing for you like it is with Saint Zack here?"

Zack pointed the top of his Pepsi bottle at Carlos. "Saint Zack. That has a nice ring to it."

Fernanda was impressed. Under that blond mop, Zack had confidence about himself and his faith. She wished she could be more like that.

The waitress hurried up carrying a bowl of ceviche in one hand and a small plate of water crackers in the other. Once the appetizer was on the table, Zack and Carlos attacked it while Alex ordered two pizzas for the group in near-perfect Spanish. Then the waitress left.

Alex pulled a laminated map from his back pocket. "I guess we should review what the schedule looks like tomorrow so we can get everything ready when we return to the Oasis."

He spread the map out between them, and they all craned their necks to look at the topographic representation of Isla Coiba.

"It looks like a big shrimp," Carlos noted.

"It doesn't look *that* big," Zack said. "We should be able to cross the island in a day or two, shouldn't we?"

The professor chuckled. "Perhaps if it was flat and had no vegetation, but Coiba is eighty-five percent virgin triple-canopy rain forest. Most of it is so dense and steep that prisoners who had escaped into the interior often were never heard from again or came stumbling back to the penal colony a couple of days later, begging to go back to work in the fields."

"Wow, you're kidding." Zack's eyes danced. "This is gonna be great!"

Fernanda thought of the trails she and her friends had hiked around Boquete when she was younger. Since then she'd spent plenty of time in the jungle, but Panama didn't have many places left that could legitimately be classified as virgin triple canopy. And on Coiba there wouldn't even be a trail to follow.

She hadn't told her mother that the packing list for this trip had specified not one, but two machetes per person. Considering that *Señora* Lerida would undoubtedly consider it unladylike to be seen near any sort of farm implement.

Fernanda couldn't imagine what her mother would say about her daughter hacking through *la selva* with a three-foot knife. That was why at home Fernanda rarely elaborated about her work.

Her mother probably imagined her behind a microscope in the

lab, when in reality Fernanda's favorite part of her studies was hanging ninety feet up in a giant ceiba tree, collecting specimens.

"The boat will first take us to the ranger station, here on the north end," Alex said, as he pulled out a red pen and pointed out the small encampment at the top of the laminated map.

At least we won't be the only people on the island.

"We'll spend an hour or so looking around and getting our permits stamped, then continue around the windward side, and put in here, at Playa Hermosa." He circled the spot with his pen. "I'd like to try to penetrate at least three miles into the rain forest from there. It's an area farthest from most of the prisoner work camps spread around the edges of the island, which means there are areas that may have never been seen by humans.

"If we can get some good specimens collected by day three, we should be able to make it back to Playa Hermosa with half a day to relax on the beach before the boat arrives to pick us up."

"That sounds awesome, Alex," Zack said. "What kinds of things do we need to watch for while we're there?"

"Well, it's important to remember that we're at least a day's journey from the nearest hospital, so we all need to be very careful. The fer-de-lance is one of the most venomous snakes around, and they are quite common on Coiba. I brought some of the antivenin, though. It's in the trauma kit. The only problem is that the antivenin itself makes the victim go into anaphylactic shock in about fifty percent of the cases. So let's make a good effort to scare away any snakes we come across."

A shiver crawled up Fernanda's spine. The standard procedure for treating anaphylactic shock was a strong dose of adrenaline, which posed its own problems. And the professor hadn't said anything about having *that* on hand.

Alex took a sip of his beer. "The crocs won't be a problem once we get inland. They stay near the salt water. Actually, the one thing to be most careful of is the monkeys."

Fernanda's brow wrinkled. "Monkeys?"

"Yes, howler monkeys. They won't hurt you, but they'll steal anything they can get their hands on. They're sneaky little buggers. I lost a pair of leather gloves to them last year."

Carlos laughed. "So if we wake up and Fernanda's gone, we know to blame it on the howler monkeys." He launched into his impression of a primate. She didn't tell him that it made him look more civilized.

A warm hand gently rested on her leg beneath the table. Fernanda turned to look at Alex and saw his smile and a barely perceptible wink.

For a moment, she hesitated, and the tingle in her spine returned. Then, returning his smile, she slid her fingers into his.

Would this be a night to remember—or regret?

Hugo sat at the bar brooding as he had for the last three hours, because he had nowhere else to go tonight. The cheap Panama brand beer was weak and nearly tasteless, but he was happy to have it since there had been none at all on the island. But what he really wanted was a hot shower and a comfortable bed.

He had come to Pizza Jamming specifically because none of the locals did. He didn't want to talk to any of the fishermen who frequented the other bar in town. Here he could pretend to be just another tourist, though he was obviously Panamanian, and pretend to be interested in perfectly worthless pastimes like the foreigners were.

Surfing? What's the point? Paddle out only to be pushed back in. And yet most of the people around him probably paid more for the airfare to get here than he had made in the last ten years. How so many people acquired such wealth baffled him.

Perhaps one day soon I will know what it is like to be rich.

Something flashed like lightning. Hugo looked up from his beer to see a beautiful chica taking pictures of her three male companions.

He studied the girl. She was stunning, and he realized that it wasn't just beer that he'd been missing on the island. She was tall and athletic, with nicely toned legs and flowing curls of black hair that reached halfway down her back. High cheekbones offset intense green eyes that made Hugo think this was a woman you wouldn't want mad at you.

Ah, but with those lips, what fun it would be making up!

Alas, it looked as if the goddess was already spoken for. The two young men at the table probably wouldn't know how to treat such a woman. But the older man—the one with the salt-and-pepper goatee—he looked at her as Hugo himself did, but with an obvious air of smugness that showed he had what he wanted, or soon would.

Hugo swallowed the rest of his beer in one gulp. No matter, he would be gone by early morning anyhow. He must catch the first bus to Santiago and be back with the needed supplies in time to make it back to the island before darkness fell. He had better get some sleep.

Rising from his stool, he turned to go, then stopped abruptly.

What was that map the man with the goatee had spread before him?

As nonchalantly as possible, Hugo sauntered toward the restroom, catching a better look at the map as he passed their table.

Coiba! It wasn't so much the presence of the map that made his blood run cold, however.

It was the location of the red circle.

He might stay out tonight later than he had hoped. Unfortunately, though, his only companions would be other locals waiting in line to use the phone.

9

The Oasis. 2130 hours

A SLIGHT GUST of wind from offshore started the palm trees swaying in the darkness as Fernanda left the large open-air eating area at the Oasis. She'd spent the past hour talking with Zack and David, the owner of the resort.

Though the sun had been down for at least two hours, the sandy path leading to the beach was still warm, and it felt good on Fernanda's bare feet. In that time, the air temperature had dropped at least fifteen degrees, giving her goose bumps. She wished she had packed something to put over the thin white blouse she wore.

She'd lost track of time. She planned to go to bed early and only went to see David to buy an extra bottle of water. Zack was there, watching a movie via satellite, and they got to talking. Soon David emerged from the kitchen and sat on one of the comfortable wicker couches. Before long the movie lost out to the more interesting conversation. Fernanda was impressed with Zack's travel experience. Since the age of eight, he had accompanied his physician father on medical mission trips around the world.

"He'd have us traveling sometimes four months out of the year." Zack shook his head. "As we speak, he's in Darfur giving out medical supplies in the relief camps."

"What'd you do about school?" Fernanda asked.

"I was homeschooled, so we took it with us."

"Wow. I've never met anyone who was homeschooled before."

Zack looked at her with raised eyebrows. "Really? Maybe it's not such a big thing here in Panama."

David brushed sand from his bare feet. "So what made your father want to do medical missions? Mine was in the foreign legion."

Zack shrugged. "Dad always said that what you have loses its value if it isn't shared. I guess he thought that meant vitamins and antibiotics too."

The moonlight illuminated the path to the cabana, and Fernanda knew she should go straight to bed. But the soft sound of the waves drew her out onto the deserted beach in front of the huts.

The night air smelled salty and fresh, and the tide was in, the soft incessant crashing of the water upon the sand much closer than it had been. She recognized the call of a gray-headed Chachalaca from somewhere up in the palm trees.

After walking over to one of the thatch-roofed umbrellas, she sat on a white plastic lounger facing the ocean and hugged her knees to her chest, thinking about what Zack had said.

"What you have loses its value if it isn't shared."

Was that what had been bothering her lately? She'd been the top of her class in prep school and had lots to be proud of…or did she? She and her family had so much, and yet everything she'd done since leaving for college had been to further her own career, to accomplish her goals. It hurt to admit it, but she couldn't remember a time when she'd made a decision based on something that didn't personally benefit her.

Fernanda thought of her father. He'd been successful in business, but what did that mean now that he was gone? Whenever people spoke of him, they talked about how kind he was. If the subject of his wealth ever came up, it was only in the context of his generosity.

Now that she was only months away from gaining her postgraduate degree, Fernanda had been having doubts—not whether or not she'd make it, but whether or not, having come so far, the title would be worth the cost. Sure, she was an expert at the classification of birds, bugs, and other jungle life, but would that be a fitting epitaph at the end of her life?

There has to be something more.

Zack's father had found it. Fernanda was still looking.

She watched the waves crashing on the shore. Each one an individual, its energy expended in a matter of seconds, leaving almost no trace on the black sand.

Something about that gnawed at her gut. She looked up at the stars. Would the wave of her own life leave any mark?

She decided she would pray about it, then it struck her that it had been a long time since she'd done so.

Lord, I'm sorry that I haven't talked to You much lately... I really don't know why. Just busy, I guess. But please help me know what my purpose is here. I love my field of study, but if I'm really honest, much of what I'm learning at university—evolution and all that—goes against what I've learned at church all my life. I know You are in control, but I need to feel it. Is this where I'm supposed to be? Help me to make sense of it all. Help me to find the life You have for me. I don't want to waste it...

Her thoughts trailed off, and she sat watching a line of high cirrus clouds scuttle across the rising moon.

"I thought I might find you here."

Startled, Fernanda turned to the sound of the voice that had intruded on her thoughts. "Oh…Alex. Hi. I guess I should be back in the cabana packing my bags."

The professor padded across the sand on bare feet, wearing lightweight linen pants and an open-collared, long-sleeved cotton shirt. "Anxious about tomorrow, eh?"

"Um, sort of."

He sat on the foot of her lounger. His face bore a soft expression with just a hint of a smile. "Don't worry, Fernanda. I'll take care of you."

"No, it's not—"

"Shhhh." He held a finger to her lips. "Listen, I'm glad we have a chance to be alone. I've been wanting to talk to you about this and haven't had the opportunity until now."

Fernanda was still catching up with his train of thought. "What do you mean?"

"Ever since we worked together on the *Nymphalis quinterus* project, I've been unable to stop thinking about you. I've never even considered pursuing a relationship with a student before."

With a student. I guess he's right. She hadn't thought of it that way. He would need to be careful if they decided to go any further than harmless flirting.

"To be honest, I've always been too wrapped up in my work to even think about anything else."

She nodded. She could relate to that. Even though plenty of men had pursued her, Fernanda had seen dating as direct competition with her studies. People assumed that just because she was beautiful, she had an endless supply of dates. But the same looks that turned heads all across campus had possibly intimidated most guys from approaching her.

He threaded his fingers into hers. "I can't help thinking that perhaps we'll both discover something on this trip—something between us."

"I-I'm flattered, Alex." It was all she could think to say, since most of her brain was occupied with a thousand questions assaulting her at once. Did she want this? He *was* a tenured professor. What would her fellow students say? Did they have to know? Alex was more than twenty years her senior. Was she ready for a relationship?

Before she could make sense of any of this, Alex leaned in and kissed her.

Her eyes went wide, and he pulled back suddenly. It was the first time she'd ever seen him get flustered. "Um, I probably shouldn't have done that." His sudden reversal gave her time to recover, and the sheepish look on his face was just so…cute.

She reached out and covered his other hand with hers. She didn't know if it was right, but she'd worry about that later. "You don't see me complaining, do you?" she said with a soft smile.

Then he kissed her again, and this time she kissed him back. The goose bumps returned, only they weren't from the breeze.

Passion welled up, and before she knew it, he'd pushed her back against the reclined lounge chair, his soft goatee tickling her face as he devoured her lips with his own.

When he started fumbling with the buttons on her blouse, the voice of caution inside her head finally became too loud to ignore. She brought her hands up to his chest and pushed.

He sat up, panting, and looked at her. "What?"

"Alex, we need to think this through."

He glanced around. "You're right. We should probably go back to my cabana."

"That's not what I meant! I mean, this…this is just too…it's too fast. I'm not going to sleep with you."

A look of frustration crossed his face. "Come on, dear. We're both adults." He tried to kiss her again.

But whatever passion she had felt was gone. She pushed him away and swung her feet off the chair. "Yes we are, which means we shouldn't act like a couple of hormonal teenagers." She stood and brushed the wrinkles out of her shirt.

He went into full back-pedal mode. "Fernanda, listen. I'm sorry if—"

"Good night, Alex. I…" Part of her wanted nothing more than to be loved by this man; the rest of her was screaming, "Run!"

She turned and hurried toward the cabanas before the rising moon's exquisite beauty could convince her to change her mind.

Joint Special Operations Command Headquarters, Fort Bragg, North Carolina. 0900 hours

"Good morning, men. Come right in and take a seat." Major Louis Williams gestured to the long conference table without letting go of the giant coffee mug that bore the label Caffeine Transfer Unit.

Rip entered the room just behind fellow NCOs Bobby Sweeney and Buzz Hogan, who plopped down in the two burgundy leather swivel chairs closest to the screen at the front of the room. Rip sat next to Hogan, and the rest of the team filed in and sat around the highly polished table.

John Cooper slid into the chair at the end farthest from the screen. "We've got everybody, sir."

"Wow, these headquarter Zoomies really have it made." Buzz gazed around the room. "When do we get a briefing area like this?"

"Yeah." Sweeney stroked his blond mustache. "We'd better keep Baldwin away from that thar fancy overhead projector, or he might just turn it into a laser cannon or some newfangled weapon of mass destruction."

Sergeant First Class Frank Baldwin smirked at him. "*You* are a weapon of mass destruction, Sweeney."

The blond master sergeant grinned and pulled out a can of Copenhagen. "Why thank you, Frank. That's the nicest thing anybody's ever said to me."

"Put that fish bait away," Major Williams growled. "I'm not going to have any half-full spit cans left lying around for the general to find."

Sweeney frowned and dropped the chewing tobacco back into the arm pocket on his digital-camo uniform. "Speaking of fish bait, you catch anything while you were home on leave, Buzz?"

"Coupla catfish out of the pond at my uncle's place in East Texas. You?"

"Nah. I was mostly helping my dad build a deck on the back of the house."

Buzz twirled a finger in the air. "Yee-ha."

"Tell me about it. His idea of a good time is digging post holes."

The door burst open, and CIA Special Agent Mary Walker entered carrying a large sheaf of papers. She was wearing a dark blue pinstripe blazer and matching skirt, her long red hair swept up into a tight bun.

"Hey, it's Agent Crash!" Sweeney drawled. "You pin on your kamikaze wings yet, darlin'?" Laughter and applause rippled through the group.

"Good morning, Sergeant Sweeney." Mary smiled sweetly as she dropped the foot-thick stack of manila folders into his lap, causing him to gasp and pitch forward in his seat. "Pass these out for me, would you please?"

John chuckled and leaned toward Sweeney. "Must still be a sore subject, Bobby."

Sweeney grimaced. "It is now."

More laughter erupted from the group.

"All right." Major Williams set his mug on the table. "Don't harass Agent Phoenix here. She saved your behinds in Lebanon. Next time she might just leave you out there."

African American medic, Sergeant First Class Joe Kelly raised his hand. "Personally, ma'am, I think using an unmanned aerial vehicle as a remote detonator demonstrates brilliant initiative. I just hope they didn't make you pay for it."

Phoenix looked genuinely surprised. "Why, thank you, Doc."

"How much was that little plane worth, anyway?" Rip asked.

Mary's pale complexion darkened. "Forty-five thousand, three hundred and ninety dollars, not including the commo gear it carried."

Whistles went up around the group. Coop raised his eyebrows. "Hope you make more than we do."

The tall CIA agent shrugged. "Well, after I pointed out what a hellfire missile would have cost, they dropped the matter."

More cheers went up until Major Williams raised a hand for silence. "All right now, at ease so we can get this briefing out of the way. I've got places to go."

Rip figured one of the major's girls had a soccer game that afternoon.

"Okay," Phoenix said, her professional demeanor returning. "I trust you all enjoyed your week off. I figured it was the least we could do after ruining your homecoming party with that false alarm. Besides, it's taken us this long to wade through all of the intel you generated in Lebanon."

She produced a small thumb drive and plugged it into the rear of the video projector. A moment later, a satellite photo appeared on the screen.

"Hey, that's Panama," Frank said.

"I'll get to that in a moment." Phoenix held up a folder. "First, let me connect the dots for you on how our intel has led us to where we stand at the moment. The good news is: we are making progress. The bad news is: not fast enough.

"When you guys hit the terrorist compound in southern Lebanon last month, you succeeded in taking out the men responsible for the bombing attack on the Hotel Rowena in February. Some of the documents you recovered from the site showed that Ansar Inshallah had much bigger plans for their stockpile of ITEB. Fortunately, those plans were thwarted."

"Score one for the homies." Rip high-fived Sweeney.

Phoenix gave them a sideways look. "Right. She pulled a glossy photograph from her file. Anyway, this is a picture of the type of bottles recovered from the terrorist stronghold. You'll notice they are clear glass, one-point-five liter bottles."

"Like a wine bottle," Coop said.

"Exactly, John. Notice that the bottle has a unique lip with three ridges on it. Other than that, it could be any high-end water bottle on the market. We're still tracking down where the bottles were made but haven't had any luck on that yet."

"Probably from China," Sweeney said. "Everything else is."

Phoenix ignored him. "We decided to focus our efforts on finding out how the ITEB got into the country, since you found no evidence of it being manufactured in Lebanon. After doing some more research on the chemical compound itself, we found that Iso-Triethyl Borane is somewhat unstable in its pure form. This means that it would most likely be refrigerated for transport, so we first checked out all of the reefers that had arrived in Sidon in the thirty days before the bombing."

Doc looked puzzled. "Reefers?"

She nodded. "Refrigerator ships. That brought up nothing, so I expanded the search to all ships that had called there, since it's a pretty small port. In fact, they had only thirty-nine ships in total arrive in Sidon in the month before the Rowena was hit.

"We checked into all of them, and only one came up suspicious. It's an old break-bulk ship called the *M/V Invincible*. What set it apart from the others on our list is that the ship disappeared shortly after the last time it called at Sidon."

Coop sat forward in his seat. "Disappeared? Where?"

"Just off the coast of Panama." Phoenix checked her notes. "About a week ago. Now, normally this wouldn't be much to go on. But we caught a break. I called the Panamanian police headquarters last night, and they told me that two nights ago a ship coming into the Pacific side of the Isthmus rescued one member of the

Invincible's crew. He was hovering near death after days adrift with no food or water.

"He's now recovering in the hospital in Panama City. Our Panama station chief sent someone to talk to the man this morning. He's in pretty bad shape and can't talk much, but he was able to look at some photos you boys took of empty crates of ITEB in Lebanon. He confirmed that they had once been on his ship. We still hope to debrief the crewmember fully, but it appears the ship was stolen by pirates who killed the entire crew except him."

Rip was incredulous. "How do you steal an entire ship?"

She started to answer, but Frank interrupted. "It's actually fairly common. I was reading an article about it recently. Happens a lot off the coast of Somalia. Pirates come up in fast boats and board the ship, kill the crew, then repaint the thing at sea and give it a new name. Then they sail the new vessel into some port and sell off its cargo. Once that's done, they either sink the ship or sell it for scrap."

"Just like a chop shop back on the block." Rip had a fleeting thought of Gabi joyriding in a souped-up yellow import but pushed it away.

Major Williams shook his head. "That's amazing. Some people's minds are just evil."

"Preach it, Major." Doc nodded.

"So where do we come in?" Coop was all business.

Phoenix turned back to the projection screen and aimed a laser pointer at the photo. "The rescued sailor seemed to indicate that a similar shipment was on board when the *Invincible* was hijacked, about fifty miles off the Pacific coast, here. If this is the case, that means we have more ITEB now in the hands of murderous criminals."

Major Williams frowned. "Wonderful."

"I'm sending you to Panama with your gear so you'll be ready when we need you. You'll go in commercial, and your kit will fly separately to be picked up at the embassy in Panama City. Travel details and a more in-depth intel brief are in the folders in front of you. You leave tomorrow afternoon."

"Er, men, there's something I need to tell you." Major Williams's usual uberconfident stare had been replaced by a sheepish look.

Rip got a strange feeling about what was coming. He'd never known his commander to act uncertain about anything.

Williams hesitated, then continued. "I won't be with you in Panama. Gonna have to go in for back surgery."

Frank let out a low whistle, and Coop raised his eyebrows but said nothing. Rip turned to the major. "What did you do to your back?"

The man looked even more sheepish. "Well, um…it was sort of a sports injury. Nothing too serious, but the docs want to fix it so it won't get any worse. I'm gonna be laid up for three weeks."

Hogan furrowed his brow. "A sports injury?"

"Yeah, well." The major put down his mug again. "Okay, listen. I hurt it playing football with my girls."

Silence reigned for a half second as everyone looked around the room at each other, and then they all burst into laughter.

Williams was laughing too. "I know, I know. It's crazy, but that Denise is a killer when it comes to anything competitive. And she hits like a truck."

Phoenix was trying to stifle a smile. "Which one is Denise?"

"My fourteen-year-old."

This time even Mary couldn't contain her laughter.

Sweeney wiped the tears from his eyes and cleared his throat. "So Phoenix, will you be our eye in the sky again this time?"

Mary was back to business as she fixed him with her gaze. "Negative. This time, I'm coming with you."

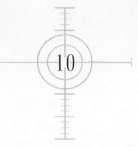

The Oasis. 0915 hours

THE SAND WAS COOL on their feet as Fernanda and Hedi stepped off of the cabana's porch and headed for the water with their backpacks. Rays of morning sunlight were filtering through the palms, and hermit crabs scuttled from their path as they walked.

Fernanda looked at her friend. "So you're feeling better?"

Hedi was back to her perky self. "I feel better. Perhaps it was that chicken soup I had for lunch yesterday that made me sick."

Fernanda feigned offense. "How can you say that about sancocho, Panama's national dish?"

"Oh, sorry."

Fernanda laughed. "Don't be. You didn't see me eating it. Besides, I thought that roadside restaurant was a little questionable. I'm glad you're better, though."

The guys were waiting for them at the water's edge, standing next to a pile of gear.

"There they are." Alex beamed as the girls approached. "The boat will be here any minute. I've got our food and other common gear divided up into individual stuff sacks. One for each of us." He gestured to the stack.

"Great," Hedi muttered. "Just what I need—more weight."

Fernanda shrugged. "It'll be a good incentive to eat."

"I don't think we need to worry about that on this trip. We might get shorter carrying these things around, though." Hedi sighed.

They dropped their packs on the sand. Alex picked up two stuff sacks and handed one to each of the girls. As he did, he leaned close to Fernanda and said quietly, "I'm very sorry about last night. Please forgive me."

She felt herself flush. "Um…thanks. Me too. I guess I just—"

"Here comes the boat!" Carlos shouted.

They all turned and shielded their eyes against the sun. Just beyond the surf break, a small fishing boat with a single outboard motor made its way toward them through the waves.

Hedi's mouth dropped open. "This is it?"

Alex laughed. "What were you expecting, a cruise ship?"

The closer the boat came, the more Fernanda had to agree with Hedi. The tiny lancha wasn't much bigger than a rowboat, with a blue tarp strung on poles to provide some shade. Even with the subdued waves this early in the morning, the little boat looked like it would surely be swamped before it reached the shore. But the pilot was skillful, and a few moments later it came within ten yards of the sandy beach.

There, he and a younger boy, who looked to be the fisherman's son, jumped out and waded the rest of the way in, pulling the boat between them as the swells rolled beneath it.

"Okay, let's do it." Alex scooped up his pack and headed off toward the water. Carlos followed close behind.

"Here, let me help you with that," Zack said, picking up Hedi's pack as well as his own. "If you want, Fernanda, leave yours there and get in the boat. I'll come back for it."

"You're sweet, Zack, but I can manage."

The fisherman and his son held the boat as steady as possible in about a foot of water while everyone passed their packs to Alex, who stacked them in the front of the boat. Then they all scrambled in and found seats amid the gear and extra fuel cans.

The fisherman and his son pushed the boat into waist-deep water and clambered aboard. Fernanda braced herself as the next wave approached. The fisherman struggled to start his outboard engine as the front of the boat rode up the surface of the wave, then crashed down the other side.

Hedi looked as if her eyeballs had doubled in size, and she clung to the side of the tiny boat with a death grip. Despite the fisherman's frenzied efforts, the motor still refused to start.

The lancha was slipping sideways in the surf. If the next wave hit them as they were, they would certainly capsize. Finally the small outboard sputtered to life, and the boat captain gave it full throttle, swinging the nose back just in time. The wave crested as it passed beneath them, dousing the group and their gear with spray.

The guys seemed to be thoroughly enjoying themselves, but Hedi was frozen in terror. Fernanda wiped the sea spray from her eyes. *I was crazy to get up early to fix my hair.*

A few harrowing moments later, once they made it past the surf break and into calmer water, Alex stood and gestured to the fisherman at the rear of the boat. "Ladies and gentlemen, may I introduce Vincente, owner of the good ship *Pescador* and the second best boat captain in Santa Catalina. Please give him a round of applause."

Fernanda was all too happy to oblige.

The white-haired fisherman's smile revealed a few missing teeth and the fact that he spoke no English. With a slight bow, he opened the throttle and the little boat sped off toward the low, dark land-mass barely visible on the horizon.

"There she is," Alex said. "That's our island."

A shiver went through her. She didn't know if it was from the cool morning air, from the thought of what lay ahead, or both. "It looks so far away."

Alex nodded. "About twenty miles from here. Actually, the word *Coiba* means 'far away' in the language of the Cacique Indi-ans who inhabited Panama until the late sixteenth century."

Fernanda nodded, impressed as usual with Alex's knowledge. She enjoyed the view for about twenty minutes as the boat sped along. Then she saw a splash about thirty meters ahead of the boat. And another. "Hedi! Dolphins!"

Hedi jumped up from where she had been sitting under the tarp at the rear of the craft. "Where? Ach!" She fell back into her seat.

Fernanda pointed at the twin dorsal fins that broke the water in unison and then disappeared again. "There. Look!"

"Sweet!" Zack shaded his eyes in the direction she was pointing.

"*¡Da palmas!!*" Vincente shouted over the roar of the outboard.

"Is that the word for 'dolphin' in Spanish?" Hedi asked, pulling herself hand over hand as she crawled to the front of the boat.

Fernanda laughed. "No, he says to clap. It must call the dol-phins." They all cheered and clapped as two more of the sleek black animals came completely out of the water.

"Ooh, they're so *fast!*" Hedi clapped. Zack was fumbling with his digital camera, trying to get a shot.

Carlos sat up, removing his earbuds and looking around. "What's going on?"

They all enjoyed the show for another minute or so, and then the pod seemed to tire and fall back. A few more jumps behind the boat, and they were gone.

"That...was...awesome," Zack panted.

Fernanda had to agree with him. *This is definitely going in my journal!*

The sun's rays warmed her back. She suddenly felt tired and checked her watch. They still had an hour and a half to go, so she turned around, put her back against the pile of gear, slid her hat over her eyes, and rested.

She thought about Alex and about what happened last night. She found him attractive, smart, and interesting. Her mother had always warned her about getting involved with a non-Christian, but really, was it all that bad if you were just dating for fun? Last night he certainly wanted more than she was willing to give, but she was an adult and could take care of herself.

Fernanda gazed through the weave of her hat and saw him staring at her. A thin smile formed on her lips.

Mother would have a fit.

She sat up with a start when the boat's small outboard motor suddenly changed pitch, screaming at twice the rpms it had been running. But rather than a corresponding increase in speed, the boat slowed like a water skier who lost his rope, settling into the vast expanse of blue. She pulled the hat from her eyes in time to see Vincente hit the kill switch on the motor.

"What happened?" Hedi's wide eyes were back.

Fernanda made an "I don't know" face, wondering if she'd been asleep. Alex stood at the back of the boat, looking down at the motor. He and Vincente were having an animated conversation, and she could hear enough of it to know that whatever had happened wasn't good.

Alex turned back toward the group, his face grim. "We've got a problem—our propeller just fell off."

Dread constricted Fernanda's throat as expressions of disbelief and frustration exploded from the rest of her team.

Alex held out a hand to quell the chaos. "It'll be okay. The captain has an extra prop. It'll just take him a little while to put it on." He shaded his eyes and scanned the rugged coastline, still at least six miles distant. Fernanda followed his gaze. No other boats were visible in any direction.

"How long is a little while?" Carlos took off his hat and gauged the rising sun with one hand. "We're going to get cooked if we stay out here too long, brah."

But Fernanda had a more pressing problem.

She'd forgotten to use the restroom before they left.

She leaned over the side and peered into the dark water. A school of large red fish passed directly beneath their boat, either ignorant or apathetic to their presence.

This could get ugly.

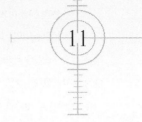

The Pacific Ocean. 0945 hours

FANNING HERSELF WITH her hat wasn't really helping.

Fernanda's watch, as well as the steadily increasing heat, told her they'd been adrift for just over thirty minutes. But her full bladder made every minute like an hour. If something didn't happen soon, something would be happening soon.

Carlos and Zack were still napping across from her, and Hedi had pulled out a book and was reading under the shade of the blue tarp. Alex was leaning over the broken outboard engine, scowling, handing tools down to Vincente, who was in the water attempting to attach the new prop.

The boat rocked gently as Zack woke up and stepped across the backpacks and other gear in the front of the boat to sit next to Fernanda. "Are you all right?"

She turned to look at him blithely, determined to preserve her dignity for as long as humanly possible. "Never better." *I love being broiled alive on the open sea with six people in a boat the size of a large picnic table.*

"Pretty hot, huh?"

Still fanning, Fernanda threw him a sideways glance and blew a sweaty black curl out of her eyes.

He blinked. "What?"

"Have you always had such a solid grasp on the obvious?"

Zack feigned offense. "Are you kidding? This is a highly refined skill. In any case, don't worry. I'm sure we'll be on our way pretty soon. If not, I say we vote Carlos off the boat and steal his iPod."

"I heard that," Carlos called without moving from his kicked-back perch on the other side of the boat.

Fernanda laughed in spite of herself. *Ooohh, don't make me laugh!*

Zack grinned. "Anyway, if worst comes to worst, the good professor can call for help on his iridium."

Fernanda crossed her legs. "His what?"

"His iridium satellite phone. He showed it to me last night. It looks like a sort of high-speed cell phone, and it works from anywhere."

She nodded. "That's comforting."

The boat swayed again as Vincente climbed aboard, dripping wet and smiling. *"Bueno."* He flashed a thumbs-up.

Everyone cheered, but nobody was happier than Fernanda. The wind had come up a bit, which made for a rougher ride. Fernanda retreated to sit in the stern, where the ride was smoother.

Hedi and Zack stood in the bow on dolphin patrol like twin blond figureheads, leaning into the forward edges as the craft bounced over the swells toward Coiba. Hedi was teaching Zack the German words for everything they saw.

Soon the island was close enough to make out cliffs rising from the sea, white spray exploding against their feet. She could see several outlying islands covered with the same lush canopy as the larger one.

As Vincente steered for the channel between the outlying

islands and Coiba, Alex pointed to the largest of the other islands. "That's Isla Rancheria."

Despite her discomfort, Fernanda was awestruck by how pristine it looked. As the boat passed between the two islands, the cliffs gave way to beaches on Coiba that seemed to stretch off to the horizon on her left, while Rancheria on her right looked so unspoiled it was hard to imagine that humans had ever set foot there.

She smiled at Alex, trying to lighten the air between them after last night. "This is going to be an amazing week."

He nodded, the self-assured demeanor once again firmly in place. "I guarantee it."

Shortly they passed a smaller group of outlying islands and a small cove came into view on the left. A short pier was visible on one end of a long arc of white sand that ended in a lone steep-sided mountain covered in lush green jungle.

"There's the ANAM station." Alex pointed to a row of low cement buildings arrayed along the coastline. "We'll only be here for a few minutes while I get our paperwork stamped."

Fernanda tried to look interested. "Sure. That's good." *What am I saying?* "By the way, which building has restrooms?"

"The washroom is in the small building with the water tank on top. It's behind the long one there." Alex indicated toward the cluster of buildings. "You can just see it beyond the covered patio."

She smiled again and picked her way up to the bow. The water had changed from an almost teal color to light aqua, and by the time Vincente throttled back the engine to approach the beach, she could see rocks on the bottom twenty feet below as if looking through liquid glass.

She didn't bother waiting until the keel hit the sandy shore. As soon as the water was knee deep, Fernanda was out of the boat and wading the last ten yards before making a beeline for the spartan his and hers washrooms behind the main building. She'd never been so happy to see an outhouse in her life.

A few minutes later, when she could finally blink and form coherent sentences again, Fernanda stepped out of the ladies bathroom and heard the sound of retching coming from the men's side.

Uh-oh. Somebody's sick. She looked around to try to figure out who the unfortunate person was but couldn't see any of their team from where she stood.

Alex and Zack were fine during the ride. Could it be Carlos?

The toilet flushed and Hedi appeared at the men's room door, looking very green.

Oh no! "Hedi, I'm so sorry you're sick. Do you think it's still the food from yesterday?"

Hedi clutched her stomach, grimacing. "Maybe. That boat ride didn't help, but I don't think that's the problem. I don't usually get motion sickness."

"I hate to say this, but our boat riding isn't over yet. Alex says we have another thirty or forty minutes to our drop-off point."

Hedi lowered her head into her hands. "Noooo! I can't get back in that boat."

Fernanda put a hand on her friend's arm. "Let me talk to Alex and see what he thinks we should do. Why don't you go lie down in one of those hammocks over there." She pointed to a tattered fishnet hammock strung in the shade of two palm trees near the boat.

Hedi nodded. "Okay." She shuffled miserably back toward the beach.

Fernanda watched her go and felt like she was witnessing a car wreck in slow motion. Why did it seem like the trip was falling apart? It wasn't just pity for her friend feeling so wretched in such a beautiful place. Hedi was the only other girl on the trip.

How am I going to do this alone?

Fernanda looked around. Zack and Carlos were nowhere in sight, probably off exploring.

The captain had anchored the boat by running a line to one of the palm trees that lined the beach. At the moment he was conversing with two other men she hadn't noticed before. They were sitting at a table on the covered patio beside the main building.

As she strolled past them, one of the men hissed at her playfully. She sat at an empty table across the patio and pretended to ignore him, even when he remarked to his *compadres* that she'd be welcome to stay on the island with him as long as she liked.

Fernanda had never been the type of girl who craved men's affections, though that was probably because she never ran short of affectionate men. As a little girl, she had become aware of the power of her looks when she learned that being cute was an easy way to manipulate those around her. But later on, when biology turned cute into sexy, the game became more hazardous, and she had to learn to be much more careful about the messages she sent.

But apparently for these two men—who she had concluded were ANAM eco-policemen after a glance at their olive drab uniforms—felt that her presence on the island was the only signal they needed. And they were still at it, throwing hard stares and lame comments her way.

This is getting really annoying.

"There you are, darling."

She jerked her head around and was surprised to see Zack coming across the patio toward her, grinning. "Wait until you see the flower I found you."

What in the world? Is everyone loco?

Then she saw Zack's subtle wink and realized what he was up to. She stood and threw her arms around his neck. "Hi, sweetie."

As they embraced, Zack whispered, "If it will help save you from the sharks over there, I'll pretend to be your rent-a-date until we get back on the boat."

"My hero." Fernanda kissed him on the cheek for added effect. She hoped she hadn't overdone it.

Alex emerged from the door marked *Administración* looking quite peeved. His expression soured further when he saw Fernanda with her arms around Zack's neck.

She felt like an idiot, but at least the bozos at the next table had gotten the message. They suddenly left.

"What happened in there?" Fernanda asked when Alex slapped a thin folder of papers on the table.

He shook his head. "If I didn't know better, I'd say these jokers are under orders not to allow anyone on the island. The boss in there insisted that we don't have the right forms and need to go all the way back to Panama City to get the correct ones before we can proceed."

The fender bender was becoming a seventeen-car pileup. "What? Why? I thought you already went to the office in Panama City."

"That's just it! I was there three days ago and got exactly what I needed, exactly like I've done the last four times I've come here. But this isn't the guy I usually deal with." He jerked a thumb toward the door behind him. "This imbecile is new, and he swears I need some different form. I don't know what his problem is."

Fernanda looked off toward the hammock that Hedi struggled to get into without falling on her head. "We have another problem."

Alex took a deep breath then exhaled heavily. "What's that?"

"Hedi's sick again."

He followed Fernanda's gaze. "I was afraid of that. She wasn't looking so good toward the end of the ride. This day just keeps getting better."

"What are we going to do if she can't make it?"

Alex pursed his lips for a moment. "Well…I imagine we leave her here."

"What? We can't just leave her all by herself!" Fernanda put her hands on her hips and thought of the soldiers who had just left.

"She wouldn't be alone. The park rangers at the station rotate through here on three-week shifts."

"Oh, *that's* comforting." She and Zack exchanged glances.

"There's a bunkhouse where she can sleep." Alex pointed over her shoulder. "Not five star, but better than where we're going to be staying. There's even a cook. And the view certainly doesn't leave anything to be desired."

Fernanda couldn't argue with that. The ANAM rangers kept the grounds nicely landscaped, and tall palms shaded the cluster of buildings on a narrow spit of land that jutted out toward Isla Rancheria. "It really is beautiful here."

"Now you can see why Noriega used to come here to party with his amigos."

Fernanda scowled. She got a bad taste in her mouth at the very mention of that era. Even though she had been in elementary school at the time, she remembered it clearly. Or rather, she remembered the change that took place when Noriega was ousted.

Boquete was well removed from the worst of that brutal regime's alleged atrocities, but even in that sleepy mountain town, Lerida Coffee had suffered and almost folded until the US invasion paved the way for a new government. It was only then that they got a true sense of what had really been happening around the country.

It was probably why Fernanda didn't do well when faced with bureaucratic stupidity. And she wasn't about to allow some spineless government hack to mess up her spring break. She thought again of the soldiers.

I know how to fix this problem.

"Did you say that the park rangers spend weeks out here at a time?"

Alex looked puzzled. "Yes. Three weeks on, one week off."

"And I bet there are a lot of things they can't get while they're here."

The professor and Zack both gave her very strange looks.

She reached out and snatched the permit paperwork from Alex's hand, then took off her hat and handed it to him. "I'll be right back."

"Where are you going?"

She gave him a coy smile. "You figure out what to do about Hedi. I'll deal with the permit problem."

"How?"

"I've got something you don't."

She ignored his protests as she marched to the door of the office. Before entering the building, she quickly pulled the ponytail rubber band out of her hair, shook her hair to its full volume, then stepped through the door.

The stocky man shuffling papers around his desk looked up with a scowl, but it soon dissolved when he saw her striding toward him.

"*Mande?* What can I...er...do for you, señorita?"

The shell-shocked look on his face told her everything she needed to know.

She flashed her best movie star smile. *Problem solved.*

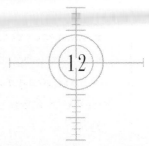

12

Washington DC. 1300 hours

THE TRAFFIC IN Washington DC was ridiculous as always. The black limousine crawled along, even though rush hour didn't start for another three hours.

"Let me out here, Bill. I'll walk back."

The driver shot him a questioning look as he pulled the limo to the curb. "It's pretty wet out there, sir. Are you sure?"

"It's okay; I won't melt."

The driver grinned in the rearview mirror. "You bet, Colonel."

Michael LaFontaine opened the door of the Lincoln and stepped onto the wet sidewalk. He'd been out of the military for more than a decade, but everyone still called him Colonel, which was just fine with him. The title seemed to open doors that *mister* sometimes wouldn't have.

He mingled with the few pedestrians who dared to brave the rain that had now diminished to barely a mist.

He loved this kind of weather. Everything seemed clean, fresh. Like a baby after a bath. It was a rare luxury in a town that too often stank of ambition and selfishness. It reminded him of why he had come here—to bring a gust of fresh air into a very dirty place.

In the military, honor was an everyday virtue. In the early nineties he had been doing a stint at the Pentagon when he was introduced to the business of politics. And what a business it was. He'd naively believed it to be public service, but it didn't take long to see that the concept of self-sacrifice in the halls of government was about as rare as a nun in a bikini.

At first it disgusted him, the glad-handing, backslapping men with pasted-on smiles and for-sale agendas. But true to his training, Michael eventually found the pony in the manure pile.

In Washington, an honorable man was a nobody unless he had money. And Michael had lots of money. So if the politicians wouldn't do what was right for simple duty, he had what it took to make them dance to the correct tune.

Some people believed there was no such thing as right and wrong, but that was crazy. One couldn't even argue the point without resorting to absolutes. But in Washington, the absolute was set by whoever picked up the tab.

The lights of passing cars reflected off the damp pavement as he walked briskly, turning north on Nineteenth Street.

The current situation with the global war on terror would have been laughable if it had happened to another country. He had invested heavily in the current administration, believing that it would prosecute this war more strenuously than the next guy. But he had been disappointed.

When it came down to it, public opinion was king, even if public opinion was stupid. So as always, Michael had to adjust the way he played the game to fit the situation. No matter, he knew how to fix this problem. It was what he did. Above all, he was a fixer.

With a casual glance over his shoulder born of his years in military intelligence, he stepped into an alley just short of Dupont

Circle and entered the nondescript office building through a service entrance.

The building was owned by an anonymous limited liability company based in the Aleutian Islands, and he had maintained a small office there for more than fifteen years, though he rarely visited it anymore. Until recently, there hadn't been a need.

After climbing three flights of stairs, Michael's steps echoed down a deserted corridor until he stopped in front of a solid wood door with a brass plate that said Fuller Global Resources, LLC.

He produced a key from his pocket, unlocked the door, and stepped gingerly over the large pile of junk mail on the floor below the mail slot. He closed the door behind him and stood in the darkness for a moment, listening. Then he reached up and pulled the thin string above his head.

There was a quiet *click-click,* and a single bare bulb burned to life, illuminating the six-foot square windowless closet in which he stood. On a shelf in front of him was an old fax machine connected to a telephone line. Other than that, the room was empty.

A single sheet of paper sat on the fax's tray. He picked it up. The paper had only three words.

Complications. 50K. ASAP.

He crumpled the paper in his fist, his jaw clenched.

This is getting out of hand.

Isla Coiba. 1345 hours

Fate had found him again.

Chombon winced angrily as the strap from his green canvas

satchel brushed the bruise on his left shoulder, made doubly stiff by the makeshift bandage Cesar had applied after the fire on the *Invincible*.

He stood on the riverbank and gazed toward where the water emptied into the sea, only a quarter mile distant. The *manglares*—mangrove swamps that grew thick between the camp and the beach—shielded their camp from the occasional ship that passed on this side of the island.

He cursed and spit on the muddy bank, as he'd done probably a thousand times since the explosion. From where he stood, the superstructure of the ship was barely visible, still smoldering. A corner of its aft deck was all that remained above water after the horrible fire that had killed five of his men and injured four more, himself included.

The ship, apparently, hadn't been so invincible after all.

He still couldn't determine what caused the fire. Cesar thought it was a faulty gas line set off by an electrical spark. That was possible, but for an explosion that size and a fire of that scope, there would have been a detectable smell, which none of the survivors claimed to remember.

At first, Chombon had thought it was a missile attack—that they'd been found out—but when no further assault was mounted, his theory had gone up with the giant plume of smoke from the ship's burning cargo.

They were fortunate the ship sank so quickly. If it had stayed afloat, the fire would have continued burning and surely given them away. As it was, they barely had time to get the wounded onto the lancha. And then the *Invincible* was gone, along with her several million dollars in lumber, the fortune they had all been counting on.

Chombon sighed and turned his sweaty face up to the sun. They would have to try again. Only now those not injured were not as enthusiastic as they had been. If he did not find a way to regain their obedience, their grumbling could turn to mutiny. But he'd worry about rebuilding their trust and admiration later.

He reached into his satchel and removed the bottle of water he'd put there earlier. When they first arrived on the island, he had taken it from the case of water on the ship. He was tired of drinking the brackish water they scooped from the river. Now was a good time to enjoy the simple pleasure of it, while he was alone and would not draw questions from the others.

He was just about to turn the cap when the thud of footsteps came through the tall grass behind him. Someone was running. He returned the bottle to his bag.

Then a frantic voice called out, "Jefe!"

Several of his men appeared, led by Enrique, the youngest member of the gang. "Jefe, come quick!"

Chombon scowled. "What now?"

"It's Armando. He's gone!"

Chombon cursed. "Where did he go?"

Enrique's glance flickered toward his compadres. "I do not know. He went only a little ways from camp to relieve himself, but he has not returned."

Chombon spit again. The idiot was most likely lost, thrashing about in the jungle looking for their camp. It was easy to get confused.

"Calm down, all of you. Armando is probably lost. We will fire some shots to guide him home." *That's it. Show them you can be a decisive and levelheaded leader.*

It was possible Armando had been bitten by a snake or eaten by a *cocodrilo,* but in either case they should have heard something. The hair on the back of Chombon's neck pricked up as he thought of another possibility.

No…impossible.

"Maybe he is tired of working here," Enrique ventured.

Chombon's tattooed hand shot out, snatching Enrique by the collar. "And if Armando has decided to give up on our plans and leave, then I will personally feed the crocodiles with pieces of him. And that goes for anyone else who desires to quit before the job is done." He looked at the others. *"¿Comprendes?"*

"Si, Jefe," Enrique said, eyes wide with fright. Chombon released the boy, and he followed the rest as they quickly retreated back down the path that led to the encampment.

Chombon cursed. Fate might have dealt him a blow, but he would not give up without a fight.

————

Isla Rancheria. 1030 hours

Fifteen minutes after entering the administration office, Fernanda dropped the signed permit forms on the table outside and gave Zack a smug look. "Done."

"What did you do?" Zack looked at her like she'd just killed an alligator with her bare hands.

"It was easy. Men are weak." She refastened her hair into a ponytail.

He looked her up and down in a glance. "I guess we are, but I'm not sure you're playing fair."

"Hey, I'm just making use of what my *papi* gave me."

Zack's eyes went wide. "You mean…"

"Coffee, you sicko!" Fernanda punched him playfully on the shoulder. "What kind of girl do you think I am?"

Zack shrugged. "Well, you said…"

She winked at him. "Gotcha."

The blond student shook his head and laughed. "I guess so! But really, what does coffee have to do with it?"

She grinned. "I simply told the jefe that my friend the professor's Spanish wasn't all that good and he had apparently made our trip sound like a scientific expedition when in reality we're just here camping for spring break. We are avid bird-watchers, so we'd like to look for some Guacamaya while we're on the island, but we aren't planning to take anything home with us, except pictures, of course."

"But we are on a scientific expedition."

Fernanda dropped her shoulders. "Okay, so I lied. It probably did no good anyway. But when I offered to send him a year's supply of Lerida coffee, the jefe agreed to allow us to camp but made me promise that we would stay away from the west side of the island."

Zack crossed his arms. "That's weird. Why would he say that?"

"I'm not sure. He just said it was off-limits, restricted."

Alex approached from the direction of the beach. Fernanda waved the permit at him. "Good news! We're cleared to go."

Alex was clearly surprised. "Really? How did—?"

"Don't ask," Zack said.

Fernanda punched him again. "It was no big deal. Anyway, how's Hedi?"

Alex shook his head. "She's quite sick. It wouldn't be wise to take her into the jungle."

"Could we stay here another day and see if she feels better?"

"No, Fernanda. I'm afraid if we lose any more time, we'll never make it into the interior and back out again. We're cutting it close as it is."

She felt as if a bucket of negative emotions had just been dumped on her head. When they were back in Panama City, the idea of trekking through the jungle had sounded like a great adventure. Now Fernanda wasn't so sure she was up to it. She hated the thought of leaving Hedi behind too. Then there was the fact that her mother would be proven right: She was going into the jungle alone with three men.

Papi would have wanted her to hold her chin up and keep moving forward. He had always been like that. When the going got tough in the coffee business, he didn't give up—he got angry. But he knew how to channel his anger into action. Fernanda wanted to be like him but didn't feel it.

Carlos came puffing up from the far side of the encampment. "Hey, guys. You got to see this. They've got a crocodile named Tito that eats soccer balls and comes when you call it!"

Her resolve wavered. "Maybe I should stay with Hedi."

Carlos looked confused. "Hedi's not coming? Man! I knew she was a weak link."

She was about to kick Carlos in the shins when Alex put a hand on her shoulder. "Hedi will be fine, Fernanda. I'll arrange with Vincente to return for her after he drops us off. He'll wait here with her until she feels better, then take her back to Santa Catalina. She can relax on the beach at the Oasis until we return. Anyway, we need you to make this trip happen. With only three of us, there won't be enough people to carry all of our shared gear."

Great. Now I'm letting someone down either way.

"Whatever we do," Zack chimed in, "we should probably do it quick before el jefe changes his mind."

"Let me talk to Hedi first." Without waiting for an answer, Fernanda trudged off toward the beach.

Her friend was swinging slowly in the hammock, staring out to sea.

Fernanda stopped and leaned against the tree to which one end was tied. "I don't feel good about leaving you."

Hedi gave her a halfhearted smile. "Ach…I don't feel good about leaving you either. But it makes no sense to take me if I'll be a burden to the team. And we both know that's what I'd be right now."

Fernanda sighed. "So you won't be mad at me if I go on the expedition?"

Hedi shook her head and stared out to sea again. "I'll be mad if you don't."

A half hour later they said their good-byes to Hedi and were back in the *Pescador* with Vincente, motoring out of the bay. Fernanda's spirits were lifted a little by the sight of Alex standing in the bow of the boat, wearing his expedition hat and looking as intrepid as anyone she'd ever seen. He had a lot in common with her father. She found Alex's demeanor irresistible.

He turned to face the group and sat on the front seat, raising his voice above the engine's whine. "All right. As soon as we get out of sight of the ranger station, we'll turn west and head for Playa Brava, which is closer than our original plan but will still allow us to arrive at our destination."

"But weren't we warned to stay away from the west side of the island?"

The professor leaned forward and gave Zack an intense look. "This is a big island. Once we're fifty yards inland, the ANAM boat patrols will never spot us. And Vincente doesn't have to go by the ANAM station when he comes to pick us up. As long as he can return without being spotted this afternoon, the rangers will be none the wiser."

Carlos grinned. "Better to ask forgiveness than permission, brah!"

Zack said nothing. Fernanda thought he looked like this trip wasn't turning out to be what he had planned either.

They motored south along Coiba's western coast for about a half hour. Then as they rounded a rocky outcropping, Vincente whistled and pointed to a long stretch of sandy beach. "Playa Brava."

Fernanda was again awed by the savage beauty of the island, though as they got closer, she realized that it wasn't quite as unspoiled as she'd originally thought. Here and there piles of flotsam that had washed up on shore were scattered haphazardly along with logs, old coconuts, and lots of other debris. Even still, the swaying palm trees and dark rocky outcroppings on both ends of the beach looked like something out of a travel magazine.

I am going to have fun, even if it kills me.

Two minutes later Vincente backed the boat into the beach. Everyone piled out into knee-deep water and started a human chain to off-load their backpacks and other equipment.

When they were done, everything was in a small pile in the shade of an almond tree just above the high watermark. Tiny hermit crabs were everywhere, leaving tracks that made it look like mice on motorbikes had staged a rally on the beach.

The waves were doing their best to swamp the *Pescador*, so there wasn't time for long good-byes with their captain. With a toothless grin and a wave, Vincente pushed the boat into deeper water, started it up, and sped off around the rocky outcropping, out of sight.

Fernanda turned back toward the lush jungle that crowded the beach. Far beyond the nearest pines, she could see dark, jungle-covered mountains with mist swirling ominously down from their peaks, and clouds gathered on the horizon.

Suddenly Fernanda felt very, very alone.

13

Isla Coiba. 2340 hours

THE NIGHT AIR hung heavy and still over Coiba, and lightning
flashed on the horizon as Nero Sancho fought to keep the large
single-engine cargo plane airborne. The Antonov AN-2 was as reli-
able a plane as any made, but it was a little like flying your house
while sitting in the attic.

The ancient Russian aircraft droned in low and slow over the
waves, aiming for the grass airstrip visible to Nero only as a lighter
band against the black canopy of the jungle. He crossed himself
hastily and said a silent prayer to the Virgin of Guadalupe, whose
icon was taped to his instrument panel.

The trailing edge of the airstrip rose and fell in the small multi-
paned windscreen, and he could barely make out the beams of six
high-powered flashlights spread out in the banana palms to signal
the end of the airstrip.

Nero tried not to close his eyes as the row of palm trees
between the beach and the airstrip loomed ahead. As soon as they
flashed by beneath the plane, he cut the throttle and let the behemoth's front wheels bounce once, then again on the rough ground,
shuddering down the short runway.

He fought to keep the wheels straight as he engaged the brakes with his left hand, still praying that the plane wouldn't hit a stump or a ditch and flip over. It shuddered to the end of the grassy strip and stopped. Flashlights bounced through the tall grass as Chombon's men converged on the plane.

Ordinarily, he would never have agreed to take this job, flying into a remote, unused airstrip in the middle of the night, bringing supplies to a group of men obviously up to no good. Especially in this place. It made him shudder just to say its name. Everyone in his hometown of Colón knew someone who had come here and never returned. Even though they had shut the dreaded prisons for good, it was illegal to land here. The island and surrounding waters had been designated *Patria Mundial*—a World Heritage site.

Nero unstrapped himself from the cockpit and climbed down into the cargo bay, unlocking the side door and pushing it open. The smell of aviation fuel mingled with that of dew and humidity and decay. A muscular black man loped toward him through the grass, carrying a large flashlight. Nero climbed down and extended his hand.

"Chombon, it is good to see you again."

"You are late."

Nero shrugged. "Aviation is not an exact science, hermano."

"You will not be able to make both trips tonight." Chombon scowled.

Nero spread his hands. "I am sorry. What can I say? We will have to try again next week. In the meantime, I've brought you something special." He led the way over to the open aircraft door, reached inside, pulled out a bottle of rum, and handed it to the gang leader. "This will solve some of your problems, no?"

Chombon examined the bottle in the light of his torch. "Perhaps. It has been a very bad week. What I really need, Sancho, is more men. I've sent a text message to Antonio about it, but it would help if you would remind him as well."

He bowed slightly. "As you wish." *There is no shortage of criminals in Colón.*

"Good. Now let's get this cargo loaded." Chombon turned and whistled. Several men ran to the tail of the plane and lifted it up, rotating the fuselage around and pointing the nose back toward the sea. Then another column of men emerged from the wood line, each carrying a crate or box. Some of the cargo required the combined efforts of several men.

Nero climbed back into the plane and flipped the button that lowered the rear cargo door. Chombon's men trudged up the ramp with their burdens, then dropped the boxes and returned for more.

While securing the cartons, Nero noticed that they contained everything from electronics to clothing, all made in Indonesia. He could guess how the products came to be on Coiba.

Get in, get out, don't ask questions. Do what you were hired to do.

As the cargo continued to be loaded, he kept an ear tuned to the approaching sounds of thunder. The lightning flashes were getting closer, and the first gusts of wind made the palm fronds rustle in anticipation of the storm.

Chombon reappeared. "If we stack things on top of each other, there would be enough room to fit all of the cargo. That would save you the second trip."

Nero nodded. "That it would, *señor.* Because with that much weight, the *Guadalupe* would never get off the ground."

Torrijos-Tocumen International Airport, Panama, 2355 hours

You've got to love the red-eye.

The double doors swung open in front of Rip to reveal a typical Latin American airport: crowded, smoky, and chaotic. The men of Task Force Valor shouldered their carry-ons and joined the air-conditioned bedlam of locals, tourists, and businesspeople, all scurrying through the lower-level terminal of Panama's Torrijos-Tocumen International.

"There's a lot of people here for midnight, y'all," Buzz Hogan drawled as they strode through the crowd.

Rip checked his watch. "Yeah, bro. We got through customs pretty quick though. Phoenix might not be here yet."

They had just arrived on the last plane from Miami for the night, and Rip fell in behind Buzz, who because of his huge physical presence, just naturally created a path through the throng of humanity.

John Cooper came up behind him. "Hey, my first team leader in the Ranger battalion was on the mission to take over this airport during Operation Just Cause in '89. He told me that two of the guys in the platoon were killed in a firefight in the men's restroom on this level."

"Wow. That's sad." Doc Kelly switched his knapsack to the opposite shoulder. "I wonder if there's a memorial or a plaque or anything."

Sweeney snorted. "In the latrine?"

Doc shrugged. "Not necessarily there, but somewhere in the airport maybe."

Buzz scanned over the heads of the crowd. "There's the latrine if anybody wants to see for themselves." He pointed to the far end of the terminal where a universal stick-figure sign hung above a green door next to the rental cars.

"Well, I'd like to check it out anyhow," Frank said. "I didn't even want to try getting around that large African woman who had the aisle seat in my row."

Doc feigned offense. "You got a problem with Africans now, cracker boy?"

Frank was unfazed at the joke. "Not in the least. It's ugly people like you who bother me."

Doc laughed and took Frank's carry-on. "Let me hold your purse while you go to the powder room, Sally."

"I'll go too," Coop said. "You guys mind watching our packs?"

"No problem, vato." Rip grabbed his team sergeant's rucksack and set it at his feet. "We'll wait for Phoenix out front."

"Good idea. Meet you there." Coop and Frank headed for the latrine.

The rest of the team walked to the exit. They moved between the Avis car rental desk and a small snack bar, then out the double doors to the covered portico. Travelers were embracing loved ones and a couple of bored policemen in starched tan uniforms stood smoking on the far side of the three-lane pickup zone.

"Wow. It's not as hot as I thought it would be."

"Famous last words, Doc." Sweeney dropped his pack on the ground and ran a hand through his blond hair.

A black Suburban with dark tinted windows rolled to a stop in front of them. The passenger door opened, and Agent Walker stepped out. "Hello, boys. Need a lift?"

Hogan grinned. "Why yes we do, little lady. Where ya goin'?"

Phoenix looked up at the bearded weapons sergeant and wrinkled her nose. "Crazy, big fella."

He laughed. "Well, you're in good company then."

Rip was surprised at the exchange. *Agent Phoenix must be warming to us.*

She surveyed the group. "You're missing a couple."

Sweeney jerked a thumb toward the terminal. "They had to visit the little soldier's room."

Coop walked up behind him. "I heard that, Bobby. Hi, Phoenix."

Rip tossed John's bag to him. "Find anything interesting?"

"Nah. Looks like they've remodeled. Frank thinks he saw a couple of patched bullet holes, but I couldn't tell."

Phoenix looked puzzled. "O-kay, I must have missed an important part of that conversation."

Doc grinned. "They were looking for signs of the fighting that happened here back in '89."

"Ah, I see. From what I've heard, most of that kind of thing is gone." She stepped to the back of the Suburban and opened the door to the cargo area. "Stash your luggage here. The pallet you packed with the rest of your stuff is waiting for you at the embassy."

Rip motioned to the figure in the driver's seat. "Who's our chauffer?"

"Oh, him. I'll introduce you in a sec."

The team piled into the SUV, with Rip ending up in the middle seat, crammed between Coop and Hogan. Phoenix jumped in the front and slammed the door. "Gentlemen, I'd like you to meet

Senior Special Agent Marcel Bucard. He's run the office here in Panama City for the last two years."

The bespectacled station chief turned to the team and gave a nonchalant wave. "Welcome to Panama." He spoke in a wheezy voice.

Rip figured the man to be in his midforties, with thinning black hair, a hawkish nose, and almost no chin. If Rip saw the man on the street, he'd think schoolteacher before spy.

Phoenix turned to face the men as Bucard pulled from the curb. "We're staying in the Euro Hotel, which is a sort of nondescript place in the city, only about ten minutes from the embassy."

"I hope this place measures up to our standards." Rip smiled. "Coop spoiled us in Beirut at that fancy German hotel."

He and Coop bumped fists. "Yeah, buddy."

Phoenix rolled her eyes. "I don't think it'll compare to the Moevenpick, but the Euro is clean, comfortable, and anonymous. And there's a nice pool out back."

"How about Internet?" Frank asked.

"No wireless, but they have a few computers in the lobby where you can check e-mail."

Frank nodded. "That'll do."

Coop turned more serious. "So do we have a mission yet?"

Phoenix shook her head. "Not yet. We were able to get more information out of the man who survived the hijacking of the *Invincible*. He confirmed that cases of ITEB were aboard when the ship was stolen. So finding that ship is our first priority. I have a couple of people working on that back in Virginia, but something tells me these guys will try and sell the ship's cargo as quickly as possible. So I plan to check out the free zone in Colón tomorrow and see if I can find anything from the ship."

"What's the free zone?" Rip asked.

"Oh, it's like a huge duty-free shopping district near the north end of the Canal. You can find anything there: clothing, big-screen televisions, bulldozers, you name it."

"Wow," Coop said. "Liz would love that."

"Well, it's only meant for wholesalers, not the general public. But there's another market near it that regular folks can shop at. The strange thing is that they built a wall all the way around the complex and will only let foreigners in. The rest of Colón is like the cesspool of humanity. Most places in that town it's not safe to get out of the car."

"Kind of like L.A., right, Rubio?" Hogan jabbed him in the ribs.

Rip shot Buzz his best "You're a redneck idiot" look. He noticed that they were driving along a freeway. In the distance, the skyscrapers' lights painted a modern skyline against the stars. He had to admit, it did look a little like Los Angeles.

"So what's the security situation like in Panama?" Frank asked from the backseat.

"I can answer that," Marcel said, slowing for a tollbooth. "The only area where there have been any problems lately is in the Darién Province, up near Colombia. Lots of problems with drug running and such. The Caribbean side of the Isthmus is generally wilder than the Pacific side. Some smuggling is known to happen out of Colón and the former military base near there: Fort Sherman.

"The bigger problem is that Panama is being overrun by the Colombians. They come here and build casinos and office buildings, all of which are good for the national economy, but they're really just blatant money-laundering schemes. The worst part is that the drug cartels have become so powerful that they are starting to influence politics. And that bodes poorly for the stability of the country. A few months ago there was a string of mafia-style assassinations right in downtown Panama City."

"The only things I want to know," Sweeney drawled, "are if the government knows we're here, and whether or not they're gonna get squirrelly on us like they did in Lebanon."

"They don't know you're here in an official capacity," Phoenix answered. "But they will before you go operational. It won't be a problem. The DEA is down here all the time, and the Panamanian government welcomes their help. From the government's standpoint, your mission will be another verse of the same song."

They were getting close to the city center now, and Rip noticed that the road traveled a very long causeway built out over the water, ending at the foot of a forest of skyscrapers.

Marcel shot Phoenix a look. "Be that as it may, I think it was a mistake to bring you all down here. One thing we definitely don't need is you men causing some sort of incident. I read the brief from your Lebanon mission, saw you were arrested by the military and shipped out of the country. Well, Panama doesn't have a military anymore, but if the Panamanian police get hold of you, they'll have you in a prison cell so fast you won't know what hit you. And there won't be much I can do to get you out."

Coop leaned over and mumbled in Rip's ear. "That's us. Just a bunch of messy guys."

After passing one more tollbooth, the causeway deposited them into downtown, and the traffic picked up quite a bit. Rip was impressed with how modern everything was. If it wasn't for

most of the signs being in Spanish, it could easily be downtown
L.A.

A few minutes later the Suburban pulled up in front of a modest hotel on a noisy major intersection. The team piled out and
retrieved their gear.

Before leaving, Marcel leaned out the window. "I highly suggest that you men do not leave the hotel until we call for you. It
won't do to have you getting in trouble with the police before we
can put you to work."

The team exchanged skeptical looks among themselves. Coop
tried the tactful route. "Uh…sure thing, sir. We'll be ready when
you need us." He gave a halfhearted salute.

The Suburban drove off and everyone looked at Phoenix.
"What was that about?" Coop asked.

"Yeah, was he serious? What are we, a troop of Girl Scouts?"
Sweeney whined.

Phoenix didn't look any more amused than the rest of them.
She sighed. "Pencil pushers. They'll be the death of our organiza-
tion yet. He's probably worried we'll lose him a promotion."

"So we're stuck here until further notice?"

She shook her head. "Actually, Rip, I think you should accompany me tomorrow. You speak Spanish, right?"

"Sí."

"Good. You can help translate and drive the rental car."

"Sure, no problem." At least he'd have something to do.

Rip hated sitting still.

14

Isla Coiba. 2400 hours

IT WILL RAIN SOON.

His matted black beard kept the buzzing *chitres* away from everything but his eyes as he lay in a patch of waist-high grass, watching. The insatiable blood-sucking gnats were unable to infest the rest of his body either, as he had long ago learned to coat his bare brown skin with mud from the river.

He had never seen anyone use the airstrip in all the years he had survived on the island, though he'd known about the runway. Rumors circulated long ago among the prisoners that a secret military training base had been built on this side of the island. And there weren't many places on the island where dry, level ground existed. He should know; he knew its rivers and ridges better than the tiny deer that roamed its dark interior.

As usual, the men were making more noise than a troupe of howler monkeys. He had heard them from the top of the ridge earlier in the day as they had prepared the grass airstrip. Now they were carrying crates and boxes to the waiting aircraft.

As a child he had seen the large metal birds flying over his village and had been terrified. He believed them to be angry animals that held evil spirits in their mouths. But prison had changed most everything he believed. He now understood that they were simply dead things driven by dead people—people who knew nothing of spirits and medicine men. People who believed in nothing that they could not see.

So when he had tired of living among them, he simply slipped away from the work camp and melted into the trackless jungle. It was no different from the deepest reaches of the Darién, where his people had lived since the dawn of time and from where he had been taken all those years ago, simply for being in the wrong place at the wrong time.

He took advantage of the racket to slither silently from his hiding place and find another, closer to where the men had hacked out a small opening in the banana palms and stockpiled their crates before the plane came. No one was in the area now. They were all straining to roll the loaded aircraft into position for takeoff.

He looked over the boxes that had not gone onto the plane. Nothing practical in them as far as he could tell. A machete lay atop one of the crates, along with a bag of some sort.

The bolsa *will be useful for keeping food from the rodents. And the machete for killing them.*

He quickly stole from his hiding place and took both items, then slipped back into the anonymity of the jungle just as one of the men was returning.

It was the younger one he had seen before. As he watched, the man picked up one of the weapons—a rifle similar to those the prison guards had often beaten the inmates with. He had no use for them.

As the young man fiddled with the rifle, the man again left his hiding place, his mud-encrusted hands finding at his side the one thing he'd taken when he left the camp those many years ago. A knife. It slid easily from its sheath as he moved up behind the pirate without a sound.

The only noise was a gurgle as the young man's lifeblood drained onto the freshly cut banana leaves. His rifle dropped to the earth with a thud. The man had not suffered.

He eased the lifeless body to the ground and felt no remorse. He had done this one a favor, as he had for the others through the years.

He spoke a greeting to the spirits on the man's behalf, then stepped over his body and melted into the jungle once again.

The young man was now free of the island.

Isla Coiba. 0100 hours

An otherworldly shriek jerked Fernanda from a fitful sleep. She lay unmoving in her jungle hammock, immobilized by fear, her heart beating like that of a hummingbird.

What…was…that?

When the screech came again, right above her head this time, she would have screamed herself—if she'd been able to breathe. The darkness under the canopy of trees sheltering their camp was so complete that even if the nylon rain fly hadn't been covering her jungle hammock, the view from her mesh-enclosed cocoon wouldn't have been any different.

Not that she really *wanted* to see what was making the horrendous noise. She was trying to convince herself that it was just a bird, since the racket was coming from high in the trees.

An enormous pterodactyl of a bird maybe.

Or perhaps a really angry monkey.

She had been sleeping—or more precisely *hiding*—in her hammock since just after dark around 7 p.m. That must have been hours ago, but she didn't want to illuminate the dial on her watch to find out, because that would entail moving.

Breathe, girl. Breathe. Whatever it is probably doesn't want to eat you.

At this rate, she'd be lucky to get an hour of sleep all night. She could never get over how noisy the jungle became after dark. The first night was always like this for her. She recognized the whirr of cicadas and rhythmic bass melody of frogs. But the rest of the hoots, screeches, thuds, and cries of predators and prey mixed into a noisy blur. Fernanda didn't think she would feel any better to know what they were, anyway.

And was that an airplane I heard?

She shivered. The small fleece airline blanket she'd brought along was about as useful as flip-flops in the Arctic. She should have listened to her instincts when she was packing. Alex's list hadn't included a sleeping bag, but she always got cold when she slept anyway. She hadn't been sure what to expect here.

The last field study she'd participated in was the *Nymphalis quinterus* study on what had been Fort Sherman, and they returned at night to men's and women's dorms in former US Army barracks. This was much different, especially when the temps dropped thirty degrees after you had been hiking through hot rain forest all day, sweating as if it were a competition to see who could die of heatstroke first.

Note to self: Next time, bring warm clothes, despite the added weight, and earplugs.

She couldn't stand it anymore. She had to move. The hammock creaked as she rolled to her side. From the soft snores coming from the other hammocks nearby, nobody else gave the screaming bird from Hades a second thought.

Why *did* she come on this trip? It wasn't just because she had a crush on Alex. *Okay, there. I admitted it.* There had to be a deeper reason. She wouldn't willingly suffer like this for any man alive.

An image of a little girl she'd seen when they first rolled into Santa Catalina appeared in her exhaustion-clouded mind. It seemed like weeks ago. The girl's dark skin offset the faded pink of her dirty summer dress. Her beautiful smile was like sunshine on the dirt path that led from a cluster of corrugated metal shacks.

As Fernanda watched the girl walk along, chewing a stalk of sugarcane, she pitied her for being born in such a place. The Lerida estate had animals that lived better than these *campesinos*. Yet in a way, she resented the girl because she was content with so little. And just knowing that she existed made Fernanda feel guilty for having so much.

Why would God give luxury to some and crushing poverty to others? It couldn't possibly be fair.

Maybe that had something to do with why she came. Maybe somewhere deep inside, Fernanda wanted to choose suffering to assuage her guilt.

Well, that's stupid.

Whatever the reason, the trip so far had been like a master's level study in human misery. When they first arrived on the beach at Playa Brava, she had been captivated by the island's tropical beauty. They unloaded their gear onto the beach, and Alex showed them the proposed route on his map. They would hike inland

toward the tallest peak, a mist-shrouded mountain he called Cerro
Torre, and make camp at its base. The area he wanted to collect
samples from lay just on the other side of the ridge.

In the hours since they first embarked on their trek inland
from the beach, she'd exerted herself like never before in her life;
hurt in places she hadn't known existed; and encountered every
biting, stinging, thorny plant known to man. Now she was
cocooned in what amounted to a suspended body bag, somewhere
in the land before time, freezing to death and hoping to survive the
prehistoric birds until morning so she could get up and do it all
over again.

Hedi was so lucky to get sick.

The screech came again. But now it was more annoying than
scary. What in the world could make such an awful noise?

The next scream came from her right at ground level. *That was
human!* Adrenaline shot through her again. She tried to peer out of
the mesh of her cocoon but saw nothing.

"Carlos? You okay?" Alex's voice sounded groggy but unfazed.

"Yeah. Sorry. I woke up and something was sniffing at my leg.
I think I scared it away, though."

Alex yawned. "It was probably just a *neque*. They're like big
mice. Don't worry. They're harmless."

"Uh…okay." Carlos didn't sound the slightest bit convinced.

Fernanda wasn't excited about the thought of giant mice roam-
ing their campsite either, but Carlos had been whining about one
thing or another almost since they landed at Playa Brava.

And he was worried about Hedi being the weak link!

But if the professor wasn't worried, then maybe she could relax
enough to get some rest. The jungle had quieted with their talking.

Perhaps she could fall asleep before the din got up to full volume once again.

She had no choice but to buck up and make the best of it. It was time to exhibit that trait her father always insisted was the duty of a Lerida. In Spanish, he called it *valor familiar.* Family courage.

She wrapped her exhausted body tightly in the fleece blanket and prayed for the sun.

Send me some of your courage, Papa.

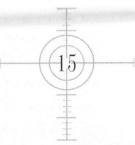

Euro Hotel. Panama City. 0630 hours

THE HOTEL LOBBY was nearly empty when Rip stepped out of the tiny elevator. He'd already gone for a swim in the pool, showered, shaved, and dressed in khaki painter's pants and a blue Under Armour shirt.

Guess the tourists decided to sleep in.

He got the once-over and a coy smile from the young woman behind the check-in desk. He acknowledged her with a simple nod and kept moving. Not that she wasn't cute, but he'd committed to sit out the gender games for a play or two, and that's what he intended to do.

If he never had another blowup like the one the other night, it would be too soon. It made him feel bad, because Chelsea really was a sincere, straightforward woman. But that was part of the problem. Chelsea knew what she wanted—and it was more than he had to give.

He walked by the bank of computers that lined one wall. One of them was occupied by Agent Mary Walker. The other by John Cooper, who looked comical as he furiously hunt-and-pecked the keyboard.

"Now, Coop, I never thought I'd see you checking e-mail on a deployment."

John never looked up, only smiled and kept pecking. "Hey, man. Love will do funny things to a guy."

"After seeing you, I believe it. Say hi to Liz for me."

"Will do."

Rip crouched by Mary's chair. "Hey, Phoenix. Chatting with your love interest as well?"

She looked up from her e-mail with a sarcastic grin. "I wish. Will you wait for me? I'll just be a minute."

Rip pointed to the door that led to the hotel's restaurant. "Tell you what, I'll get us some coffee. How do you take it?"

"I've already had some, but you go ahead."

Rip nodded and pushed through the door into the restaurant. A bar with stools separated the dining area from the kitchen, and booths lined the opposite wall under windows that looked out onto the busy Via Espana, where traffic was already thicker than the humidity.

He slid into a swivel chair at the bar and smiled at the middle-aged waitress, who looked like she'd been on duty all night.

"*Buenos días,* señora."

"Buenos días. *¿Algo para tomar?*"

"*Café negro, por favor.*"

She nodded. "*Como no.*"

Five minutes later he paid for his coffee and a banana and was climbing into a taxi with Phoenix. "US embassy, por favor," she told the driver.

Mary turned to Rip. "Our friend rented us an economy car. It'll be waiting for us there."

"No problem. What's the name of the place where we're going?"

"Let's talk about that when we get to the embassy, shall we?" Phoenix shot a glance at the taxi driver, who appeared to be listening only to the blaring Reggaeton emanating from the car's sound system.

"Oh, right. Sorry." *Guess I just failed Espionage 101.*

She smiled. "Don't worry about it."

Rip didn't ask any more questions as they rode to the embassy, which was located on what had once been Fort Clayton in the canal zone. Nowadays, Phoenix explained, it had been renamed *ciudad de saber*, a sort of "gated community" for artists, scientists, and other foreigners coming to Panama for various projects.

"The former embassy was downtown and right on the street. This one is well off the road, much less vulnerable."

When they neared their destination, Rip could see what she meant. The embassy didn't exactly say "Welcome to America." Instead, it looked like a maximum-security prison, several stories tall and set on the side of a hill at the end of a long, winding driveway.

"Tell him to let us out here," Phoenix told Rip, who relayed the command to the driver. They stepped onto the curb near the first guardhouse, staffed by rent-a-cop Panamanian security guards.

After paying the driver, she and Rip walked to the guardhouse and showed their government IDs. A moment later, the young guard waved them through.

"That was easy," Rip commented.

Marcel was waiting for them in the marble lobby, looking nervous as he had the night before.

"Here are your car keys. And I received this intel when I arrived this morning." He handed Phoenix a manila folder. "Our analysts at Langley found the information on the rest of the *Invincible*'s cargo when she disappeared. It appears the main cargo was lumber, but there were several containers aboard as well, mostly filled with consumer goods."

Phoenix looked frustrated. "Doesn't sound like much of a break."

"Well, maybe this will. It took me more man-hours than I had to spare, but some of my people were able to dig up this PDA with a Compact Flash card RFID reader, then program it with the codes of the products you're looking for." He handed her the small gizmo, which looked like Rip's own handheld computer with a flat plastic antenna sticking out of the top of the unit.

"How does that work?" Rip asked.

Marcel sighed. "RFID readers send out an electronic signal that causes any radio frequency ID chips nearby to send back their data." His nasally voice took on a tinge of annoyance. "If you two get within range of any of the products you're looking for, the PDA is set to alert you."

"What's the range like?" Phoenix turned the unit over in her hands.

"With this antenna, not very far. You'll have to be within maybe twenty-five meters."

"I'd like to get at our pallets, if possible. Phoenix said last night that you have them here?"

Even more annoyed, Marcel looked at Rip. "What for?"

Rip shrugged. "I figure if we're going to Colón, it won't hurt to at least have a handgun."

Marcel shook his head vigorously. "No way. No weapons. Langley would have my hide if anything happened."

Rip shot back. "Oh? But they won't mind if we come back in a box because we got attacked and couldn't defend ourselves?"

Marcel reddened. "I am *not* having this conversation." He turned on his heel and strode off down the hall.

Phoenix looked up at Rip with a grin. The girl was unshakeable. "I should have warned you. Agent Bucard didn't score high on the personality test."

Rip tried to bore holes in the man's retreating back with his stare. "He must have ruined the curve on the 'cover your behind' exam."

She laughed. "Probably. I've seen lots of people like him in this business. There aren't a lot of risk takers out there anymore, you know?" She turned and exited the building.

Rip followed. "How about you? Are you a risk taker?"

She pretended to be insulted. "Sergeant Rubio, are you flirting with me?"

"Er, no, ma'am. I just wanted to know if you were okay doing this mission unarmed."

"I'm fine with it," she said, the playful look still in place. "People go shopping in Colón every day without a handgun. What makes you think we need one?"

He frowned. "Just to be prepared. You never know what will happen."

She put on a no-nonsense look that Rip found strangely attractive.

"It doesn't always take a gun to be prepared." She headed down the steps. "Stay here; I'll bring the car around."

Rip was officially freaked out. He really wasn't trying to, but it was almost like he couldn't *help* flirting with Phoenix. He didn't want to be attracted to her, but he was all the same.

Ack! I can't turn it off!

It wasn't that she was unattractive. Quite the contrary, actually. She was smoking hot, like a red-headed, Scotch-Irish version of Angelina Jolie. And from what he'd heard, Phoenix didn't need to carry a gun. Somebody said she'd been a champion kickboxer.

Some guys might not find that attractive in a girl, but Rip liked the confidence it had obviously given her. She carried herself in a way that screamed "capable" without making her seem mannish or intimidating.

He wasn't going to think about this right now. Romance existed in a different room of his brain, and he had a lock on that room at the moment. He would relate to her as a person if it killed him.

Phoenix drove up and hit the button to roll down the passenger window. "You ready?"

"Yep. You want me to drive?"

"Sure, go ahead." She put the car in neutral and set the hand brake, then slid nimbly across to the passenger side. "But it's a stick."

"No problem." He walked around to the driver's door.

Ten minutes later they were on the main north-south highway that ran from Panama City to Colón. Rip tuned the radio to one of the ubiquitous salsa stations, and for a while they rode in silence.

Once they got out of town, the countryside opened up to rugged mountains covered with flowering trees, palms, and tall grass. In between, campesinos living in small pueblos went about the chores of daily life—washing, working, and walking—without paying much attention to the two lanes of heavy traffic that rumbled past their simple concrete-and-thatch homes.

A lot of trucks were on the road, hauling everything from pineapples to ponies to people. The only thing they seemed to have in common was a lack of proper emissions. By the time they reached the outskirts of Colón, Rip's eyes were burning from the lingering clouds of diesel smoke that hung over the entire route.

"The Zona Libre should be coming up on our right." Phoenix consulted her map. "At seventy acres, I'd think it will be hard to miss."

Rip turned down the radio. "Okay." He swerved to miss a huge pothole. "What are we looking for exactly?"

"Only information, really. If we can find something else that was on that ship, maybe we can trace it back to the ship's location now."

"I see. Find the ship, find the ITEB."

"In theory. It'll put us one step closer anyway."

As they neared the city center, the traffic and roads continued to get worse. "I think I see the cranes from the port up ahead." Rip pointed to the angular structures jutting above the ramshackle rooftops of businesses lining the road. "The free zone has to be close to that."

She nodded. "You know what I don't get is the billboards. Ever since we got within thirty miles of Colón, there have been signs nonstop advertising stuff here at the free zone."

Rip shrugged. "So, what's strange about that?"

"If you notice the models, all of them are American women. Like that one, there." She pointed to a large billboard advertising cowboy boots, featuring a white woman wearing little else. "Why no Latina models?"

Rip thought for a moment. "The Catholic church."

"Really? Why?"

Rip kept his eyes on the road while he explained. "Look, Latino culture is very Catholic and very conservative. To see our women dressed like that would be offensive."

"But white women in lingerie is okay?"

"Well, apparently so. I mean, you see white women running around dressed like that all the time on television. It wouldn't surprise me if the people here, on some level, see American women as cheaper, easier, than Panamanian women."

She bristled. "That's not true!"

Rip held up one hand. "Hey, don't punch me or anything. I said it's just a theory."

The red-headed agent pursed her lips. "Well, you have a point. But I wonder what seeing all those perfect white-skinned models does to the self-image of the Panamanian girls."

"What do you mean?"

"It's just that in America, girls see those ads and maybe aspire to that level of beauty, which leads to all sorts of problems. But would it be worse if you knew it was impossible to ever look like that because your skin was the wrong color?"

Rip shook his head. "Got me. Guys don't think that way."

"Well, girls sure do."

A short time later, Rip motioned to a large fenced area on their right with warehouses visible inside. "Hey, is this our place? I think I see a gate coming up ahead."

Phoenix peered at the approaching guardhouse. "I think that's it."

They turned in under a large concrete arch that read: Zona Libre, Panama, in blue letters on a white background. A heavyset black man with a pockmarked face and a shotgun stepped from a guardhouse, which sat on their left under the arch. He held up a hand for them to stop. "Buenos días."

"Buenos días," they answered.

"Welcome to the Colón free zone." The guard spoke Spanish

with a pronounced Caribbean accent. "What is the nature of your business here today?"

"We just want to have a look around," Rip answered in Spanish.

"You are tourists?"

Rip glanced at Phoenix. "Yes, just tourists."

"I'm sorry, then you cannot come in."

Fantastic. Now what? Rip turned to Phoenix. "He says that tourists aren't allowed in."

She reached into her purse and brought out a ten dollar bill. "See if this changes his mind."

Rip looked at the money. "You're serious?"

Her eyes bored into his. "Do I look serious?"

Rip took the bill and held it up to the guard. "We really would like to see the free zone. We've heard it's very interesting. Are you sure no tourists are allowed inside?"

The man smiled. It was clear this was exactly what he had hoped for. He took the bill and put it in his breast pocket. "I can make special exceptions for you, mi amigo."

"I thought so."

The man stepped away from his window and waved them through.

She sighed. "If only everything in life was that easy."

Rip shook his head. "I can't believe we just bribed that guy."

Phoenix looked nonplussed. "I'm told it's a fact of life down here. It's the cost of doing business."

From inside, the Zona Libre resembled a city more than a shopping mall. A grid of narrow streets crowded with every imaginable kind of delivery vehicle separated each city block, most of which were occupied by what looked like gigantic outlet stores.

"Seems like you can find a little bit of anything here," Rip said. "Do you know how the prices compare to the States?"

Phoenix shrugged. "Marcel said that you don't actually come here to shop for individual products. Rather, wholesalers come here to view the goods available and then order by the container load."

"So they probably won't be having a spring hijacking sale here with items from the ship?"

She laughed. "They actually might. I mean, this place would be ideal for selling the stolen goods en masse, because it would give the sellers a certain amount of anonymity and allow them to get rid of the entire load of goods at one time, as opposed to trying to sell them retail."

Rip nodded. "Makes sense."

"Which is why I suggested we visit."

He stopped the car at the curb in front of a giant store selling clothing. Very few pedestrians were on the street, aside from the workers who were scurrying around loading and unloading trucks. "So where do we start?"

She pulled the palmtop computer from her bag. "Let's just drive around first and see if we get any hits."

"Okay." Rip put the car in gear. *This is going to be like looking for a needle in seventy acres of cacti. But it beats sitting at the hotel.*

Two hours later, a hard rain was falling when they again pulled to the curb. Rip stretched. "Well, it was worth a try, you know?"

Phoenix sighed. "It was a long shot anyway. The traffic here is like Washington on the Fourth of July."

"Yeah, except everyone is driving a delivery truck. So what do we do now?"

She set the PDA on the dash. "How about some lunch?"

"Sounds good. I haven't seen any restaurants in here, though. We might have to go into Colón to find something."

She turned in her seat. "I saw a street vendor selling food back that way about a block."

"Are you crazy? You want to eat food from a Panamanian street vendor?"

She grinned. "Sure, why not?"

He rolled his eyes. "I can think of several reasons. Not the least of which is amoebic dysentery. Besides, you don't strike me as the type who would eat on the street."

Phoenix raised her eyebrows. "Hey, frying kills everything. I'm not afraid. Are you?"

Rip shook his head. "All right, *hermana.* We'll eat street food. But don't say I didn't warn you." He put the car in gear and made a quick three-point turn.

"Man, that's what I call rain," Rip said as he parked across the street from the vendor, who had a booth against the wall of a warehouse and was busily deep frying something.

Phoenix peered through the rivulets on the windshield. "Tell me about it. It's like driving through a car wash, only without the brushes."

"Okay, you stay here, and I'll run over and secure our chow. It looks like you have a choice of something brown—fried or fried."

"I'll take fried. Here's a ten."

"Don't say I didn't warn you." Rip jumped out of the car and dashed across the busy street to the shelter of the portico where the vendor had his stall, sheltered from the rain on one side by a blue plastic tarp.

The man was just fishing a batch of crusty *empanadas* out of a vat of oil that looked long overdue for a change and stacking them with a pile of similar fried pastries on a greasy plate.

Mystery meat pies. Wonderful.

Rip was trying to decide if he wanted to know what the pies were filled with when another man walked up and asked for him. *"¿Qué tipo son?"*

The vendor pointed to one side of the plate. *"Estos son de carne,"* then to the other side, *"Y estos de pollo."*

Beef or chicken. Actually, it doesn't smell half bad. While Rip made up his mind, the other man paid for his order and walked several steps away to eat it. Then the vendor looked up from the vat-o-grease and said, *"Dígame."*

Rip ordered two of each and was amused when the total price came to one dollar. The man was reluctant to break Phoenix's ten dollar bill, so Rip fished around in his pocket for some ones. He heard her honking the horn at him as he did.

Sheesh! The girl can't even let a guy pay for lunch. Wait until she finds out why!

He took the warm paper bag from the vendor, absently wondering if the hot grease would really be enough to kill any nasties that might have been in the meat. He turned back toward the car and prepared to dodge puddles again when his heart almost stopped.

The car was empty.

16

Zona Libre, Colón, 1155 hours

DOMINGO BEDOYA LICKED the last of what would likely be his only meal that day off his greasy fingers. He watched with interest as the red-headed *gringa* sprinted down the opposite side of the street. The scene got more interesting when the athletic Latino caught sight of her and dropped his just-purchased bag of empanadas to give chase.

Domingo had scoured the sidewalks all morning for enough change to purchase the meal he'd just eaten. And here this man just threw away a bag full of food. What was it like to care so little about life's basic necessities?

The vendor was watching the commotion too, so he paid no attention to Domingo when he retrieved the bag, then quickly crossed the street and hid behind a box truck, stuffing one of the still-hot empanadas in his mouth.

At the end of the block, the clean-cut Latino caught up with the woman, and Domingo watched them having an animated conversation, standing in the rain. At first he decided they must be lovers in an argument. But then he realized that the woman had been chasing the white cargo van that had just pulled into the open garage belonging to his former employer Señor Hu.

He had unloaded trucks for the elderly Chinaman before

being injured in a nasty fall from a loading dock. Señor Hu was incredibly well connected within Zona Libre, and Domingo held out hope that the shrewd businessman might be compassionate enough to hire him for something, anything that would give him enough money to eat. But Señor Hu was not an easy man to persuade.

He decided to save the rest of his pastry windfall for later. He did not know when his next meal might be, so it wouldn't do to waste his good fortune. He glanced again in the direction of the *gringos* and didn't see them anymore. Suddenly worried the man might come back for his bag of food, Domingo stepped from behind the box truck and hurried off in the other direction.

He passed the car that the gringos had gotten out of and glanced in the passenger side window. There on the dash was an electronic device. Perhaps a large cellular phone? *No, it has too many buttons, is too big.*

He knew he shouldn't do it. Somewhere deep inside a brief skirmish ensued between the rules he'd been taught at the Catholic orphanage as a boy and the gnawing uncertainty of his present situation.

It was a short-lived battle. A glance up and down the street showed few people in his immediate area. No one was paying attention to him. *Sometimes it is good to be a nobody.*

He quickly opened the door and took the device, then closed the door again and walked away. He had no use for whatever the gadget was, but he could sell it for enough money for some new shoes and a month of food, at least.

Or better yet, maybe this is my ticket to an audience with Señor Hu.

Domingo opened the paper bag and ate another empanada. Despite the rain, it had become a beautiful day.

———

Isla Coiba. 1200 hours

Thwack!

Zack's machete deftly sliced through a young banana palm, and as it toppled, water seeped quickly up from the four-inch stump.

"See? I told you." The mop-headed college student grinned. "Water."

All the time I've spent in the jungle, and I never knew that! Fernanda gave him a dubious look as she sat on her backpack several feet away, sweating. "Okay, but is it drinkable?"

"I dunno. Let's find out." Zack stuck his machete in the ground and bent over the stump, out of which water was still flowing.

"Zack! Are you sure you want to…?"

He spit it out. "Bitter. Yech."

Fernanda rolled her eyes. "Maybe we should refrain from putting things in our mouths when we don't know if they are poisonous or not."

Zack spit again. "Where's the fun in that?"

"Sure. Don't think of it as dysentery. Think of it as 'the Coiba diet.'"

Zack laughed. "Good one. There are people in the States who are stupid enough to pay for something like that." He flopped down next to his backpack.

The shade from a stand of tall palm trees shielded them from the worst of the midday sun's rays, but not from the oppressive humidity. Cicadas whirred unseen in the tall grass of the clearing to their front, bordered by seemingly impenetrable stands of banana palms.

The still air made the sweat that soaked through their clothing useless for cooling but great for attracting the interminable flies, and Fernanda waved at them absently with her hat as they buzzed around her head.

"How much longer do you think Alex and Carlos will be?"

Zack shrugged. "Alex said they'd be back inside of an hour unless they found water. And I sure hope they did. I'm down to my last quart." He sloshed a half-full water bottle. "How much do you have left?"

Fernanda thought for a moment. "Probably about a liter and a half. I gave one bottle to Carlos before they left. I figured if they were going to climb to the top of the hill, he'd need it more than me."

She peered up the hillside behind her and could see less than thirty feet up the steep bank through the dense foliage in the direction the two men had taken.

Zack gave her a serious look. "So how do you feel about being here?"

She brushed a spider off of her sleeve. "What do you mean?"

"Aside from it being tougher than we thought, we're kind of breaking the law by being here, aren't we?"

"I guess so. But in Panama, you're probably always breaking one law or another."

He nodded. "Sure, it's like that in the US too. I don't know how you feel about God and all, but I get kind of worried whenever I find myself doing something I know is wrong."

She wasn't sure how to respond to that, so she said nothing.

"Do you go to church or anything?"

Fernanda looked up. "Sure. I'm a Christian."

"Really? You mean like Catholic, or what?"

"No, my family is Protestant."

Zack pointed at her with both outstretched hands. "Well, there you go. Doesn't it bother you then, breaking the law like this? I mean, the Bible says that the government is there to do us good."

It does? Fernanda pursed her lips. "But in Panama, most of the laws don't make any sense."

Zack threw a pebble at his shoes. "I used to think the same thing about the rules my parents gave me too. I guess what worries me is that I think God put laws in place to keep us out of trouble, and when we go outside of those laws, we choose to give up God's protection to some extent."

Fernanda was starting to feel uncomfortable. "Hmm…I never thought of it like that."

They sat in silence for a few minutes, listening to the buzz of insects and screech of what seemed like a thousand different birds.

Fernanda reached into her backpack and pulled out her journal. *Might as well keep up with this while I've got the time.*

Coiba: Day 2. I finally got some sleep last night once the rain hit and quieted the jungle animals. Aside from being claustrophobic and sort of cold, the hammocks did a great job keeping us dry. According to Alex's Global Positioning thingie, we've made it over two miles inland from the beach and have found the edge of the triple-canopy rain forest. Now all we need to do is cross a steep ridge, and we'll officially be in the interior of the island.

So far, this is harder than I ever expected, but at the same time, it's incredible to think that aside from a few prisoners who may have explored this part of the island (since most of them lived on the other side), we could be the only people in history to set foot on this place. Pretty amazing to think that's possible in the twenty-first century. If I had known how strenuous and uncomfortable this was going to be, I'd never have come. But now (at least while I'm resting in the shade of a palm tree), I'm glad I didn't know.

Fernanda looked up to see a bright purple hummingbird hovering in front of her, practically within arm's reach. She gasped. *A violet sabrewing!* She could clearly see its black face and iridescent green tail as it floated there for a few seconds, then was gone.

I just saw the most amazing sabrewing hummingbird! It gives me a strange, almost guilty feeling to think that I may be the only person who will ever see that particular bird. Like I've been given a special gift…a rare privilege, for no particular reason.

In fact, it seems like my whole life has been this way. I can't help but feel like God can't love everyone the same when He plays favorites with people's lots in life. Zack said that what we have loses its value if it isn't shared. Can that really be true?

He also mentioned that he felt uncomfortable breaking the law to be here. I don't know… We're not here to hurt anything, so is it really that bad?

Zack jumped to his feet. "Scarlet macaws! Look!"

Fernanda jerked her head up just in time to see two brilliant splashes of red swoop low over the treetops, headed straight for them. When one of the dazzlingly colored birds screeched as it passed overhead, she recognized the sound immediately as that of the late-night visitors that had nearly scared her to death.

"Here they're called *guacamayos!* Ooohh! They are *so* pretty!" She shaded her eyes to get a better look. The birds looked like flying rainbows—their backs displaying rows of yellow, blue, and green feathers. The pair screeched again before passing out of sight beyond the trees.

"Wow." Zack shook his head. "Just wow."

Fernanda couldn't have put it any better. She was still hot and sore and exhausted, but if that was the price of admission to see things like this, it was worth every steamy, muddy step.

A moment later, Carlos and Alex came thrashing back into the clearing, panting from exertion. Carlos dropped his pack and said between gasps, "Water."

Zack and Fernanda set the pack up and opened the top pocket to get at the now-filled water bottles that Carlos had taken along.

Alex also dropped his pack and was bent over, hands on his knees, catching his breath. "Don't drink it yet. Give the iodine time to work."

Once the two had recovered, Alex went on to describe what they'd found. He unfolded his map, then pointed toward the steep hillside to their west. "The area we're looking for is just over the other side of this ridge. But Carlos and I couldn't find any good water sources over there. And since it's about four hundred feet of vertical elevation to cross over, the best thing to do would be to cache our gear on this side, then hike up and over the ridgeline without the extra weight."

He indicated the spot on the map with a stalk of grass. "We'll take only water and our collecting bags and tools, spend a few hours getting what we came for, then cross back this way and make camp on this side, closer to our water supply."

Zack was studying the map. "That'll definitely make the hiking easier, but is there a way to safeguard our gear from the monkeys?"

Alex nodded. "We'll secure all of our packs together and tie them to a tree. The monkeys are smart, but they haven't yet learned how to untie a square knot."

Fifteen minutes later, the team was laboring up the hillside armed with only their machetes and water bottles. While the angle of ascent kept getting steeper, Fernanda endured the burning in her thighs with the consolation that at least they weren't in the hot sun or slogging through swamp. The deep humus underfoot made the slope even more difficult to traverse. *Why does everything have to be slippery?!*

It took nearly an hour to reach the top of the ridge, because they had to take so many breaks to catch their breath. Going down the opposite side wasn't much easier, what with the combination of treacherous and thorny plants and slippery footing. The dense canopy high above them shaded out so much sun that the forest floor looked to be in a sort of perpetual twilight.

They moved without speaking, for the most part, and Fernanda concentrated on not slipping. She was convinced that if she lost her footing, she wouldn't regain it until she hit a black palm tree or the swamp at the bottom of the ravine. Neither option sounded appealing.

"Hey, Alex," Carlos called out. "What kind of…?"

"Shhhh." Zack suddenly held up a hand, and everyone stopped and fell silent. "Did you hear that?"

Nobody spoke for a moment, listening. Then Fernanda heard a rustling sound. Something was moving in the thick jungle below them.

"What is it?" she hissed. Alex shook his head slowly.

Fernanda clutched her machete and peered through the shadowy undergrowth. She began moving her head this way and that, hoping to catch a glimpse of whatever animal they might have scared up.

Then she slipped.

A scream escaped her lips as her feet shot out from under her. She landed on her back, which sent her sliding out of control down the steep hillside.

The dense undergrowth seemed to claw at her as she careened out of control. Then a few seconds later, she came to rest at the foot of the slope. She got to her knees, thankful not to have met any thorny trees on the way down.

But the relief disappeared when she looked up into the black face of a man she did not know.

Fernanda's scream echoed through the forest and sent birds to flight in all directions. She heard shouts above, but before she could scramble away, the man took a step forward and seized her roughly by the arm, pulling it painfully back behind her.

She cried out again, this time in rage. Pivoting her body so she was facing the leering thug, she brought her free hand around and dug her nails into the already scarred flesh above his eye.

He roared and released her arm, and Fernanda lashed out with her foot and kicked him in the groin.

He grunted and bent double, but when she turned to flee, his hand shot out and grabbed her ankle. She fell flat.

Fernanda rolled onto her back and started to rise when a crushing backhanded blow connected with the right side of her face. Stars burst in her head, and she sunk back to earth, stunned.

There was a crashing in the underbrush above her, and she saw Zack and Carlos half running, half sliding down the embankment like a couple of insane mud-surfers. "Leave her alone!" Zack called.

She looked back at her attacker and, for the first time, noticed the enormous black pistol in his hand. She screamed and closed her eyes as the man raised the pistol from his waist. "No!"

The shot exploded above her head, so loud she thought her eardrums had burst.

17

Zona Libre, Colón. 1205 hours

"MARCEL IS GOING to kill me if we don't get that PDA back!"

Beads of rainwater splashed off the hood of the rental as Phoenix pounded it with her fist and uttered a string of profanities that almost made Rip blush despite his years in the military.

He swiveled his head around, looking for anyone who might be the thief to no avail. He put a hand on her shoulder. "Okay, look. Walk me through what happened."

The CIA operative inhaled deeply, visibly taking control of her emotions. "I was waiting for you in the car, and all of a sudden the device started beeping like crazy. One look at the screen and I realized that it had picked up the tags on the products from the ship. So I looked around. I mean, we weren't moving, and the only thing that had changed was the white truck passing by. I tried to get your attention, but you were busy with the food."

Rip slapped his forehead. *Duh! The empanadas.*

"So I just jumped out of the car and ran after the truck. At the end of the block here, it turned into that big white warehouse, and the door closed behind it. Then you showed up."

Rip scanned the street again. "Well, it probably won't do any good to ask if anybody saw anything, but it's worth a try. You stay with the car. I'll get us some more food, and see if the vendor saw anything while I'm there."

"No, I'll come with you. I'll just lock the car this time." She reached across and locked the driver's door, then her own, and then slammed it and joined Rip on the sidewalk. "Let's try this again, shall we?"

Several minutes later they were munching on warm pastries filled with beef and cheese. They actually weren't half bad. The fact that the two of them were soaked to the bone probably made them that much better.

As Rip expected, the food vendor had been distracted by Rip running after Phoenix and hadn't seen anyone near their car. Rip didn't bother asking anyone else.

"What do we do now?" He wiped the extra grease on the paper bag the merchant had given him.

Phoenix looked up from her makeshift meal. "How about we see if we can find that truck."

Rip grinned at the way she politely covered her mouth when she spoke. She could be so in-your-face and confident one minute, and so demure the next. Mary Walker was definitely a complex person.

"Any reason why we couldn't simply walk into the white warehouse and pretend to be interested in whatever they have to sell?"

She shrugged. "I don't see why not."

He nodded toward the end of the street. "Let's do it, then."

As they walked, the sun appeared momentarily, and it quit raining. Instantly, steam started rising from the pavement, and the humidity was almost suffocating. At the end of the block, a large white building occupied the corner across from a six-story edifice that, judging from the gigantic half-dressed white women whose pictures adorned the outside, was the home of a lingerie company. The building they were interested in had a grimy storefront on one side with a wide sidewalk, and a grungy sign hung above it that read: ODMAI Ferretería.

"They sell hardware," Rip said.

Phoenix had her game face on. "Makes sense. I want to see what they have to offer."

Rip pasted on a smile as he pulled open the glass door that led inside, then whispered. "Just let me do the talking."

The dimly lit "showroom" wasn't much larger than Rip's hotel room, but its walls were lined with pegboard holding various kinds of tools, machetes, hoses, and such. Against one wall leaned a piece of plywood upon which were various sizes and styles of boot soles, each with a crudely scrawled price taped to it. A television was propped on a desk in the back of the room, tuned to a Panamanian game show, but no one was around to watch it. Rip and Phoenix found themselves alone.

Rip pointed to the boot display and snorted. "I wonder if the devil comes here to buy soles."

She gave him a serious look. *So much for comic relief.* He cleared his throat and called toward the back. *"¿Buenas tardes? ¿Hola?"*

No answer. Rip felt his hackles rise. A door in the far corner of the room stood ajar. He crossed to it and peered into a long, dark hallway.

"¿Hola? ¿Hay alguien aquí?"

Nothing. The place smelled like a gas station bathroom.

He started to turn around when Phoenix pushed past him and went striding confidently down the hallway. Somewhat flustered, he followed quickly behind.

She reached the door at the far end and opened it like she owned the place. The two of them stepped out into the warehouse proper and saw a cluster of six men gathered around a desk, speaking excitedly. The moment the two of them stepped through the door, however, all conversation ceased.

Rip took in the scene in an instant—crates and boxes stacked almost all the way to the corrugated metal roof; the white box truck parked near the still-closed garage door; and five rough-looking laborers gathered around an older well-dressed Asian man, seated at the desk with an ornate cane in one hand.

But it was the man's other hand that contained the one thing that surprised him most.

The PDA!

The precariousness of their situation hit him in an instant; their agreed-upon cover of being interested in purchasing hardware was blown. They were outnumbered, and if the men had understood what was on the PDA, the entire mission might be compromised.

Phoenix didn't miss a beat, though. She strode to the desk where the Asian man was sitting, bent over, and looked the surprised man directly in the eye. Without blinking, she said, "I believe this is mine, thank you."

She picked up the device, turned on her heel, and walked past Rip and back through the door. Everyone, including him, watched in stunned silence.

Rip realized what had just happened and quickly followed Phoenix into the dark hallway. When muffled shouts told them that the men in the warehouse had also regained their senses, he and Phoenix broke into a run. Rip pulled a display case over on his way out the door, hoping to slow their pursuers.

When they hit the sidewalk, the rain had begun again in earnest, pounding on the parked cars and hot pavement like a million snare drums.

"This way!" She took off up the street in the opposite direction from where they'd come.

Rip quickly caught up with her and grabbed her arm. "Wait! They know which car is ours."

Mary's blue eyes widened under her matted, wet hair, and they both sprinted back toward the vehicle. They made it halfway down the block when Rip turned and saw the workers pouring out of the Asian man's building like bees from a hive that had just been kicked.

"Hurry!" Rip fumbled in his pocket for the keys and got the driver's door open without looking back. Behind him, Phoenix vaulted over the hood of the car, sliding across, and then tumbled inside the moment Rip got her door unlocked.

He fired up the engine, threw it into reverse, and backed into the car behind them. When he pulled out into the street, Rip could see several men running toward them, some brandishing crowbars and one with a machete.

"Hold on!" He threw the car in reverse again and accelerated to the corner, where he had to slam on the brakes to keep from hitting a man on a moped.

"Go, Rip!"

"I'm going!" He gunned the engine, turned the wheel to the left, and spun the car into the intersection. Then he put the car into second gear, floored the gas pedal, and popped the clutch. Smoke from his tires mingled with steam from the pavement, but the car didn't accelerate fast enough.

The man with the machete reached them and took a savage swipe at their left rear tire as the front wheels finally gained traction and the car sped away.

Unfortunately, the streets were so crowded with people, cars, and delivery trucks, that the men on foot nearly had the advantage. Rip weaved through the tangled maze of traffic, honking at pedestrians with one hand and steering and shifting with the other. But every time he looked in the rearview mirror, the pursuers were still there, running down both sides of the street.

"And Marcel didn't think we'd need a handgun," Rip muttered under his breath.

"Just drive!" Phoenix craned her neck to see out the back window.

"How do we get out of here?" Rip shot back, realizing that they had failed to formulate an escape plan.

She pointed to the right. "Turn here."

Rip jerked the wheel and careened around a corner, then slammed on the brakes to avoid a large delivery truck that was occupying the entire street.

Rip clenched his teeth and threw the car into reverse again.

The men on foot rounded the corner and then dove aside just in time to keep from being flattened by Rip's vehicle as he reversed through the intersection and kept going for another block before spinning into a tight J-turn.

Rip turned into an alley, then right onto another street, and then they were on the main thoroughfare, less than a football field from the free zone entrance.

"Oh, thank God," Phoenix said.

Rip crossed himself. *I'll second that motion.*

Five minutes later, once they were back on the road to Panama City, Rip felt like he could start breathing again. He accelerated to get ahead of a diesel-smoke-belching truck.

Then, just as they rounded a corner, the back tire blew.

18

Amador Causeway, Panama City, 1740 hours

"SO THEN THE TIRE blows out, and I almost lose it on this turn, you know? I don't know how we kept from flipping over the embankment." Rip shifted uncomfortably in the cramped confines of the taxi. "Hey, Coop, mind getting your elbow out of my ribs, ese?"

"Here we are, boys." Phoenix, sitting in the front, indicated for the driver to stop.

The aged minivan coasted to a stop in front of an open-air restaurant at the water's edge. Buzz Hogan pulled the side door open and unfolded his six-four linebacker's frame from the taxi, followed by Rip, John Cooper, Frank Baldwin, Doc Kelly, and Bobby Sweeney, all complaining about the cramped conditions.

"Next time, I'm springing for a second taxi." Sweeney stretched.

"At least we don't have all our gear, like that time in Lebanon," Hogan said. "Now *that* was cramped."

Phoenix finished paying the driver and closed the passenger door. She shook her head in mock disgust. "You guys are a bunch of whiners."

Coop was peering at the lit sign in front of the establishment. "*Restaurante Mi Ranchito*—Causeway Amador. Is this, like, Mexican food?"

Phoenix shook her head. "No. Marcel recommended it for classic Panamanian fare." She indicated the view of the canal with a sweep of her hand. "And for the atmosphere."

Rip couldn't argue with that. Their taxi had taken them to the end of the causeway at the mouth of the Panama Canal, where open-air *palapas* shading each table gave a fantastic view in both directions—of ships passing beneath a colorfully lit bridge on one side and the Panama City skyline across the bay on the other.

A light breeze brought cooler air in from the Pacific, and a lively salsa band was playing in the restaurant's bar. Rip took a deep breath of salty air and watched the sunset flare over the Pacific like a curtain of fire. He had definitely been on worse deployments.

"What's the name of those islands out there?" Frank pointed to the far end of the causeway.

"That used to be Fort Grant, I believe," Phoenix said. "It was used for coastal defense during World War II. The land side of the causeway, over near the bridge, was Fort Amador, and they built this causeway in the early part of the twentieth century with earth that they excavated when building the canal."

"And then we just gave it all away in 2000," Sweeney said wryly, shaking his head.

Phoenix shrugged. "It was a money-losing venture anyway, from what I've read."

Doc Kelly noted the steady traffic traveling the brightly lit causeway. "It certainly looks like the place is popular now."

She nodded. "Definitely. Most of the former US canal zone has been renovated into high-end retail and tourist attractions. You wouldn't believe the size of some of the boats that dock at the yacht club over there." Phoenix pointed to the marina visible in the distance.

"Well," Hogan slapped his belly with one hand, "let's quit talking and start eating!"

Ten minutes later they had been seated around an oversized table at the far end of the patio of the Mi Ranchito. The waitress brought their drinks, took their meal order, then left.

Coop leaned forward and rubbed his hands. "Okay, I want to hear how the rest of your fact-finding mission went today—before Rip almost crashed the car."

Rip gave Phoenix a crooked smile. "Do you want to give them the rundown, amiga, or should I?"

She sighed. "The good news is, we found some of the products from the hijacked ship."

Coop raised his eyebrows. "Really? What's the bad news?"

"Well, we were compromised in the process." She proceeded to tell them about losing the PDA, and Rip filled in the details on how they got it back.

"You should have seen her, man. Phoenix just walked right up to those guys like she was some kind of pro-wrestler chick, then picked up her PDA and left. Once the thugs realized what had happened, everybody went ballistic."

Laughter erupted around the table. Buzz Hogan slapped his thigh. "I bet you left that part out when you explained what happened to Marcel."

Rip nodded, smiling. "Let's just say that when we turned in the rental car, we conveniently forgot to mention the tire in the trunk with the machete slash in it."

The theme from *Mission Impossible* sounded from Mary's purse. The men quieted down until she produced her cell phone, then they burst into laughter again.

"Excuse me." Rolling her eyes, she rose and moved to a less noisy spot to answer the call. At that moment, the waitress reappeared with a tray of steaming entrees and began distributing them around the table.

Rip took a sip of his lemonade. "So what did you guys do today?"

Coop sat back to make room for the plate the waitress was placing in front of him. "Nothing much. Went shopping downtown for a while. I demonstrated my fine navigational skills, Frank displayed his knowledge of Panamanian history, Doc surprised us all by speaking exceptionally good Spanish, and Buzz and Sweeney demonstrated their ability to eat everything in sight."

"Plus we all picked up some new civvies," Doc chimed in. "A brother can get an entire wardrobe down here for less than what you'd spend taking your lady to a nice dinner in the States."

Rip took a bite of ceviche. "I thought Marcel said to stay at the hotel."

Sweeney snorted. "You know what I always say: if you aren't breaking the rules, you're not trying hard enough."

Phoenix returned, looking serious. "Hey, Rip. That was Major Williams. He said your mother called the shop today looking for you. She needs to reach you right away."

Rip frowned. "That doesn't sound good."

She held out her phone. "You can use my cell if you'd like to call her. Just, you know, don't mention where you are, of course. Dial 0-1-1 and the number."

Rip set his napkin on the table and took the phone. "Thanks." He rose and moved to a secluded section of the path that ran along the water in front of the restaurant, dialing the number as he walked.

His mother answered just before the machine picked up. "¿Hola?"

"Mami, it's me."

"Euripides! Where are you?" He could hear desperation in her voice.

"I can't say, Mami. What's wrong?"

"It's Gabi. She didn't come home last night."

A ball of ice formed in Rip's gut. *Stupid girl!* He grimaced. "You haven't heard from her?"

"No, mijo. I'm worried. Should I call the police?"

Rip thought for a moment. "Do you have phone numbers for any of her friends?"

"A couple, sí."

"Okay, call them, and see if anyone knows a guy named Chaco. See if you can find his number. I have a feeling Gabi'll be with him." Rip clenched his fists at the thought of his baby sister with that thug. The picture made him nauseous.

His mother cried on the other end of the line. "I'm losing her, mijo. My baby girl."

The ball of ice in his gut shattered, and tears suddenly filled Rip's eyes, surprising him. "It'll be all right, Mami. Just..." *Just what? What can you do?*

An image flashed in his mind of John Cooper sitting across from him at the Waffle House, head bowed in prayer.

"Just pray, Mami. Okay?"

His mother hesitated. "Of course. You pray also, my son."

A single tear escaped. What if it was too late to pray? "I will, Mami," he croaked. "I will."

He hit the End button on the phone and dropped it in his pocket. Rage welled up within him until he thought he'd have to scream to let it out. Instead, he picked up a rock and flung it at the sunset, as far out into the water as he could.

God, what's the problem here? It was more of a child's tantrum than a prayer. He didn't know what else to say. He also didn't know why God would listen to anything he asked, but Rip hated the feeling of being helpless.

The phone in his pocket played its tune again. He fished it out and answered it. *"What."*

"Hello? Who is this?" Marcel's voice was on the line.

"Sergeant Rubio."

"This is Agent Bucard. Is Phoenix there? It's urgent."

"Just a second." Rip took a moment to push the anger and frustration into a corner of his mind. He'd have to deal with that later.

He walked back to the table and handed Phoenix the phone. "Marcel's on the line. He says it's important."

"Maybe he needs help finding his sense of humor," Sweeney quipped before stuffing a large forkful of roasted chicken into his mouth.

She gave him a sideways glance and excused herself to take the call. Rip took his seat and dug into his almost cold plate of fish. Even still, his first bite of the local specialty—called Corvina—was nothing to complain about.

Frank looked up from his food. "Everything okay, Rubio?"

Rip shook his head. "It's my sister, bro. Mom says Gabi didn't come home last night."

"Ooohh. The girl's gone wild," Sweeney said, grinning.

Rip dropped his fork. "Shut up, Bobby, or you'll be sucking your next supper through a straw." He was in no mood for joking.

The stocky southerner raised both hands in mock surrender. "At ease there, Staff Sergeant. Don't get your undies in a wad."

Rip looked at Coop. "And you wonder why I don't like to talk about things."

Phoenix reappeared at the table. "Okay, guys. It looks like we're getting somewhere. I think we have a mission."

Buzz slapped his thigh. "All right! That's what I like to hear. Tell us."

She rolled her eyes at the big Texan. "Not here, Buzz. Let's finish eating, and then we'll hop a taxi back to the embassy."

"Nope." Sweeney held up a hand. "Two taxis."

Forty minutes later, Task Force Valor sat expectantly around another table, this one in a conference room on the third floor of the embassy.

Agent Bucard burst through the door in his signature rumpled suit with his signature facial expression—peeved. Phoenix entered behind him, cool and professional in a form-fitting black crewneck shirt and olive drab tactical pants. They both carried a sheaf of papers.

"Good evening, men. I hope you enjoyed your little jaunt downtown today." Marcel scowled. "While you were playing tourist, the rest of us were working."

Rip noticed Mary's barely contained smile as she stood next to the balding station chief. The guy needed a good beating with a happy stick.

"We reported our findings in Colón this morning to Panamanian intelligence," Phoenix said. "Within three hours the police raided the warehouse in the free zone and arrested several men, one of whom is a private pilot. The man confessed to picking up a shipment of stolen goods on the island of Coiba, off the Pacific Coast."

Marcel cleared his throat. "Our agency is very familiar with this island, which until recently served as a maximum-security prison for Panama's worst offenders."

From the way Bucard said it, Rip got the distinct impression that there was more that the lanky station chief wasn't saying.

Coop raised his hand. "How big is this island? Could they hide an entire ship near there without being spotted?"

Phoenix pulled an eight-by-ten color satellite photo of the island from a folder, passing it around the group. "It's very possible. Coiba is about three times the size of Manhattan, and except for a few park rangers and eco-police, it's completely uninhabited. There are plenty of secluded bays that would accommodate a ship the size of the *Invincible*."

"So what's the mission?"

"We think the pirates who stole the ship are hiding out on the island, and they are obviously trying to sell off the cargo as quickly as possible. Once that's finished, they will either reflag the ship and sell it for scrap or scuttle it. Since we believe the ITEB was onboard that ship, then capturing that cargo before it leaves Coiba is imperative. If we can retrieve the ITEB intact, it might lead us to the supplier or manufacturer."

"Didn't the ITEB we captured in Lebanon help with that?" Frank looked puzzled.

"Only partially for two reasons. First, the explosives you captured were not in their original shipping containers, which could have provided us with additional clues, and second, owing to the political red tape when dealing with the Lebanese government, we weren't able to get as close a look at it as we would have liked."

Coop smirked. "Who says the ITEB hasn't already left the island?"

Phoenix leaned over the table. "It may have. That's why we need you and your team to find out. The pilot claims not to have seen anything matching our description of the explosive, and his claim holds up based on what the Panamanian authorities found in Colón. But time is of the essence here. The pirates have to know that time is not their friend."

"So what's the time frame for the raid?" Frank asked.

"You leave tomorrow night."

Expressions of surprise and disbelief erupted all around the table. Sweeney shook his head, laughing. "You CIA folks aren't real big on planning, are you?"

She held up a hand for quiet. "Like I said, time is of the essence. Now this will be a fairly straightforward reconnaissance and raid. The plan is to insert you near the pirate's camp and have you try to determine their strength and, if possible, the location of the ITEB."

Sweeney leaned back, folding his hands behind his head. "Too bad we can't just send them a little present with a Spectre gunship. One of those flying battlewagons could take out every one of those pirates and mow the grass at the same time."

Phoenix smiled. "But why let the Air Force have all the fun?"

Rip studied the map. "This is a really big island. How are we going to know where to start looking?"

"And rugged. It could take us weeks to cover the area on foot," Coop said.

Marcel cleared his throat again. "We know where the plane picked up the shipment."

"Because the pilot told you?"

"Not exactly."

Hogan seemed confused, as did the others. "What's that mean?"

Phoenix and Agent Bucard looked at each other. "Go ahead, tell them," she said.

Marcel did his throat-clearing thing again. It was starting to get annoying. "What I'm about to tell you is classified Top Secret and does not leave this room, understand?"

Nods and grunts of assent went around the room.

"There are only two airstrips on Coiba. One is near El Centro, which was the village where the penal colony's administrative offices were situated. Today a few policemen are stationed there to prevent squatters. The other is across the island in a very remote area away from the work camps, here." He held up one of the photographs of the island and pointed to the spot with his finger.

Rip tried to make sense of that. "But why would the Panamanians build an airstrip in the middle of nowhere?"

Marcel dropped the photo back on the table. "The Panamanians didn't build it. We did."

Now Rip was really confused. "What? You lost me."

The station chief nodded. "The CIA once had a training base

on the island back in the early '80s. The base was built to train
Contra rebels from Nicaragua in infantry tactics, then send them
back to fight the Sandanista government."

Frank let out a low whistle. "I remember reading about that
whole mess. Didn't Congress forbid the US government from helping the Contras?"

Bucard glanced down at his paperwork. "Yes, well, technically.
But that was before my time. Suffice it to say that we are pretty certain the pirates are using the old airstrip for pickups. Their camp
can't be far away since no roads exist on that side of the island."

Doc spoke up. "So how do we get in?"

"Very simple," Marcel said. "We will have a boat drop you off
in that area tomorrow night. You can sneak up on the pirate
encampment before dawn and then radio us with your findings."

"Whoa, hold up." Coop raised a hand. "From the aerials here,
it looks to me like that area is mostly triple-canopy jungle."

"What's your point?" Marcel looked peeved.

"My point is that movement at night in the jungle is not
possible."

Marcel smirked. "Do you mean to tell me that your team of
crack commandos can't even walk in the woods at night?"

Coop stared him down. "With all due respect, sir, what I'm
saying is that you obviously have no idea what you're talking about.
I went through one of the final jungle warfare training classes at
Fort Sherman before they closed it down in late 1999. I've been in
the jungle at night. There isn't even enough light under the jungle
canopy for night vision to work."

Marcel's face reddened. "Don't presume to tell me what I know
and don't know!"

"Then don't presume to tell me how to run my mission." Coop's tone was icy, unwavering. "You've given us the objective. We'll take it from here. Task Force Valor plans its own mission execution."

Marcel looked like his head was about to pop. He picked up his folders and turned to leave. As he yanked the door open, he sputtered, "Your commander will hear about this!"

The door swung shut with a hiss and a muted click. For a moment, the room was silent. Then Phoenix's face cracked into a smile, and the rest of the team burst into laughter.

Sweeney slapped Coop on the back. "Way to tell'm, boss!"

Phoenix was trying to maintain some semblance of profession-alism. "Okay, quiet down please. Master Sergeant Cooper, what do you see as the best course of action to get this mission accomplished?"

"Well, it's going to take some more map reconnaissance and discussion, to be sure. But I can tell you one thing: We won't be inserting by boat."

"Oh yeah…" Sweeney's eyes lit up. "I feel a HALO blast coming on!"

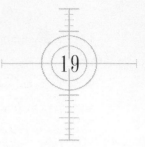

19

Isla Coiba. 2400 hours

FERNANDA HUDDLED ON the muddy jungle floor as the rain pelted her, running in cold rivulets over her shivering body and mingling with her tears.

The plastic zip ties dug painfully into her bound wrists, but it was so dark that she couldn't even see them if she pulled her hands up in front of her face. What she wouldn't give to be back in her apartment in Panama City, awakened by a passing bus to find that this was all just a nightmare.

But to be awakened, one had to fall asleep, and that wasn't going to happen to her this night.

A soft moan came from somewhere to her front, though she still couldn't see anything.

Zack.

Her ears still rang from the gunshot. She could see him clutching his side, eyes wide as he fell next to her in a heap at the feet of the thug with the big black pistol. Fortunately for Zack, the bullet had only grazed his rib cage, leaving a nasty bloody gash.

The thug hadn't been alone, because when he fired his pistol, the rest of the men with him opened fire as well, shooting wildly toward the top of the ridge. Then they were surrounded by nine ragged, dirty men, most of whom carried wicked-looking weapons.

The dark-skinned one with the scar above his left eye was apparently the leader. The other men called him Chombon.

She could hear Carlos behind her, whimpering softly in his sleep, bound as she was, hand and foot. He had surrendered immediately when Zack was shot, skidding to a halt with his hands held high. But that hadn't spared him from a few rifle butts and brutal kicks as the thugs led them away.

"Fernanda?" Zack's voice croaked softly in the darkness. "Are you awake?"

She sniffled, then whispered, "Yes."

They had been ordered not to speak. She'd seen a guard huddling under his poncho against a tree a few feet away before night fell, so she spoke as quietly as possible.

"Where do you think they're taking us?"

Wet leaves rustled. Zack must be trying to scoot closer to her. Then the noise stopped, and he said nothing.

She strained to hear any movement from their guard, but the only sound was huge raindrops slapping the palm fronds on their way to the jungle floor.

Finally, Zack spoke again. "They must be taking us to their camp. I counted nine of them and didn't see any gear other than their weapons and water bottles. We must have held them up so they were unable to get back before nightfall."

Fernanda could have used a drink from one of those water bottles. Despite the rain, her mouth was dry and her head hurt from dehydration. Each of their dangerous-looking captors carried a water bottle tied with a loop of twine that he slung over his shoulder.

She took a ragged breath. "What will they do with us?"

Zack hesitated. "I don't know. I'm trying to figure out what they were doing here in the first place."

Fernanda had wondered the same thing. After being captured, they walked for a little less than three hours, but being herded along by this group of armed ruffians had been slow going.

She thought at first that they must be a band of prisoners who had missed the boat off the island when the penal colony was shut down two years earlier. But the weapons they carried were shiny and new, some sort of assault rifles like the terrorists wielded in movies. Where would prisoners get such weapons? No, they must be terrorists themselves, or pirates, perhaps.

Zack grunted as he tried to move closer still. "Don't worry, Fernanda. I don't think they got Alex."

Alex! The professor hadn't followed Zack and Carlos down the hill when she fell, and she feared that he had been hit by the hail of gunfire up on the ridge. If he escaped, though, perhaps he was able to return to their backpacks and call for help.

Something inside her felt like he had abandoned them to the brutes and run away. But that was silly. Alex had no weapon. He would simply have been captured and beaten, or maybe shot, like the other two. If he had escaped unhurt, he was their only hope.

She tried to sound confident. "He should have found his way back to camp fairly easily with that GPS thing he has."

"Alex wasn't carrying the GPS. I was. I dropped it when I got shot." Regret filled Zack's voice.

Despair clawed at her. *Oh, no…*

Without the handheld location finder, Alex would certainly have a much harder time finding their camp.

A tiny light flashed suddenly from a few feet away. *The guard!*

She could see Zack's body, curled into a fetal position only an arm's length away. The light came closer, and the guard hissed, *"¡Cállate!"*

Zack's body convulsed as the guard's boot slammed into his stomach. *"¡Silencio!"* Then the light went out, and she cried silently as she closed her eyes and listened to Zack retching and gasping in the darkness.

She must have fallen asleep, because when she opened her eyes, the rain had stopped and the faint glimmer of a misty twilight filtered through the trees. The guard's dark form sat unmoving against a tree about six feet away. He was sleeping.

Footsteps rustled behind her, and a rough hand stroked her cheek. She turned her head and stared into the cruel, scarred face of Chombon. Welts above his right eye were still visible from their scuffle yesterday.

Anger and fear warred within, keeping her silent. She simply glared at him as his hand traced the curve of her jaw and he leered back.

He spoke softly in Spanish. "Do not worry, *linda*. I will take good care of you when we get back to my camp. It is not far." The look in his eyes left no question as to his meaning, and he chuckled lustily and stalked off to rouse the other men.

Oh, God. Help!

It was without a doubt the most fervent prayer she had ever uttered.

Within moments the men were all awake, and obviously eager to get back to their camp. A skinny man with squinty eyes and an incredibly dirty white baseball cap approached them. He cut the plastic zip ties at their feet, his gaze lingering on Fernanda as if she were a sports car or a hanging *cabra* in the meat market.

It made her feel naked, dirtier than she actually was, and with still-bound wrists, she pulled at her shirt, hiding herself as much as possible.

Carlos looked pitiful, with puffy eyes and his matted black hair caked with mud. As the squinty-eyed man cut the bonds on his feet, Carlos rasped, "¿*Comida,* por favor?"

The man laughed heartily and spit at Carlos, then walked away.

The three of them stood, eager to be out of the mud and moving again. Fernanda never thought she'd look forward to the heat of the day, but the rain and wet ground had chilled her to the core.

If it hadn't taken every ounce of energy she possessed to simply get to her feet, Fernanda would have plunged headlong into the jungle. As terrible as the night had been, the thought of what lay ahead was too horrific to contemplate. But she had to. Zack and Carlos might be fortunate enough to simply be murdered, but her fate would be much worse.

Oh, Lord, I hope that Zack and Carlos don't see it happen!

She willed herself to stay strong, but she could not get the memory of Chombon's face—and that *look*—out of her head. It made her feel as if she were covered in cockroaches.

Papa would say, "Leridas do not give up!" I must fight and not give them the power they so desire…

But what if they violate me to the point where I don't want to go on living? Please, God, just be merciful. Let them murder me instead!

She tried not to think of what they might do. Even if Alex had survived to call for help, it might not arrive in time.

With a curt command from their leader, the group began moving again. The captives were prodded into line somewhere near the middle of the column. They walked single file, proceeding slowly as the men in front hacked a path with their machetes. The wet, rough palm fronds pressed in on both sides, scraping at them like an endless green car wash, continuing to drench them even though it was no longer raining.

Fernanda tried to pray again, but the tangled emotions inside were thicker than the unbroken wall of vegetation through which they struggled. She found it almost impossible to form coherent sentences in her head.

Zack struggled to stay on his feet, stumbling along in a barely conscious state. His side was bleeding again, and his shirt was black with the thick ooze of blood, attracting flies by the hundreds.

God, please help Zack.

She wasn't sure how long they had been trudging along in silence. But it was much hotter now, and they had moved out of the steep triple-canopy jungle and into a grove of banana palms so thick she could not see the man in front of Zack, who was ahead of her.

She had been trying to ignore the fact that she had a full bladder, but it finally became so unbearable she had to ask for a potty break.

The man walking behind Carlos was more heavyset, which made him look a little less ruthless than some of the other men. Fernanda turned to him and politely asked if she could take a moment to relieve herself.

The man gave a raw chuckle, called to Chombon at the front of the line, and described in graphic terms why they needed to stop. Her face flushing, Fernanda stared at her feet and said nothing.

She was afraid that her request would be denied. But what if she was forced to do her business in full view of not only the thugs, but Carlos and Zack, too?

Fortunately, Chombon called back, "Roberto, take her back on our trail a little ways. But don't go far."

The heavyset man smiled at her and motioned behind him with his rifle. Gratefully, she slipped past him and walked to the rear of the column, enduring the lascivious ogling of each man she passed.

Ten feet beyond the last man in the column was all it took to get the privacy she needed. Unfortunately, Roberto clearly had no intention of letting her out of his sight. She stood there looking at him for a second. When he simply stared back, she sighed and held out her wrists, still bound with the plastic flex cuffs. "At least cut these off so I can go quickly."

Roberto sneered at her. "And what will you do for me, mami?"

She blinked back tears. She had always been able to use her beauty as a tool to get what she wanted. Now it was coming back to bite her. She had never felt so humiliated.

And it will only get worse. Please, God. Help!

"*¡Ándale!* Hurry!" Roberto was getting impatient.

Anger rose in her. *Fine.* If Roberto wouldn't cut the restraints, she'd keep them on. And if he got his thrills from watching her, she'd have to live with it. She waved a fly away from her face and ignored Roberto's stare as much as she could.

Suddenly gunfire erupted from the front of the column, so loud that Fernanda nearly jumped. From the surprise on Roberto's face as he whirled to the sound, he must have been startled too.

Then one of the other men shouted, "*¡El hombre de Lodo!*"

20

THE MUD MAN?

More firing sounded up ahead, and whatever "the mud man" was, the mention of it clearly scared Roberto. The rotund man jerked the weapon he carried to his shoulder, facing away from the trail. She flinched as he loosed several bursts into the surrounding foliage, firing blindly into the jungle.

Each of the criminals was firing his weapon at something. Instinctively, Fernanda dropped to a crouch. Catching a stray bullet at this point would only add injury to insult.

Behind her, she noticed a trail she hadn't seen before. Actually, it was more like a tunnel, perhaps three feet high, possibly made by some animal through the dense thicket.

This was her only chance to survive.

She looked back at Roberto, who was still firing burst after burst into the jungle on the other side of the trail. His back was to her.

Go, girl. Do it!

With a deep breath, she plunged into the thicket headfirst.

Hot tears stinging her face, she scrambled as fast as she could crawl, ignoring the pain in her wrists from the zip ties.

Within seconds, Roberto screamed in rage. He noticed she was gone.

Fernanda tried to move even faster, without looking back, knowing she couldn't outcrawl the bullets from Roberto's rifle.

Please don't let them hurt too much!

But the bullets never came. Perhaps he was more afraid of what Chombon would do if he killed her. Instead, she heard Roberto cursing and thrashing through the dense tangle of banana palms and thorny vines as he gave chase.

Her arms and legs ached with exertion, and her lungs were about to burst, but Fernanda pushed herself even harder, frantic to get away. A few feet farther, she fell headfirst into a narrow creek bed that crossed the path.

She landed on her back, knocking the wind out of her. The water had cut a path into the sandy soil nearly as deep as she was tall, and the rain-swollen creek ran swiftly at the bottom, winding out of sight.

Struggling to her feet and gasping for breath, she could hear Roberto hacking through the undergrowth with his machete, screaming for help from the others. The firing had stopped, but more shouts sounded as the rest of the party realized she had escaped.

Lightheaded from lack of oxygen, she struck off blindly, splashing her way downstream. Around the second corner, she encountered a jumble of logs and debris, piled up even with the steep banks on either side. It would be nearly impossible to climb with her hands still tied. The only gap was where the stream flowed through near the far bank, but she couldn't tell if it was large enough for her body.

There wasn't time to think of something else. Bracing herself, she waded down into the flowing water, feeling the current pulling her downstream. The hip-deep water was cold, but she hardly noticed. She put her hands out in front of her, sank down so her chin was all that remained above the water, and let the current carry her toward the logjam.

Lifting her feet off the bottom, she let them slip through the logs beneath the surface. But her body stuck fast, and though the stream continued through a gap in the debris, it wasn't large enough for her body. She struggled against the force of the water, to no avail. It crushed her against the logs, like a giant filter designed to strain her out of the flow of the river.

Fernanda kicked and choked on a mouthful of water as the rushing current splashed over her head. Reaching down with her still-bound hands, she felt a log at her waist, beneath which her legs were already through. Fighting panic, she took hold of the log, grabbed a lungful of air, then pulled with all her might.

Her pursuers' shouts disappeared momentarily as the rushing water filled her ears. Her body began to slip through the hole beneath the waterline, and with another frantic heave, she shot through to the other side.

A few too many seconds later, she came to the surface, choking and gasping for air. She dragged herself miserably up onto the bank and sank to her knees, feeling like she was going to throw up.

She could hear the men's shouts and an occasional gunshot, but they were farther away now. Still, she forced herself to her feet and stumbled down the creek bed, then noticed a place where a smaller stream trickled in from her right. She decided that up there would be less exposed than staying in the larger streambed.

Again she dropped to her knees and elbows and pushed her way up into the small tunnel in the thick foliage created by the rivulet. She flinched as some sort of large rodent crashed off through the undergrowth, disturbed by her movement. After about twenty yards, she stopped and lay panting, listening for her pursuers.

She could still hear them, shouting and cursing at one another, and though she feared the pounding of her heart would give her away, for the first time she began to believe that she might have actually escaped. Relief washed over her, and she stifled a sob.

The thought occurred to her that they might be able to follow her footprints in the soft sand of the streambed and eventually find her if she didn't keep moving.

But which way to go? She looked around. It made sense that if she followed the creek downstream, she'd eventually reach the coast. And what then? Flag down a passing ship? Not likely. Plus, she had no gear. No, her best hope was to find her way back to their camp, where there was food and water, and hopefully, Alex. But the camp was on the other side of the tall ridgeline that they'd crossed, which meant uphill travel.

She had no machete, to say nothing of the fact that her hands were still painfully bound by the plastic restraints. She looked down at them. Her wrists were discolored and swollen where the zip ties had dug into her flesh, and blood oozed from the cuts inflicted during her getaway.

I'd better do something about that. She didn't want to add infection to the problems she was facing. She dipped her hands in the water, washing the grime from her cuts as best she could. She had to find a way to get the flex cuffs off, that was for certain.

She tried rubbing them on several nearby rocks but was unable to find one sharp enough to cut the plastic. Upon close inspection, she realized that the ties were narrow and fairly cheap, probably not intended for use as personal restraints.

She got an idea. Picking up a stick the size of her ring finger, she slid it under the zip tie on her left wrist. Then, with much difficulty, she twisted the stick, using her chin and fingers together in an attempt to break the tie. But she couldn't stand the pain and had to stifle a cry as she released it. The stick fell to the ground.

Her breathing was coming in ragged, painful gasps. She fought back tears. *Think, Fernanda, think!*

Then another idea surfaced. She picked some thick palm fronds from above her head and pushed the leaves under the flex cuffs, pulling them through with her teeth. There wasn't much space, but after a short time she had padded one wrist with leaves all the way around. Then she picked up the stick and reinserted it.

Twisting, the ties tightened again, but with the added padding of the thick green leaves, the pain was bearable. She twisted until the plastic tie snapped.

She lay back and put her head on the ground, panting. *Thank You, God.*

After washing her free wrist in the stream, she repeated the process on the other arm until she was free of the other cuff.

No time to celebrate. She had to move. But now that the adrenaline was fading, an incredible thirst settled in. She looked at the trickle of water. They had been filtering and treating their water since the start of the expedition. She certainly didn't want to catch some kind of nasty gastrointestinal parasite, but she had to have water to survive.

The risk of dehydration was worse than the risk of dysentery at this point. Besides, the water looked clear and wasn't stagnant.

Fernanda crawled to where a small pool had formed, put her lips to the water, and drank. She had never tasted anything so refreshing.

The sound of rustling through the palms made her sit up, wide eyed and frozen. They were coming her way!

As quietly as she could, she picked her way uphill, forced to remain on her hands and knees for the time being to keep from rustling the foliage overhead. Eventually, the palm thicket gave way to a forest of black palm, and she was able to walk upright again.

She tried to get her bearings. Nothing around her looked familiar, or worse, all the jungle looked the same. She'd never been very good with directions anyway. After all she'd just been through, she barely knew which way was up.

How much more can I handle?

Fernanda remembered the conversation she'd had with Zack about being outside of God's protection. Tears stung her eyes again.

I'm sorry, God. Maybe it was wrong of us to come here. But please forgive me and help me find my way out of this. Please!

Somehow, she felt a little better. She might not know where she was, but between kidnapped and lost, she'd gladly take lost.

The endless monochromatic green of the jungle told her, however, that if she didn't get rescued soon, she might change her mind.

Isla Coiba. 0940 hours

The man knelt next to the creek and scooped a handful of mud. He daubed it over the oozing wound on his thigh. The bullet had only grazed him. Still, he must be more careful.

The black-skinned one and those who followed him were not

skillful enough with their weapons to hit a lame deer from ten
paces, but they made up for it by sheer volume of wild, unaimed
fire. And an unaimed bullet could kill him the same as an aimed
one.

The one that escaped has just been here. The depressions in the
mud made it clear that this place had hidden the skinny one who
had run away.

He cupped his hands in the water and drank. As he did, his
eyes fell on two white circles, lying next to the creek in front of him.
He reached out and picked them up. They were stiff but flexible,
made of a material he had seen before but that did not grow in this
place. They were shaped like the bracelets worn by the women in
his tribe. But these were broken.

He placed them in the canvas satchel that hung across his
chest. Maybe he would find a use for them.

He picked up the machete he had taken from the outsiders. He
would follow the escapee. It was always easiest to catch his victims
alone.

Perhaps this one would soon join those whom he had freed
from the island.

21

Congressional Country Club, Outside Washington DC. 1130 hours

MICHAEL LAFONTAINE QUICKLY ended his cell phone call as the limo driver opened his door for him. As he stepped into the crisp sunshine, he could hear that the event inside was already underway.

"Good morning, ladies and gentlemen. I'm Judge Eugene Sanders, member emeritus of the West Point Society of DC, and I'd like to welcome you all to our nineteenth annual spring brunch. Please enjoy your meal."

Polite applause rippled though the airy banquet hall. A four-man jazz ensemble began to play and white-shirted wait staff bustled about carrying trays of grilled Norwegian salmon and chicken breasts stuffed with Maryland crab.

Michael entered at the rear of the hall, giving a handshake to a senator here, a pat on the back to a general there. He made his way between the large round banquet tables and across the glossy parquet floor to the head table next to the podium. He sat next to the judge, who gave him a conspiratorial stare. "I was sort of hoping you'd show up."

He tipped his head toward the judge, speaking through his smile. "Now, Gene. You know how much I love the spotlight."

Sanders picked up a crystal water glass and took a sip. "Exactly."

Michael regarded his rotund former West Point classmate, who looked somewhat rumpled in his standard black tuxedo. Then again he had never seen Gene Sanders wear anything else. Michael leaned closer and whispered, "How do you like your little side job, consulting for the National Imaging and Mapping Agency?"

The judge almost choked on a mouthful of chicken. "Michael, it is my goal to someday understand how you get your information. That is supposed to be a secret."

"And it is, my friend." He patted Sanders on the back. "It is. But still, it must be interesting work."

Sanders wiped his face with the napkin from his lap. "To tell you the truth, it's quite disturbing. If you knew the level at which people can be monitored—from space, even—it would make you want to board up every window in your house."

Michael cocked an eyebrow at him. "Is that so? And you're helping them wade through the legal ramifications of being able to spy on little old ladies in their bathrobes?"

Sanders snorted. "Something like that. But really, I feel for the analysts there, who spend their days watching death and mayhem, via various methods, around the globe. It has to wear on a person to watch horrors like the killings in Sudan in real time on a television monitor, knowing there is nothing you can do to stop it."

Michael nodded. "That would be tough. But while I have your ear, let me ask you a favor, Gene."

"What's that?"

He pulled a card from his breast pocket with a single word scrawled on it. "If you get a chance, have one of those analysts of yours find me a recent aerial shot of this place."

Sanders took the card, pulling his glasses from a breast pocket. "You're kidding, right? You want me to lose my job?"

Michael shook his head. "No, no, no. I'm not asking you to task a satellite or anything. But NIMA has the best maps on the planet. I'm just looking for a good shot of a place where I may purchase some land. If you run across anything that could help me, I'd be very grateful."

Not to mention that I was instrumental in your judicial appointment...

The big man frowned and pocketed the card. "I'll see what I can do, Colonel, but don't get your hopes up."

"I have faith in you."

"Well, don't."

A few minutes later, Sanders rose and went again to the podium. The crowd quieted. "Ladies and gentlemen. I trust you are enjoying the food and fellowship. It is now time to present our Distinguished Member Award for this year."

He unfolded a piece of paper and adjusted his glasses. "To give you a bit of background on it, the West Point Society of the District of Columbia and the National Capital Region presents the Distinguished Member Award to West Point graduates who have made significant contributions..."

Blah, blah blah. Michael surveyed the room. His assembled classmates might have gone on to careers in business, politics, or the military, but their time at the academy gave them all something in common—a penchant for success. Or perhaps West Point simply attracted those who had those qualities already. Maybe both. What disturbed him was that other thing the men before him had in common. They were *all* politicians, really. Their wives might have come along today for the food and the gossip, but the men were here for one reason only. In polite circles they called it networking. He called it "social espionage."

Sanders was still blathering on. "…with the qualities that West Point strives for in keeping with its motto: 'Duty, Honor, Country' while making significant contributions to West Point, to their class, our society, or their community…"

It's a wonder they're all not facedown in their quiche by now.

"This year's candidate is a classmate of mine, who has gone on to great heights in both his personal and professional life. As founder and CEO of a large pharmaceutical empire, his company's research has saved countless lives, and his generous donations as overseer of his company's charitable foundation have improved the lives of many more.

"He is heavily involved in lobbying for political reform here in Washington and has probably done more to encourage the government to increase benefits for our men and women in uniform than anyone in the last thirty years. He is also known to be the single largest contributor to the Wounded Warriors foundation, which provides aid to severely injured soldiers. Not only that, but I hear he plays a mean game of handball."

Laughter rippled through the crowd as Judge Sanders refolded the sheet of paper and took off his glasses. "I'm pleased to present to you this year's Distinguished Member, my friend and fellow cadet from the West Point class of 1969, Colonel Michael LaFontaine."

The crowd roared in applause as Michael stepped to the podium, accepting Gene's handshake with one hand and the engraved walnut plaque with the other.

When the applause died down, Michael pulled his own set of notes from the pocket of his tuxedo jacket and cleared his throat.

"Thank you, Gene, and thanks to the society for this great honor. I'd like to take a few minutes to talk to you about something that the judge alluded to just now. Something I am quite passionate about. That is, our armed forces and the situation in today's continuing war on terror. Mostly because this is the only gathering of people in Washington DC who might actually agree with me on some of what I'm about to say."

Polite laughter arose from the crowd.

"Last month, a Palestinian Muslim extremist walked into a World Bank meeting in Beirut, Lebanon. The diplomats were there to discuss ways to make that country better and to help it to continue the process of rebuilding after the long civil war that tore the country asunder. But the Palestinian extremist, by way of thanks, detonated a bomb that murdered twenty-six people and injured scores of others.

"Many people ask what would possess someone to hate so deeply that he would perform such a despicable act, not upon the combatants of an opposing military, but upon peaceful civilians. I believe that this kind of activity is not the result of hate. It is the result of cowardice."

A two-star general in the front row raised his glass. "Here, here!"

Michael acknowledged the general with a nod. "This was the act of radical Islamists. This group of people hates everything about us—they hate our very way of life. They say they are a peace-loving people, but that's only partially true. They believe in a peace that is accomplished at the end of the sword, by force. But if theirs is a

worldview of peace, it is not one of love. They have no love for anyone, including themselves.

"Fortunately, in every era there have been brave and good men
who were willing to do the dirty work necessary to keep evil men
at bay. Make no mistake—this has never been, nor will it ever be
anything less than a gruesome task. Since evil men understand no
language other than violence, good men must open the dialogue
and finish the argument in that language."

A few spouses looked somewhat uncomfortable by this kind of
talk, but Michael could tell that, for the most part, his audience was
hanging on his every word.

"Since its founding, our country has been populated by
men who weren't too squeamish to do this dirty work. It's something that has caused other countries, even our allies, at times to
consider us to be slightly less than civilized. But there's no denying the fact that because America has been willing to roll up its
sleeves and get its fists bloody now and then, the world is a better place today."

Several men, including the general in the front row, looked like
they were about to start shouting in agreement.

"I'm concerned by the trend in this country toward pacifism.
Perhaps it's a natural result of a postmodern consumerist culture,
which is always trying to sell us the notion that we deserve a safe,
comfortable life in order to sell us something designed to reduce the
stress of our existence.

"What does this have to do with terrorism? Because our culture is no longer willing to entertain the distasteful business of war,
which requires copious amounts of dirt, sweat, and blood, we are
not winning the war on terror. We are, at best, holding the dogs at

bay. But if we were willing to meet them on the field of battle instead of simply keeping them outside the walls of our comfortable society, we could destroy them once and for all.

"If our country wants to be rid of the terrorist threat, we must be willing to pay the price to accomplish that. You don't stop a fanatical coward with conciliatory half measures. You must be willing to pull out all the stops, to pay whatever price necessary to win. Anything less is not only inefficient and counterproductive, it's a slap in the face to those brave boys and girls we send into harm's way."

The crowd roared its applause. Michael stood quietly until the clapping had died down.

"My godson, John Cooper, is one of those boys. Last month he and his team almost lost their lives, not because of a tactical failure on their part, but because of bureaucratic cowardice. And that is a travesty. As leaders ourselves, we must commit to each other that we will pursue the course of honor and encourage our elected representatives to do the same."

He folded his notes and paused, looking at the faces in the crowd. "Ladies and gentlemen, I pledge to you, I will continue to do everything within my power to keep our elected officials' collective eyes on the ball. We must win this war. There is no possibility of appeasement. Thank you."

Michael stepped away from the podium and took his seat, paying very little attention to the standing ovation he was receiving. His mind was already on to other things.

Some people craved applause. He craved change. Now that he had accomplished what he came to do at this banquet, it was time to leave.

Judge Sanders was back at the podium making some sort of yada-yada remarks, and shortly the band began playing again, which Michael took as his cue to head for his limo. But getting there required running the gauntlet of congratulatory well-wishers between the head table and the doorway at the back of the hall. Reluctantly, he pasted on his best smile and waded into the back-slapping, handshaking throng, shrugging off questions from several people about whether or not he would be chosen as the next ambassador to Russia or perhaps some country in South America.

Gene caught up with him in the foyer. "Leaving already, Michael?"

"I'm sorry about that, old friend, but duty calls."

"What's that supposed to mean? What are you up to now?"

"I've an important meeting this afternoon, that's all." He winked at the judge. "I have to get some facts in order so I can pretend to know what I'm talking about."

Sanders laughed as they descended the outside stairs to where Michael's black stretch limo was waiting. "I suppose so. But I've been meaning to ask you something."

"Shoot."

"You're known as a pretty die-hard conservative. But I saw where you gave a hundred forty thousand to various liberal democrats last year. How does that square with what you're trying to accomplish?"

Michael put a hand on the limo's door handle and turned back to his friend. "That's simple, Gene. If you want people to listen to you, you must make it worth their while to do so."

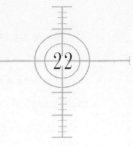

22

Panama City, Panama. 2200 hours

THE FLAME FROM the expensive nickel-plated Zippo lighter disappeared with a decisive flick of the wrist and a *click,* plunging Oswardo's face back into shadow.

He leaned back in the booth in the darkened poolside café, causing the torn and faded patent leather to groan with his weight, and took a long pull on the Cuban cigar. He exhaled. The café was nearly empty. It must have been a nice place at one time, long ago, but not now.

Still, vestiges of its former glory remained. Twin eight-foot swordfish statues, their paint now faded, spouted water into the murky pool that he wouldn't have swum in on a bet. A mural of gaudy mermaids swam along the walls on either side of the pool, probably added sometime during the era when the hotel catered mostly to American GIs and their paid escorts. The AIDS epidemic had ruined that business even before the United States left Panama.

Good riddance.

The majority of the restaurant's patrons had already retired for the night. Only one other man remained, and his attention was on the attractive young waitress bustling about the kitchen, her black hair pinned loosely atop her head with a pencil. She looked bored with the young man's attempts to woo her as she busied herself with cleaning up the area behind the bar.

She saw Oswardo watching her from across the room and pursed her lips at him, a decidedly Panamanian way of asking if he wanted something. He shook his head and took another drag on his cigar.

The cell phone on the table in front of him began playing the ridiculous American rap song that his son had programmed into it several months ago, the last time he was home. He almost never came home from college anymore unless he wanted money. And he never called.

Ah, well…it is your own fault. You were always too busy to pay much attention to him.

He snatched it up, annoyed, and pushed the button. *"¿Mande?"*

"Oswardo! I am here at the hotel. Where are you?"

"By the pool. Hurry up, *idiota*. I have been waiting almost an hour."

"Be right there."

Young Remi was his most valuable asset in the city government, someone he could always rely on to get the job done and who was just as reliably late to every occasion. But the light-skinned mulatto's position in the Panamanian Ministry of the Interior virtually guaranteed that he would show up eventually, because Oswardo had enough incriminating evidence on the mid-level civil servant to put him in prison for life. It was the best kind of relationship to have with a government official.

The dirty glass door to the hotel lobby burst open, and Remi entered, looking very out of place in his finely pressed pinstripe suit. As usual, he was furiously chewing a small wad of gum. Most uncouth in the circles where Remi worked, but one supposed it was in lieu of other, more harmful vices. He spotted Oswardo immediately and bustled past the waitress and her admirer to take a seat opposite him in the booth.

"You couldn't find a nicer meeting place than this? I'll be lucky if my car is still outside when I return!"

Oswardo eyed him coolly. "Would any of your friends come here?"

"Are you kidding? *Never.*"

"Exactly."

Remi ran a mottled hand over his close-cropped black hair and chewed even faster. "You have a point."

"Then please—" the older man laid his palms on the grimy table—"tell me what you have found. I must return to Colón tonight to meet another shipment that arrives tomorrow morning. I have found a buyer willing to pay handsomely for the full remainder of my product, and I have much to do to prepare my lab before the shipment arrives."

Remi nodded. "I learned this evening that our special police forces raided a warehouse in the Zona Libre and found items that were on the *Invincible.* The products were apparently flown there from Isla Coiba."

Oswardo tapped the ashes from the end of his cigar. "Isla Coiba? Are you sure?"

"I am only telling you what I was told."

He took another long drag, thinking. "Where is the closest port to the island?"

"Santa Catalina. But it is not a port, just a fishing village."

"Do you have anyone who can find me some men with weapons and boats there?"

Remi shook his head. "I might be able to get boats. Don't you have your own men?"

"Yes, but they will be busy with this new shipment. I cannot afford to spare them."

The younger man nervously rubbed his hands together. "I have a man in Puerto Mutis who owes me a favor. Perhaps he can recruit some men there. Many of the fishermen used to be guards on Coiba. I will see what I can do, but it will be very expensive. And they will need arms."

Oswardo stubbed out his cigar. "Arms are not a problem, of course. You find the men; I will find the money. Call me when you have something. We will need at least twenty who know how to use a gun."

Remi swallowed hard. "There will be great risk. Are you sure there isn't someone else—"

Oswardo stopped him midsentence with a dismissive wave of his hand. "You know how to keep yourself distanced from these things. Besides…" He pulled from his coat pocket a device made of black plastic, no larger than a raisin, and rolled it across the table to Remi.

"What is it?" Remi peered at it in the half-light emanating from the pool.

"My latest invention. What does it look like?"

"Like the cap that one removes to put air in one's tire."

Oswardo nodded. "Very good. Except this cap contains just enough explosive to give a car a blowout when triggered by a remote detonator. A perfect way to make someone's death look like an accident, no?"

Remi swallowed his gum.

Oswardo picked up the device and rose to leave when Remi put a sweaty hand on his arm. "Amigo, don't forget that the *policía* have this information, and there is something else. I have reason to believe that the American intelligence people have taken an interest in this too. It's very possible that they are mounting an operation as well."

Oswardo bent and gave him a steely look. "Then you had better get busy. I want my shipment back."

Isla Coiba. 2300 hours

Pain shot up Fernanda's left leg as she tripped over yet *another* log. The vines and ferns and thorny bushes seemed to reach for her in the darkness, and she flailed her arms to try to fight them off.

She reached down to rub her tender shin, and something alive scuttled across her hand, causing her to add her own squeak to the cacophony of noises from animals and bugs that had emerged once the sunlight disappeared.

It was insane to be moving at night, but she couldn't bear the thought of bedding down here in the swamp. Not only was the ground spongy and wet, but there were too many creepy-crawlies, like the one she'd just encountered.

But despite being in the lowlands, she had been unable to find another source of running water since she left the stream. And her thirst was becoming all-consuming.

Every muscle in her body hurt. The oozing mud sucked at her boots, as if she were wading in wet concrete. The vines and thorns tore at her hair and clothing. Before dark it had been as if she were a flea lost on the back of a big, wet, green dog. But now it felt like the jungle itself was a living, malevolent entity, bent on her destruction.

But it still beat the alternative. An image of Chombon's leering face appeared in her mind, devouring her with his eyes. She pushed away a sob and thought of Carlos and Zack. Where were they now? Were they still alive?

And Alex! If only she could find their campsite, she imagined him waiting there. No matter what had happened between them, he would protect her. She wanted to cry out, to call his name, but that would certainly give her position away to the evil men who took Carlos and Zack.

But she would not make it there tonight. She was lost—plain and simple. Lost with no food, water, or shelter. And even if Alex had been able to summon help, there was a very real chance that they would never find her.

I will die here.

That thought surrounded her, clawing at her mind like the vines and thorns did her body. How she wished for a machete. She sank down and sat on the log.

God? Have You abandoned me too?

Tears rolled down her cheeks. Water she couldn't afford to waste but couldn't stop. "I'm sorry, God, for treating You like You weren't important."

Fernanda realized that she had been talking out loud, but it felt good to hear a voice, even if it was thin and full of despair.

"I'm sorry for not living the way I should. So much of my life lately has been wrapped up in the pursuit of insignificant things.

This trip was supposed to be an escape from my problems. But now, in this place, I see how silly and meaningless so many of my problems were.

"Please lead me out of this place. I'm afraid! I don't want to die here. Please protect Zack and Carlos. And Alex." A wave of conviction swept over her. "I'm sorry for what happened between us. Please protect Alex too."

She wiped her eyes and looked around. Though she couldn't see a thing around her, a patch of sky was visible above. Through the hole she could see stars, almost blindingly brilliant compared to the complete darkness around her.

She stood on the log for a better look, steadying herself by holding on to palm fronds on either side.

If only I could fly.

It felt good to have her feet on something solid. Slowly, she felt her way down the log. She moved toward the gray area of the trunk at its base. As she got closer, she could see that a clearing of some sort was beyond the twisted roots of the tree, silhouetted against the lighter blackness of the sky.

She stopped and stared, wishing she could tell if the clearing consisted of dry ground. At the end of the trunk, she climbed down to find herself in waist-high grass on dry ground, woozy from exertion.

Though she was still intensely thirsty, she would find no water tonight. She had to rest. Finding water would be the first order of business when it got light.

Wading through the tall grass, she moved to the middle of the small clearing, as far away from the evil jungle as possible. There, she sank down, exhausted, but grateful to be out of the swamp.

Thank You, God. Help me find some water tomorrow. And please send help.

She curled up in the grass next to a bush and fell asleep.

Isla Coiba. 2330 hours

The whirring of the tree bugs had resumed after her passing. They did not normally stop their thrumming when he passed by. Nor did the forest animals quiet their calls, not for him. If they sensed his presence at all, they did not perceive him as a threat, because he was one of them. Not like the outsiders.

The man stood in the murkiest shadows on the edge of the clearing and wrestled with emotions that he'd forgotten even existed.

When he first caught up with the skinny one, it had been to do what he had always done—to gain strength for his own journey by freeing the spirit of another. He had never considered the killing to be evil, but good—like setting a bird free from its cage, especially in a place like this. But when he saw the skinny one up close, something had changed.

It had been so long since he'd set eyes on a woman that it wasn't until she passed directly beneath him, standing motionless in a tree, that he realized she was more than just a skinny man.

The realization brought back memories long buried by a thousand sleeps, memories of his village, of his mother and sisters, whom he'd fought to protect when the outsiders came with their saws to steal the very forest they lived in.

But his blowgun had not been able to compete with the outsiders' weapons. Their blowguns, which required no breath, had found him. He still had the scar where their dart had pierced his shoulder. And while he had been wounded, the outsiders drained the blood of his sisters, taking the women's life force for themselves.

Part of him felt that he should drain the blood of this woman—his people would have called the skinny girl *mali*—and make up for what had been done to his own family. But another part of him believed that the reason the spirits had allowed him to be taken away from his home and brought to this place was that he failed to protect his own sisters. Perhaps the way to redeem himself was to protect this one.

So he kept the knife in its sheath and followed *la mali* to see where she went. But she moved like a wounded animal, crashing through the bush with no direction, walking in circles. She clearly did not belong here, and if she did not find water soon, she would die.

But he could not show himself. He had lived alone for so long that he had almost forgotten his own language and certainly did not know hers. He'd even forgotten his name. How could he meet someone if he had no name to give?

The man's hand fell to the bag he had taken from the pirate camp. The bottle he had taken was still there, the cap on the end holding in the water. Its constant bumping had put a bruise on his thigh. He did not need it, because water was everywhere on the island. He had almost broken the bottle several times, thinking the shards might be useful for making spears. But now he knew what to do. The mali did not know how to get water. She could use the bottle.

Without a sound, he padded softly over to where she was sleeping. He stood looking at her dark form, curled up like a child. The conflicting emotions came to him again. But he put them away. He had chosen his path, and he would stay on it. He slid the bottle from the canvas bag and laid it next to her, then slipped away.

23

Over the Pacific Ocean. 0400 hours

A BLAST OF COOL night air hit Rip in the face as the rear door of the C-130 opened with a hydraulic whine. Lights from scattered villages along Panama's Pacific coastline sparkled like diamond chips scattered on black velvet. The glowing pinpoints of light ended abruptly at the water's edge, some thirteen thousand feet below, and picked back up again as stars on the horizon.

Rip stood in the aircraft's darkened cargo bay with the rest of Task Force Valor, lined up on the ramp in two columns, waiting for the jump command. He watched the stars waver and blur in the superheated prop wash from the aircraft's four powerful turboprop engines.

The ride to a drop was always a good time to think, since the roar inside the plane's unpressurized cabin precluded any sort of discussion that couldn't be accomplished with hand signals.

While the rest of the team had been trying to catch some sleep in the hour since they'd boarded the plane at a remote corner of Albrook Airfield, Rip had been thinking a lot about Gabi, worrying.

Couldn't his sister see that she was gambling with the rest of her life? And for what? The girl was smarter than that. She'd always been top of her classes, an A student. And now she was dressing like a prostitute and staying out all night. She was barely a teenager!

He hated the powerless feeling it gave him, being here while this was happening. Hated it so much he'd actually considered leaving the Army for the first time in his career.

It had always been a foregone conclusion that he would complete his twenty years with the Special Forces. He couldn't imagine any other job that would appeal to him. But maybe the nonstop, back-to-back deployments were getting to him. Maybe he needed a break, some time to help his family straighten things out. Gabi needed him. His mother needed him.

But what bothered him the most was that the situation with his sister had forced him to look at the whole concept of his own love life from a totally different angle. He'd watched over her when their mother was at work ever since she was just a few years old. She hadn't known a father but had come to her big brother for many of the things she needed from a dad: acceptance, advice, and affection. He'd never been as close to anyone as he was to Gabi. Without a doubt, he wouldn't hesitate to die for her. There had never been a girlfriend he would have said that about.

But he could see now that his girlfriends had been part of the problem. Gabi saw the way he went through women. Suddenly the idea that his cavalier attitude toward dating had been harmless fun was being shot full of holes. It wasn't harmless. Gabi learned how to let a man treat her by watching her brother. And the realization was like a kick in the gut.

Rip was jerked back to reality by Bobby Sweeney, who turned to him and patted his chest harness, a smile evident under the black Pro-Tec helmet and jump goggles. Rip looked down at his own rig—the full-body harness that secured the MC-4 parachute to his back and the rucksack clipped to his waist. Earlier that night when they were given this mission, he had gone through his gear, carefully considering each item, trying to decide what was essential and what could be left behind.

It was just a reconnaissance at this point. They were to infiltrate the island and put eyes on the pirate's camp to determine their assets and how many men they were dealing with, as well as whether or not the ITEB was still present there. Phoenix had informed the team that a platoon of Panamanian special police would be tasked to assist, as well as a pair of US fighter planes from Texas. But for the time being, it was simply a sneak-and-peek mission.

The plan was to HALO into a clearing near the pirate base just before dawn. As soon as it got light enough to move, the team would stash the majority of their equipment and move in on the camp. Once they were in place, they'd radio the information they gleaned back to Phoenix. If they were going to hit the camp, she would be the one to make the call.

After rechecking all of his buckles and straps, Rip flashed a thumbs-up at Sweeney, who gave an "okay" sign and turned back toward the ramp. John Cooper was on it, kneeling near the starboard hydraulic cylinder, peering at the sea below. As jumpmaster on this mission, it was his job to check the winds and spot for the drop zone.

Coop stood and held up an index finger. *One minute.*

Rip's pulse quickened. This was the kind of thing he had signed up for when he joined the Special Forces. But this was no Hollywood jump done under perfect conditions just for fun. This was the first time he'd parachuted into a real-world mission. He shifted his weight from one foot to the other and rotated his head back and forth, like a boxer getting ready for a fight.

It was always possible that he wouldn't come home from this, from any mission. He'd been shot in the chest in Lebanon, and the ceramic plate on his body armor was all that saved his life.

But they didn't bring body armor on this mission.

He'd made a habit of telling himself at the start of every mission that it could be his last. Every soldier thought it; Rip just made a point to bring it to the surface and face the fact, to make it okay in his mind before he went into battle. Somehow doing so made it easier to do his job. He had to be ready to lose in order to be able to win.

But something was different this time. He really *wanted* to come back from this mission. If he didn't come back, his sister wouldn't have anyone to set her straight.

He was surprised and angry at the fear he felt. *This isn't the time to think of this.*

Coop signaled thirty seconds. Jaw clenched, Rip forced the fear from his mind. Almost as an afterthought, he crossed himself. *God help me.*

Coop had taken up his position at the head of the stack, and Rip tightened it up, pushing forward until he was touching Sweeney's pack tray.

Beside him, Hogan let out a yell over the roar of the plane. "Let's do this, y'all!"

Coop's right hand counted down from five. At zero, the team charged off the end of the ramp as one and disappeared into the night.

———

C-130 rolling down the strip...

Three miles above Coiba, six black shapes exited the C-130 and plunged into the night in a tight formation. Rip arched his body hard, stabilizing himself in the slipstream while honing in on the muted green chem-lights the rest of the team wore on their Pro-Tec helmets. For some reason, an old cadence from airborne school ran through his head.

Sixty-four Rangers gonna take a little trip.

The air was cool at this altitude, and the beginnings of twilight formed in the eastern sky. From this vantage point, Rip could see the curvature of the earth on the horizon. He never got over the feeling that free-falling gave him.

The difference between riding in a plane and free-falling was sort of like the difference between riding in a boat and swimming. It felt more like floating than falling, especially at night with the absence of any visual cues. But it was floating at 120 miles per hour, and that feeling of speed was what made his adrenaline flow.

Stand up, hook up, shuffle to the door...

Being careful not to collide with any of his teammates, he flew toward where two of them had already linked up, not surprised that he recognized Hogan by his big head, even in the darkness.

With his left hand, Rip latched on to the big Texan's right arm and pivoted slightly toward him. A moment later, he felt a hand catch his right arm in the same manner. Within a few seconds, all six men were falling together in a circular formation, just as they had rehearsed on the "dirt dive" practice run on the tarmac before climbing aboard the plane.

Jump right out and count to four.

The plan called for the team members to open their chutes a little bit higher than normal, because they needed more time under canopy to steer themselves to the small clearing chosen as a landing zone.

Rip checked his altimeter. They were already passing through twelve thousand feet. Directly below, he could see a single pinpoint of light, which he assumed was coming from the ranger station on the north end of the island. Other than that, the only lights he could see were in the distance on the mainland.

Twenty seconds later, he could just make out the black shape of the island. Coop was directly across from him, distinguishable by the backlit GPS strapped to his forearm. At four thousand feet, Coop waved the formation off, and everyone released his grip on the man next to him. Rip spun his body away from the group, tracking into open space so he wouldn't hit anyone when he deployed his chute.

If my chute don't open wide…

After one last check of his altimeter, Rip reached back with his right hand and found the pilot chute secured to his hip. He compensated for the movement by bringing his left arm up over his head.

I've got a reserve by my side.

He flung the pilot chute away from his body and waited for the reassuring jolt of his main canopy catching air. He felt the familiar tug of the Para-Flite MC-4 parachute leaving the pack tray on his back and then…nothing.

He looked up and his heart almost stopped. Instead of a beautiful square canopy silhouetted against the night sky, he saw an ugly, snarled mess streaming above him by only one riser.

His hand flew to the harness near his left shoulder, confirming his worst fears. Only one riser was still connected.

If that one should fail me too...

Rip could almost feel the ground rushing up at him, but it felt as if his mind went into slow motion. That little guy in his brain was screaming that time was running out—the malfunctioning parachute had done very little to slow his rate of descent.

Look out below, I'm coming through.

He fought off panic. There wasn't time to think about what he should do, only time to react with his training.

Look, grab, look, grab, arch, pull, pull. He'd done the drill a million times in HALO school and hoped he'd never had to use it. Rip grasped the quick release for the remaining riser connected to the harness on his right shoulder.

Jerking hard on the release, he felt the main canopy detach, and he was again in free fall. Then just as quickly he pulled the handle at his side to deploy the reserve parachute, which fluttered then opened with a satisfying pop.

Rip checked the inflated canopy and started breathing again. Everything was in good order. But then he looked down.

He had another problem.

He'd lost so much altitude that the rest of his team was still somewhere far above. Not only that, Rip wasn't sure he had enough altitude left to find and land in the agreed-upon clearing.

Peering off to his right, he could just make out three patches of lighter gray surrounded by the black jungle, illuminated by only the faintest sliver of moon. From the map reconnaissance they'd done during the briefing, he recognized the clearings. They looked sort of like a lopsided Mickey Mouse head—one large round area with two smaller "ears" nearby. The plan called for the team to land and assemble in the large clearing.

But as he turned his parachute toward the clearing, he realized that he was far too low. Even with his canopy's forward motion of up to twenty-five miles per hour, it would be tough to make the drop zone from his present position and altitude.

There didn't appear to be much wind aloft, and he got a sinking feeling as he looked between his boots at the black jungle below. If he landed in the trees, he might find himself hung up, too high to climb down the lowering line for his rucksack, and most likely lost.

He tried not to even think about the likelihood that something might get broken in a tree landing. The rest of the team could ill afford to spend hours trying to rescue him, and doing so might easily compromise the mission.

He kept the chute pointed at the clearing, willing his canopy to stay aloft. *Come on... Come on! A little gust of wind would be real nice right about now!*

But it wasn't happening. He was just too low to make it to the large clearing. The smallest of the three was much closer, though. With a little luck, he might actually make it there. It was probably more than a kilometer from where he needed to be, but at least it wasn't trees. He aimed his canopy that way.

The clearing was tiny, perhaps only ninety feet in diameter, roughly equal to the height of the trees surrounding it. Even under perfect conditions, it would be a difficult target to hit. But at night, with combat equipment, it would be a miracle if he didn't break something.

Rip fought the urge to pull the quick release on his rucksack, which was meant to be lowered on a fifteen-foot line prior to land-ing, because he wasn't out of the woods yet—literally. If he landed in the trees, he wanted every ounce of protection on his legs.

The tops of the trees reached out for him. *This is going to be close!*

He pulled his feet up to miss the topmost branches of one tree on the edge of the clearing, then dumped air in order to keep from smashing into the trees on the opposite side of the clearing.

The ground rose up much too fast. He braked at the last sec-ond, pulling both toggles all the way down to his knees.

But it wasn't enough.

A large bush loomed in front of him just as his boots entered the tall grass and impacted earth. Not bothering to try to make a standing landing, he took a lesson from his static line airborne training all those years ago and kept his feet and knees together to absorb the shock, trying to execute a textbook Parachute Landing Fall.

Once his feet hit the ground, he pivoted and rolled onto his side with a grunt, but the forward momentum caused his feet and the heavy rucksack to continue over his head, and he rolled a sec-ond time, tangling up in the static lines.

But this time he rolled onto something besides earth.

Something alive!

A bloodcurdling scream shattered the night.

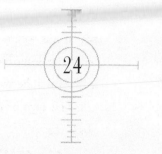

24

Isla Coiba. 0450 hours

THE MAN'S LONG, matted hair flew behind him as he leapt from the tree, landing on all fours like a jungle cat. As soon as he heard the scream, he knew that the girl was in trouble. They had come for her. How had he not heard them? No matter. He would not let them take her again.

His lithe form made almost no sound as he moved swiftly though the undergrowth like mist in the wind. His bare feet pounded toward the clearing where he had left her.

Another scream came, this one more terrified than the last. He quickened his pace, bursting into the open. He charged ahead, pushing away the thought that the evil men's blowguns might find him again.

Then he spotted something in the sky and stopped so abruptly that he nearly forgot what he was doing there in the first place.

Something was floating down out of the sky. He counted. *Five somethings.* Like bats, only much, much larger. He had never seen anything like them; they did not exist in his world.

Spirits. They are black, evil spirits.

Fear gripped him like never before in his life. They were coming for him. To punish him for not protecting her.

He turned and ran as fast as he could. It was too late for the girl. It was too late for him. He would hide. It was the only thing he could think to do. They had come to steal his life force. Better to die in hiding than to let the spirits consume him with one crunch, like a beetle. No, he would go somewhere that they would never find him.

He ran like the wind and didn't look back.

Oh no! He's found me!

Fernanda's scream echoed off of the mountainside, sending sleeping birds to flight. She had no time to contemplate *how* he had found her, but she had been dreaming about Chombon's filthy, vile face leering at her when he pounced.

She pushed him off of her and lashed out with both feet, hearing the man grunt as she kicked him in the chest. She had no idea whether his intent this time was murder or rape or both, but she had endured too much to give up without a fight. With a guttural cry, she raked her fingernails at his face again, surprised when she instead caught something hard, something…plastic? Was he wearing a hard hat?

Vines were everywhere, draped over her, all around her, as if someone had come along in the dark and wrapped her up in them. *Wait, not vines… Is this a net?*

She flailed both arms, trying desperately to get away. But he rose and threw himself on top of her. A fist crashed down on her temple, sending an explosion of pain through her head. She brought her knee up as hard as she could, and he gasped and rolled off of her, groaning.

Still seeing stars from the blow and nearly delirious with fright, she rolled to her stomach, trying to claw her way out of the net. She heard him rise behind her, cursing in Spanish. But before she could get free, one of his heavy, muscled arms snaked around her neck, and from the corner of her eye, she saw the glint of a knife in the other.

She closed her eyes. "No! Please!"

Suddenly, he froze. "What did you say? You speak English?" It was not Chombon's voice, but he was choking her.

Chombon doesn't speak English!

"Yes, I speak English. Please let go of me!"

The man released his hold a little. "Who *are* you?"

"My name is Fernanda. I'm a college student."

He let go completely and pushed her away. "What are you doing here?"

She rolled over and got to her knees, facing him. His face was painted in light and dark stripes. He still held the knife warily as he regarded her. He wore some sort of uniform and a helmet, and was that a parachute?

"I'm on spring break. What are you doing here?" she spat out.

Is he a...a soldier?

"Spring break?" His voice was incredulous. He shoved the knife back into a sheath on his chest. "You've got to be kidding me."

Fernanda gasped as a group of parachutes—black silhouettes against the lightening sky—sailed past, high above the treetops.

Did they come to rescue us?

"Tell me the truth, chica. How did you get out here?"

She answered him with a sob. This man, whoever he was, hadn't come to kill her.

25

Colón, Panama, 0500 hours

THE SILVER TOYOTA PRADO and its obese but well-dressed driver bumped over the steel decking that moments earlier had been lowered across the lowest chamber of the east flight of the Gatún locks.

Oswardo waved at the tired security guard as he passed, then continued to the far side onto what had been a United States military reservation. In his rearview mirror, the sun was rising over Gatún Lake, giving even the filthy cesspool known as the city of Colón a fresh, almost baronial look.

Fort Sherman. For decades the 9,300-hectare swath of jungle had served as the US Jungle Warfare training center, only to be abandoned on January 1, 2000. And the moment they left, Oswardo was there, planning a way to profit from the country's windfall.

That stupid rap music blared again from his cell phone. Rather than try to navigate the narrow road beyond the canal in the dark while talking, he pulled off on the shoulder and picked up the device.

"¿Sí?"

Remi's overstressed voice answered. "I only have a moment, but I knew you would want to hear this. A colleague in the national

police phoned and said that ANAM received a satellite phone call
from a scientist stranded on Isla Coiba. He claims that his team has
been taken captive by armed thugs."

Oswardo thought for a moment. "So that confirms that the
pirates are hiding out on Coiba?"

"Possibly."

"Then you should move forward with all possible speed with
our recovery operation, Remi. My man in Chame will supply them
with the tools they need. "

"We will be ready very soon. But there's more. Apparently
there is a woman at the American embassy just recently arrived in
the country, who has been asking Panamanian intelligence lots of
questions regarding Coiba."

"Claro, the Americans always want to put their fingers in
everything. Why does this surprise you? Do you think they know
something about this problem of ours?"

"That is also possible. The same contact told me that the raid
on the warehouse in the free zone was part of a joint operation with
the Americans—and that Americans were at the scene before the
police arrived."

Oswardo chewed his lip. "They could simply be helping the
authorities track down pirates, as they have helped the police deal
with drug trafficking in the Darién."

"Well, I just thought you might want to know."

Oswardo shifted in his seat. "It is appreciated, my friend. Let
me know if you hear anything more." He hit the End button and
dropped the phone on the seat. It rang again, and with an exasper-
ated scowl he snatched it back up. "What!"

The familiar gravelly voice of his newest customer came on the line. "Good morning, Oswardo."

He quickly changed his tone of voice. "And a good morning to you, sir. To what do I owe the honor of this call?"

"What is the status on our order?"

"We are on schedule. Processing should be complete by early next week. I also have some new products that might interest you."

"Ah…unfortunately, our timetable has shifted. My carrier will be in port in Colón within forty-eight hours. Can you have the product for me by then?"

"What? Forty-eight hours!" He feigned surprise. Customers always did this. He could be ready in twenty-four hours but wouldn't let his customer know.

"If you can have it ready by then, I will pay an extra ten thousand."

"Make it twenty and I'll guarantee that you will have it as soon as your ship docks in Colón."

"Very well. Did you receive the initial payment?"

Oswardo winced. Who knew what agencies might be listening? "We should not discuss this now. I will have some information sent to you via secure e-mail." He finished the call, then pulled a pen from his pocket and scrawled a reminder to himself on a scrap of paper.

Pulling back onto the road, he steered his vehicle toward old Fort Sherman. As he drove the winding, overgrown road, which had fallen into disrepair like everything else the Americans had abandoned to Panama, the conversation he'd had with Remi bothered him more and more. The Americans had a large interest in slowing the deluge of drugs headed for their borders. But piracy? A knot formed in his gut.

His new operation was very lucrative, but for a while it would be a risky one. The religious zealots who attacked America in 2001 had done a great disservice to the global arms trade, and he had felt the effects in his own wallet.

This new product would have a limited lifespan. Governments around the world would sooner or later come up with technology to combat its effectiveness. In Britain, it took only hours after the plot to get liquid explosive aboard jetliners for that window of opportunity to slam shut.

Fortunately, there were still many uses for his pet project.

These days the US was, at least in public, devoting much more attention to its ridiculous "War on Terror" than it was to the drug trade. Perhaps this interest in the *M/V Invincible* was an indication that they were cracking down on piracy as a part of their larger objectives. But if they found the stolen shipment of his new product in the process, that might end his run of keeping his name out of the papers—and destroy the opportunity that had recently presented itself: to be finished with this dangerous business for good.

This time he didn't bother pulling to the side of the road; he just stopped. There would be no traffic to block. Retrieving his cell phone, he dialed a number and put the phone to his ear, hoping he hadn't yet passed out of range.

When Remi answered, he said, "*Oye*. Has your man alerted the American embassy about this stranded scientist yet?"

The line was quiet for a moment. "Of course not. It's not even six in the morning yet."

"Good. I have an idea."

Isla Coiba. 0500 hours

What the...?

Rip's mind reeled as he stared at the crying figure of a woman before him, whom he had nearly killed with his combat knife. Once in Ranger school he had gotten so exhausted that he started hallucinating—Salma Hayek appeared with coffee and doughnuts for him one night on a patrol. He was no less surprised now.

But this was no hallucination.

He struggled to comprehend what had just happened. *Wasn't this island supposed to be deserted? And what is a woman doing in the middle of the jungle, alone?*

The girl was still on her knees, sobbing into her hands with a couple of static lines from his parachute draped over one shoulder. Her black hair was a tangled mess, and her clothes—what he could see in the predawn darkness—were torn and dirty.

"Tell me again how you got here?"

She tried to answer through her tears. "I...we were taken by...by..." She moaned and began crying even harder.

Rip unstrapped his carbine. *Did she say* we?

He started to worry that her crying could be heard by anyone within a quarter mile. "Shhh, it's okay. It's going to be all right." He reached down and disconnected his rucksack, then popped the quick releases on his harness. Then he moved closer to the girl to try and comfort her.

She pulled away. "Don't touch me!"

He backed off a little. "Whoa, chica. Listen, I'm not going to hurt you, okay? I'm an American soldier, and I need you to tell me what's going on here. I can help you if you tell me what happened. But please stop crying." He hated to see girls cry.

He waited a moment as she composed herself. Even with the wild black mane and torn clothing, he could tell that she was very pretty. She looked to be a little younger than he was.

She touched a swollen left eye and sniffed. "You hit me!"

"Oh, sorry about that." She hadn't exactly been the welcome wagon herself.

She took a deep breath. "Okay. My name is Fernanda Lerida. I'm a master's student at FSU in Panama City."

"You're an American?"

"No. I'm *Panameña*. My family owns a coffee business in Boquete."

"What are you doing on this island?"

"I'm part of a research team. We…we were here to collect moths. But some men showed up and captured us. Well, Alex got away, but—"

"Who's Alex?"

"My…he's the professor leading the expedition. Anyway, the other two in our group, Zack and Carlos, are still with them— whoever they are."

Rip scanned the clearing. "We think they're pirates."

"Pirates?"

"Yep. Go on."

She thought for a moment. "I escaped from them but got lost and ended up here. Did Alex call you to come rescue us?"

Rip's radio headset crackled in his ear. "Hey, Rubio? You okay?"

It was Coop. Rip held up an index finger to Fernanda. "Just a sec." He pressed the transmit button on his radio. "Yeah. But you ain't gonna believe what happened, bro."

"We saw you had a malfunction. What happened?"

"That's not what I'm talking about. Wait until you see what I found on the ground."

"Do you need help? We're about a klick south of you in the big clearing."

"Negative. I'll come to you. But be advised, I have encountered one Panamanian female and will be bringing her with me."

"Yeah, right."

"I'm serious, Coop."

"What?"

"I'll explain when I get there."

He glanced back at Fernanda. She had disentangled herself from his shroud lines and was studying him with a look that told him she was still trying to decide if she was hallucinating too.

"How many soldiers are there?"

"There are six of us."

"Did you come to rescue us?"

Rip frowned. "Not exactly. We didn't know you were here. But don't worry. We'll get you out. It just might be a while. Give me a few minutes to roll up my chute, then we'll go meet the others."

She sniffled again. "Okay."

Rip shook his head. *This is surreal.*

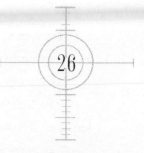

26

Isla Coiba. 0505 hours

A BATTLE BETWEEN relief and disbelief was raging in Fernanda's mind—and disbelief was winning.

How could this be? An American soldier, falling out of the sky? She watched him busily collecting up his parachute. He said he was here to help and that her kidnappers were pirates. But she was still wary. He had, after all, attacked her.

"You didn't tell me your name."

He stopped for a moment and looked at her, then smiled. "Sorry. Staff Sergeant Rip Rubio, US Army Special Forces."

Her brain was still playing catch-up. "Uh…nice to meet you. Are you Latino?"

"Sí." He unbuckled his helmet and dropped it on top of his parachute.

"*¿De dónde?*"

"I was born in L.A., but my family is from Mexico."

Fernanda sat down and watched as he scooped up his chute and harness in a bundle and stuffed it underneath a bush. Then he pulled a small pair of binoculars from his backpack and hung them around his neck on a cord. He produced a cap from his pocket and put it on, then swung his rucksack onto his back and picked up his rifle, which was much more compact than the ones the pirates had carried.

"If there are only six of you, you'll be outnumbered. There are more pirates than that."

He went to one knee in front of her, balancing the gun across his other thigh. He took off his hat and scanned the clearing as he spoke. "That's good to know. I need you to tell me everything you know about them, but let's go find the others first, okay?"

It had gotten a bit lighter in the last few moments, though it would still be perhaps half an hour until the sun rose. Staff Sergeant Rubio was very athletic, with stark, chiseled features and very intense eyes that made her feel like he could handle anything. For the first time since the capture, she allowed herself to think that maybe things would turn out all right.

"Okay, Staff Sergeant Rubio, I'm ready." She rose to her feet, aware of how dirty and disheveled she looked. Her clothes were torn and caked with mud, and she smelled like swamp.

"Hey, call me Rip."

"Okay, Rip. Let's go."

He turned and started moving toward the edge of the clearing. She started to follow, then kicked something in the tall grass. Looking down, she saw the glint of a glass bottle, about the size of a wine bottle.

She bent and picked it up. It looked clean and new and was full of water. She suddenly remembered how thirsty she was.

"Hey, Rip. You dropped your water bottle. Mind if I have a drink?" She struggled to twist the bottle's cap.

"Don't open that bottle!" Rip rushed toward her. It startled her so much, she dropped the bottle.

"No!" Rip launched himself at her, and she screamed as he drove her to the ground, landing on top of her.

So he isn't a good guy after all!

She pushed him away, struggling desperately to beat him off of her. Pawing at the ground, one hand found a large stick, and she picked it up and swung it at him, landing a solid blow on his left shoulder.

He sat up astride her and quickly pinned her arms with his own. "Whoa! Whoa, hermana. Chill out for a minute, would you?"

She struggled like a wildcat. "Get off!"

"All right, look. I'll get off you, but you have to promise to stop hitting me."

She tried to bite his arm. "Yeah, right. If you think I'm just going to let you assault me, you're wrong."

He jumped off her and backed away. She struggled to her feet and circled him warily, holding the stick like a club in both hands.

"Where did you get that thing?" Rip kept his distance while looking in the grass for the bottle.

"You dropped it."

"No, I didn't."

"It was lying right there on the ground."

"Okay, let me explain. That bottle may be very dangerous. Help me find it."

She kept circling him like a boxer. "Look, if you don't want to share your water…"

"Listen to me! I'm here searching for some bottles just like that one. They're filled with liquid explosives!"

She stopped circling. "What?"

He spotted the bottle and picked it up carefully. "Holy smokes. How did this get here?"

"I'm telling you, I found it on the ground!"

Rip looked up at her. "If this bottle had broken, we'd both be dead."

She gave him a dubious stare. "I think you're *loco*."

"No, I'm telling you, this is just like some bottles we found in Lebanon last month, and I promise you don't want to be around when this thing gets opened. It's like…*whoosh!*" His eyes went even wider.

She dropped the stick. "Well, I don't know how it got here."

He shook his head. "This mission just keeps getting weirder." He rubbed his shoulder. "Man, chica, you pack quite a punch."

"Yeah, well, I'm getting tired of being assaulted."

He grinned. "Hey, sorry about that. You want some water?"

"I'd love some, if you promise not to tackle me."

Still looking at the bottle, Rip absently unclipped a small tube from the shoulder strap of his rucksack. "Here, bite on the end of this."

Her thirst overcame her wariness, and she did as he instructed. The water had a slightly plastic taste, but she could feel its coolness spreading throughout her body. *Wonderful.*

As she drank, Rip pushed a button on what looked to be a walkie-talkie on his side and spoke into a small microphone he'd hung from one ear. "Valor One, Valor Five."

She was standing close enough that she could hear the answer crackle in his headset.

"This is Valor One, go."

Rip keyed the microphone again. "Be advised, I've recovered what I believe to be approximately one liter of ITEB, over."

"Say again, over?"

"I have a bottle of the stuff, Coop. We found it on the ground."

"Rubio, if this is one of your pranks, I'm going to have your hide. Do we need to come to you?"

"Negative, we're on our way to your position. And it's no joke, bro. We'll be there in approximately one-zero mikes, out."

He looked at her, grinning slightly. "Well, chica, now that you've drunk all my water, I guess we should be going."

Fernanda blushed as she pulled the hydration tube out of her mouth. "Sorry. Thanks though. I was dying of thirst."

"No problem. Are you okay to walk?" He surveyed her ragged clothing, and she flushed some more.

"I'm fine. Much better, actually."

Rip removed his pack and tucked the bottle inside. Then he shrugged back into it and pulled a compass from his pocket. He pointed toward the far end of the clearing, where the mist-shrouded mountains were just becoming visible in the distance. "Okay, then, let's go that way."

They waded through the tall grass and were soon wet from the waist down from the dew. She did her best to keep up with the lithe soldier, though his confident strides made it difficult. Within moments, they were both perspiring heavily.

At the edge of the clearing, they encountered a nearly impenetrable wall of undergrowth. After several unsuccessful attempts to plow through it, Rip mopped his brow and spat out, "This is stinkin' thick!"

Fernanda, who had opted not to follow until he was successful, stood several yards away looking at the dirt under her fingernails. "Tell me about it."

Rip took off his pack and pulled out a small machete. Then after several minutes of hacking a path through the vines and branches, he reshouldered the load. "Okay, now let's try it."

Once they got into the shade of the towering hardwoods that surrounded the clearing, the way opened up a little. They crossed a small brook that ran clear and cool over a sunken creek bed, and she grimaced at the irony of how close she'd been to good water the night before.

A short while later they emerged into a much larger clearing, and she heard a short whistle coming from the tree line on the other side. But Rip didn't head toward the whistle. Instead he turned and skirted along the edge of the clearing.

"Where are you going, Rip?"

He turned to her and put a finger to his lips, then whispered, "We can't go across the middle of the clearing—too exposed. Just follow me and try to be quiet, okay?"

She wouldn't make a very good soldier. "Oh, sorry."

Several minutes later they'd covered the distance to the other side of the clearing. Fernanda could hear the faint sound of surf in the distance. Then she heard the whistle again, quieter this time. At first she didn't see anyone, then a soldier stood from underneath some trees and waved them over. His camouflage uniform matched Sergeant Rubio's, and he had the same green-and-black stripes on his face.

They walked into a tight circle of five men, all facing outward on one knee. She studied their painted faces. Their wide-eyed looks were tempered by an underlying seriousness that didn't make her feel any less out of place.

A tall, rugged-looking soldier stood and walked to where Rip had gone to a knee again. "I'm glad to see you in one piece, Rubio. When I saw that you had a malfunction, I prayed for you all the way to the ground. I was sure you were going into the trees."

Fernanda was surprised to hear a soldier talk that way, and from the expression on Rip's face, she gathered he was too. Once she realized she was the only one of the group who was standing, she went to a crouch.

"Hey, uh, thanks, Coop. Look what I found." Rip jerked a thumb toward Fernanda.

The muscular soldier took off his cap, revealing a head of black hair. He looked at Fernanda and then back at Rip. "Man, I thought you were kidding!"

One of the other soldiers, a black man, turned toward them and chuckled. "Dude can't go anywhere without picking up girls."

"At ease, Doc," Rip said with a frown. "Gentlemen, this is Fernanda, uh..."

"Lerida," she finished for him.

"Right."

The black-haired man extended a hand. "Hi. I'm Master Sergeant John Cooper. Don't mind Doc Kelly there. He jokes with everybody. How did you get here?"

"She's a Panamanian." Rip answered for her. "A student at the university in Panama City. She's part of an expedition here, and the rest of her team is being held by the pirates."

One of the other men, this one shorter with his hat kicked back to reveal a shock of blond hair, spoke up. "*Wonderful.* Just what we need."

Fernanda couldn't tell if his sarcastic tone was in reference to her team being captured or to her being here.

"That's Sweeney," Rip said. "He's just mad because he was born a redneck."

"Shhh!" John held up a hand for silence. Everyone froze. The faint whine of a motor floated across the clearing from somewhere beyond the trees. Its volume increased as it came closer and then cut off.

Doc hissed, "Is that a car or a plane?"

"It's a boat," she said. "The way he turned the motor off, they do that when they coast in to the beach."

"That would make sense," a clean-cut soldier whispered from behind John. "The beach is that way." He pointed a gloved hand in the direction of the sound.

Rip leaned over to Fernanda. "That's Frank Baldwin, weapons sergeant."

"Sounds like the pirates are getting a visitor. I wonder what for?" John asked.

"Who knows, bro? But wait until you see this." Rip pulled off his pack and retrieved the glass bottle, then passed it to him.

Muted exclamations came from every man in the group. The looks on the other men's faces chased away any lingering doubts that Fernanda had about whether Rip had been telling the truth.

"You seriously found this just lying in the grass," John said.

Rip shook his head. "No, Fernanda did. The first time I saw it, she was about to open the thing."

She shrugged sheepishly. "I was thirsty."

"Well, opening that bottle would have fixed that problem for good," the blond redneck commented.

Doc put a hand on her knee. "Somebody was looking out

for you, honey. How long have you been running around out here?"

Fernanda had to think for a moment. "We got here four days ago. The pirates took us the day before yesterday, and I escaped yesterday afternoon."

Sergeant Cooper pointed to the biggest man in the group, one who hadn't spoken yet. "Buzz, get on the horn and give Phoenix an update on all we've found so far. We need to get this show on the road. And ask her what to do with this bottle. It's my understanding this stuff is pretty unstable."

"Roger that." The big man sounded a little like John Wayne in the old American movies she sometimes watched late at night. He took off his pack and started producing electronic gadgets from it. She assumed it was the radio and its accessories.

John turned to the others. "Okay, here's what we're going to do." He pulled a map from his pocket and spread it between them. "We're here." He pointed to the map with a blade of grass. "Sweeney, you and Hogan circle around to the east and see if you can get up on this hill right here."

Fernanda noticed that the map had the same type of topographic lines on it as the one that Alex had used.

Alex! Where are you right now? Should she ask the team to look for the professor? But apparently they had a plan already.

John continued. "Frank and I will go southwest toward the beach and see if we can get some intel on that boat we heard. Rip, you and Doc stay here with Fernanda and the gear. And keep commo with Phoenix."

"What? Come on, vato. Don't leave me on rucksack patrol!"

"Hey, Staff Sergeant." John's tone was calm but firm. "Let's just focus on getting the job done. We don't have much time."

Rip clenched his jaw and looked away. "Sorry, bro. That was out of line."

Buzz took off a headset he'd been speaking softly into for the last several minutes. "We got a problem, boys. Phoenix went to a meeting, and Marcel is running the show until she gets back."

A muted collective groan arose from the group.

Buzz continued. "And he's sayin' we need to postpone the recon until she gets back."

"He does, does he? How long will that be?"

Buzz held out the headset. "At least an hour. And he wants to talk to you, Coop."

Whoever Marcel was, he wasn't popular with this bunch.

John shook his head and walked over to Buzz. He reached inside the big man's pack and clicked off the radio.

"We just developed communications trouble. Get your gear. Let's move."

An image of Chombon's vicious face came to Fernanda, and she shuddered.

Please, God…help Carlos and Zack hold on just a little longer!

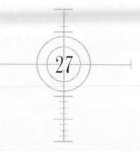

27

Casco Viejo, Panama City, 0600 hours

I REALLY DON'T HAVE time for this.

Mary Walker locked the door of Marcel's Jeep Cherokee and stepped out onto the street as she dropped the keys into her pocket. Life in the small plaza had yet to awaken. It sat in the heart of Panama City's old town. When Marcel drew her the map, he said this quarter was known as Casco Viejo.

His contact in the Panamanian intelligence had never wanted to be seen coming to the US embassy, he said. So when Marcel called to say there was something important to pass along concerning the mission to Coiba, she had no choice but to meet with him.

It would take some time for Task Force Valor to get assembled on the ground and move into position. If she hurried she would certainly be back in time to monitor their reconnaissance, and Marcel could handle things until then.

She had already been up for more than twenty-four hours and could use some sleep, but as long as the team was on the island, rest would have to wait. In the absence of Major Williams, she was feeling the weight of responsibility for commanding the team.

Mary wanted to accompany them on the mission, despite the fact that she wasn't HALO qualified. But she had learned from the mission in Lebanon how vital it was to have an advocate at headquarters to keep the bureaucrats and politicians out of the way.

The operative said it was urgent, and any operational intel concerning the mission was priority one. So she'd hastily borrowed Marcel's Jeep and driven the ten minutes through early morning traffic to the Plaza de la Independencia near the presidential palace in the old city. By her estimation, she would be able to meet the operative and be back at the embassy within an hour.

She did a quick survey of the people in the plaza. Some policemen on the opposite side, a few street vendors setting up for the day, and a homeless man sleeping on a park bench. Brightly colored four-story tenement buildings surrounded the plaza, looking fresh and clean in the early morning light.

And here and there half-naked children played and women hung laundry on the balconies above the street. A large whitewashed cathedral, which looked to be at least a couple hundred years old, occupied the far end of the plaza, and mature trees in between were in full bloom with bright purple flowers. Mary wished she had brought her camera. Since she only had her cell phone, she used it instead.

After taking a few pictures, she put the phone in her pocket and pulled out a folded slip of paper, annoyed at her own handwriting. It was so scratchy that even she had a hard time reading it. She was pretty sure it said *Calle 6a este*. It must be nearby; this was where Marcel told her to park, after all.

In less than a minute she found what she was looking for—a chipped and faded sign mounted on the brick wall of one of the tenement buildings that read *6a E*.

The side street was completely empty except for a few parked vehicles. Marcel had given her directions to the Panamanian operative's safe house, a second floor flat in the dingy green building. She set off toward the entrance.

The street was red brick, and the buildings, though freshly painted, were very old. The doors to the tenements opened directly onto the street.

She heard a vehicle coming behind her and stepped as close to the building as possible so it could pass.

But it didn't. There was a squeal of brakes, and Mary turned in time to see a bald, muscular black man and two others jump from a white box van and rush for her.

There was nowhere to go. She turned to run but a heavyset Panamanian with a handlebar mustache blocked her escape. Anger rose in her as survival instincts kicked in.

It's a trap!

Without waiting for the men to converge on her, she charged the third man, a short, stocky thug leering at her with a mouthful of bad teeth. She spun on the ball of her left foot and launched a roundhouse kick that connected squarely with his jaw, which sent the goon reeling, minus a few of the rotten teeth.

She pivoted to face the other two, just in time to notice something black and plastic in the bald man's hand as he thrust it at her torso. She twisted away and brought an open palm up hard into his nose, but it was too late. A jolt of electricity shot through her, and every muscle in her body contracted at once.

She dropped hard to the pavement, and the bald man stepped forward and sent another shock of intense pain through her body.

His bloody face was the last thing she saw before she blacked out.

Isla Coiba. 0610 hours

"Please! We have no reason to lie to you."

"¡Cállate!" Chombon swung the bamboo rod once more, and it landed with a *thwack* across the shoulders of the blond American boy.

"Aaaaagghhh!" the boy cried.

The pirate leader didn't speak enough English to know whether his hostage was being truthful or insolent or delirious. But Cesar did, and all Chombon cared about was keeping the boys scared and miserable enough to tell him anything he asked.

Another of his men appeared in the doorway, silhouetted by the morning sun. He looked from the bruised and bloody captives kneeling in the center of the moldy concrete floor to Chombon standing over them. Jorge gulped and said, *"Perdón, Jefe. La lancha viene."*

Hugo and his boat—finally. Chombon wiped the sweat from his brow and tossed the bamboo rod in the corner. "Bueno." He crossed the room in three swift strides and, instructing Jorge to watch over the captives, hustled down the trail toward the beach.

He had been waiting eagerly for the arrival of Hugo's boat. His last message had promised four new men, recruited by his contact, Manuel.

When he arrived at the beach, Hugo and the other four were struggling to unload the lancha as it bobbed in the surf. They were young and tough looking—probably longshoremen from the port who were tired of the dangerous and low-paying work loading and unloading cargo on the docks.

Hugo had also secured some better weapons: two belt-fed RPK machine guns from Colombia. They would make his small fleet that much more formidable when they struck again. And they would have to strike soon.

He had paid handsome bribes to the so-called "eco-police" at the ranger station to have them keep the occasional yacht and live-aboard dive boat away from his secluded cove. But the presence of the research team was proof they couldn't keep everyone out. The area was becoming more and more popular with divers and sport fishermen too.

There was even recent talk of cruise ships docking on Coiba. He'd heard that Mick Jagger and other celebrities often trolled other islands around Coiba in their multimillion-dollar yachts. Perhaps soon he and his men would take one of these yachts for their own.

The loss of the girl made Chombon want to kill something. He had been looking forward to her company. If he had not been shorthanded, he would have cut Roberto's eyes out as an example to the others. But she was most certainly dead by now, and if she wasn't, she would be soon. The horrors of the jungle would not respect her beauty or her sex.

Many prisoners had thought they could escape the torturous life of the forced-labor farms instituted on Coiba during the eighties. But they had all either died in the jungle or come crawling back, half dead, a short time later.

All but one.

He and the one they called the Mudman had been prisoners on the island at the same time. But Chombon had never known of him until the man escaped into the jungle and began killing prisoners. Then everyone knew the Mudman. They said he was one of the Wounan—a primitive and reclusive Indian tribe from the jungles of the Darién.

After laborers were found with their throats cut, the man achieved something of a mythical status. But it spoke volumes about how little the guards cared about the *encarcelados* that they never made a serious attempt to stop him.

Perhaps, like most of the prisoners themselves, the guards believed that it was only a matter of time before the jungle took care of the psychopathic killer. Nobody expected the man to actually survive out there. But many years had passed, the prisons closed, and now it was obvious that they had been wrong.

El hombre de Lodo was still out there—and now he was stalking Chombon and his men.

But the hunter was about to become the prey. His men had devised a trap for the Indian, and for once even his men had done the work quickly and without complaint. Once the Mudman walked into their trap, they would visit upon him the worst terrors they could imagine, then turn their attention to more profitable endeavors.

There was also the issue of the captives. The men wanted to simply kill them and make it look as if the malevolent jungle had claimed more victims. But Chombon decided it would be more profitable to hold the boys for money, even if it meant abandoning their camp. This would not be easy, but he saw opportunity where others saw only problems.

The boys could likely be ransomed for good money, especially the American. And there were many criminal elements in Panama whom they could pin the blame on or negotiate a deal with. The trick was to hide the captives away someplace on the mainland, then make contact with their families as soon as possible.

If it was believed that the entire party had been captured, it might buy them weeks, even months, of negotiating for the hostages' return. That would take the heat off of their hiding place long enough for Chombon and his men to make one more big score—and this time cash out. By the time the authorities figured out that the chica was dead, the pirates would be living large in Brazil or Ecuador or anywhere that money would let you be whoever you wanted to be.

Chombon reached the water's edge and waded into the waves where Hugo held on to the boat to keep it from being sucked out in the undertow or rolled in the surf.

"Buenos días, amigo." The shaggy campesino waved a greeting from the bow of the lancha.

"Good morning, Hugo. I am very glad to see you, my friend. We must talk."

Hugo jumped into the waist-deep water next to him. "What do you need, Jefe?"

"We have captured the team that your phone call warned us about. I need you to take them to the mainland and put them somewhere while I make arrangements."

Hugo brightened visibly. "You have the mamacita?"

Chombon scowled. "We did, but Roberto, the idiota allowed her to escape."

Hugo's face fell. "That is a great loss. She would have been very entertaining, no?"

"Not for you."

"Ah, well. Now she will be no diversion for either of us. What a waste. So it is just the other three then?"

Chombon's anger increased. "Three? What three? We only found two: the American and the skinny boy."

"You did not find the older man?"

"What older man?"

"The one with the goatee?"

"No. But I must ask the other two why they did not tell me about him." Perhaps he had not applied the rod strongly enough.

"Well, even with only the two, this is a big favor you ask. Moving supplies is one thing, but keeping prisoners? Very risky. I do not want to end up back in prison, amigo."

Chombon grabbed Hugo's shirt and twisted, glowering into the smaller man's bloodshot eyes. "Do not forget, *amigo*, that if it weren't for me, you would never have left this island alive the first time."

Hugo let go of the boat momentarily, putting his hands up in surrender. "You are right. I will do as you ask. My humble *casita* near Bahía Honda will suffice. It has no facilities, but nobody ever comes out there. It will be a perfect place."

A broody calm returned to Chombon. He let go of Hugo's shirt. "Yes, that will work for now. But we must move quickly. Stay here, and I will have them brought to you."

Hugo bowed his head slightly. "As you wish, Jefe."

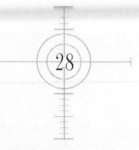

28

Isla Coiba. 0700 hours

DOC KELLEY KNELT over a sitting Fernanda and daubed at her swollen eyes with an alcohol wipe. "Hoooey, girl, you look like you got drug behind a train! Who did this to you?"

"That would be me, bro." Rip wondered if she resented him for it. "I guess you could say we met by accident."

Doc clucked disapprovingly. "You beating up the honeys now, Rubio?"

"Actually, Rip isn't responsible for this side," Fernanda lightly touched her right eye. "Chombon did that."

Well, at least she doesn't sound mad.

Doc looked concerned. "Who's Chombon?"

"He's the pirate leader." She shuddered slightly. "They're not nice people."

Rip was surprised by the anger that rose in him at the thought of a man hitting this girl. Thoughts of Gabi tried to enter his mind, but he pushed them away.

Compartmentalize, Rubio. Focus on the mission.

He reached into his rucksack and pulled out a brown pouch, passing it to Fernanda. "I bet you're hungry. When was the last time you ate?"

She took the plastic pouch. "Thank you. I don't remember the last time I had food. What is this?"

Doc pulled out a large knife and helped her open the bag. "It's an MRE, which stands for Meal, Rejected by the Enemy.'"

Rip laughed. "Don't listen to him. They're not bad."

Fernanda dumped its contents on the ground and picked up the individually wrapped pieces, reading their labels. "Omelet with cheese and vegetables. Applesauce, carbohydrate enhanced. Strawberry dairy shake powder, fortified with calcium and vitamin D."

"See?" Doc asked. "A veritable cornucopia of goodness."

She tore open the applesauce. "Anything will be goodness right now."

As she ate, Rip and Doc plied Fernanda with questions about herself, and between ravenous mouthfuls, she told them about her family, the Lerida coffee business, and her work at the university in Panama City.

Eight minutes later, after she had downed the last of the strawberry dairy shake, she sighed. "I didn't realize how hungry I was. Thank you again, Rip."

"No problem, chica. We'll get you off this island just as soon as we can."

"But you're not here to rescue us?"

Doc spoke up. "We're really not supposed to talk about it, hon. It's not..."

"She already knows about the ITEB, Doc. Look, Fernanda. We're a covert unit, so please remember that when you get back. A lot of people could really be in danger if word got out about what we're after here."

She nodded, studying her hands in her lap. "I just hope Carlos and Zack are okay. And Alex."

Rip tried again. "We'll do our best to get them out. What were you guys doing out here anyway?"

Fernanda sighed. "Alex is a professor of biology at FSU. He's been doing research on this island for years. There are hundreds of endemic species of plants and animals here, and he believes that somewhere in the island's interior could be the cure for AIDS or cancer or who knows?"

Rip didn't want to look stupid, so he pretended he knew what *endemic* was.

Doc was now checking Fernanda's eyes with his penlight. "Hmm…no concussion. That's good. So this island's full of stuff that doesn't exist anywhere else?"

Fernanda nodded. "Nobody really knows what's in the interior, but there are unique birds, plants, and animals all over this island. What we were actually after were butterflies and moths. Alex wanted to see if we could find some species never catalogued before, so we were trekking to the interior rain forest where nobody has ever been."

"And he invited you along to join in the fun?" Rip tried not to lay the sarcasm on too thick, but the girl flashed him a sideways look anyway.

"Yes, actually. We all wanted to come."

Rip back-pedaled. "Oh, I see. And the other two? Carlos and…"

"Zack. Carlos is my cousin, and Zack is one of the professor's students, here for a semester from the States."

"So he's an American?" Doc's eyebrows shot up.

"Yes, well, so is Alex, technically."

"And how about you?" Doc asked. "Your English is almost perfect."

"I studied at Ohio University for two years. My father said that if we were going to be successful in the global exporting business, we had to learn to speak proper English."

"So where did you grow up?"

"I was born in Chiriquí, in the mountains near Costa Rica. But I live now in Panama City."

"So you aren't planning to work in the family business?"

She shrugged. "I work there sometimes, and once I finish my degree, well, who knows?"

Coop came on the radio in Rip's ear. "Valor Five, this is One. We have eyes on the beach, over."

Rip looked at Fernanda. "Hold that thought." Then he keyed his mike. "Roger, One. Anything to report?"

"There's an open boat of some kind, about ten yards off the beach in shallow water. One person with the boat. Three more men sitting on the beach with a few boxes of what looks like ammunition. Plus three AK-74 carbines. Frank is getting digital pictures for Phoenix, over."

"You want me to tell Marcel?"

"I suppose we should. Better to ask forgiveness than permission, right?"

"Roger that. Out."

Rip waited a few seconds, then keyed the microphone again. "Valor Three, this is Five. What's your status, over?"

"We found the camp but can't get good eyes on it yet, break." A few seconds passed, then Sweeney came back. "We're moving to a higher position to get a better look, over."

Fernanda stood. "Do you mind if I go back to that creek we found and freshen up a bit?"

Rip looked at her. "Um, actually, that's not a good idea right now. We should stay together."

Doc spoke up. "How 'bout I give you a pack of wet wipes. You can go back into the trees over there for privacy, but stay where we can hear you holler if something happens."

"I guess I can live with that. Thank you." She took the package offered by the medic and moved off into the trees.

When she was out of earshot, Doc said, "That's one tough girl."

Rip nodded. "No kidding. She about beat the snot out of me twice."

"Well, she's been through the ringer, that's for sure. But do you believe her story about the ITEB?"

Rip shrugged. "Why would she lie, bro? You don't think she's a pirate, do you?"

Doc chuckled. "If so, she's the best lookin' pirate I've ever seen." His smile turned to a frown. "I suppose anything's possible. We'd better keep an eye on her."

"Nah, that doesn't make sense. She's wandering the jungle, all alone and beat up. I say her story is believable." At least he wanted to believe it.

"I don't know, but the part about finding the bottle doesn't make sense. She just found it? In the middle of this?" Doc spread his hands to take in the tall grass, jungle, and mountains. "I mean, that stuff's unstable, right? If it sat out in the sun for too long, it'd detonate, wouldn't it?"

Rip chewed his lip. "I don't know. Maybe a pirate dropped it. Who knows?"

"I'll be interested to see the report on that bottle."

"Absolutely, bro. Me too." Rip walked to the satellite radio and turned it back on. Immediately the receiver crackled. "Valor, this is base, come in, over."

He keyed the headset. "This is Valor Five. Go."

Marcel's nasally voice sounded through the headset speaker. "Where have you been? We've been trying to raise you for half an hour!"

"Sorry, base. Communication issues. We got them fixed now, over."

"What's your status?"

Rip thought for a moment, then keyed the mike. "We have recovered one bottle of ITEB and rescued one hostage so far. The pirates have a boat on the beach, with at least four people, ammunition, and weapons, over."

"*What?* I specifically instructed you to stand fast until further notice! I'm going to file an official reprimand with your commander over this!"

Doc had been leaning close, listening. "He makes that sound like a bad thing, doesn't he?"

Rip rolled his eyes. "Roger, base, official reprimand. Good copy. Will keep you informed of our progress. Over and out."

He held the headset away from his ear and let Marcel rant for a few seconds before shutting the radio off again. "Dude is scaring the birds."

Doc chuckled, shaking his head. "That guy must have gotten beat up a lot when he was little."

"Or something. You'd think he'd be glad we're making progress. Let's hope Phoenix gets back soon."

Coop beeped in on Rip's headset again. "Valor Five, this is One. The boat is now leaving with four men on board. They didn't load any cargo in the boat, so I don't think they're moving the ITEB. We're going to let it go, over."

Rip could hear the craft's motor from where he stood. "Good copy, One. We've earned an official reprimand already. Keep up the good work."

He could imagine the look on John's face as he called back. "Will do. Out."

Fernanda walked back into camp, looking refreshed despite the bruises on her face. She must have used her fingers to comb her hair and pulled it back into a ponytail. Rip was surprised, not just at how attractive she was all of a sudden, but at how she seemed to be taking this all pretty much in stride.

She smiled at Kelley and returned the packet of wet wipes. "Thank you, Doc. I feel a hundred percent better. I wish I had my hat, though. These chitres like to buzz around my head."

Doc waved one of the pesky gnats away from his own head. "Is that what you call these things? They're so small, but man, can they bite!"

Rip had noticed them too. "Yeah, they're like flying devil spawn of a mosquito and a crocodile, you know?"

His radio crackled. "Valor Five, this is Valor Three. We have enemy contact and are taking fire, over!"

"Sweeney and Buzz!" Rip jumped up, and before he could respond, the sound of gunfire drifted to them through the trees from the direction of the mountains. He punched the button on his radio. "Five here, do you need backup?"

He could hear the urgency in Sweeney's voice, as well as

heavy gunfire as the weapons sergeant shouted, "Affirmative! Buzz is hit!"

Doc's face was grim as he snatched up his aid bag and weapon. "Let's go, buddy."

Rip was already moving. He hit the button on his mike again. "We're on our way!" He turned and pointed at Fernanda. "Stay put, chica. We'll be back."

The rusty metal chair Chombon had been sitting on crashed to the floor when he jumped to his feet. Outside the crumbling concrete barracks, the sound of gunfire echoed off the mountain, drifting through the holes in the walls where windows once had been.

He looked over at Cesar. "They've got him. Call every man. Go!" He snatched up the new RPK machine gun that Hugo had brought and slapped a circular metal 75-round magazine into its receiver. He was going to end the Mudman problem once and for all.

He pounded down the dirt path between mango trees toward the supply hut. El hombre de Lodo had been stealing food from them, and that was where they had set their ambush.

The Mudman would run as soon as the bullets started flying, but Chombon had planned for that. The path of least resistance away from the ambush led down one of the sunken creek beds, which during the rainy season were rushing rivers but now were mostly dry. His men had found the Mudman's footprints in the riverbed and knew this was the way he came.

This time, Chombon would be there to greet him as he fled.

He cut behind the latrine hut and crashed through a stand of banana palm, barely slowing down. A few seconds later he was at the lip of the washout. He threw himself down in the prone position and extended the bipod legs on the machine gun. At six hundred rounds per minute, the heavy 7.62mm slugs would cut the psychopathic Indian in half.

Chombon grimaced and took aim down the washout. The firing continued less than one hundred meters in front of him. His men were mowing down the jungle. Their fire discipline was dismal, but it would have the desired effect. He was ready.

Less than a minute later, he heard the sound of running feet approaching and gripped the weapon's stock tightly with sweaty hands. But wait. Something was wrong. The sound was approaching from the wrong direction! Someone was running *toward* the sound of the firing!

He swung the machine gun around in time to see a uniformed man charge around the bend in the riverbed. It was not the Mudman, but this man was undoubtedly an enemy. He lined up the sights and squeezed the trigger.

Chink. Nothing happened. *A jam!* Chombon tossed the fouled weapon aside and roared, launching himself at the soldier from the edge of the washout.

The man tried to raise his own rifle, but Chombon hit him high and drove him to the ground with the weapon between them. Chombon screamed in rage and smashed his forehead into the man's face in a vicious head butt. All of the intense frustration of the last week boiled over. If he ever did actually kill a man with his teeth, this would be the one.

29

PAIN EXPLODED IN Rip's brain as the huge black-skinned man landed on top of him, crushing the M-4 carbine to his chest and knocking the wind out of him.

Without the heavy aid bag that Doc was carrying, Rip had outpaced the medic and was a good fifty yards ahead. As he struggled for breath, he realized that even though Doc would be here in less than twenty seconds, by then it might be too late.

Dizzy from the blow and fighting the blackness creeping in from the corners of his vision, Rip released his grip on the weapon and brought both hands up, grabbing his assailant around the neck.

He could smell the man's sweat and sour breath, and he pushed for all he was worth on the stubbly, scarred face. As he did, the man landed a blow with a ham-sized fist that glanced off the side of Rip's head. Then the other fist crashed into his right eye socket, and he saw stars once more.

Rip had been in plenty of fistfights, but he'd never been hit this hard. This man was strong—too strong. Rip pushed for all he was worth trying to dislodge his attacker, who slammed his forehead into Rip's face a second time. Things started to get fuzzy as more blows followed, one after the other.

Rage welled up inside him. *I will not die this way!* No way was some punk going to take him down.

The thug was going for another head butt when Rip grabbed his attacker's greasy hair and smashed his elbow into the man's nose. The man cried out in pain and rocked back, and Rip used the momentum he'd created to shove the pirate off of him and struggle to his feet. He could taste his own blood and feel it coursing down his face, but that only served to fuel his anger.

As the dark-skinned man launched at him again, Rip clasped his arms around his attacker's head, forcing it downward while bringing his knee up as hard as he could.

The man's arms flailed and clawed as Rip's knee thrust the stock of the rifle, still slung around his neck, into the man's face once, twice, three times. On the fourth, the man loosened his grip and sat down hard. A well-aimed kick to the side of his head put him out cold.

The giant man had barely flopped over on his back when Rip grabbed for the carbine, slick with both of their blood, and made a woozy attempt at looking around the edges of the ravine they were in, searching for more attackers.

At that moment, Doc came huffing around the bend and stopped short at the sight of the two blood-soaked combatants. "Whoa, what happened?"

Rip dropped his weapon to the ready position across his chest. He bent at the waist and dry heaved, resting his hands on his knees. He wiped his sleeve across his face, and it came away covered in crimson.

Between gasps, Rip said, "Dude jumped out at me…when I came…around the corner." He started shakily toward the continued firing. "Come on…got to help Sweeney."

Doc caught up with him in a few steps and grabbed his sleeve. "Hold up, Rubio. At least catch your breath, or you won't be any good when you get there. Here." He held out a green cotton bandanna.

Rip took it and wiped the blood from his face. "I'm okay, Doc. We've got to…"

Both men froze as the sound of heavy weapons firing reached their ears.

That's coming from the beach!

This wasn't the *pop-pop-pop* of automatic weapons fire, but a much louder, deeper sound.

Doc cocked an ear toward the water. "That's a large-caliber machine gun."

There was a huge explosion nearby, and the ground shook. Things were getting worse by the second. Rip's radio came to life again. "All units, this is Valor One. We've got a large force approaching the beach in several boats—approximately twenty men. Looks like an assault force of some kind. We are in the line of fire and are going to be pinned down if we don't pull back, over."

They both ducked as something whooshed over their heads and exploded into the hillside. "That was a LAW rocket! Where did that come from?" Rip asked.

Doc looked at him and said exactly what Rip was thinking. "This is getting out of hand."

Then Sweeney came on the radio. "One, be advised. The forces that were engaging us have just stopped firing and pulled back. We're going to try to make it back to the rally point, over."

Doc nodded. "Something big is happening over there." He keyed his radio. "Sweeney, what's the status on Hogan, over?"

"Just a scratch. We're coming your way."

Rip put a hand on Doc's shoulder. "You stay here and wait for them. I'll go help out Coop and Frank."

"Gotcha. See you back at the rally point. And keep the bandanna. You're going to need some stitches on that cheek."

As Rip stumbled back down the washout, Doc called after him. "You want me to put some flex cuffs on this yo-yo?"

"Absolutely!"

Rip jogged back into the rally point five minutes later and found Fernanda lying on her stomach behind his rucksack. She looked up at him, wide-eyed. "Something sailed through the trees above me and cut down a palm frond." She pointed to a large branch on the ground next to her. "I think they're shooting at me!"

Rip took a knee next to her, panting. "I doubt it, but you did the right thing by taking cover."

"What happened to you?"

"I got jumped by a big pirate dude." He yanked the CamelBak tube from his rucksack and tried to take a drink, then remembered that Fernanda had drained it already. So he went digging for water in John's pack next to his, ducking as heavier weapons fire cracked by above them.

"What did he look like?"

"Ugly guy, dark skin, big hands."

"Did he have a scar above his eye?"

"Uh…yeah, I think so."

Her mouth dropped open. "That was Chombon!"

He spit out the drinking tube. "Really? The pirate leader?"

Fernanda scrambled over to him, taking the bloody bandanna from his hand. "Let me help you with that."

Rip winced and started to protest as she wet the bandanna and daubed the blood from a gash on his cheek. "Listen, Fernanda, I'll—"

"Did you kill him?"

He shook his head. "I don't think so. Doc's got him flex-cuffed and...oh, here comes Coop and Baldwin." He pointed across the clearing, where his fellow operators ran toward them in a low crouch.

A moment later they made it to the tree line where Rip and Fernanda waited. Both were breathing hard and drenched in sweat.

"Where's everyone?" Coop asked.

"Doc is on his way with Sweeney and Hogan."

"Are they okay?"

"You know as much as I do. Doc stayed behind to help with Buzz."

Coop looked grim. "What happened to you?"

"He got in a fight with Chombon, the pirate leader!" Fernanda spoke up.

"What?"

Rip spat blood on the ground. "I was on my way to help Sweeney, and this *tipo* jumps out of the bushes on top of me. It was like an ultimate fighting cage match."

Just then, Doc and Sweeney came back in with Hogan bringing up the rear, limping a bit. The tall Texan was grimacing in pain, but Rip couldn't see any blood.

He groaned as he took a knee in the circle. "Them turkeys put a hole in my lucky pair of trousers."

Doc shrugged off his aid bag. "Where? Do you need a bandage?"

"Aw, Doc, leave me alone. I'm okay." Hogan grimaced. "It just grazed the inside of my thigh, felt like a hornet got me. It was a little too high for my likin' though, if you know what I mean."

Doc peered at the rip in Buzz's pants leg. "Yow."

"What'd you do with Chombon, Doc?" Rip asked.

"The ugly guy? We flex-cuffed him but had to leave him. The ground fire was getting pretty intense there, and I don't think we could have carried him. But you must have knocked him a good one, he's still out."

Rip grunted. "Good."

Sweeney looked at Coop. "So what's the plan, boss?"

The tall team sergeant listened for a moment. More shouts and explosions drifted from the direction of the camp. "I think we're safe here for now. Let's stay out of it for the time being and see what happens. Oh, and Sweeney, you'd better let command know what's up."

"What are you going to do with the bottle I found?" Fernanda asked.

Coop scratched his stubbly chin. "We need to transport it back to have it analyzed. Our people will see if they can get any clues as to where it's being made. The shape of that bottle is fairly unique, so they might be able to trace it that way."

Frank spoke up. "I would suggest that we try and find a way to cool the bottle some before we move it too far. Phoenix said that it may become less stable when it's not refrigerated."

"How are we gonna do that? I plumb forgot my beer cooler," Sweeney said.

"How about the creek?" Fernanda asked. "It's probably twenty degrees cooler than the air temperature."

"Good idea," Doc said. "But it might be even better if I wrap it up in my poncho liner with a couple of cold packs."

"Do it." Coop pointed to Sweeney. "Bobby, get on the horn quick."

"Roger that, boss." Sweeney went to make the call.

The sounds of a firefight continued, interspersed with concussions from grenades and a few shouts.

Coop turned to the rest of the group. "Okay, look. I'm not sure why, but there's a major skirmish going on over there right now. I have a feeling that if the rest of the ITEB was there, it may have been destroyed."

Fernanda sat up. "You've got to go save Carlos and Zack!"

Coop held up a hand. "That's part of the plan, Fernanda. But I don't know if this is a turf war we've stumbled into or what. We can't just walk into the middle of it. So we'll have to lay low and wait until help arrives. Maybe we can get in just before the airlift comes."

"How are we going to do that?" Rip asked.

"Helicopter," Doc said from behind him.

"What?"

Doc was kneeling next to Hogan with an ear cocked to the sky. "I hear a helicopter."

Sweeney pulled the radio headset away from his ear. "This guy Marcel is about to blow a gasket. He says that the Panamanian special police are on their way with two Hueys. When he didn't hear from us, he assumed the worst and sent in the cavalry."

Rip could hear the choppers now too. "Well, what do you know. Marcel might have done something right for once."

"But you can bet we're going to hear about this later," John said grimly.

Just then two olive-green helicopters thundered over their heads and banked sharply toward the camp. Rip could see the blue and red Panamanian flag painted on their sides, distorted by the heat signature from their engine exhaust. Green-helmeted door gunners leaned out the open side doors and their belt-fed machine guns spat flame at the camp below.

"They're lighting them up!" Rip said.

Coop stood, a scowl on his face as he shaded his eyes against the sun. "Idiots! They're going to hit the ITEB, or worse—the hostages! Sweeney, see if you can contact them and tell them to cease fire!"

"On it, boss."

Coop took off his cap and squinted toward the choppers. "I wish we could see what's going on."

"Hey, we can!" Frank dove for his rucksack and rummaged around inside, coming out with a shiny metallic bullet the size of his fist. "The HUNTIR. You remember me trying it out on the range? I brought two of them."

"Sweet. Put that thing up in the air!" Coop said.

Frank quickly set up the small battery-powered LCD screen that would receive the video feed. Then he loaded the HUNTIR round into the barrel of his M203 grenade launcher and clicked it shut.

Frank stepped out into the tall grass and pointed his rifle at the sky. "Here goes nothing!" He pulled the trigger.

There was a loud *whoomp*, and Frank ran back to the receiver. Everyone crowded around the monitor and saw nothing but a blue screen.

"I don't think it worked, bro," Rip said, as he peered up at the sky.

"That figures," Sweeney commented from his post near the radio.

"Just give it a second," Frank said. Then the screen went to gray static, and a surprisingly clear image appeared. Everyone cheered and slapped Frank on the back. The image was upside down, though, so he turned the screen over.

Rip could see the light green overgrown expanse of banana and coconut trees, ending at the darker green, much taller triple-canopy forest that began at the foot of the mountain. The image swung back and forth as the camera gently oscillated under its small parachute, but he could clearly make out plumes of smoke rising from the camp.

The camera must have been rotating under canopy, because the image panned around to show the field where the team was. They were closer to the camp than he'd thought. Then the image rotated to show the bay and four open boats, which had been driven right onto the beach.

"It looks like they're leaving. See there!" Frank pointed to one of the boats, and Rip could barely make out the figures of several men trying to push it offshore.

"Here comes one of the helicopters!" Fernanda ran out into the field and waved excitedly at the helo.

"No!" Rip bolted toward Fernanda, hitting her with a flying tackle just as the door gunner in the helicopter opened fire, chewing up the ground with a stream of fire from his machine gun, right where Fernanda had been standing.

The helicopter went around for another pass, and Rip half carried, half dragged Fernanda back into the tree line.

She was shaking all over. "You…you saved my life."

Rip's intense eyes flashed up at the helicopter as he helped her up. "Hey, don't sweat it. Maybe you'll return the favor someday."

Sweeney was shouting profanities into the radio as they both collapsed under cover.

"Sweeney, tell them to cease fire."

"I *am* telling them!"

"Everybody down!" Coop commanded. They all hit the dirt as the chopper flew by again, raking the tree line with tracer bullets. They thwacked through the undergrowth above their heads. The LCD screen Hogan held exploded in a shower of fragments.

"Aaagghh! I'm hit!" the big Texan cried.

Coop turned to Buzz. "What? Again?"

"Pop smoke!" Sweeney screamed. "Red smoke! Now!"

Frank fumbled with his harness and pulled the pin on a soda can–sized canister, then tossed it overhand out into the tall grass. Seconds later there was a *pop*, and then a plume of red smoke wafted up with a hiss.

The helicopter banked and circled away from them, then resumed firing on the camp.

Doc was already working over Hogan. "Hey, we got a bleeder here. Frank! Give me a hand!"

Buzz was lying on his back. "Aw, Doc, I'll be all right."

Doc's face was serious as he handed Hogan a canteen. "Shut up and drink water, Buzz."

Sweeney looked up from the radio. "They say that three enemy speedboats are fleeing toward the mainland. The rest have either run into the jungle or been killed."

"Ask them if they have someone who can intercept the boat," Coop said.

"I did. The eco-police from the north end of the island are on their way right now." Sweeney listened to his headpiece for a few seconds. "They're going to do one more turn around the camp looking for stragglers, then come get us."

"Tell them I want one of those birds on the ground, right here, right now!" Veins stood out on Coop's face as he knelt next to Hogan, whose leg was now covered in blood. "Hogan needs a medevac. And that trigger-happy door gunner will be lucky if I don't beat him to a pulp."

"What about Zack and Carlos, John?"

Sweeney cursed. "Don't start, lady."

Fernanda responded with a torrent of Spanish. Rip had never heard anyone so eloquently describe Sweeney's upbringing.

Coop stepped in. "At ease, Bobby. Listen, Fernanda. Your friends are a priority; I promise." He took off his cap and used it to wipe the sweat from his brow. "We'll make sure the Panamanian special police look for them, but right now we've got to get Buzz out of here. If they or the ITEB is here, I'm sure these guys will find it."

Rip doubted that either was still much of a possibility, but he didn't want to say it. Fernanda nodded, but Rip could tell by her face that she was thinking the same thing.

Frank spoke up. "Here comes the chopper."

The slick green Huey slid in low over the treetops and dropped into the clearing in front of them. Rip knelt and pulled Fernanda down as the prop wash blasted them with tiny particles of dust.

As soon as the skids touched down, a half dozen soldiers in olive fatigues jumped out and took up positions around the chopper. A short man with captain's bars on his epaulets jogged toward the team. Rip figured he was the officer in charge of the PSP troops.

Coop put his cap back on. "Let's pick up and go. Doc, get Buzz ready to move."

"Roger."

The captain held a hand out to John. "I am Captain Estevez. My men have—"

Coop picked up his and Hogan's rucksack and jerked his head toward the chopper. "Let's go, men." He ignored the captain and ran for the chopper.

Without a word, the other four men picked up their fallen comrade and hustled after their team leader.

Once Buzz was loaded on the helicopter, Rip looked back to see Fernanda having a hurried conversation with the captain. The man nodded and waved his troops over, calling out commands to them and pointing toward the camp.

Rip jogged back to where the man stood. "Fernanda, we've got to go." He nodded at the Panamanian officer. "You'll have to excuse my team sergeant, sir. He gets pretty bent out of shape when somebody shoots at us."

To his credit, the captain was very apologetic. "I am extremely sorry for the mistake," he said in Spanish. "My helicopter will take your comrade directly to Panama City."

"I want to stay to see if they find Alex, Zack, and Carlos."

Captain Estevez shook his head. "It would be better for you to go, señorita. Otherwise there will not be room for all of my men in the second helicopter. Here is my card." He produced a business card from his pocket. "Call me at police headquarters in Santiago when you return and leave your number. I will let you know what we find."

Fernanda looked reluctant but agreed. She thanked him, then followed when Rip turned and jogged back to the waiting chopper.

Cooper stuck his head out the door. "Shake a leg, Rubio! We got another problem." He pulled the intercom headset off of his head.

"Marcel says that Phoenix went missing."

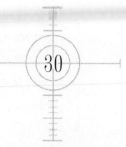

30

THE HELICOPTER SHUDDERED as it rose out of the clearing, flattening the tall grass and making the nearby palm trees bend, as if trying to get away from the screaming green machine.

Lord, please help them find Zack and Carlos!

Fernanda clung to the nylon webbed seat next to Rip, who crossed himself as the chopper climbed above the treetops. Seeing him do that surprised her somewhat, but she found it strangely reassuring. When he saw her looking at him, he gave her a solemn thumbs-up. She managed a weak grin in return. It was her first time in a helicopter.

Her heart lurched as the front of the chopper tipped forward and headed straight for the trees at the far end of the clearing. Just when she was ready to brace for the crash, the craft swept up, cleared the trees, and she could see an aquamarine cove ringed by a wide, tan strip of beach, bisected where a sluggish green river emptied into the sea.

Out in the bay, she could make out the dark outline of something beneath the water. At first it looked like a huge submerged rock, but as the chopper got closer, she saw something protruding from the water.

A ship!

The aft section was closest to the surface, and she could just make out *M/V Invincible* painted on its sunken stern as they passed above it.

The irony of the name struck her as funny, and she was horrified to find herself giggling at a time like this.

The helicopter banked inland, and Fernanda's giddiness went away as she looked straight down out the open door. Below her, several plumes of smoke rose skyward from still-burning huts, and Panamanian soldiers searched around the edges of the pirate camp for stragglers. In a clearing in the center of camp, the second helicopter sat with rotors stilled.

As their helicopter drifted higher, she could see mountains in the wild interior blanketed with lush forest and the clear blue waters pounding the rocky cliffs at its periphery.

Is the rest of my team still alive in there somewhere? Did they escape, God? And what about Alex? Wherever they are, please, protect them. Let them be found.

The higher the helicopter flew, the less menacing the island looked. When they cleared the tallest peaks and turned north toward Panama City, the island had regained that innocent, idyllic appearance. Like a place where people would go to relax on the beach or enjoy an afternoon surfing. But now that she had experienced the island's raw malice, she doubted if she'd ever hear the name Coiba again and not get a chill down her spine.

What a horrific few days this has been. She looked down at Hogan, lying on a stretcher on the floor, an IV bag hanging from the barrel of his gun as Doc worked over him. Buzz gave her a weak smile.

These men were amazing. This had been the worst experience

of her life, and yet these soldiers signed up to do things like this on a regular basis.

Despite the blood crusted around Rip's nose and the cut under his left eye, she found him very attractive. It wasn't about his looks; it was more the way he carried himself, like he knew exactly what to do in every situation, not to mention that he had bested Chombon. And as they sat side by side in the cramped confines of the aircraft, she found she liked the closeness, perhaps because he had come to her rescue and being with him felt safe.

He leaned closer and shouted in her ear over the *thwop-thwop-thwop* of the rotor blades. "Our embassy just radioed that they contacted your family. Your mother will be waiting for you when we land at Albrook."

Fernanda nodded. She would be very glad to see her mother, of course, but how long would it be before she heard an "I told you so"?

The last few days had given her lots of time to think, and she decided that if she ever got off that island, she would try harder to get along with her mom. Fernanda never really talked to her mother about her father's death. What a strain it must have been to lose a husband. Something about her ordeal on Coiba helped her to see that she and her mother had allowed their grief to drive them apart instead of closer.

She shouted at Rip, "How long is the flight?"

He held up an index finger and told her to hang on. He squeezed the button on his headphones and spoke to the pilots. Then he pulled the microphone back out of the way. "We have to stop in Santiago to refuel, so it will be at least two hours until we get to Panama City."

She sighed and looked out across the vast expanse of the Pacific.

She had lots to sort out from the last few days. She had to call Tía Magali, Carlos's mother, and get a message to the Oasis at Santa Catalina to tell Hedi about the ordeal. The expedition wasn't due back for two more days, so Hedi probably had no idea what had transpired.

But that would have to wait. For the next few hours there was nothing she could do, and suddenly she felt very, very tired. She leaned back, closed her eyes, and let her head droop onto Rip's muscular shoulder, hoping he wouldn't mind too much. The rhythmic beating of the helicopter's blades and the warm breeze coming through the open door lulled her to sleep.

Fort San Lorenzo National Park. 2000 hours

It is almost time.

Oswardo listened to the barely audible hum of the generator as he stood looking at the woman through the tiny window into the massive steel door. He was sweating, despite the fact that the temperature in the dimly lit hallway never rose above 68 degrees.

The smoke from his cigar mingled with the earthy smell of old concrete and the strong odor of new paint. He looked at his watch again. It would never give him the answer he sought.

But how much time is left before it is found out?

He was so close to the payoff. He wanted nothing more than to be done with this phase of his life—to be rid of the spoiled wife and children, the responsibilities, all of it—and start a new life, unencumbered. If only he could hold things together for another twenty-four hours or so.

The American woman sat unmoving in the corner of the room, head on her chest and arms handcuffed to a metal pipe running up the wall. It wasn't immediately clear if she was conscious, but she was alive.

Kidnapping the American woman had been a desperate move, something he regretted doing. It would certainly mean the US government would be out in force trying to find her.

That was bad, but not as bad as if they *weren't* looking for her. Because then they would be looking for the pirates and might discover his shipment, which he still hoped to recover.

He had never harbored any delusion that he'd be able to keep his operation a secret forever. But all he needed was a bit more time, enough to finish this last batch of product, which even now was being extracted from its diluted state in the lab one level above him.

The final shipment of his new product had been purchased sight unseen by one buyer, and at a price six times what the first batch had sold for. That kind of profit exceeded his wildest expectations since the product's spectacular debut in Lebanon recently. Once this shipment was processed, he could afford to walk away and disappear. He already had his new name chosen and had been shopping for a nice, large rancho in Argentina or Ecuador—someplace where enough money could ensure privacy and comfort for the rest of his life.

He had little choice about where to hide the American. He had to keep her away from his legitimate businesses and the many workers he employed. He could have hired someone to take her, but few who would agree to such a job had the fortitude to do it right and keep it a secret. Besides, everyone had a price, and there were few he trusted enough not to bail if the stakes got too high.

No, he had decided to bring the girl here himself.

She probably expected someone to come soon and interrogate her. Or draft a ransom note to send to her superiors. But if she held any such hopes, she would be disappointed.

Nothing personal, gringa. Just business.

He looked down at the device in his hand, and adrenaline surged as it always did when he completed a prototype. Oswardo had always been good with his hands, a tinkerer, but when he learned that men would pay him handsomely for his creations, his hobby took on a whole new dimension. It made him feel potent, like a god, with the power of life and death in his hands.

As for the woman, this latest device would bring death quickly. She should be thankful, really. Which was worse? To die old and feeble, fading away in a home for the aged, nothing but a worn-out version of your younger self? Or to be living in this world one minute and enter the next in the space of a micro-second? She would feel no pain, and she would have served his purpose for her—to delay the gringos until he could finish his work and disappear.

Oswardo had put forth an incredible amount of resources to keep his real business private. Why not take advantage of that privacy and use it to safeguard this secret as well? The place was undetectable by air, unreachable by sea, and forgotten on land. If it was good enough for the lab, it would do to hide the girl.

The United States had always used Panama like a cheap mistress. After conducting their hazardous live-fire exercises here for decades, they pulled out in 2000, leaving behind training areas so contaminated that the land would never again be arable. They left ranges littered with unexploded ordnance and hundreds of millions of dollars' worth of abandoned structures, many of which had been left to rot in recent years.

But Oswardo saw it as a good thing.

Because when the product was completed, he would destroy the entire operation, and it would look like yet another example of American carelessness. The environmentalists would wring their hands and call for an investigation, and they would find little more than a smoking hole in the jungle. And if they managed to find the woman's DNA in the rubble, there wouldn't be anyone left to blame because Oswardo would have ceased to exist.

He turned the handle on the door, pulled it open softly, but didn't enter. The woman's head jerked up, revealing the dirty rag that had been over her eyes since the street thugs he hired to capture her had put it there.

"Who's there?"

He didn't answer. Oswardo entered the room and regarded her for a moment. She was strong and beautiful. Her figure was quite feminine but not the stick-thin of models on the billboards. If he had more time, he might make better use of her…

"I am a United States citizen, and I demand to be taken to the embassy immediately."

He smiled slightly and held his tongue. No. Unfortunately, he did not have the time. He must get back to the city before daylight. He crossed to the pile of boxes and bottles stacked against the far wall of the room, directly beneath the laboratory upstairs.

The crates of Semtex were overkill, considering the number of artillery shells and other ammunition he'd stockpiled, but he wanted to be absolutely certain that when it detonated there wouldn't be enough left of the lab for them to trace anything to him.

This bunker had been built to withstand a naval bombardment from without, but it would never stand up to a detonation of this size from within. He placed the device on top of one of the boxes and quickly set about connecting detonation cords to the blasting caps he'd already prepared and inserted among the charges. When he was finished, he took one last look at his handiwork and turned to leave.

"What do you want with me?"

Oswardo chuckled, then switched off the light. He walked out of the room and carefully shut the door behind him. The woman said nothing more. Perhaps she knew.

He reached into his pocket and produced a small vial, dabbing the white powder from it onto the back of his hand. He needed to be alert in order to drive back to the city. He put his hand to his nostril and inhaled deeply.

A sense of well-being washed over him.

It won't be long now.

He trod back up the crumbling concrete stairs, reveling in how alert and strong he was.

The lab was small, occupying only one windowless room that was mostly filled with the nitrogen chamber, a glass-enclosed box where the product was bottled.

Oswardo watched the team of three scientists beginning the extraction process on the last batch of product. A pang of conscience stabbed at the thought that these intelligent men—whom he'd lured with enormous sums of money and in one case, photos of the man with his mistress—would meet their fates in tragic accidents.

His valve-stem caps were already in place on each man's vehicle, and once everything else was done, the job would be almost an afterthought. It was an unavoidable cost of finishing this business.

He shoved aside his conscience once again. *Ah, well, nothing personal.*

Five minutes later he was slogging through the mud to his silver Prado, eager to get back to the city before dawn. He had to finish wrapping up the loose ends of his life so that none of it would follow him when the project reached completion.

As soon as he was back in range of the cell tower in Colón, he called to check his messages.

Halfway through the first message, he had to pull to the side of the road because he was shaking so badly.

It was the last thing he ever expected to hear. He had to fish the vial from his pocket and sniff some more of the powder it contained.

It was a good thing he was going to start a new life. This old one was in shambles.

The attack had failed.

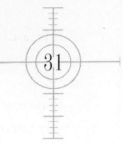

31

AS THE CHOPPER PASSED over the brilliant blue slash of the Panama Canal, Rip watched it winding across the lush carpet of jungle and was amazed at the scale of it. From his vantage point twelve hundred feet above the Bridge of the Americas, it was hard to imagine that the gleaming ribbon of water hadn't always been there.

Through the headphones he wore, Rip heard the pilots coordinating their approach to the airfield. It wouldn't be long now. It felt like a punch in the gut every time he looked down at Hogan, lying pallid on the stretcher with an IV in his arm. From the concerned look on Doc Kelly's face as he worked over the lanky Texan, he knew Buzz's injury was worse than it looked.

And now Phoenix was missing too. Rip hated the feelings brewing inside him, a toxic mix of anxiety, anger, and helplessness. The helplessness was the worst, which made him want to *do* something about it. Inside he was pacing like a caged animal.

But outside he sat still because Fernanda was still leaning on his shoulder, asleep. Just like Gabi used to do when they rode in the backseat of his mother's old Cutlass Supreme on the way to the beach. Mama liked to picnic there on summer Sundays after church. He had looked forward to those days, and it had made him feel like a man when Gabi used his shoulder as a pillow. He missed that.

Fernanda had the same silky black hair too, loose strands of which were whipping about in the wind coming through the open doors.

The chopper hit a downdraft over the canal and shuddered, waking Fernanda. She sat up and looked around. "Are we almost there?"

In answer, Rip pointed to the ships passing through Miraflores locks in the distance.

The aircraft banked hard, and Rip could see the airstrip at Albrook, its hangars nestled up against a forested hill, with rows of red-roofed former military barracks still lined up dress-right-dress along the edge of the airfield. As the Huey shot its final approach, he could see an ambulance waiting at the far end of the tarmac.

The moment the skids touched pavement, Rip and the rest of the team were out of the bird, each taking one corner of the stretcher, fighting the rotor wash to deliver their wounded comrade to the ambulance.

Doc climbed in with Hogan and the doors closed. Then Coop trotted back to the helicopter to retrieve his rucksack.

Rip followed. "Let me help you with that. We need to get that bottle someplace safe."

Coop nodded. "And cold. Hey, who's that with Fernanda?"

Rip turned around and saw Fernanda embracing a distinguished-looking older woman and a muscular blond girl standing just inside the hangar with Marcel. He shrugged his own rucksack into place. "I dunno, bro. I'm glad we got her back here in one piece, though."

"Me too," Coop said as they carried John's ruck between them into the hangar. "At least the mission wasn't a total loss."

They carefully set the bundle in an empty corner of the hangar just as Frank and Sweeney approached with their gear. "You two keep an eye on the ITEB and our gear," Coop said. "Rip and I'll report to Marcel and see what he plans to do next."

"Roger that, boss." Sweeney dropped his rucksack and sat on it.

Marcel was still conversing with the older woman. When they got close enough, Rip heard her saying, "…and she always does the accounting for Lerida Coffee during the harvest season, though she seems to prefer looking at bugs in the jungle."

"Mama, this is Sergeant Rip Rubio. He's the man who found me."

Rip stepped forward and extended his hand. "*Mucho gusto, señora.*"

Fernanda turned to Coop. "And this is Sergeant John Cooper. He's the *comandante* of the team."

John smiled and shook the elder Lerida's hand. "Um…team sergeant, actually."

The woman smiled politely. "I am very grateful to you. Of course, if Fernanda had listened to me, she never would have gone to that terrible island in the first place."

Rip tried to relieve Fernanda's discomfort. "Well, uh, I'm glad she was there. She was able to give us some valuable information, and without her, the mission would likely have been a failure."

Marcel scowled and shook his head. Apparently Rip was talking too much. Fernanda brightened a little, though. "Oh, and this is my friend Hedi! She was supposed to be with us on the island, but at the last minute she had to stay behind."

"And now I'm very glad I did." Hedi looked at Coop like he was a movie star. "I've never met an American commando before."

Everyone laughed except for Marcel, who cleared his throat. "*Doña* Lerida, I'm very sorry, but I must insist that your daughter not share the details of this operation with you or anyone for the time being. It is absolutely essential for the safety of these men."

Señora Lerida nodded. "Will you allow me to contact my husband's brother to let him know that his son is missing, at least?"

Marcel frowned. "I suppose that is reasonable. Now, we have much to accomplish this evening. I hope you understand?"

"Certainly, Señor Bucard. Thank you for alerting us that Fernanda was safe and for bringing us here to meet her. I cannot tell you how worried we were."

Marcel bowed slightly. "Of course." He turned to Fernanda. "Miss, we may contact you in the next day or so for an official debriefing, if you don't mind."

"No problem," Fernanda said, her face downcast. She looked up at Rip. "Will you all be looking for Carlos and Zack?"

Marcel interrupted. "I'm afraid they're not at liberty to discuss their mission at this point, miss." But he wasn't looking at her—he was scowling at Rip, who stared back icily. This guy was really getting on his nerves.

Marcel held out a hand in the direction of a Marine security guard standing near a white Chevy Tahoe with diplomatic plates. "Ladies? Shall we?"

Rip and Coop walked with them toward the vehicle. On the way, Fernanda whispered something to Hedi, who handed her purse to her friend and then hurried up next to Marcel. Hooking her arm through the station chief's, she smiled up at him. "Agent Bucard, I'd love to take a tour of the embassy sometime. Do you do that sort of thing?"

While Bucard sputtered to find a suitable way to fend off the blond German, Fernanda pulled a pen from Hedi's purse with one hand and took Rip's hand with the other.

The pen tickled his hand as she began scrawling numbers on his palm, whispering, "This is my cell phone. That first number is a six. Call me if you can. I'll be here in the city if you need anything."

She dropped the pen back into the purse, and Rip watched her lithe figure gliding toward the vehicle. Then she stopped and turned back to him. "And Sergeant Rubio?"

He arched an eyebrow at her in reply.

"Thanks."

Rip tossed an easy salute in her direction. Would he ever see her again?

Panama City, 0437 hours

Each revolution of the ceiling fan made a slow *tick-tick-tick*. The noise competed with the clock on the shelf in Fernanda's apartment, both reminders of each second that passed while Alex, Carlos, and Zack remained missing.

She lay on her back on the bed, unable to sleep despite the fact that she was completely exhausted. The room felt confining and oppressive. The absence of the jungle sounds, which had driven her so crazy, now made it feel like she was stuck in a mausoleum. Anxiety clawed at her, and being alone only made it worse.

The clock on her bedside seemed frozen.

As she and her mother had climbed into the black sedan ten

hours earlier, she asked the balding embassy official named Marcel if he had any information on Alex. His curt answer was that the professor had indeed made a frantic phone call two days ago, but nothing had been heard from him since.

Hedi offered to stay after accompanying Fernanda to her apartment, but she knew that if Hedi stayed, they'd be up talking all night. And Fernanda hadn't felt up for that. So after making Fernanda promise to call her first thing in the morning, Hedi went back to the dorm.

When exactly is first thing, anyway?

Tick-tick-tick. 4:39 a.m. The clock was mocking her.

Lord, please be with Carlos and Zack right now. Keep them safe and let them be found quickly. And Alex...please help him survive and be found too. I still feel badly about what happened between us. If I had done the right thing earlier, made my faith clearer to him, I doubt anything would have happened. Please forgive me.

She thought of Rip and the rest of the team—men who had risked their lives to take down the pirates and who had protected and rescued her. The tall one with the beard had even taken a bullet in the process.

Please take care of Rip and his friends. I don't understand everything about why they are here, but guide them to their goal and keep them alive.

Fernanda sighed. Though it felt good to pray, like getting the worry out of her head so there'd be room for other thoughts, she wanted to do more. But what?

"What you have loses its value if it isn't shared."

She opened her eyes. Why had she thought of that? Zack's words echoed in her head. *Did You bring me that thought, Lord? If so, what do You mean by it? What do I have to share that will help this situation?*

Frustrated, she threw the sheet off of her body and swung her legs over the side of the bed. She got up and padded over to the small table in her kitchen where her laptop lay. She opened the screen and punched the power button, then turned to the stove and set the kettle on to boil. As sacrilegious as it was for a Lerida, she normally didn't drink coffee, but this morning would be an exception.

Once the computer booted up, Fernanda opened her Internet browser. She laid her forehead on the table while the modem screeched out a handshake with the ISP. What was she going to do? Ask Google, "Where have the pirates taken my friends?"

She checked the Web site of *La Prensa*, Panama's main daily newspaper. A search for the word *piratas* returned only a review of the latest *Pirates of the Caribbean* movie.

Fernanda cradled her head in her hands. *What was the name of that ship?* Iguana. Indonesia. Indigo. *Grrrhhh! What was it?*

She got up and ground some coffee beans—Lerida Organic Estate—into a French press and poured the boiling water over the grounds.

Ignacio. Investigator. Inversion. She was going to go insane.

Stop thinking about it. That was what she had to do. Her subconscious would remember if she left it alone for a while.

She sipped her coffee and considered the previous twenty-four hours. An involuntary shiver went through her as she realized just how close she'd come to dying. What had been an abstract, nebulous concept, had in the past few days become almost a living entity, something that had pursued her on the island. If Rip hadn't shown up when he did, she certainly would have tried to drink the bottle of "water" she'd found that morning. And if it was really some kind of explosive… Fernanda shuddered again.

She thought about the athletic Latino sergeant who had literally dropped from the sky into her life. Was it only twenty four hours ago? It seemed much longer. He'd saved her life, what, two, three times in less than a day? And he'd gone face to face with the man who had terrorized her—and won. Perhaps she was just a sucker for a man in uniform, but there was more than the intense eyes under long, dark lashes that attracted her. Rip had a purposeful hardness in his face, a white-hot focus that she found more attractive than any physical asset could ever be.

But there was something else as well, though she couldn't quite put her finger on it. Was it something in the way he acted? Or in how he looked at her? She couldn't say. Whatever it was put a warm spot on her heart and a cold knot in her stomach. Fernanda hoped she'd have another opportunity to see him and figure out why.

Invincible! That was the ship's name! *Thank You, Lord!* The coffee must be working. She pulled up her browser again and searched the *La Prensa* Web site for the ship's name.

She hit pay dirt in point-three seconds.

A merchant ship due to enter the canal at Miraflores locks failed to arrive last Wednesday at its scheduled time. The ship was reportedly named the *M/V Invincible*, a twenty-seven-year-old break-bulk carrier flagged in Liberia. According to canal records, the ship has visited Panamanian ports six times in the last three years to take on cargoes of sugar, coffee, and bananas.

An official for the Panama Canal Authority told *La Prensa* that after the ship failed to arrive as planned and would not respond to radio calls, a search plane was sent to look for the *Invincible* along her charted course, but they found nothing.

Officials are not speculating publicly on the ship's fate but would not rule out the possibility of foul play. A formal search-and-rescue operation is being mounted.

The middle of the paragraph jumped out at her. *"Cargoes of sugar, coffee, and bananas."*

She drummed her fingers on the coffee cup, thinking. Then she closed the laptop, went to her bedroom, and got dressed. Maybe a cup of coffee and a sunflower-print sundress wouldn't chase away her feelings of uselessness, but doing something about it might.

Okay, Lord. One thing I can share is my brain. The more people who are working on this case, the quicker it will be solved.

Six minutes later as she stepped to the rain-slick sidewalk in front of her apartment building, she still had no idea how she would find her friends, but one thought kept tumbling around in her mind, daring her to pursue it and see where it led.

Casa Lerida exports twenty percent of Panama's coffee.

32

THE CITY WASN'T fully awake yet, and traffic was light in the predawn darkness. After finally hailing a cab, Fernanda had the elderly driver take her to the FSU parking lot where she'd left her Nissan.

It was kind of surreal to see it there, across from Zack's car, and remember the sense of excitement they'd all shared less than a week earlier as they waited for their adventure to begin. She felt like a different person now—as if the Fernanda who had laughed at Zack and Hedi's antics on this very spot was only someone she once knew. She paid the cab driver and then climbed out of his car and into hers. With a last look at Zack's beat-up taxi, she headed for the Lerida Coffee offices in Paraiso.

On the way, she passed the gates of the *Ciudad del Saber*, the site of the new US embassy. Was Rip there with his team? As they were leaving the island, she'd asked him who Phoenix was. He politely evaded the question. He simply said, "She's a friend of ours." Was she a girlfriend? Fernanda actually knew very little about Sergeant Rubio. He wasn't married, or at least he hadn't been wearing a ring. But was he seeing someone?

She shouldn't even be asking these questions. It was likely she'd never see him again. Why did that thought cause such tightness in her chest?

Hopefully he'd call her. She'd given him her number after all. If only there was some way for her to contact him as well. Fernanda pushed the thought from her mind as she pulled into the parking lot of Lerida Coffee. Hers was the only car in the lot.

She let herself in the building via the front office. It smelled of green coffee and paperwork, just like Papi's office in Boquete. And for a moment she felt a pang as she was transported back to that much simpler, more carefree time in her life.

A dim hallway stretched out toward the back of the building where the warehouse was, with an open administrative area on the right and several offices on the left. The first office belonged to her uncle. *How much does he know of what has happened?* Tío Edgar had always been friendly to her, if only in a distant kind of way.

She sat at a desk and fired up the computer. Maybe if Lerida Coffee had traveled on that ship, she could use the company's records to find out more about the ship and its cargo and find a clue as to why the ship was hijacked in Panama.

And then what? Talk about a long shot. At least I'll feel like I'm making an effort to help my friends. It was a small consolation.

Once the database was booted, she started with a simple query in the shipping field, searching for the name *Invincible*. The search returned empty.

She sighed. For all their wizardry, computers were still as dumb as a post. They could make lightning-fast calculations of infinitesimally large numbers but still couldn't think for you.

Furrowing her brow, she tried again. This time inserting wildcard characters into the search: **Invincible**.

Nothing.

She thought back to the *La Prensa* article. It said that the ship was a break-bulk carrier. That meant its cargo was mostly noncontainerized. Lerida Coffee was almost always shipped in containers these days.

An order would come in, and a truck would arrive in Boquete with one of the long metal boxes. A troop of Guaymi Indian men would show up and load the container to the roof with bags of green coffee, each of which probably weighed as much as they did. When the container was full, it would be sealed and the truck would take it to the port.

But very small lots might have gone on a pallet, which would more likely travel aboard a break-bulk carrier.

She looked back into the database and searched for odd lots, those too small to be containerized. There were only four in the last six months: orders to Bilbao, Lebanon, Istanbul, and Toronto. She sent the report to the printer.

Lebanon! Hadn't Rip said something about that?

Fernanda pulled up the order for Lebanon. It still didn't specify the ship. It told only the product amount, the shipment date, the destination, and the amount paid.

She printed the report on all of the orders from that time frame. Scanning it she didn't see anything out of the ordinary, not that there would be anything on the report that would help her find her friends.

Why am I doing this anyway? This is crazy. She dropped her forehead to the keyboard, tears brimming in her eyes.

Wait a minute. Something about the order wasn't right. She looked up and scanned it again. Then she went back to the report with all of the other orders from that time frame.

Then it hit her. *Why did we pay so much?* The amount paid to send the break-bulk shipment to Lebanon almost exactly equaled the amount that they'd pay for a regular containerized shipment. That didn't make sense.

She flipped through the report again. The other break-bulk payments were less than a third of the regular container price. *Why would…?*

"Fernanda?"

Her head jerked up. A burly older man stood in the office doorway, regarding her with a look of shock on his face.

"Tío Edgar!"

Her uncle approached, arms outstretched, his face melting into a smile that was completely at odds with his personality. "I can't believe you're here!"

Fernanda stood and tentatively accepted his embrace. He smelled of smoke and cologne and hugged her more tightly than she would have liked.

"I am so sorry, *sobrina*. I only heard last night."

He must be worried sick. When he pulled back, still holding on to her hands, she could tell even in the dim light that his eyes were bloodshot and puffy. *He must have been crying too.* In fact, her uncle was more disheveled than she'd ever seen him.

"I'm…I'm sorry about Carlos." The words caught in her throat. "I've been here racking my brain trying to figure out how to help find him. I just wish…" The emotion returned like a storm, flooding her eyes as she tried furiously to compose herself.

Edgar clucked softly, offering her a handkerchief. "Don't blame yourself for what has happened. If I had known you were going to that cursed island, I would have warned you to stay away."

"Mother did that—" Fernanda dabbed at the tears—"and I didn't listen."

"Well, I have faith that Carlos will be found. And I am very glad that you were not hurt in the attack. Now why don't you go home and recuperate for a day or two."

She was suddenly very tired, as if speaking with Edgar had broken through the strange emotional blockade that hadn't allowed her to sleep. "Thanks, Tío Edgar. You are right. I don't know why I even came here."

His telephone rang as he led her to the door. "I'm glad you did, chica. Times like these make you realize the importance of family. Please let me know if you hear anything." He opened the front door for her and then hurried into his office and shut the door.

Fernanda started for her car, then froze.

The attack!

Edgar's words suddenly came back to her with the force of a summer squall. *"I'm glad you weren't hurt in the attack."*

How did Edgar know about the attack? Hadn't Agent Bucard insisted that they tell no one what had happened? She hadn't even discussed that with her mother, so how else could he have known?

Then she remembered the reports, still sitting on the printer.

Her heart was pounding. Something was definitely wrong here. She needed to take another look at those reports.

As quietly as possible, she returned to the front door and eased it open. Tío Edgar was in his office talking on the phone. He seemed angry.

She slipped in the door and, praying that he wouldn't see her, went right to the printer and retrieved the reports. She stole a glance into his office on the way out, breathing a sigh of relief when his back was to the door.

As she hurried across the parking lot, the sky was much lighter than it had been when she'd entered the office. She hoped Rip would call sometime today, and not only because she wanted to know if they'd found anything that might lead to Carlos and Zack. Actually, she craved the feeling his presence gave, like everything would turn out all right.

As she passed Edgar's SUV, a flash of red on its grille caught her eye. She stopped. Looking closer, she froze, staring in disbelief.

It can't be…

Her hands shook as she reached for the small dead butterfly and peeled it from the Toyota's radiator. There was no mistaking it—she'd spent hours studying the bright red wings edged with an iridescent purple that classified this definitively as belonging to the new species Alex had discovered.

Nymphalis quinterus!

For a moment she almost forgot her exhaustion as a wave of adrenaline surged through her. *What is it doing here? Does this mean it exists outside of the habitat where we first discovered it?* It was possible, sure, but *here*? In Paraiso?

Her brain registered for the first time how muddy the vehicle was. Where had her uncle been? He wasn't the kind of man who would enjoy off roading. In fact, the only reason he drove an SUV was for the added comfort it provided on the poorly maintained roads in the city.

Her head was spinning. Had Edgar been to Fort Sherman?

She remembered the dusty roads they'd traveled to reach the research site. But that had been in the middle of the dry season.

Now that it was starting to rain every day, the roads through the jungle would be nothing but mud.

But what would Edgar be doing in the jungle? She ran her finger along the vehicle's bumper. The mud was caked on top but still gooey underneath.

This is fresh.

She rolled up the reports and put them under one arm, then carefully cupped the little butterfly in her hand and hurried to her car.

Something definitely wasn't right here.

She just needed time to figure out what it was.

She was almost home before she remembered the inconsistency in the reports. *Could it simply be an error?* She could check the accounts next time she went to the office and be sure. But what if it wasn't a mistake? Tío Edgar was the one who made the orders. In fact, he was responsible for most of the day-to-day financial transactions. Could he be siphoning off money for himself?

Mother said that business wasn't so good this year, but from the number of orders she'd just seen, Lerida Coffee should be having one of its best years ever. Should she call her mother immediately and tell her…what? That she'd gone the entire night without sleep and then gone to the office before dawn and found a slight discrepancy in the records?

Fernanda shook her head. She was going crazy. Edgar had always been a little eccentric, but he wouldn't steal from the family. But even if he was embezzling money, what did that have to do with the butterfly she'd found? And how could *that* have anything to do with her friends, who might possibly have perished in the initial attack?

She pulled through the automatic gate behind her apartment
building and coasted to a stop in an open parking space. Her heart
was beating so fast she couldn't think. She rolled down the window
and forced herself to breathe deeply.

How could Tío Edgar be involved with this? Nothing she could
come up with made sense.

She pulled the parking brake and grabbed her purse with the
butterfly specimen carefully tucked inside.

Something was up with Tío Edgar. *And I'm going to find out
what it is.*

33

US Embassy, Panama City, 0800 hours

RIP WINCED AS the medic poked at the Steri-Strips she'd applied to his face the night before. Why looking at them wouldn't have sufficed, he didn't know, but he sat bare-chested on the gurney and waited with resigned patience while the embassy's matronly physician's assistant examined the wounds on his head.

He wasn't as sore as he thought he'd be, but with a fairly purple right eye and a nose still swollen from Chombon's vicious head butt, Rip couldn't help hoping the pirate leader looked even worse.

The hot shower he'd taken back in his room at the hotel last night had been better than any of the medic's ministrations, but when he called home to check on Gabi, it felt like he was getting beat up all over again.

Gabi had returned home after two days, his mother said, and then added that she'd promptly kicked the rebellious teenager out of her home. "The way she talks to me, Euripides, I just cannot live with it," she said through tears.

His family was falling apart, and there was nothing he could do about it.

"Where is Gabi staying now?"

"She went to Tía Teresa's. But that woman will probably only make things worse."

Rip's mother had never gotten along very well with her late husband's younger sister. "Give me the number, Mama. I'll see if she'll talk to me."

This is loco. What can I do while I'm way down here?

The pain from his recent altercation was nothing compared to the burning in his chest because of Gabi. What surprised him most was the realization that the ache was jealousy. He was resentful of the punk that Gabi was hanging with. Obviously he didn't feel for her like Chaco did, but he was jealous just the same. He felt the old bitterness creeping into his heart. The two men who should have been there for Rip's family—his father and his stepfather—had both put their personal pleasure and comfort ahead of the needs of the family.

And what bothered Rip the most was that he could see himself repeating the pattern. Gabi needed a daddy. What would her father think if he saw what his selfishness had done to his family so many years later? Probably nothing.

Rip couldn't help getting angry when he saw the effect on Gabi. It was clear she was just looking for affection, and the men who should have been there to give it to her, weren't.

Including me.

What made it worse was that his attitude toward women mimicked his father and stepfather: Women weren't something to be treasured; they were something to be collected, like cars.

It was no use blaming his actions on his upbringing. If the Army had taught him anything, it was that. *You take responsibility for your situation, even if it isn't your fault.*

On a deeper level, something told him that his cavalier attitude toward women would, in the end, bring him neither lasting pleasure nor satisfaction. *But neither will taking a lifetime vow of chastity.*

"No sign of infection," the medic said, shifting her poking and probing to his shoulders and back. "You're going to have a scar though."

"A real man's tattoo." Coop's voice came from the direction of the door.

Rip turned slightly and saw his team sergeant ambling toward them, grinning.

"Good news," Coop continued, stopping at Rip's side. "Buzz's surgery went well, and they said he'll make a full recovery."

Rip exhaled and closed his eyes. "That's a relief, bro. How long will he be in the hospital?"

"Hold still, Staff Sergeant," the PA insisted.

Coop shook his head. "Probably about three days. Then they'll send him back to Bragg. He'll be on light duty for a week or two."

Rip flinched again and tried not to glare at the PA. "You know, I really didn't think it was that bad when I first saw him."

Coop shrugged. "Doc said the bullet clipped a nerve and came within a hair's breadth of a major artery. It could have been much worse. You about done here? We have a meeting with Marcel in a few minutes."

The PA nodded. "You can go."

Rip jumped up and dressed quickly before she changed her mind, then followed Coop out of the infirmary. Outside it was so hot that Rip wondered if someone had left the door to Hades open.

The main embassy building stood on the other side of a small, perfectly manicured flower garden. As the two men worked their way toward the rear door of the embassy building, Coop said, "Feels like it's going to rain."

Rip just grunted.

"What's the story with your little sister? Did you talk to her yet?"

Rip stopped and regarded his friend. "No, I didn't. How did you know I was thinking about her, bro?"

Coop put a powerful arm around Rip's shoulder, making him wince again. "That's why they pay me the big bucks, man! Don't worry, though. I hear the reenlistment bonuses are going up again. You'll make out like a bandit when it's time to re-up."

"Who says I'm going to re-up?"

Now Coop stopped and stared. "Seriously? You thinking about leaving the team?"

"Thinkin' about it. Yeah."

"Because of your sister?"

Rip shrugged. "Not necessarily. A guy's got to settle down sometime, you know? I'm just thinking how nice it would be to find a good woman, settle down, and actually be there for my family."

"Don't you see what we're doing as being there for your family?"

Rip's brows furrowed. "No."

"Look, buddy, you do a job that most people couldn't do. And you're good at it. Can you imagine what it would be like if ITEB made it into the States somehow? You've got to see the broader picture. You save your sister every day."

Rip shook his head. "I'd like to believe that, bro. But even if I am, how long does it last? I can't do this job forever. And while I'm here focusing on the 'broader picture,' the narrower one is going to pot. I can't let that happen."

"I understand what you're saying, I really do. But do you seriously think you can give your sister what she needs? Even when kids have their fathers at home, they still rebel at this age."

"Gabi's looking for love in all the wrong places, ese."

"Sounds a little like her brother."

Rip just stared at him. "I can't believe you just said that, Coop."

John raised one hand slightly. "Hey, no offense, buddy. What I'm trying to say is that you—her brother—can't give Gabi the love she really needs. Only God can do that. And based on the conversation we had at the Waffle House awhile back, you need the same thing: To know that your heavenly Father loves you in spite of everything. To know that you don't have to earn His love. You can't give that kind of love to Gabi—or any woman—if you don't understand it yourself."

A stab of anger hit Rip in the chest. *What right does he have to say that?*

Eyes narrowed, he turned on his heel and headed for the guard station at the rear of the building. "I don't have any choice, Coop. If she doesn't get it from me, she'll get it from Chaco. I can't let that happen."

34

Outside Panama City. 1100 hours

THE BLACK TAXI shuddered and jolted along behind a smoke-belching truck loaded down with bananas. Hopefully Zack wouldn't be mad that they'd taken his car. Actually, Fernanda hoped he would get angry. To do so, he'd have to come home alive. And though she tried not to show it to Hedi, the thread upon which her hope was riding strained a little closer to the breaking point.

She'd doubted her German friend would even agree to go along with this crazy idea. But Hedi was frustrated too, and after what happened the last time Fernanda went off without her, Hedi wasn't about to let her do this trip alone.

"You're right, Fernanda. Too many things don't add up with your uncle. But what does it have to do with Coiba?"

Fernanda shook her head. "All I know is that when I talked to Mother, it seems that things are worse than I thought."

"How?"

"Well, the numbers she gave me from the company bank account don't square with what I'm seeing in the database for the last several months. I guess nobody noticed sooner because Tío Edgar takes care of shipping and accounts payable."

"Didn't your mom want to know why you were asking?"

"I just told her I was cleaning up the database to get my mind off the last few days. But she knows something's up. She said that when she noticed a spike in operating overhead several months ago, Edgar blamed it on increased fuel costs."

But from what Fernanda could see, transport costs couldn't account for all of the increase. Nor could it account for Edgar spending time in the jungle of what used to be Fort Sherman, now the Fort San Lorenzo protected area near Colón, if in fact that was where he picked up the *Nymphalis quinterus*. And that appeared to be the case, since he was driving back that way now.

They'd decided to take Zack's car since Edgar wouldn't recognize it. Then they sat outside the Lerida Coffee offices for two hours. Hedi watched while Fernanda napped until he came out and got in his SUV.

So here she was, trailing her own uncle in a "borrowed" car, speeding north along the highway to Colón. Her stomach was uneasy, and half a nap gave her that herky-jerky feeling, like her brain was always one step behind. Even driving with the windows down and radio blasting wasn't helping.

She gave Hedi a grateful smile. "I'm glad you decided to come with me. I don't think I could have done this by myself."

Hedi nodded. "I want to do whatever we can to bring Carlos and Zack home. At least this way I feel like we're *trying*, even if nothing ever comes of it."

Fernanda agreed. She wanted to feel like she was contributing to the side of justice, though it might have nothing to do with her friends.

She edged carefully over to the left far enough to confirm Edgar's SUV was still there, five cars ahead. She'd been hard pressed to keep up with him on the poorly maintained two-lane road. In fact, she'd never driven so fast in her life. By the time they made it to the outskirts of Colón, she was glad for the traffic congestion.

Hedi pointed. "Hey, there he goes!"

Edgar veered to the left near the sign that pointed to the canal crossing at the Gatún locks. Fernanda followed. She knew the road well from the two weeks she'd worked on Alex's project the previous year.

Traffic was lighter on the road that wound down to the canal crossing. Fernanda hoped that the wait wouldn't be too long. The crossing was only open between ships, and sometimes it took more than an hour of waiting in line before the metal ramps were lowered in front of the lock's huge doors to let vehicles pass.

Edgar was really speeding now. His SUV kicked up leaves and gravel as he blasted down the straightaway and careened around each corner. The little taxi strained to keep up but failed. She'd never known Edgar to be so reckless, and if her mother had seen it, she'd have words for her brother-in-law.

They were approaching the Gatún locks. When the road finally straightened out for the last quarter mile before the canal, she saw the small cloud of dust left by the SUV far ahead. The gates must be open, since the line of cars that normally waited on this stretch of road wasn't here.

Fernanda floored the accelerator to try to close the distance with the Toyota. As she neared the gate, the SUV braked hard before reaching the crossing, then edged onto the metal bridge that crossed the 110-foot lock.

Almost there! She tried to coax more speed out of the whining automobile, already shuddering like a kite.

But it was no use. Before she reached the crossing, the guard was closing the high chain-link gate across the road. She probably said a few words she shouldn't have as she slammed on the brakes and screeched to a stop just in front of the sign that read *Propiedad de la autoridad del Canal de Panama. Prohibido entrar sin autorización.*

"Oh no! What do we do now?" Hedi wailed.

The guard eyed the girls with interest from his post on the opposite side of the high chain-link fence, which was topped with a tangle of razor wire. Beyond him, her uncle's SUV powered up the ramp on the far side of the canal, then turned left and disappeared behind the lock.

She smacked the steering wheel. A tirade of Spanish followed.

"What'd you say?"

Fernanda blushed. "Oh...sorry. I'm just frustrated."

"What's on the other side of the canal?"

"Really the road only goes to the old base. But once we get through the gate, there are lots of side roads, most of which used to lead to various military training sites, I think. But most of the work we did on the *quinterus* was at the very end of the road, near the ruins of *Fuerte San Lorenzo*.

"What's that?" Hedi asked.

"Oh, it's an old pirate fort on a bluff overlooking the Caribbean. It's really neat in a spooky kind of way. There are still old cannons pointing out to sea and ramparts that look down on the mouth of the Chagres River."

Hedi's eyes went wide. "A real pirate fort? Wow!"

Fernanda nodded. "Yeah, they say it was conquered by Captain Morgan himself back in the sixteenth century. We'll have to go see it someday."

"Do you think that's where your uncle is headed?"

"I can't imagine what he'd be doing there, but he must have been close to end up with a specimen of the *quinterus* in his grille."

They waited, watching in frustration as a ship nosed its way out of the lock at a snail's pace and headed for the Caribbean. Fernanda wanted to scream.

A full thirty minutes later, she was beside herself as the gate finally opened. The bored guards looked on as she forced herself to maneuver slowly down the narrow drawbridge. Once clear of the canal, she gunned the engine and sped away.

Three minutes later she passed the guardhouse for the entrance to Fort Sherman. It was empty, and the wooden barrier was propped open. With her anxiety at a rolling boil, she turned left at the sign that said *Parque Nacional San Lorenzo*.

"How far is it to the fort?" Hedi asked.

"About four miles after the pavement ends."

Hedi peered up at the sky. "It sure looks like it's going to rain."

Fernanda nodded. "It's that time of day."

After about half a mile, the pavement ended, and they bumped along as quickly as the rutted dirt road would allow. It was in worse condition than Fernanda remembered. The jungle closed in on both sides, and soon they were traveling in a lush, dark green tunnel. Moss-covered vines hung from the trees over the road, and brightly colored land crabs scuttled away from the vehicle as it passed.

Hedi had the window down and was hanging her head out the window. "Oooh, it smells so good here. Hey, I see a monkey!" She jabbed a finger skyward.

Fernanda was straining to see what she was pointing at when it started raining hard. It was as if someone had turned the nozzle on a giant fire hose. Hedi pulled her head inside and quickly rolled up the window. Fernanda switched on the windshield wipers; they were of little help.

She slowed a bit. "Great. Just great."

She rounded a bend and felt the tires begin to slide—just a little but enough to nearly cause her to panic. The look on Hedi's face as she gripped the dashboard didn't help. Enormous puddles sprang up out of nowhere, and avoiding them required so much concentration that she almost forgot why they were there.

"Look out, Fernanda!"

She slammed on the brakes and the car slid. It stopped abruptly with a crunch. She couldn't even see what she'd hit. "What is it?"

Hedi wiped at the dirty windshield. "I think you ran over a fallen log."

Fernanda shifted into reverse and gunned the engine. The car didn't move. She dropped her head to the steering wheel, honking the horn. "This is bad. I forgot how poorly maintained this road is. We always brought a four-wheel drive before. This car will never make it, especially in this rain."

Hedi put a hand on her arm. "I'll take a look and see if there's any way to move the log, Fernanda. Get ready to try it again."

Before Fernanda could protest, Hedi opened the door and stepped into the downpour.

She opened the driver's side window a crack and watched through the pounding wipers as Hedi made her way to the front of the car.

"I'm going to try to move it!" Hedi stooped and lifted, grunting like a power lifter. The log in her arms was larger than her leg. Just as quickly, Hedi dropped it again. Mud splattered in all directions, including on Hedi.

Fernanda pulled the parking brake and stepped out into the rain. Obviously this was a two-person problem.

"I'm sorry!" Hedi shouted over the storm.

"Don't be! We can do this together!"

The log had lodged under the grille of the car. It was at least fifteen feet long, but working it back and forth together they were able to pull it out in a matter of minutes. By the time they rolled the log to the side of the road, they were both drenched and covered in mud. They slipped and slid their way back and fell into the car, laughing hysterically.

"Are we crazy, or what?" Hedi asked.

Fernanda shook her head. "I just hope we can get out of here." She released the brake, put the car in reverse, and headed back toward civilization.

Hedi wiped a spot of mud off of Fernanda's face. "I guess we owe Zack a car wash." She giggled.

Fernanda laughed. "I think we're going to need one ourselves!"

When they got to the gate, a guard was manning the post. He stepped from the guardhouse, hunching under a plastic poncho as he motioned for them to stop.

She rolled the window down just enough so they could talk. He peered in the window at the two wet and muddy women. He arched an eyebrow but said nothing about their near-drowned appearance.

"Buenas tardes, señoritas." The guard looked to be in his late teens and was wearing camouflage fatigues over a lanky frame, all covered with a cheap transparent poncho.

Fernanda stifled a grin. "Buenas tardes."

"*Lo siento*, señorita. I'm sorry, but you must pay now to enter the park."

She cocked an eyebrow at him. "But we are leaving, not entering."

He smiled. "Yes, well, I was busy when you came in, or I would have collected the fee then." He shrugged. "I sit here every day and get very few visitors, and the moment I'm busy..."

She smirked at him. "Busy sleeping, perhaps?"

He looked sheepish. "But, no. I was...er...using the latrine."

Fernanda and Hedi could no longer contain their laughter. To her surprise, the guard just chuckled and shook his head. She reached for her purse. "How much is the fee?"

"*Dos balboas,* por favor."

That gave her an idea. She fished a ten from her wallet and held it up. "Have you noticed a silver Toyota Prado coming in and out recently, driven by an older gentleman?"

He nodded. "Sí, señorita. I see him many times in the last few months. But I do not know his name."

She smiled. "He is my uncle, and I was trying to find him, but the road is too muddy for my little car. Do you know where he goes in the park?"

"I would not know. My job is just to collect the entrance fee. But he is not a tourist, so I would assume that he is working at one of the batteries."

The batteries! She'd completely forgotten about them. Alex had told her once about the defensive gun emplacements that were built along the coastline on Fort Sherman before World War II to protect the canal.

"So, what kind of work do they do at the batteries?"

The boy shrugged. "I have never been inside one. But I know at least one of them is used by the Panamanian military and one is used by scientists of some kind. There has been more traffic than usual in the past few days, so I think they may be doing some construction."

"Ah, well, thank you very much." She handed over the ten.

The boy beamed from ear to ear. "It is my pleasure, señorita." He went to the gate and lifted the barricade, waving at them as they drove away.

The drive back to Panama City went quickly. They tried to make sense of the new information they'd garnered.

"Edgar still owns his pharmaceutical company, I think. Maybe he's just doing some research on a new medicine or something."

"But that wouldn't explain the missing finances, would it?" Hedi asked.

Fernanda shook her head. "No, nor would it explain his knowledge of the attack or the coincidence with the boat to Lebanon."

"Maybe you should talk to the authorities about this."

"I could, but I don't really think they'd take it seriously at this point. There's just not enough evidence."

"How about your mother?"

"I would, but I promised Rip I wouldn't talk about the mission details with anyone. I've told you, because I trust you to keep a secret. If my mother knew the story, it'd be in *La Prensa* by tomorrow morning. She talks to everybody."

Hedi shrugged. "How about Rip then?"

Fernanda was silent for a moment. Yes, Rip would know what to do. In fact, he might be the only one who could help her make sense of the chaos in her head.

She nodded. "Good idea, Hedi. But first I have to find him."

35

US Embassy, Panama City.

THE DOOR TO THE second-floor embassy conference room swung shut with a muted *click*. Perched on the end of the conference table with his back to them, Doc Kelly was talking with Frank and Sweeney, standing by the window. From the looks on the two men's faces, Doc was briefing them on Hogan's condition.

Doc turned when Rip and John entered. "Hey, Rip! Glad to see the PA let you out of there. What'd she say?"

Rip was in no mood to talk, so he just shrugged and slumped down into one of the swivel chairs at the table.

Coop spoke up. "The medic said he'd have a scar, but otherwise he'll be fine."

Doc hesitated. "Oh…well he doesn't look too excited about it."

Rip wanted to give a witty comeback but didn't have the energy. "What's the word on Phoenix?"

Doc shook his head. "Nothing. That's why you're here. Me, I'm headed back to the hospital to sit with Hogan. I'll call the embassy if anything changes." The black medic picked up his gear and left the room.

Sweeney spit a stream of tobacco into a paper cup. "I get the feelin' that there's something more going on here than just a bunch of pirates out on Gilligan's island."

Coop nodded. "I think you're right. But what? That assault force had some pretty heavy weapons. I mean, who has LAW rockets and forty millimeter grenades? And that boat had a .50 caliber machine gun mounted on it. You don't just pick up those things at your local gun shop. Who do you think they were?"

Still standing by the window, Frank answered. "Could be Columbians. Supposedly there are lots of narcotics traffickers around here."

That made sense to Rip. "Okay, but what would *narcotráficos* want with Phoenix?"

Coop shrugged. "Got me. I guess we'll have to wait for Marcel to get here."

"Hey, Rubio. Isn't that Fernanda down there?"

Rip's head whirled around toward Frank. "What?"

Frank was peering outside. "That girl, down by the gate. She looks a lot like Fernanda."

Rip moved to the window, followed by everyone but Sweeney.

"See there." Frank pointed. "It looks like she's talking with the gate guard."

He couldn't be completely sure, but the dark-haired woman certainly looked like her. As they watched, she turned and hurried down the street away from the embassy.

"What's she doing?"

Frank frowned. "I'd say she was trying to get in and they turned her away. They don't let just anyone into the compound."

"There's one way to find out." Rip dug in his pocket, glad he'd thought to write her number on a card in his wallet before he showered last night. "I'm gonna call her cell phone."

"There's a phone over here." Sweeney indicated a small table in the corner of the room.

Rip had just picked up the handset when Marcel burst through the door. "Take your seats, all of you. You've wasted enough of my time already."

"Grumpy today, isn't he?" Sweeney muttered.

The conference table shook as Marcel's fist slammed down on it. "Who do you think you are?! You soldiers come into my city and think you can just go around wreaking havoc?" He turned on Coop. "Do you realize how much this idiocy has cost the taxpayers, Master Sergeant?"

Rip sighed and dropped the phone back into its cradle. He thought of Hogan and had to stifle the urge to jump over the table at the pear-shaped CIA agent and separate the man's ears from his balding head. He looked back at Coop, who was surprisingly cool and collected.

Frank had taken a seat and was staring at his hands. He didn't like confrontation. Sweeney was following the exchange with an amused smirk, as if he were sitting in his living room watching WWF SmackDown.

Coop's voice was that of a quiet professional, a marked contrast to his opponent. "I'm the team sergeant here, Agent Bucard. I'm responsible for any decision that—"

"You're not in command! In the absence of Agent Phoenix, I am." Marcel seethed. "I'm also the guy who has to clean up after you yahoos once you've finished setting the whole country on fire!"

Coop stood up and leaned across the table on his fists, blue eyes boring into the station chief. "And I'm the guy who makes sure

Task Force Valor isn't jerked around by someone who doesn't have a clue about what's happening on the ground."

Marcel's head was about to pop. "I ordered you to postpone that reconnaissance!"

Coop's face was set like red granite, radiating intensity. But he still didn't raise his voice. "You also ordered in the Panamanians, who proceeded to wound one of my men and could have killed the hostages, not to mention destroying any remaining ITEB." He returned to his seat. "The bottom line is this, Agent Bucard. As far as I'm concerned, you're not in our chain of command. And if you disagree, I suggest you take it up with our headquarters at Fort Bragg."

"That won't be necessary," a voice boomed from the back of the room. Everyone whirled to see a burly man in blue jeans and a hunting shirt standing beside the open door. Rip gaped in amazement. "Major Williams!"

"Who are you?" Marcel demanded.

"Lou Williams. I'm the commander of Task Force Valor."

"It's about time somebody showed up to corral these loose cannons. Your men have—"

Williams put up a hand. "Now hold on there, partner. I understand Agent Phoenix has gone missing, and whatever has happened up to this point needs to take a backseat to finding her, wouldn't you agree?"

Marcel floundered some more. "But...I mean, well..."

The major leaned toward Marcel a little, lowering his voice. "You know, if she's not found soon, it'll certainly reflect poorly on your station, don't you think? So why don't we all work together to get this problem solved?"

The tension drained slowly from the room as Marcel began flipping through folders on the table. "Yes…yes of course."

Rip smirked. *He's more worried about his reputation than he is about Phoenix.*

"All right then," Williams said. "Why don't you tell us what we know about Phoenix."

Marcel sighed, collecting himself. "Very well. Agent Phoenix left here just before dawn yesterday morning to meet with one of our counterparts in the Panamanian intelligence service. She never arrived. We have no hard evidence that she was abducted—no ransom notes or claims of responsibility. But her vehicle was found parked near the site where the meeting was to take place, so we presume she made it that far. So far, there are no witnesses who can tell us what happened. But since we haven't heard from her, I'd say it's likely she was kidnapped."

Coop frowned. "How many people knew she was going to that meeting?"

"Don't even insinuate that I've compromised operational security, Master Sergeant."

Major Williams intervened. "Nobody's accusing you of anything. But besides you and the other agent, could anyone else have known?"

Marcel scratched his head. "Nobody on our end knew, but the Panamanian intelligence is notoriously corrupt. Anyone with enough money who wanted to know what was going on could probably find out."

Williams nodded. "Okay, then, it might not just be a random kidnapping. I assume you've got people looking for her?"

"Of course, but she's only been gone a little over twenty-four hours. We haven't had time to shake all the bushes to see what falls out," He gathered up his papers and moved to the door. "Major Williams, I'd like to speak to you privately, if you don't mind."

"Okay, I'll be right there."

As soon as the door closed, Williams broke into a smile. "Did you miss me?"

Exclamations broke out around the room, and the major went around and shook hands with each man. Rip wasn't normally a hugging kind of guy, but when the major embraced him, his relief in seeing the commander allayed any awkwardness he might have felt. "I thought you were going to be laid up, sir?"

The major feigned offense. "Shoot, them sissy doctors said it'd be weeks. I'm fine. Besides, nothing like a little time in a tropical paradise to help me recuperate, right?"

"Have you seen Buzz yet?" Coop asked.

"Yep. Went right to the hospital from the airport. I'm getting him on a flight back to the States tonight."

The team spent the next half hour getting their commander up to speed on all that had happened. When they finished, the major said, "All right then, it looks like until we get a lead of some kind, we're in a holding pattern. I don't want you to worry about that Marcel character. I'll deal with him. Coop, you and the men go back to the hotel and wait for the word. I'll work with the folks here at the embassy, and as soon as we know something, we'll send someone for you. So get some rest and don't go anywhere. If this thing breaks open, things are going to get hot in a hurry."

That was one order Rip would gladly obey.

Thirty minutes later, John, Frank, Sweeney, and Rip walked into the lobby of the Euro Hotel. John immediately peeled off toward the computers set up along the wall. "Gonna check my e-mail. I'll stay here if you guys want to get some chow. I've got some food up in my room."

"Tell Liz we said hi, loverboy. And give me the room key." Frank held out his hand.

"You're just jealous." John smiled as he tossed Frank the key.

Rip caught the elevator up to his and Doc's room on the fifth floor. Deciding to go for a swim, he started to change. While emptying his pockets, he found the card with a phone number scrawled on it.

Fernanda! Oh, man! I almost forgot! He sat on the bed and turned the lamp on over the telephone, then began to dial her number.

He dialed three digits, then hung up. *What are you going to say? Hey, were you looking for me today? Man, if that doesn't sound like a line.*

But what if she *was* looking for him? After the trauma she'd been through, why would she want to see him again?

She told me to call her. He frowned. *What's wrong with you, Rubio?* He retrieved the handset and dialed the number.

On the fourth ring, her voicemail picked up. "Hola, por favor *deja un mensaje.*"

After the beep, he said, "Hi, Fernanda, it's Rip. I…I was just wondering how you're doing. Give me a call tonight if you get this. I'm at the Euro Hotel, room 210." He left the phone number for the hotel and hung up.

After changing into his swim trunks, he pulled back the curtains over the window and looked out at the pool. The only people out there were an amorous couple who looked more interested in swapping slobber than swimming. Disgust mixed with a tinge of loneliness, and he wasn't sure which bothered him the most.

Good grief. I can't get away from it.

The phone rang. Rip dove over the bed to answer it. "Hello?"

"Rip, it's Fernanda."

He couldn't believe she called back, or how good it felt to hear her voice. "¿Qué pasó, amiga?"

"Oh, Rip. I've been trying to find you."

"Was that you at the embassy today?"

"You saw me? Why didn't you call sooner then? They wouldn't let me in!"

He chuckled. "I would have—I meant to! But I was busy getting chewed out."

Her voice sounded urgent, almost frantic. "Rip, listen. We need to talk. I have some information that might be related to your mission."

"You do?"

"I think so. Can you meet me?"

Rip's brow furrowed. "Well, not really. I mean, we might get the call any minute, you know?"

"What if I come there?"

Rip could only imagine the remarks he'd have to put up with if the guys saw him on a date when they were still technically on a mission. But she sounded desperate, and any information at this point would be helpful. It wasn't a difficult choice to make.

"There's a restaurant in the lobby of the hotel. Can you meet me there in fifteen minutes?"

"I can be there in ten."

"Okay, I'll get us a table." He ended the call and sat staring at the telephone. *Whoa. What's up with that?*

He stood and put his pants back on.

Only one way to find out.

36

FERNANDA ENTERED THE brightly lit restaurant from the noisy street, clutching her purse as she scanned the tables, half of which were occupied. Rip sat in a booth by the window, sipping from one of two glasses on the table. He was dressed in blue jeans and a blue-and-white striped cotton shirt with the sleeves rolled up. Quite different from the camouflage she'd seen him in last. But the cut under his eye was still apparent as he raised a hand to catch her eye.

She looked around. Not as private as she would have liked, but it would have to do.

The thought crossed her mind as she hurried to the table that despite the once-over she'd given herself in the taxi, she probably looked awful. But anything would be better than the last time he'd seen her. At least now she was clean.

He stood and smiled as she approached. "Hola, amiga. That was fast." His demeanor was easy, confident, and casual. It made her feel like they had been friends for much longer than two days.

She stepped forward and kissed him lightly on the cheek, then felt herself blush when she remembered that in America a hand-shake was more appropriate for someone you'd just met.

He didn't seem fazed by it, though. *Well, he is Latino, after all.*

He stepped back. "You look…different."

She smiled. "That's a good thing, I hope."

"Claro que sí." He motioned for her to sit. "I got you a drink."

She looked at the frosty glass filled with a frothy white beverage. "What kind is it?"

"It's like a banana milkshake. Do you like them?"

She laughed. "Sure! It's called a *batido*. All Panamanians love them."

He took the opposite side of the booth. "Good. Hey, I'm sorry I didn't call earlier. Things are pretty loco up there, you know?"

She nodded. "Well, you'll definitely think I'm crazy when you hear what I've got to tell you." She looked around the restaurant, feeling sort of silly for lowering her voice. "Since we're not supposed to talk about what happened, you're the only one I could go to."

He gave her a warm smile. "I'm glad you did. But I'm not sure what I can do to help. Tell me what's going on."

Fernanda took a deep breath. "I did some checking, and my family's company, Casa Lerida, S.A., may have transported coffee on the ship that was stolen, the sunken one we saw as we left the island."

Rip shrugged. "Okay."

"I know, a coincidence. But when I went into our database to look at that shipment, there was a problem. We paid far too much for the amount of coffee shipped."

He shook his head. "I'm still not getting where this is going."

Fernanda held up one finger. "Just wait. Since my father died, my uncle Edgar is the one who makes those arrangements and handles most of the finances for our company."

"That must have been hard for you."

She was getting frustrated. "No, listen. I think my uncle may

be involved in stealing money from our company. And get this—
he knew about the attack."

"What attack?"

"The attack on the…" She lowered her voice. "The attack on
the island!"

Rip's eyebrows came together. "He did? How?"

Fernanda put both hands on the table and whispered, "I don't
know! I didn't tell anyone."

Rip steepled his fingers and thought for a moment. "So, how
do you think he's involved?"

"I was hoping you could help me with that. I mean, why did
he pay so much for that coffee shipment? Could Tío Edgar have
used our account to pay for something else to be shipped to
Lebanon? Like drugs or something?"

Rip shook his head. "Then what incentive would he have to be
involved in attacking a ship that was *returning* from there?"

Fernanda hadn't thought of that. She chewed her lip. "I…I
don't know."

"Hold up." He sat up straighter in the booth, his eyes taking
on an intensity that hadn't been there before. "Do you know when
the ship last went to Lebanon?"

She pulled the printed reports from her purse. "Sure. Our shipment went out on March 6."

He said nothing for a moment and seemed to be calculating in
his head. "That was about a week before…" He snapped his fingers. "Stay here." He got up and left.

What just happened?

She sat alone and sipped the batido, looking around at the
other patrons, none of whom seemed interested in her. She had

that feeling again, being here with Rip. That feeling like everything
was going to be okay. And it was as refreshing as the frozen drink.

He returned a moment later with John Cooper. They slid
into the booth opposite her, and this time she remembered to
offer a handshake only. John took her hand and smiled. "You
don't look anything like that wild woman we found out in the
jungle."

"Yes, well, I feel much better too."

"So Rip says you have some info for us?"

She went through the story again, with Rip putting a word in
here and there. She got a little better understanding of what had
made the light come on in his head when she explained the timing
of the shipment to Lebanon and the extra cost.

"But wouldn't that discrepancy have been picked up on by
someone else at the company right away?" John asked.

She shook her head. "We send out hundreds of orders during
that time of year. Most of them are containerized. The only way I
caught this is because I did a search for noncontainerized orders,
which isn't something anyone would normally do."

"So the last shipment went out in March?"

"Right. March 6." She sipped her batido.

Rip leaned closer to John and said quietly, "About the time we
were meeting up with Liz. Which means that if the *Invincible* had
another shipment for…you know…then they wouldn't have been
there to pick it up."

John nodded. "Return to sender."

"Right, bro."

Fernanda wanted in on the secret. "Who's Liz?"

Rip hiked a thumb at John. "Coop's girlfriend."

Fernanda blinked. *Hedi's going to be disappointed.*

John waved a hand. "Long story. Hey, Rubio. Could you order me one of those shakes? They look good."

"Sure. Be right back." He rose and walked to the bar.

Fernanda took advantage of his absence to ask a question that had been bugging her. "So, is this Phoenix person Rip's girlfriend?"

John smiled. "No, nothing like that. We sort of work together. Anyway, Rip has sworn off girls for the duration."

Fernanda's eyebrows shot up. "Oh."

Rip returned and took his seat. "Your batido will be here in a sec. So what if this uncle of yours is somehow involved with the *Invincible*?"

"Well, here's the rest of the story. My uncle has apparently been sneaking off to the Caribbean side of the isthmus a lot recently. Spending time out in the jungle on the old Fort Sherman base."

John perked up. "You don't say? I was there in 1999. I hear it's a national park or something now."

"Officially, yes. But as far as our business is concerned, he doesn't have any reason to be over there, and he's never said anything to us about it. So something is suspicious, I think."

John cocked an eyebrow at Rip. "I have to say this is a long shot, but it's time we took this info to the major."

Rip finished off his batido. "My thoughts exactly."

"Then lemme out, and I'll go make the call." He nudged Rip out of the booth. "Thanks for thinking of us, Fernanda. I hope something comes of it. I'll be back in a few minutes. Don't let Rip drink my shake!"

She smiled. "Okay."

When he had gone, she said, "John's a nice man."

Rip nodded. "The best. I'd follow him anywhere. So how did you figure out your uncle was going to Fort Sherman?"

"You won't believe it—a butterfly told me."

He laughed at her. *"Es una broma, ¿no?"*

"Nope. No joke. Like I told you before, I'm studying to be a lepidopterist, a scientist who specializes in the study of moths and butterflies. I know, that sounds crazy, until you realize that of the two hundred thousand species of lepidoptera in the world, almost half of them are found right here in Panama. And we're discovering new species all the time. It's a really interesting field."

He shrugged. "And so you talk to them?"

Laughing, she said, "Nothing like that. I found a rare species of butterfly in the grille of my uncle's car. Alex discovered it last year on Fort Sherman, and as far as we know, that's the only place where it exists."

"Who's Alex?"

She hesitated. "He's my…" *My what? Friend? Mentor? Lover?* She settled for, "He's a professor at the college." She stared out the dirty window and added quietly, "And he's still out there on Coiba somewhere."

In all the excitement, she hadn't dwelt on that for some time. Talking about it reminded her of what a mess her life really was.

"What's the matter?"

Apparently Rip noticed. She looked into his dark eyes and chiseled face and found herself wanting to tell him everything but was afraid to tell him anything. "Nothing. I'm…I just hope my friends are found soon."

Rip was quiet for a moment, then smiled. "I know what John would suggest."

"What would John suggest?"

The full force of his gaze hit her dead on. "He'd say we should pray about it. Just the other day he was telling me how prayer helped him trust God with the intangibles."

She was shocked. "Is he a Christian?"

Rip nodded. "Yep, got religion on this last deployment." She detected a note of sarcasm.

Fernanda crossed her arms. "Well, I think he's right."

"Really? Do you pray too?"

"Not as much as I should, maybe…" She pinned him with her gaze. "How about you?"

The intensity in Rip's eyes clouded over, and he seemed suddenly sad.

"Rip, I'm sorry. I didn't mean—"

He held up a hand. "No, it's not that. I guess I was just thinking that I need to pray as much as anyone, especially recently. I just…"

"Just what?"

When he looked at her again, his eyes were softer. "I guess I don't really know how. I mean, I learned all kinds of prayers as a kid—the *Ave María*, the *Padre Nuestro* and the *Gloria*—but none of those really apply to my situation right now, you know?"

"So you're Catholic?"

He shrugged. "If being dragged to church every week as a kid makes you Catholic, then I guess I am."

Something in his tone, his unexpected vulnerability made pity well up inside her. "So what's your situation right now? If you don't mind sharing with someone you hardly know."

He stared at her for a moment, as if weighing a great risk. Fernanda waited. Then he said, "Okay, amiga. Maybe you can help me with this, give me a woman's perspective. Here's the problem." He went on to explain the situation with his mother and his sister.

Fernanda listened with a growing sense of empathy; she herself had a younger sibling, her brother, Marcus. Even though she and Marcus had never been as close as it sounded like Rip was with his sister, she could imagine how hard it must be to be so far away, unable to help when it was needed.

"The thing is," Rip said, "she has no dad to give her the love she needs. And since he's not there to give her that affection, she's gonna get it from Chaco or any other punk who pays her some attention. And there's nothing I can do to stop it, short of quitting this job and moving back home."

"You would do that for her?"

His jaw was firmly clenched. "I don't want to, but if that's what it takes, I'll do what I've got to do, you know?"

She reached out and put a hand on his. "You're a good man, Sergeant Rubio. I will pray for you. But you can do it too. Just talk to Him, like a friend. I think God will answer, one way or another."

John stuck his head through the open restaurant door. "Hey, buddy, let's get a move on. Taxi's on its way to get us."

Rip pulled his hand from under hers. "Thanks, chica. I'm sorry to dump on you like that. But right now I have to go."

She stood with him, wondering if he meant anything by the way he removed his hand. She hoped not. "No problem. I enjoyed getting to know you a little better. Maybe we can talk more later?"

He smiled. "I'll call you when I can, okay?"

A surge of adrenaline surprised her. "Great. Talk to you soon!"

And be careful, Sergeant Rubio.

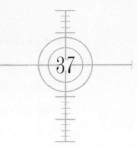

LIGHT BECAME LIQUID. Fish of all kinds swirling around the hulking form of the ship, which had come to rest at a forty-five degree angle after plunging nose-first into the seabed. The stern was just below water level at high tide, and the myriad of sea creatures had already accepted the ship's presence, making their homes on the rusty metal skin.

Fernanda was weightless and happy as she swam among them. Below her, the deck of the ship disappeared into the murky depths, its hatches tightly shut and everything in its place. It was as though they had lived there for a hundred years. Looking up, she gazed in awe at the schools of opalescent sea life between her and the shimmering aqueous orb of the sun.

Tap, tap, tap.

A flash of vermilion caught her attention on the ship's railing. She swam in for a closer look, and when she recognized it, the shock was like nothing she'd ever known.

A...butterfly?

Impossible. Butterflies didn't swim. Yet this one was. While she watched, incredulous, the little creature drifted from its perch and slowly moved its wings, propelling forward. She followed it down the deck, captivated by the delicate shade of red, much darker and richer than the *quinterus,* like the inside of a fresh strawberry.

Tap, tap, tap.

Fernanda looked around. *Where is that noise coming from?*

There it is again!

Distracted, she followed the tapping sound over the side of the ship. *A porthole!*

Tap, tap, tap.

Dread rose in her throat. She didn't want to find out what was making the noise, but she couldn't keep from looking. She drifted down toward the window, but it seemed no matter how deep she swam, she couldn't reach it. The water around her was dark and cold before she floated over the porthole in the side of the ship.

And then her heart stopped.

¡Papi!

Her father was floating on the other side of the glass. He smiled.

He's still alive! I have to get him out!

But she needed air. Her lungs burned, and Fernanda clawed frantically at the porthole. It was rusted shut. Her father shook his head and frowned.

Tap, tap, tap.

She could hold her breath no longer. She shot to the surface to get a breath. *Hold on, Daddy!*

When she broke through the surface, the sun was gone. She was alone, sitting on her bed, drenched with sweat and gasping for breath.

Tap, tap, tap.

Fernanda's heart gave another jolt, and she shook her head to be sure she wasn't still dreaming. But no, the sound was real.

Someone was knocking on her door.

She stumbled out of bed and quickly donned a black silk robe over her the tank top and shorts.

On the way to the door, she bumped a half-eaten plate of noodles off the hall table, shattering the dish on the floor. That, at least, served to awaken her enough to remember what day it was. Even so, she had to stare at the clock in the entryway for a moment before it registered that it was only 6 p.m.

Maybe it was the drowsiness that kept her from checking the peephole before opening the door; normally she'd never think of such a thing. But this time, she turned the lock and pulled the door open about halfway.

The man's poorly lit form was not immediately familiar. But when he spoke, Fernanda decided she must still be dreaming after all.

"Hello, Fernanda."

It can't be! Her brain was saying his name, but her mouth refused to comply. When she did finally say it, the sound came out as a whisper. "Alex?"

He stepped into the light of the entryway, revealing sunken cheeks, a week's worth of stubble, and a weak smile. "I never thought I'd see you again, my dear."

Her knees went weak. "I thought...Alex, you made it!"

"I did." His tired voice still contained the faintest spark of the old confidence.

She threw her arms around his neck and cried.

He returned her embrace with an eagerness that matched or exceeded hers, and they held each other for a long moment in silence.

When he released her, he stepped back and lowered his eyes to the floor. "Fernanda. I…I'm sorry."

She wiped her eyes. "Don't be sorry, Alex. I'm just so glad you're alive."

He gave a mirthless laugh. "And I you!"

"Are you all right?"

He said nothing for a moment, then looked up. "May I come in?"

She led him by the hand into the kitchen and put a pot of water on to boil. "Have a seat at the table there. My sleep schedule is still a mess. I don't know if it's day or night half the time."

She sat across from him and was again overcome by emotion. Half laughing, half crying, she pulled a wad of tissues from a nearby box and tried to restore some semblance of humanity to her face. "I'm sorry. I still can't believe you're here. How did you get off the island?"

Alex's eyes bore a tortured, faraway look. "I saw him."

"Who?"

"The Mudman, Fernanda. I saw him."

"What?" More confused than surprised, she suddenly caught her breath. *The pirates.* "El hombre de Lodo."

Alex nodded and swallowed as if his mouth were full of cotton. "It was the most terrifying moment of my entire life," he croaked.

"The Mudman is real?"

Alex spoke automatically, as if he was reliving the nightmare in his head. "It was shortly after you three were captured. I was lying on the ground under a dense thicket, trying to decide if I should go after you or go for help. I'd been there for—I don't know how long, it could have been hours. Then all of a sudden, a man's bare feet passed directly in front of me without any sound. I froze. A second later I could see all of him. He was naked but for a loincloth and covered in mud. His hair was long and matted, as was his beard. He took a few more steps, then stopped."

He said nothing for a moment, and his eyes darted around the room, as if talking about it would bring the apparition back.

"I knew immediately who it was. I've heard the legends. The Mudman kills anyone he finds in the jungle alone."

"What happened?"

"Fernanda, he stopped and looked directly at me. Our eyes met. Then he turned and disappeared into the jungle. I never heard a thing."

"*Hijo de la mañana,*" Fernanda breathed. "What did you do?"

"I ran. From that moment until I stumbled into the ranger station yesterday, I was haunted by that image. I knew he was stalking me. It was a miracle that I found the satellite phone after two days of searching. Then I set out for the ANAM station. Every night when the darkness forced me to stop, I would lie there just waiting for him to cut my throat. I think if I had stayed in that jungle for one more hour, I would have gone insane."

He grabbed her hand so suddenly it made her jump. "I did some serious thinking about my life over the last week. I've had lots of successes, but there's something missing. It's like there's this hole in my life. I guess I just realized that my profession isn't enough. Money isn't enough. Recognition either. If I had died out there on Coiba, all that the world would have had to remember me by would be a few butterflies and an obituary."

Something moved in Fernanda's soul. *You know what he needs. Tell him.*

The intensity was back in his eyes. He clutched her hands tightly with his. "Fernanda. I want you to marry me."

If he hadn't been holding her hands, she would have fallen out of the chair. Her eyes went wide. "What?"

"Listen, I know it's sudden, but I also know that you are what I need. I want to share my life with someone, have children, leave a legacy. Fernanda, you are the one. I love you."

She gulped. "Alex, I…it's just…"

He got up and moved around to her side of the table. Kneeling next to her chair, his eyes pleaded with hers. "Fernanda, it was the thought of you that kept me going. You gave me something to live for. I need you in my life!"

Tell him.

The kettle was boiling. She looked at him for a long moment, trying to regain her mental footing. "Let me get that."

He moved aside as she stood and went to the stove. With her back to him, she prayed silently. *Lord, help me!*

When she turned off the stove, the kettle's whistle wound down like an air raid siren. She took a deep breath and was about to turn around when Alex's hands gently encircled her waist as he pulled her close. "You will make a good wife, Fernanda," he breathed into her ear.

She turned to face him, suddenly uncomfortable at how close his face was to hers. "Alex," she couldn't look him in the eye, "I can't fill the hole in your heart."

He pulled back slightly. "What do you mean, darling? Of course you can."

She shook her head. "I know this isn't what you want to hear right now. But your emptiness comes from having nothing in your life that is bigger than yourself."

He sighed. "What?"

Why is this so hard to say? "It's…God, Alex. You need God." It came out as a whisper. She looked up at his raw, unshaven face. He blinked.

"You're joking, right?"

"I wouldn't joke about something like that."

He let go of her and sat down abruptly, staring at her with an incredulous grin like she had just told him she was secretly in love with Barney the dinosaur. "I never imagined you saying such a thing."

That stung. Had her faith really been so hidden? "I'm sorry I didn't say so sooner."

He got up from the chair and paced like he did when he was giving a lecture. "I came here, Fernanda, to pour out my heart to you, to profess my love for you." He stopped and glared at her. "And you use my vulnerability to foist your religion on me? I mean, if you feel you need it, that's fine for you. But what I'm talking about has nothing to do with whatever collection of myths you choose to believe. I'm giving you a chance to be my life partner! Imagine the research we could do together, what it would do for your own standing in the scientific community. This is the chance of a lifetime for you! Don't let your religion cloud your thinking. You're smarter than that. You're beautiful and sexy and tough— don't give up your shot at the life you've always wanted."

Now it was Fernanda's turn to blink. She could see him clearly now for the first time. He wasn't proposing marriage as much as he was a merger. Suddenly she understood that to him, she wasn't a treasure to be guarded; she was a trophy to be hunted. And being in this man's crosshairs was not a comfortable feeling.

She took a deep breath. "I don't know exactly what I want right now, Alex. I need to think."

He smiled again, like the wise professor explaining a complexity of science to a first-year undergraduate. "You think too much, dear. Let me hold you, and you'll know it's right." He spread his arms and moved to embrace her.

She put a hand out to stop him with as much grace as she could muster, which wasn't much. "Not now, Alex." She went to the front door and opened it.

He followed her, his demeanor much softer but not quite contrite. She put her back to the wall to allow him to pass. Instead, he stopped in front of her and stroked her cheek.

"Come, come now. Let me stay with you tonight, my love. I've been alone too long." He dropped his hands to her waist, letting them slide sensuously down to her hips. "I promise, you won't regret loving me."

"That's not love, Alex. That's sex."

She punctuated her statement by shoving him out the door. Once it was closed, she put her back against it and cried.

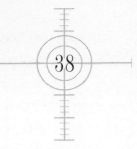

38

US Embassy, Panama City, 1815 hours

MOST OF TASK FORCE Valor was asleep in the briefing room on the second floor of the embassy when Major Williams burst through the door, carrying an armload of folders.

"All right, we got something!" he exclaimed, though Rip noticed the man wince slightly as he dropped the paperwork on the table.

"How's your back?"

Williams gave Rip a wink. "Not as painful as working with some of the folks around here." Sardonic chuckles arose from the group. "Anyway, Rip, the information your little friend brought us has yielded a few items of interest that we're going to check out." He opened a folder and produced a stack of satellite photos and passed them around the room.

"What're we looking at?" Coop asked.

"It's called Battery Davis." The major motioned for the men to be seated. "It's on what used to be Fort Sherman. There are seven batteries there in all, but this one is of interest."

"Am I the only one who doesn't know what a battery is?" Sweeney drawled.

"Yes," Frank said under his breath, to the snickers of the rest of the team. Sweeney punched him in the arm.

"Okay, here's a little history lesson." The major ignored their antics. "As I understand it, sometime prior to World War I, the United States began constructing coastal defenses to guard the entrances to the canal. As time went on, these grew into an elaborate series of bunkers and coastal defense guns. They were utilized as such until after World War II when the government decided to decommission them. Fort Sherman, since it sits at the entrance to the Caribbean side of the canal, had several of these bunkers."

"Are we talking like fortified concrete fighting positions here, or what?" Sweeney said.

Williams shook his head. "More than that. These batteries were underground complexes, some of which could quarter hundreds of men at a time and were completely self-sufficient. There were radar towers, artillery batteries, and underground medical facilities, among other things."

Coop snapped his fingers. "We did a training mission on one of those when I was here for Jungle Warfare school in '99."

Williams nodded. "Right. The military continued to use many of these batteries in various capacities until we pulled out in 2000. Then the Panamanian government abandoned several of them and sold a couple others to various research agencies."

"So what does all this have to do with ITEB?" Frank asked.

"First things first." The major got out his reading glasses and pointed to a clearing in the center of the photo. "This area is apparently one of the bunkers that was abandoned, which means it should be empty now."

"Let me guess; it's not," Coop said.

"Satellite imagery shows activity around the site over the last six months."

"And that's where Fernanda's uncle has been going?" Rip asked.

"We don't know that for sure. Other than Fernanda's information, we don't have any idea where he's been. But in the process of checking, we did find something interesting: Uncle Edgar is the founder of a Panamanian pharmaceutical company called Panagen."

"I thought he ran the coffee company," Rip said.

"Apparently he took that over when his brother died. But he still owns Panagen. And when we had some analysts take a look at that company's output over the last year, a few things didn't add up. First of all, they haven't taken any new drugs to trial in over two years."

"Doesn't sound too profitable," John said.

"Right. But that could partially be explained by the fact that Edgar has been too busy running the coffee business lately. But here's where it gets really suspicious. Our guys at Langley looked up Panagen's purchasing records. They turned up information in one case from an unexpected source."

"What's that?" Sweeney asked.

"Apparently, the US government held some pretty large yard sales in 1998 and 1999 in anticipation of pulling out of the country. Everything from vehicles to hospital bedpans—hundreds of millions of dollars' worth of stuff from US bases went on the auction block. Panagen made substantial purchases of scientific and medical equipment from these auctions and picked up some pretty high-tech lab equipment at fire-sale prices."

"Sounds like good business management," Frank said.

"Sure it was. And here's where the report went over my head," Williams grinned. "But I'll give you the English version, as best I

can understand it." He took a deep breath. "Iso-Triethyl Borane is
a liquid that explodes on contact with oxygen. Right?"

"Pyrophoric," Frank said.

"Whatever. So this chemical gets used by computer chip makers,
and guess who else: pharmaceutical companies. But it's never transported or used in its explosive state. That is, it's normally diluted with
another chemical that keeps it from being explosive. You follow?"

Rip nodded. *So far, so good.* Sweeney didn't look so sure.

Frank raised his hand. "What's the chemical that it's combined
with?"

Williams consulted his notes. "You would ask that, Baldwin.
Lessee…here it is. Hexane."

Frank shrugged. "Never heard of it."

"Me neither. But see, while it's mixed with hexane, ITEB won't
explode. It only becomes poly…pylo…"

"Pyrophoric," Frank said, grinning.

"Yeah, that. Anyway, it'll only blow up if the hexane is
removed. To do that, it's mixed with some sort of powder or something."

Frank was reading ahead in the report. "A nanopolymer."

Williams put his report down and took off his glasses. "You
want to do this, Frank?"

"No sir. Sorry. Please continue."

The glasses went back on, and after clearing his throat, the
major continued. "It's mixed with a *nanopolymer—*" he glared at
Baldwin—"which absorbs the hexane molecules and leaves the
pure ITEB, ready for bottling."

"Wouldn't this have to be done in a vacuum?" Coop fingered
his copy of the report.

Rip could tell Frank wanted to answer the question but was biting his lip instead, consternation creeping across his face.

Williams shook his head. "Not a vacuum; it just has to be done in an environment where there isn't any oxygen. So they use some other gas, like nitrogen."

"Oh," Coop said, as he went back to the report. "So they would have to mix the liquid into this nanopolymer, which absorbs the hexane and is then filtered out, leaving pure ITEB."

The major's eyebrows shot up. "Wow. You've been paying attention."

Coop dropped the report on the table. "Yes, but you still haven't explained how we know that Panagen is our culprit."

The stocky commander sighed and removed his reading glasses, setting them on the table. "Have you ever seen one of those photographs of, say, Abe Lincoln, that is made up of thousands of other tiny photographs?"

Rip spoke up. "You mean like a collage that when you look at it from far away makes a picture of something else?"

"Exactly. Well, if you look at the individual pictures, you'd never see old Abe. But taken together, the sum of the parts, you can see him clearly."

"I get you," Rip said, nodding. "The bunker, the equipment, the knowledge of the attack, all that adds up to our man, Edgar, being the maker."

"That's right," Williams said. "Oh, and one more thing: Panagen has been purchasing a fair amount of this nanopolymer in the last year."

"Why didn't these high-speed CIA yahoos just check to see if they've been buying ITEB too?" Sweeney asked.

"That was the first thing they checked. But that's the strange thing. None. Why would they be buying the stuff if they aren't buying anything to use it with? The answer is: They're getting their boom juice somewhere off the record."

Rip was tapping his pen on the desk, eager to get on with the mission. "So where are they getting their ITEB?"

The major pinned him with his gaze. "That, my boy, is what you all are going to find out."

"When?"

Williams stood with difficulty and picked up his glasses off the table. "You're going in tonight."

———

0240 hours

The two-and-a-half ton Daewoo cargo truck sat idling in the mud outside the battery, belching diesel exhaust that burned the eyes and throat. The man supervising the loading of the last of the ITEB was irritated at how long it was taking.

He was Edgar Oswardo Lerida, but not for much longer. He'd chosen his new name, and as soon as the product was transferred to the ship he'd made arrangements to meet off the coast at sunrise, he and his boat would be headed for Colombia, then on to Argentina and a new life.

Distant thunder signaled the approach of yet another rainstorm, and its rumbling competed with the guttural howls of a troupe of monkeys somewhere in the jungle nearby.

The bottles were safely packaged in foam-lined cases that gave no indication as to their contents, so he had to keep reminding the three longshoremen from Colón to be careful. As far as Oswardo was concerned, supervising the howler monkeys would have been less trouble.

After much coercion, the last case was finally strapped down inside the covered bed of the truck. Oswardo stood on the running board and pulled himself up even with the driver.

"Bueno. ¿*Estamos listo?*" the man asked.

"Sí. Everything is loaded. When you reach the road, turn right and keep driving until you reach El Fuerte. When you reach the fort, take the road that bears to the right. It ends at the beach, and a boat will be waiting there. But I want you to wait until I arrive before moving or unloading the boxes."

"Why don't you just ship them out of the port in Colón?" the driver asked.

"The less you know, the better it will be for you!" Oswardo snapped. "Do as I say, and you and your men will be paid in cash once the boat is loaded. And remember, you are to speak of this to no one. ¿Comprendes?"

"Sí, señor," the driver said, obviously not wanting to do anything to upset his employer.

"Very well. Ándale. I will be along shortly."

The driver popped the clutch, causing the behemoth to shudder and lurch off down the muddy track leading to the road.

Oswardo winced and glowered after it. Idiota. Even though he'd found the chemical makeup of the compound to be more stable than the textbook said it should be, it still became more volatile when it wasn't refrigerated. And he lived in fear that too hard a jolt would crack one of the bottles. If that happened, it would be all over.

The loss of the shipment on Coiba still stung, being that he'd been offered such an incredible sum for his remaining product. As for the truck driver, Oswardo didn't dare tell the man just how valuable his cargo was, lest the man and his companions decide to make off with it.

He sighed. They wouldn't get far if they tried. He'd arranged for the pickup near Fort San Lorenzo to save the risk of driving the product past the guards at the entrance of the park and through the security surrounding the canal.

Once the truck was out of sight, Oswardo turned and walked through the still-open steel door of the bunker, which was set into a concrete wall in the side of a small man-made mound of earth.

He made his way through the cramped, acrid-smelling lab and down the concrete stairwell to the lower level. It was time to activate the device he had built just for this occasion.

The woman had somehow worked the blindfold off her head since the last time he left, and it lay crumpled next to her on the floor when he entered. Not that that surprised him. She had been sleeping but woke up immediately when he unlocked the door.

Blue eyes flashed at him from beneath unkempt red hair when the dim fluorescent bulb lit up the room. Apparently the hours since he'd last seen her hadn't broken her spirit.

"Who are you and why are you holding me?"

He chuckled, savoring the feeling it gave him, being here. He carefully snubbed out his cigar before crossing to the pile of explosives. "My dear, you have been watching too many American movies. There is no reason for me to tell you my business. I will only be a moment, and then will leave you in peace."

With his back to the CIA agent, Oswardo opened an ammo

crate and removed a few RPG rounds from it. On the black market they were worth several hundred dollars apiece, and the rest of
the ordnance upon which they were sitting would easily have
brought more than fifty thousand. But with the ultimate payoff so
close, it wouldn't have been worth the risk of trying to unload
them. Instead, they would serve to ensure that there would be no
recognizable evidence of this place.

From his pocket, he produced a simple electronic kitchen
timer, which he'd modified for his purposes. He took hold of the
electrical leads protruding from the device and connected them to
two wires protruding from a control box he'd constructed from an
old car alarm.

He set the timer for two hours and ten minutes, then started
the countdown. Then he placed the timer inside one of the boxes
and closed the lid, unwinding the wires as he carefully set the box
on the floor next to the doorway.

Bueno. He hit the timer on his watch. Now he would know
just when to be looking back at the horizon from the boat.

Oswardo carried another empty wooden case over to the far
corner on the opposite side of the door from the first one. Then he
reached into his pocket and removed a small green circuit board to
which he'd soldered a tiny photocell, both purchased over the
counter in the market in Colón.

Wrapped around the silicon circuit board was six feet of thin
wire. He unwound it and ran the twin leads over to the control box.
Once they were connected, he carefully arranged the circuit board
on top of the box that contained the timer. It was propped up
against a block of Semtex explosive with the photocell facing the
opposite wall beyond the door. The one-pound weight of the plas-

tic explosive on the wires was enough to hold the tiny photocell perfectly immobilized.

This accomplished, he stood and surveyed his work, steadying himself momentarily on the stack of crates as a bout of lightheadedness overcame him. He needed another dose of the powder, but that would have to wait.

The woman had been watching his movements with interest. "You're going to blow it up."

He ignored her.

He checked all of the connections one last time, angry with himself for the difficulty he was having concentrating. Then he walked to the far corner where he'd put the other wooden crate. From his breast pocket he produced a small, simple laser pointer. This device would serve a special purpose—as insurance to make sure she couldn't escape if she somehow figured a way out of the handcuffs. The chances of that happening were slim, but she was a CIA agent after all. Who knew what they were trained to do.

He smiled and relit his cigar. *Perfecto.*

He set the laser pointer on the box and secured it with a strip of tape to keep it from rolling. Then he made sure the power button on the device was locked in the "on" position.

Next, he got down on the floor next to the crate and carefully aligned the red dot, which now played along the far wall. The red beam was invisible as it crossed the approximately ten feet of space before showing up as a bright red spot on the photocell.

Oswardo stood once more, sweating. "And now, gringa, I must leave. Please don't concern yourself with this." He took in the pile of explosives and ammunition with a sweep of his hand. "You will be free of this place soon."

It wasn't exactly a lie.

"Please, tell me one thing?" she asked softly.

He turned and regarded her, savoring the feeling of power he had over her. "What is it, my dear?"

"Tell me what time it is."

He thought for a moment. He supposed there could be no harm in granting her last request. He looked at his watch. "It is three in the morning. And now, if you'll excuse me, I must go."

Chuckling to himself, he left the room. Swinging the steel door closed, he left it unlocked and retrieved the tiny remote arming device that he'd salvaged from the car alarm. Sighting it through the window, he took a deep breath and prepared to press the button that would arm the device.

Adrenaline surged through him. *The power of life and death.* If it wasn't set up perfectly, he'd be dead before he knew about it.

He pushed the button.

39

Over Panama. 0422 hours

FIFTY-SIX MINUTES to first light.

Rip squinted into the wind coming in the door of the unmarked Black Hawk helicopter as it blasted through the night at 165 knots. The chopper was shrouded in mist from the dark jungle below. Forward-looking infrared radar allowed the pilots to fly nap-of-the-earth as the Special-Ops chopper thundered north from Panama City less than a hundred feet above the treetops, flying toward the Caribbean coast and Fort Sherman.

The pilots' eyes showed as diffuse green circles behind state-of-the art ANVIS Heads-Up Display night-vision goggles that illuminated their tight, emotionless faces. All of their concentration was focused on the dimly lit instruments, since there were no visual cues outside the cockpit to keep the ten-million-dollar aircraft from slamming into a forested hillside on the way to their objective.

Rip's stomach lurched to his throat as the chopper dropped suddenly out from under him. He held on to his safety sling and squinted into the wind coming in through the open door. As the aircraft broke through the cloud cover, he saw off to the right what appeared to be a brightly lit multistory building in the middle of the jungle, which confused him until he saw the reflection of the lights on the water.

A container ship! The canal!

The chopper plunged to within ten feet of the water, hurtling along so close to the surface that the aircraft left a wake, and Rip could smell the fish.

Frank, John, Sweeney, and Doc all broke into grins at the same time. Sweeney, who was sitting next to him, howled in his ear over the roar of the rotor blades. "Hoooo boy! Now this is what I signed up for!"

Rip gave him a thumbs-up and nodded.

The previous several hours had been a whirlwind of activity. Though the mission wasn't given final approval until six minutes before the chopper's wheels left the tarmac, the team had used what time it had to check and recheck their equipment, study the plans of the battery, and rack their brains planning for every possible contingency.

After an apparently lengthy argument between the major and Marcel, who was responsible for coordinating with the Panamanian national police, the government reluctantly agreed to send a ground platoon of special commandos to set up a blocking position on the road leading into the national park where the bunker was located and to provide backup support if the team got in trouble. After the foul-up on Coiba, Rip sincerely hoped that wouldn't be needed.

Coop leaned forward and pulled his headset off one ear. "Six minutes!"

Sweeney clapped Rip on the shoulder and removed a magazine from his ammo pouch, tapping it against his helmet before slamming it home in the receiver of his SOPMOD M4 carbine. He shouted in Rip's ear again, patting his weapon. "I'm glad we're usin' these again!"

Rip nodded, reaching over the fourteen-inch circular breaching saw on his lap to load his own weapon. They'd decided to bring the rotary cutoff saw after studying the layout of the bunker with plans that had been hastily dug up in the nearby canal archives by an embassy employee.

Coop tapped Rip's shoulder and pointed to the thick green polypropylene rope coiled on the floor like an enormous snake.

Rip quickly unfastened his harness and felt around on the rope, which was as thick as his wrist, until he located the chemlights taped at intervals one foot, three feet, and five feet from its end. He bent the small plastic tubes and felt the glass ampoules inside break, which lit the now-all-business faces of his fellow commandos in a subdued greenish hue.

Then Rip pulled the thick leather work gloves from the cargo pocket on his left leg and put them on. Without the weight of the saw, forgetting the gloves would make the ninety-foot slide to the ground the most painful ninety feet of his life. But with it slung across his back, forgetting the gloves would surely be deadly.

Coop stood and grasped the loop where the rope was attached to a boom on the cargo bay ceiling. The boom extended three feet out the right side door. Once the team had completed their planned fastrope insertion, the pilot would pull a lever to release the rope, allowing it to fall to the ground. He yanked on the loop to ensure the release hadn't been pulled prematurely.

Coop pressed a hand to the headset he wore, listening to the pilots. He held up two fingers. "Two minutes! Get ready!"

The team struggled to their feet, jostling each other unintentionally in the cramped confines of the aircraft. Rip grimaced when the saw impacted his knee as he swung it around behind him.

He steadied himself against the bulkhead. The helicopter climbed back up to treetop level as they reached the edge of the lake, and he could see the lights of Colón in the distance. But the g-forces from the sudden jump in altitude only added to the weight of Rip's gear, and his thighs were beginning to burn. After the ship's reflection on the calm water, the dead black jungle flashing by below looked bottomless and evil.

Coop hung out the open side door, spotting for the insertion point, which from the sat photos was directly in front of the bunker. It was the only clear spot between the objective and the ocean, almost a kilometer away.

Rip didn't like the idea of inserting this way, even though fast-roping made it possible to put the entire team on the ground in only a matter of seconds, but the noise of the chopper would kill the element of surprise.

Whoever was occupying the bunker would have a bit of time to lock the door, destroy evidence, or—detonate the ITEB, in which case Hogan would be the lucky one for only getting shot.

Coop peered down at the ground, talking to the pilot on his headset, and the helicopter began to flare as the pilots reduced speed. John held up his hand, thumb and forefinger an inch apart.

Thirty seconds... Rip lined up behind his team leader and felt Frank crowding him from behind. The tech sergeant shouted in his ear. "Let's do this for Buzz!"

Rip nodded and released his weapon long enough to make the sign of the cross. It felt more sincere than it ever had before. *So why not try a prayer? Fernanda said God would answer. Okay, God. If You're listening, keep us safe on this one, please. And be with my family too…over.*

The chopper shuddered and flared to a full ninety degrees. He held on tight as the tail rotor pointed at the ground, and for an instant the horizon went vertical. A lighter patch of earth stood out below them, surrounded by trees now waving frantically, trying to escape the powerful ground effect of the helicopter. Then Coop kicked the coiled fastrope out the door.

Rip braced himself and leaned out of the bird, grasping the rope tightly in both gloved fists. The colored chem-lights were already visible, lying apart from each other, which assured him that the helicopter wasn't too high above the ground.

"Go!" Coop shouted in his ear, slapping him on the shoulder. Rip swung his feet out onto the rope. He pivoted toward the aircraft so that the saw on his back wouldn't catch in the door. Gravity took over, dragging him toward the earth. He picked up speed even as he clamped down hard on the rope with hands and feet, trying to slow his descent.

A glance skyward showed Frank already on the rope above him. The chopper's rotor disk, glowing with static electricity, framed its body with a phosphorescent ring.

By the time his feet impacted with wet earth, Rip's hands were burning despite the gloves. He hit hard in a patch of tall grass, crumpling away from the rope and doing his best to roll aside before Frank's boots made contact with his helmet. But the saw foiled his efforts, and when its handle punched him between the shoulder blades, he didn't even have enough breath left to curse.

Fortunately, Frank let go early and leaped the last few feet, landing next to him instead of on top of him. He rolled and was up and running before Rip gained his feet again. Sweeney landed just behind him, followed by Doc and finally Cooper.

At first Rip wasn't sure which way to go, then he realized that everything from where he stood was downhill. Apparently they'd been dropped directly on *top* of the bunker instead of in front of it.

"This way!" Coop dashed down the trail Frank had created. The other men were less encumbered than Rip, which left him bringing up the rear. The helicopter had already dropped the rope and was circling out to sea to await further instructions.

As soon as it was gone, the whirr of crickets replaced the whine of the rotors. Rip was breathing hard as he hustled through the tall grass, encountering the rest of the team stacked up on a concrete wall set into the side of the hillock that they landed on.

"Rubio! Fire up the saw. We've got a locked door."

He quickly slung his M-4 and unclipped the saw from his harness. Setting it on the ground, he pulled the starter cord twice, and the machine roared to life.

Frank's tactical flashlight illuminated a very large padlock on a steel door, covered by an unlit concrete portico. Rip revved the engine and placed the circular blade against the hasp. A shower of sparks, three seconds, and they were in.

Rip stepped back and cut the engine, then clipped it again to his harness and picked up his carbine. Frank had already yanked open the door, and Coop at the front of the stack charged into blackness, peering inside through the binocular NVGs mounted on his helmet. Immediately following were Sweeney and Doc, who had his .45 caliber pistol at the ready.

Rip dropped his own goggles over his face and went inside, with Frank bringing up the rear.

An eerie silence greeted the team as they cleared a long subter-

ranean hallway. It was completely empty. Coop poked his head
through a door on the left, then whispered, "Clear."

The team's shuffling feet echoing off the walls was the only
sound. It smelled of paint and stale earth. Each man automatically
reached up and flipped on the tiny infrared illuminator on his goggles, necessary because of the complete void of ambient light.

They found several other doors, none of which were locked.
The doors led to other small rooms that the team cleared in short
order. Some had maps on the walls or extra furniture piled in the
corners, but few looked recently used.

"Looks like nobody's home," Doc whispered in Rip's ear.

They reached a second thick steel door like the one at the
entrance. This time, Coop turned the handle and simply pushed it
open. Sweeney ducked inside and cut left. There was a crash and a
muttered curse as he ran into a table full of equipment. The rest of
the team entered the room single file, weapons at the ready, and
Doc remained outside as rear security.

Several quiet exclamations of "clear" were heard. There were no
people, but the room wasn't empty. When Rip stepped inside, his
goggles illuminated a thirty-foot square chamber filled with tables
piled with flasks, tubes, and other scientific gear. In the corner was
a large box with a glass pane set into it, and a row of five-foot steel
bottles was lined up against the far wall.

Frank was inspecting them. "I think we may have something
here. The writing on these bottles is Cyrillic."

"I've got a stairwell," Sweeney said.

Coop spoke up. "Frank, you and Bobby check it out."

Frank hurried to where Sweeney stood, and the two disappeared from sight. Rip moved to the top of the stairs to cover them.

The short stairs led to a dark hallway. Rip could see his teammates' lights moving around below, but nothing else. Other than
his own heartbeat, it was as quiet as a tomb.

Stop them.

Then a shout rang out from below. Adrenaline exploded
through Rip's body as he heard Frank say, "We've got a body! I
think it's Phoenix!"

Rip pounded down the stairs. Rounding the corner, he flinched
as Frank's ultrabright tac-light came on, illuminating the entire
length of the short hallway and the steel door set into one end.

He flipped up his goggles, seeing his teammates peering
through the small window in the door as he sprinted to their side.

"Phoenix! Hey, Mary! Can you hear me?" Frank pounded on
the door.

"She moved!" Turning, Sweeney shouted back toward the
stairs. "Phoenix is alive!"

"Get the door open." Frank reached for the handle.

Something shouted in Rip's head. *The easy way is always mined!*
The thought was too loud to ignore. "Stop! Don't open it!"

Both Sweeney and Frank turned to look at him.

"Hold on, bro." Rip held up one hand. "I have a bad feeling
about this. Check the door."

Frank's enthusiasm waned a little. "That's probably not a bad
idea."

"Yeah, remember what happened in training?"

Footsteps sounded on the stairs as Coop and Doc came to
investigate.

Rip stepped up to the window and pulled out his tactical flashlight. Its xenon beam illuminated a crumpled red-haired woman

chained to a pipe in the far corner of the room, squinting up at them as if she'd been awakened from a deep sleep.

Excitement and dread mixed in his chest to make breathing difficult. *That's Phoenix, all right.*

Then her eyes went wide, and she tried to say something, but Rip couldn't hear her through the door. He turned to the other men. "Shut up for a minute, man! She's talking."

The team listened. Phoenix was shaking her head. Then she croaked, "Don't open the door!"

Rip craned his neck to peer through the little window, shining his light around the inside of the room. In the corner opposite Phoenix, he spied the pile of explosives, and his mouth went dry.

"Guys, this place is wired to blow."

40

Panama City

HELP THEM.

Fernanda sat straight up in bed. Until that moment she'd been enjoying her first real sleep in a week, brought on by a shower and a mug of chamomile tea.

What is it? She looked around the darkened room, straining her ears for any sound other than the *tick-tick-tick* of the overhead fan. Nothing. But what had awakened her?

You must help them.

It was just a whisper of a thought, but the command was unmistakable. She blinked and rubbed her face with one hand, annoyed with herself for not being able to turn it off—the worry, the sense of dread. She looked over at the clock—4:37 a.m.

She flopped back down on the pillow and shut her eyes tight. *Just stop thinking. You have to stop these thoughts from twirling around. Let it go!*

She pulled the pillow over her head, trying to shut out the need to constantly be doing something. She had to get some rest or she would die.

I've done all I can. What more can I do? She couldn't stand the helpless feeling. Just days ago she'd lamented about having so much, but now it seemed that everything she had was worthless.

Nothing she owned could fix the situation for Zack and Carlos. Not her money, not her looks. Not even her education. Hope for her friends being found alive was waning by the hour.

The whisper got louder.

Help them.

She pulled the pillow back and sighed. "What can I do?" She didn't feel wealthy anymore. Or smart. She felt like the little girl back in Santa Catalina—dirty, hungry, poor beyond words.

God had never felt so far away.

"What you have loses its value if it isn't shared."

Was that it? She'd never shared her faith? Could faith lose its value?

You admit to being a Christian, but have you ever told anyone why?

A tear rolled down her cheek, losing itself in her hair.

But I'm a good person! I don't drink, sleep around... Isn't that enough proof of my faith?

Just having to ask the question was all the answer that was necessary. She rolled over and buried her face in the pillow.

Hedi was a good person too, but she'd never been to church. In fact, lots of people avoided vice for a thousand different reasons apart from a faith in God, so was her life really that different? What is faith worth, really, if it's nothing more than a convenient excuse to pass on a beer now and then? If she was a health nut instead of a Christian, wouldn't her life look the same?

She'd never told Hedi what being a Christian meant to her. Or Carlos or Alex. How many hours had she spent with them in the last year? Had she ever once mentioned to either of them the relationship with Christ that had changed her life?

Or to Rip?

"What you have loses its value if it isn't shared."

Fernanda thumped the mattress with her fist. "How?" The question echoed off the walls of her tiny bedroom. "How do I share it with them? I might never see any of them again!"

Pray. The prodding was more insistent this time.

Her heart pounded in her rib cage, almost as if it had an urgent message to deliver.

Pray? How is that sharing my faith?

An image flashed in her mind, an image from the island.

It was Rip, smiling at her just after she thanked him for saving her life. What had he said?

"Maybe someday you'll return the favor."

Understanding hit her with the force of a blow. *This is urgent.*

She had to pray. Now.

She swung out of bed and went to her knees.

"Just leave me and go!" Mary's hoarse voice pleaded through the door.

Rip and Coop looked at each other. "We both know that's not going to happen," Coop said. "But maybe we shouldn't keep everyone down here, just in case."

Rip nodded. "I'm staying, bro."

"Me too," Frank said.

"I ain't leavin, boss," Sweeney drawled.

"I guess we're all staying then," Doc said.

Coop shook his head, his face a determined block of granite. "Look, men, there's not room for everyone down here. I know we all want to stay, but we still have work to do. Frank, I want you to go up and photograph everything in sight, get some video, then get outside with that camera. Sweeney, go back outside with Doc and pull security while you send the major a sitrep. Tell them we're going to need a medevac one way or another. Rip and I'll figure out a way to get her out."

Nobody budged for a moment. Then Frank pulled the camera from his vest and held it out to Coop. "I respect your wishes, but I think you have to admit that I know more than anybody about these kinds of devices. So I should stay with Rip and you take the pictures."

Coop stared for a second, his expression intense, his jaw muscles tight. "Okay. You're right." He took the camera and headed down the hall. "Sweeney, Doc, let's go. Frank, I'll be back to check on you two in a few minutes."

Doc Kelley and Sweeney both frowned at each other. Then the medic looked back at Rip and Frank. "You guys stay safe, okay?"

"Yeah, git 'er done," Sweeney said, as he slapped Rip on the shoulder. The two turned and jogged back upstairs.

"All right, bro. What are we going to do?"

Frank sucked his teeth for a second. "Let's see what Phoenix can tell us."

Rip dropped to the prone and shone his light under the door. There was about a quarter-inch gap. "Hey, Phoenix, it's Rip. Can you hear me?"

"Don't open the door, Rip. There's a laser beam across it that will detonate the explosives." Mary's voice was shaky.

"Okay, just tell me exactly what you see."

"First tell me what time it is."

Frank checked his watch. "It's 4:53."

"There's only a few minutes left. Please go. There's no way you can get in here before it explodes."

Rip shook his head. "Just tell me what you see. Hurry."

Mary quickly described the setup. "I can't see much now, though, because the lights went out. But it's just a cheap laser pointer. The batteries might go out any second anyway."

"How far is the beam away from the door?" Frank asked.

"It's hard to tell. Maybe four inches?"

"Far enough to get the door open a crack?"

"Maybe. Like I said, I can't see it now."

Frank pushed to a sitting position and leaned against the wall. "If breaking the laser beam will set off the explosives, there's no way for us to get the door open unless we can move the laser to the other side of the door without moving the beam. That would be nearly impossible, and I wouldn't even try it without being able to take a good look at the diode that it's pointed at. Some of those things can get pretty tricky."

Rip sat up too. "We have the saw. Why don't we just cut a hole in the top of the door above the laser beam and climb in that way?"

Frank shook his head. "That's too risky. If even one piece of debris from the door falls through that beam, we're toast. Even smoke or sparks could set it off. If the beam was up high, we could cut under it, but as it is…"

Rip snapped his fingers, then dropped back to the prone, speaking under the door. "Hey, Phoenix, how high off the ground is the laser?"

"He set it on a box, but it's still pretty low. Maybe eight inches?"

Rip looked up at Frank. "What if we cut a few inches off the bottom of the door? That would give us enough room to get a look at what we're dealing with."

"That might work, but even the vibration from the saw could set off the explosives. You want to run it by Coop?"

"Nah, let's get on with it. She said he used a standard laser pointer. We don't know how much time those batteries will last." He stood and reached for the saw. He knocked on the door. "It's gonna get loud for a minute, Phoenix!"

Then the light came on. Literally. The bare bulb in the hallway burned to life, and the fluorescent lights inside the room flickered on.

"Hey, how about that?" Frank said. "Light!"

Coop's voice echoed down the stairs. "I found the generator. How's it coming down there?"

"That will help!" Frank shouted back.

Rip stood up and looked through the door at Phoenix. "Hola, chica." He smiled.

"Get me out of here."

"Yes, ma'am."

"Listen." Phoenix brushed her hair away from her face with her still-bound hands. "I can see it better now. The laser is about four inches away from the door. You might be able to get it open just a little. I'm not sure how that will help, though."

Rip looked down at Frank. "Want to give it a try?"

"Sure. Everybody's got to die somehow."

"Shut up, bro." Rip carefully turned the knob on the door and shouted at Phoenix. "I'm going to open it a couple of inches to see what we're dealing with."

"Be careful!"

Rip eased the door open about an inch. He and Frank peered through the gap.

"Okay." Frank looked carefully at the device. "I see it now. Looks like a rudimentary photocell. A cheap one at that. That's the good news. It's not very sophisticated. The bad news is, it's tiny."

"How do we disable it?" Rip asked.

"We don't have time. The light hitting the cell keeps the current flowing, and when the light goes out, the impedance is greatly increased and the current stops. That must be what triggers the detonator. If we could move the laser, maybe we could get the door open and get Phoenix out."

Rip thought for a moment. "What if we point a different laser at it? Would that set it off?"

"A second laser? Like your laser target designator?"

"Why not?"

"That might work. But there'd be no way of knowing until we actually tried, and if we're wrong…"

Rip was still sweating. "We're going to be in trouble any minute anyway, bro."

"Okay, but our designators are infrared. That won't do it. We need a visible laser."

Rip's eyebrows shot up. "Sweeney has one on his pistol."

"I'll get it." Frank turned and dashed up the stairs.

Rip ran behind Frank to the top of the stairs, where he found Coop still taking pictures. "How's it coming?" He asked Rip as Frank ran past him out the door and down the hallway, yelling for Sweeney.

"Get out, John! This thing could blow any minute!" Rip

started tossing equipment on the floor, looking for something that would hold Sweeney's laser stable in the correct position.

"What are you looking for?"

"A stable platform for the laser!"

Coop looked around him. "How about this?" He held up a wire clamp made for holding test tubes over a Bunsen burner.

Rip snatched it out of his hand. "Perfect. Now get out, bro. Seriously!"

Reluctantly, John jogged off toward the surface just as Sweeney came puffing down the corridor, disassembling his pistol on the run.

"Where's Frank?" Rip said.

"Shut up. Take this." Sweeney handed Rip the laser pointer.

The two men pounded down the stairs to the room where Phoenix was. "We're gonna get you out, Mary!" Sweeney shouted through the door.

"Gimme your tape, Bobby."

The muscular sergeant produced a small spool of green duct tape from his vest. "You're lucky I carry all this high-speed stuff."

Rip looked at the spool. "I hope this is enough."

Dropping to their knees, the two soldiers taped the firing laser into the articulated clamp, then carefully slid it through the crack in the door.

"Hurry!" Mary pleaded.

Sweeney lined up the laser beam so it pointed exactly at the photocell.

"How stable is it?" Rip asked.

"As good as we're going to get at this point."

"Do you really think it'll work?"

Sweeney gave him a grim smile and wiped his brow. "'It's appointed unto man once to die, and after that the judgment.'"

"What?"

Bobby shook his head. "Come on, man. Didn't you ever go to Sunday school? It's in the Bible."

Gallows humor notwithstanding, Rip really wasn't sure if he was ready to die. He said nothing for a long moment.

Am I ready? What will Mama do? And Gabi?

He looked back at Sweeney. "I never thought I'd hear you say that, but we're in it now, bro. So let's do it."

Rip looked through the window again at Phoenix. "Okay, chica, we're coming in. We'll try to get you out as quickly as possible, all right?"

"Get on with it." There was a note of resignation in her voice.

Rip held his breath and grasped the door handle, then pushed. The door swung inward.

Nothing happened.

"Gracias a Dios." It was the most sincere prayer Rip had ever uttered.

"Let's go!" Sweeney pushed the door open and went to Mary. "Get the saw, Rip."

He picked up the cutoff saw and carried it inside.

Bobby was inspecting Mary's wrists. "We don't have time to try and get the cuffs off. There might be a secondary timer on the explosives. Just cut the pipe, and we'll worry about the cuffs later."

Rip hefted the saw. "Get ready, Mary. This is gonna get loud." He pulled the starter and the saw roared to life. Sparks flew as he applied the blade to the metal pipe, making two quick cuts above and below her hands. Sweeney caught the piece in the middle and slid it out of the way.

Before he even had a chance to shut off the saw, Mary was already running for the door. "Come on!"

The two men pounded after her, up the steps, where she stopped to gape at the laboratory. "Oh my…"

Sweeney grabbed her arm and pulled her to the exit. "We got pictures! Keep going!"

Rip checked his watch as they ran out the door and down the hallway. 5:04 a.m.

As they sprinted into the first rays of morning, a rumble sounded in the earth.

41

Isla Coiba. 0545 hours

THE WIND SIGHED through the trees on the island, making them undulate in waves that matched the sea far below. The guttural shouts of a troop of howler monkeys floated down from the ridge overlooking the sea.

Birds of every color, impossibly bright, swirled in carefree circles overhead like sparks from a bonfire, their varied calls mixing into a riotous symphony of color and sound.

On the horizon, God was busy painting a masterpiece in an explosion of citrus hues as the morning sun exploded out of the horizon.

He stepped over the twitching body of the dark-skinned one, having said hello to the spirits on the man's behalf. This one had fought his release from this world particularly hard, despite his bound wrists, which had been tied with the same sort of bracelets the girl had broken.

The dying man gurgled a farewell to the island, and the Indian was alone again. He wiped his blade on a leaf and returned it to its place at his side. Then he picked up the machete from where he had left it.

After one last look at his victim, he turned and walked slowly to the rock that overlooked the edge of the earth. Far below him, the bitter water crashed against the rocks, singing to him in its own way. He let the song carry him back to his people, his village.

He would never see them again, for his life force was weakening. He was old, too old to hunt much longer. He had eluded the death-spirits for a time, but he could not run from them forever. They would find him.

He looked at the machete. It was heavy, and he did not like it. Besides, he had no way of keeping it sharp. He had survived for years without one, so with an underhanded toss, he watched it fall down, down, until it was swallowed by the waves.

Looking up, he saw birds silhouetted against the bright red orb of the sun as it crawled slowly out of the sea. He wished that he had been braver. Then perhaps he could have joined his fathers in the sun when it was his turn to leave the island. Now it would not be so.

But for the time being, he was at peace with himself and with his destiny. With one last look at the rising sun, he turned his back on it and melted into the jungle.

Panama City. 1800 hours

The waitress in the don't-bend-over skirt leaned across the table to set the heavy platter of cheese-drenched french fries down where everyone could reach it.

The Artist Formerly Known as Prince crooned from the speakers overhead, a little too loud for Rip's taste, not to mention about ten years behind the times. Actually, he would have much preferred to celebrate at one of several other restaurants anchoring the

Multicentro Pacifico mall in downtown Panama City, but he and Fernanda had been outvoted by Hedi, Bobby, John, and Frank.

Nothing was going to ruin his mood tonight, though. It wasn't just that surviving a life-or-death situation tended to make a guy appreciate everything a bit more. He put down the glass of Coke he'd been sipping and looked over at Fernanda.

She looked fantastic, sitting next to him in a simple scoop-neck yellow T-shirt and jeans. As far as he was concerned, she couldn't have looked better in an evening gown.

A pang stabbed at him. Was it regret at having sworn off all the mushy stuff? In reality, he was enjoying the fact that he could relate to Fernanda as a friend. An unbelievably attractive woman, but a friend just the same.

She saw him staring and pursed her lips at him.

"What's that mean?" Rip asked.

"What?"

"That lip thing you just did."

Fernanda laughed. "Oh. It's like, 'what's up?'"

Rip nodded. "I was thinking how glad I am you came along, chica."

She gave him a demure smile. "You mean tonight?"

"I mean at all."

She blushed. "Well, thanks for calling tonight. I would have been sad if you'd left without saying good-bye."

"No way. And make sure I get your e-mail address before we take off."

"I will. Have you heard anything about Sergeant Hogan?"

"Apparently Buzz is doing very well. He'll probably be out of the hospital by the time we get back."

"Thank God for that. I've been worried about him."

Rip raised an eyebrow. "What about your two friends? Any news?"

Fernanda shook her head. "I spoke with the jefe in Santiago this afternoon, and he said they've searched the entire island of Coiba and are fairly certain that Carlos and Zack were taken off the island at some point. But then, they haven't found Chombon either, and we know he was there. It's just so thick, so remote…"

In all the excitement, Rip had forgotten how much grief Fernanda had to be dealing with. Tears brimmed in her eyes. "I'm sorry, amiga. I guess this situation didn't turn out so great for you." He slid a napkin over to her.

She waved it off. "No, that's okay. I haven't given up hope. This whole thing has been so crazy. I mean, to think that Tío Edgar has been leading this secret life—and now he's a wanted criminal!"

Rip nodded. "I hope they catch him too. How's your mother taking all this?"

"I don't know if she's madder at Edgar for embezzling money from Casa Lerida or at herself for not noticing. But she'll be fine. She's a very strong woman."

Rip smiled. He'd always heard that a girl's mother was the best measure of what she'd turn into. "Maybe that's where you get it."

Sweeney spoke up from the other side of the table. "It's really too bad Mary couldn't come. She's kind of the guest of honor, you know?"

Coop shrugged. "Yeah, but actually, Fernanda should hold that title. We'd have lost everything—including Mary—if it hadn't been for her."

"Here, here!" Doc raised his glass, and the other men followed suit.

"To Fernanda!" John said.

Rip looked at her as he raised his Coke with the others. He caught her eye and said, "You did good."

Fernanda grinned. "Thank you, but I still can't believe Tío Edgar was involved with all of this." She shook her head.

"Hey, what did I miss?" Hedi returned from a trip to the ladies' room and sat between Fernanda and Frank.

"We were toasting Miss Lerida for our success," Sweeney said, as he stuffed a cheese fry into his mouth.

"Oh. Well, let me get a picture." Hedi pulled her digital out of her purse. "Raise your glasses again."

Everyone laughed, and this time, Fernanda raised hers too. Hedi stepped back and blinded everyone with the flash as she captured the shot.

A waiter walked up behind the blond German girl. *"¿Quiere que lo saque de todos?"* He pointed at her camera.

Hedi scrunched up her face and looked at Fernanda. "That was too fast. What did he say?"

Grinning, Fernanda said, "He asked if you wanted to get in the picture too."

"Oh no, gracias." Her German-accented Spanish almost made Rip cough soda through his nose. *"Miro…no…parece feo…* Ugh! Tell him I look terrible in pictures."

Fernanda and Rip both laughed at that.

Coop spoke up. "Come on, Hedi. Let's get one with all of us. Hey, Frank, did you bring the team camera?"

"As a matter of fact, I did." Frank pulled the ruggedized Olympus digital camera from his go-everywhere daypack. He handed it to the waiter and tugged at Hedi's belt. "Come on, Hedi. Sit down and smile and it'll all be over before you know it."

"If you insist." She took her seat and threw an arm across Frank's shoulders as they turned toward the camera.

The waiter snapped the photo and started to hand the camera back, but Hedi stopped him. "Oh, wait! Take another one, and this time let's all make a funny face."

The waiter shrugged, then stepped back to get the shot. Fernanda looked at Rip and rolled her eyes until he made a face at her that started her laughing.

Then just before the waiter snapped the shutter, Hedi kissed Frank on the cheek! The flash went off, and the whole group exploded in laughter. Frank shook his head as he wiped the lipstick from his face.

Everyone had to see the picture. Rip snatched the camera and switched it to display mode, then he and Fernanda hooted at the expression on Frank's face in the picture.

"Let me see!" Hedi grabbed for it.

She looked at the screen. "Hey, this isn't the right pic—I must have hit a button or something."

Frank leaned over. "Oh, you advanced back to the first shot on the card. That's from the island."

Coop's smile disappeared. "Frank, she shouldn't see those."

Frank reached for the camera. "Sorry, hon, those are classified. Lemme get it back to the one you wanted to see."

"Wait! Wait!" Hedi pulled the camera away from him and stared intently at the screen. "That's Zack and Carlos getting in that boat! What are they doing with Hugo?"

Rip looked quickly from Hedi to Coop to Fernanda. "Who's Hugo?"

Hedi pointed at the screen. "That's Hugo. This slimy guy who hangs out at the pizza place in Santa Catalina." She looked at Fernanda. "He kept trying to pick me up when I was waiting there for you."

Fernanda took the camera and peered at the screen. Her eyes went wide. "That *is* Zack and Carlos. We've got to alert the authorities! Hedi, does this man live in Santa Catalina?"

She shrugged. "He must. He was at Pizza Jamming almost every night. He kept trying to buy me drinks one night and told me that I should go with him back to his villa overlooking the ocean. I assume it was nearby."

Fernanda looked pale as she reached for her purse. "I need to make a few phone calls. Please...don't wait on me." She stood and hurried toward the exit.

Rip looked in astonishment at his buddies around the table. "No way that just happened."

42

Turbo. Colombia. 1830 hours

SEAGULLS CIRCLED NOISILY over the docks in the tiny town of Turbo, just across the Panamanian border into Colombia. The boat for Cartagena would be leaving shortly.

The throwaway phone rang three times before Edgar realized the noise was coming from his own pocket. He'd finally gotten around to changing it to a normal ring, but without the stupid rap music, he hardly recognized the sound. A pang of sadness stabbed him as he thought of the son he would never see again.

His spirits brightened when he heard the voice on the other end of the line, speaking English.

"I have confirmation that the product is en route, Oswardo."

"Yes, yes." He smiled broadly. "Everything went according to plan. When can I expect the rest of the payment?"

"When the ship arrives and I take possession of the product."

"Bueno. You should see it within the week. It's been nice doing business with you."

"As with you," the voice said. "You're sure there is no more of this product anywhere?"

"Believe me, if I had any more I would certainly have sold it to you. But tell me, why are you so anxious to have it?" *And to pay six times what I could have gotten anywhere else?*

"Ah, that, my friend, is outside the scope of our relationship."

He figured as much. "Very well, amigo. I am not going to have this phone number much longer. But I will be sure to fax my new number to you when I get one."

"You do that, Oswardo. Good-bye."

He punched the button to end the call and stared at the black plastic device. It was the last tie he had to his old life.

In one swift motion, he flung the phone out across the water. It skipped twice, then disappeared. He had been wanting to do that for a long time.

He turned back toward the docks, inhaling deeply of the salty night air.

It's good to be free.

———

Washington DC. 1825 hours

Spring rain pounded on the terrace outside Michael LaFontaine's office window, all but obscuring his view of the White House. But he glared at it anyway, fuming.

Cowards. All of them.

He steepled his hands, brooding in silence, everyone else having already gone home for the day.

He'd lost count of the millions he'd spent trying to get the bozos in Congress to act decisively in the war on terror. Most of them were far too worried about saving face with the public to make the tough decisions. And the upshot was that the brave men and women who volunteered to fight the enemy were relegated instead to the role of international baby-sitters, their efforts thwarted by knock-kneed politicians who hoped somehow to defeat the enemy without actually offending him.

And because of this political squeamishness, the American people had forgotten that there was ever any threat to their security.

He picked up the report he'd been reading. Most Americans now spent more than four and a half hours each day in front of the television.

Fat, dumb, and happy. It was the only way one could describe them. They were sheeple, nothing more. Mindlessly consuming whatever pablum the media dished out, far more concerned with who won this week's *American Idol* than with preserving the greatness of their country. Most of them made no more use of the priceless gift of freedom than the average prison inmate. Freedom was simply cushioning to pad their behinds as they blithely watched TV.

I'm so sick of watching the terrorists manipulate the media in order to receive sympathy from the very people they want to destroy. Doesn't anyone else see it?

It was a brilliant strategy, really. Defeat your enemy by distracting them from the goal. Convince them that their own leaders are the evil ones, make them forget that the threat is real. Appeal to their civility and use it as a weapon against them.

He wadded up the report and threw it across the room. He knew what it would take to turn the tide of public opinion. Problem was, nobody had the courage to do it.

Nobody but Michael LaFontaine.

Multicentro Mall, Panama City, 1830 hours

Fernanda's heart raced as she dug in her purse for the card that Captain Estevez had given her on the island. She found it and quickly dialed the number for his office in Santiago. Her heels clicked on the polished marble floor of the mall, and the reverberating music from the Hard Rock Cafe faded behind her.

A police sergeant on duty at the Santiago headquarters answered the call and said that the captain was gone for the day.

Frantic, she told him who she was and that she had urgent information about the case. "Please. Is there someone you can send to Santa Catalina to check it out?"

"I cannot send anyone, señorita, but I will call *el Capitan* at his home. I'm sure he will want to hear of this. He can send someone to Santa Catalina. But tell me, how did you come upon this information?"

Fernanda stopped. *Didn't John say all of this was classified?* She didn't want to get Rip in trouble, but wasn't finding Zack and Carlos more important?

She did her best to straddle the fence. "The…um…Americans found some information on the island that showed he was involved." She hoped it was enough to satisfy him.

"Bueno, I will call the captain right away."

Her body tingled all over. "Thank you so much, *Sargento.* Please let me know if you find anything." She gave the man her number and hung up.

A voice sounded behind her. "There you are."

What are you doing, Rubio?

Rip waved and offered a hopeful smile when Fernanda turned to the sound of his voice. He'd followed her because he had to—he couldn't stomach the thought that she might leave to look for her friends and he wouldn't get to say good-bye.

His apprehension melted away when she smiled back.

"Hey." She slipped her phone back into her purse. "That was the police station in Santiago."

"Everything all right?"

She nodded. "It looks hopeful. They're sending someone to Santa Catalina to check it out."

"Great." There was an awkward silence. Rip cleared his throat. "Um…want to take a walk?"

"Sure. Let's go out on the terrace."

Even though it went against his self-declared girl hiatus, warmth filled his chest as she slid her hand into his and led him out on a wide balcony overlooking Avenida Balboa. The traffic was relatively light, and a recent rain left the air smelling fresh and clean.

Fernanda smiled. "Something makes me think that this is the clue we needed to find Carlos and Zack."

"How can you be so sure? They haven't been found yet."

She pursed her lips. "I don't know exactly how to describe it. It's like a whisper from God in my mind."

Rip said nothing. In fact, he felt suddenly uncomfortable.

"What's the matter?"

"Oh, um…nothing. I was just thinking about something that happened the other night when we found Phoenix. We were going to open the door to the room where she was, and it was like something told me not to do it."

"You mean, like a hunch?"

Rip shook his head. "More than that. Almost like someone was talking to me."

"That's just what I'm talking about. I woke up at like four thirty that morning with the same thing. It was like the Holy Spirit woke me up and told me to pray for you."

His eyes went wide. "Really? Did you?"

"Yes. Yes, I did. I prayed that you'd be safe."

Rip ran one hand over his stubbly head and gazed out over the city. "That's about the time we found Phoenix, amiga. I guess your prayer worked, because if we had opened the door, none of us would be here now."

She smiled. "I guess I shouldn't be surprised. Because if you hadn't been here tonight, we wouldn't have seen those pictures."

"Unbelievable."

She cocked her head to one side. "Is it really?"

"Really what?"

"Is it really so unbelievable that God would help us when we ask?"

Rip studied the moon's reflection off the Pacific Ocean, barely visible between two skyscrapers across the street. *That's a good question. Is it really such a crazy idea? People a lot smarter than I am seem to believe it…and there's no denying what happened the other night.*

Actually, when it came down to it, somewhere along the line he'd acquired a strange sort of aversion toward spiritual things. Somehow it seemed that if you had to rely on God, you weren't man enough to get the job done alone.

But as he thought about the situation with Gabi and his mother, he knew deep down that John was right. He couldn't give his sister what she needed, because he didn't have it himself.

Something else came to mind—an image of John at the Waffle House, praying. What was it he'd said? *"I'm man enough to pray…"*

There was no denying that John was a man's man. And if he needed God to make it in life, what hope did Rip Rubio have of going it alone?

He looked Fernanda in the eye. "No, amiga. I guess I have to believe it."

Her gaze dropped to their intertwined hands. She stroked the back of his hand with her thumb, saying nothing. He could sense she was struggling with something.

"What, chica?"

Her eyes showed a vulnerability that pierced something in his soul. "I'd like to ask you something, because I don't know if I'll ever see you again. I hope you won't think I'm a freak or anything. But even if you do, I want you to know that I have so much respect for you and for the job you do." She turned away slightly, and tears welled up in her eyes.

He gently turned her face back to his. "Anything, Fernanda. Ask me anything."

She pulled him over to a bench and sat down. He sat next to her.

"Okay, Rip. Do you believe that God loves you?"

Now it was his turn to look away. Images of his past flooded his memory—the fights; the string of meaningless love interests, pursued for little more than momentary pleasure. Even the dirty work he'd had to do as a soldier.

Something hardened within him. "You know, to be totally honest, after some of the things I've done, that's pretty hard to believe."

"Do you believe Jesus is God's Son and that He died on the cross?"

He shrugged. "Sure. I can believe that." It came with the upbringing, after all.

She put her hand on his arm. "Why would He have chosen to do that if it wouldn't have accomplished anything?"

Rip furrowed his brow. "What do you mean?"

"Jesus did it willfully. If He is God's Son, He didn't have to die that way. But He did it to show His love for us. There's a verse in the Bible that says God demonstrates his love for us, in that while we were still sinners, Christ died for us."

While we were still sinners. The same images flashed through his head, only now he saw Christ in the background, being flogged for every deed. Something about that image hurt—bad. The knot in Rip's gut tightened until tears blurred his own vision. He turned away, hoping Fernanda wouldn't see.

She put a hand on his shoulder. "Rip, God loves you and has a plan for you. He wants to give you the desires of your heart. But you have to give it to Him first."

"How?" His voice was only a whisper.

For the moment they were alone on the balcony. Fernanda gently turned him so she could look him in the eye. "Tell Him, Rip. That's how. Pray and tell Him you need Him in your life. I can pray it with you if you want."

Conflicting emotions tore him to shreds inside. Part of him wanted nothing more than to surrender himself, to give up the driver's seat of his life and let God take the wheel. But another part was screaming that the change would mean giving up the comfort of being his own man. Sure, there was a lot of misery where he was, but who knew if giving God control wouldn't be even worse?

An image of his father came to mind. Suddenly Rip realized that the man's biggest failing wasn't the infidelity; it was the unwillingness to put his family ahead of his own personal pleasure.

So are you going to be any different?

That stung. Anger jumped into the emotional fray. Anger at his father, and anger at the similarities he saw in himself.

No. I won't be like him. I can't.

The time was right. Comfort wasn't worth losing himself and his family.

He met Fernanda's gaze. "Okay, amiga. Let's do it."

She covered both of his hands with her own. They both bowed their heads. Fernanda began, and Rip repeated her words phrase by phrase. "Father, I admit that I don't deserve Your love, but I believe that Your Son, Jesus, died in my place."

It's hard to believe anyone could love me that much.

"And I give my life to You now."

Take it, God. It's a wreck, but if You want it, You can have it.

"Forgive me of my sins."

The words caught in his throat.

Fernanda's voice trembled. "Give me a new life and guide me in Your ways."

Rip sobbed quietly. *I want to change…please change me.*

"Give me new life and guide me, Jesus. I receive Your gift of eternal life. *En el Nombre de Jesus.* Amen."

A sweet sense of well-being oozed like warm honey into the depths of his soul. He raised his head and saw Fernanda's tears through his own. And he suddenly understood that surrender had been the only thing standing between him and victory.

Rip wiped his tears on his shirtsleeves. "I must look like an idiot."

She reached out and stopped him. "Not at all. It takes a real man to do what you just did." She hugged him tightly.

He hugged her back. Her soft hair smelled wonderful. He pulled back and looked at her. There was something incredibly special about this woman, and a frantic thought hit him that he might never see her again.

"Fernanda, I…"

"What?"

Their eyes met, faces only inches apart. Part of him wanted nothing more than to touch his lips to hers. It would have been the most natural thing to do. But somehow it wasn't right.

"I want to kiss you right now."

"And?"

"I want to, but I'm not going to. It's too cheap. You deserve better than that." The truth was, nothing could be more intimate than what they had already shared. Kissing her now would have been like putting frosting on a diamond ring.

She smiled and glanced at their hands. "Well, I won't say part of me doesn't want you to, but you're right. It's too soon."

He put his hands on her shoulders. "For once I want to have a relationship with a girl based on something other than physical attraction. I like you so much and want to give us the chance to get to know each other as people, not just bodies, you know?"

She nodded. "Maybe it's a good thing you're leaving tomorrow. E-mail is a wonderful thing."

His laugh was more heartfelt than any he could ever remember. It was like he'd won the lottery. No, it was even better than that.

"I guess that means I'm going to have to learn how to type."

Author's Note

I first set foot on the island of Coiba in the first days of 1990, during what would be my last combat mission of Operation Just Cause. Even then, as a twenty-year-old team leader with the 75th Ranger Regiment, I found the island mysterious, intriguing, and revolting all at once.

When we arrived, we met with no resistance, and soon found that the vast majority of the prison island's leadership had fled to the mainland, leaving only a handful of lower-ranking guards and approximately three thousand inmates. I have never seen more miserable human living conditions before or since.

We found thousands of sick and starving men, all claiming to be political prisoners. (Very few of them actually were.) The men were herded into a large corral intended for livestock and were fed military Meals Ready to Eat while they waited their turn to be interviewed by Special Forces linguists to determine their identity and status.

In the back hallway of the penitentiary, we discovered a man in solitary confinement. He was being held in a cell that was essentially a concrete box—fifteen foot square without windows, furniture, or plumbing. He was fed once a day through a small slit in the solid steel door.

Not surprisingly, after seven months of living in his own filth and not seeing daylight, the man had gone insane. With some difficulty, he was persuaded to leave the cell so he (and it) could be searched. When he emerged into the sunlight, he cried—not for joy, but in pain. The sunshine physically hurt him, and he begged to be returned to his filthy hole.

My squad was tasked to keep an eye on some of the prison guards on the island. We were located in the only town on the island, called simply El Centro. We were just across from a two-story white house that reportedly belonged to the island's governor. He and his family had fled before we arrived. So while two of my privates stood watch, I walked across the street and kicked in the governor's door, looking for something to eat.

Combat is strange like that.

I was elated to find a large, well-stocked pantry. My buddies and I were tired of Army food. I set to work and soon whipped up a feast of scrambled eggs, sausage, and fruit. Loading it up on plates, I carried the meal outside and served it to my men.

They promptly voted me governor of the island.

So for three days, I got to sleep in the governor's king-sized waterbed.

Fifteen years later, I returned to Panama with my wife. I was just beginning work on the Task Force Valor series and thought Panama might be a good place for the second book to be set.

Getting back to Coiba wasn't easy, but we finally found a fisherman who agreed to take us. When we motored into the bay near El Centro, at first I didn't recognize the place. The town was essentially in ruins and looked nothing like it had when I'd visited before.

After we waded ashore, however, slowly the mental images began to return. We encountered some policemen stationed there to discourage squatters, and they were decidedly unhappy with our presence. But as I spoke with them, I told the story of being elected "governor" of the island. As I did, their countenances changed, and I was suddenly a VIP. Connie and I were ushered on a grand tour of El Centro and met some of the last remaining prisoners there.

These experiences and hearing the prisoners tell of the island's legends, like the Mudman, solidified my decision to make Coiba a centerpiece of this novel. On a subsequent expedition in March 2006, my team and I discovered the remains of a purported former CIA training camp in the jungle on a remote part of the island. This became the pirate hideout.

These experiences taught me that the best part of writing fiction is finding the hidden thread of truth in which to wrap the story.

You can follow my adventures around the globe at www .livefire.us.

I'd love to hear from you. Feel free to send a note to Chuck@TFValor.com.

If you've been touched by the sacrifices given by our men and women in uniform, please consider a donation to the Wounded Warrior Project at www.woundedwarriorproject.org.